LOST AND FONDUE

AVERY AAMES

WHEELER
CHIVERS

This Large Print edition is published by Wheeler Publishing, Waterville, Maine, USA and by AudioGO Ltd, Bath, England.

Wheeler Publishing, a part of Gale, Cengage Learning.

A Cheese Shop Mystery.

The text of this Large Print edition is unabridged.

Other aspects of the book may vary from the original edition.

Set in 16 pt. Plantin.

LIBRARY OF CONGRESS CATALOGING-IN-PUBLICATION DATA

Aames, Avery.
    Lost and fondue / by Avery Aames. — Large print ed.
       p. cm. — (Wheeler Publishing large print cozy mystery)
    ISBN-13: 978-1-4104-4077-8 (softcover)
    ISBN-10: 1-4104-4077-X (softcover)
    1. Cheese shops—Fiction. 2. Providence (Ohio : Township)—Fiction.
3. Large type books. I. Title.
PS3601.A215L67 2011
813'.6—dc22   2011025558

BRITISH LIBRARY CATALOGUING-IN-PUBLICATION DATA AVAILABLE

Published in 2011 in the U.S. by arrangement with The Berkley Publishing Group, a member of Penguin Group (USA) Inc.
Published in 2012 in the U.K. by arrangement with The Berkley Publishing Group, a member of Penguin Group (USA) Inc.

U.K. Hardcover: 978 1 445 87105 9 (Chivers Large Print)
U.K. Softcover: 978 1 445 87106 6 (Camden Large Print)

Printed in the United States of America
1 2 3 4 5 6 7 15 14 13 12 11

LOST AND FONDUE

To Jackson. This one's for you.

ACKNOWLEDGMENTS

Thanks are owed to so many who have helped me on this journey.

First, thank you to my husband, my port in the storm. You keep me on course. To my sister and the rest of my family for your love. To my critique partners Krista and Janet for your honesty and creativity. To my blog pals at Mystery Lovers Kitchen and Killer Characters for making me think outside the recipe box. To my Cozy Promo pals for a great forum where new ideas are welcomed. To my Sisters in Crime Guppies and subgroups for your endless enthusiasm. To Kim Lionetti and the Bookends Literary Agency team for your counsel and friendship. To the Berkley Prime Crime team of Kate Seaver, Katherine Pelz, Kaitlyn Kennedy, Teresa Fasolino, and Annette Fiore Defex for your vision and your artistic talents. To Dana Kaye and your publicity team for such attention to detail.

7

Thank you to bookstore owners everywhere, but most particularly to those who have welcomed me on this journey. Thank you to librarians. Over the years, you have inspired me to read and to share my love of reading with others.

And last but not least, thank you to all my readers. Thank you for your emails and comments on my blogs or social networking posts. You make me smile on a daily basis.

CHAPTER 1

"The Ziegler Winery will be the perfect site, Charlotte. So historic!" Meredith, my best friend since grade school, twirled in the middle of The Cheese Shop, arms spread wide, the flaps of her red raincoat fluting outward. Moisture from today's rainfall sprayed off her like a sprinkler. "With just a pinch of *mystère*."

I shuddered. "More than just a pinch."

"Fiddle-dee-dee!" Meredith spun again, bubbling with the kind of excitement I expected from a kid on Christmas, not a thirtysomething elementary school teacher.

"Whoa, whirling dervish." I reined her in before the zippered corners of her jacket could slaughter every display I had set out. April was the best time of year to add fresh touches to Fromagerie Bessette, before tourist season kicked into high gear. I'd added amber-colored tablecloths embroidered with spring motifs to all the display barrels, and mounded them with wheels of tasty Gruyère and decorative containers of pesto, mustards, and jams, as well as tasty crackers made of goji berries and pistachios. My grandfather, Pépère, said I was inviting disaster, putting the jars out where little children could accidentally whack them in passing. But children weren't what I was worried about at the moment — Meredith and her unbridled enthusiasm were. I steered her to a safe place.

"Just think what turning the abandoned winery into a liberal arts college will do for our town," Meredith went on.

Bring an odd assortment of lookie-loos, that's what. A few months ago, a handful of Providence teachers and a band of concerned parents decided that Providence needed a college. They invited potential donors to join the quest. Meredith not only suggested that they convert the Ziegler Winery into the college, but that they hold a fund-raiser there.

Back in the late eighteen hundreds, Zachariah Ziegler, one of Providence's first mayors, landed on the idea to build a winery. Not just an ordinary winery, a mock castle with spires and towers. Its sprawling grounds, befitting a king, dwarfed the nearby Quail Ridge Honeybee Farm. Then

Ziegler's wife went insane. She killed her son and committed suicide. Soon thereafter, Ziegler shut down the operation. In 1950, upon her father's death, Ziegler's daughter deeded the winery to the town of Providence and hightailed it to New York. The town council suggested the winery be boarded up.

"Oh, did I tell you?" Meredith leaned in close, as if expecting to be overheard. She couldn't be. It was only seven A.M. I didn't open the shop until nine. "*Vintage Today* has been at the winery all week giving it a facelift. But, shhhh, it's a secret."

Vintage Today was a home makeover show that didn't know the word *understatement*. I could only imagine what they'd do with the winery's oak-paneled tasting rooms and the musty cellars.

Meredith removed her newsboy-style cap and fluffed her tawny hair. "Isn't it exciting? We'll have so many new faces. Professors and administrators and —" She cut a sharp look toward the kitchen. "What's that?"

"What?" My heart did a jig.

"That incredible smell."

I chuckled at my overreaction. Talking about Ziegler's Winery had put me on edge. "Honey-onion quiche," I said. In addition to selling cheese, The Cheese Shop offered homemade quiches. I tried to come up with a new recipe every week. Today's was made with honey from Quail Ridge, applewood-smoked bacon, sweet Vidalia onions, and Emmental cheese to give it a nice bite. The first batch was minutes from coming out of the oven.

"I have to buy one before I leave."

"I'll give it to you, compliments of the house."

"You're the best. Anyway, where was I?" Meredith tapped her lower lip with her index finger. "Right. The big bash to celebrate. I know it's short notice, since it's tomorrow, but I thought we'd add mariachis at the entrance."

"I adore Latin music, but why mariachis?"

"They're festive. Maybe some of your grandmother's actors will dress up in serapes and sombreros and carry guitars."

Something this avant-garde would be right up Grandmère's alley. In addition to being town mayor, she ran the Providence Playhouse, which put on a mixed bag of productions, to say the least.

"They won't have to play the guitars, of course," Meredith went on. "They'll pretend. Karaoke style, you know. Piped through speakers. I'll have the gals at Sew Inspired Quilt Shoppe help me decorate.

Doesn't it sound fun?" She painted the air with her fingers. "And we'll have a scavenger hunt to look for the buried treasure."

"That's a rumor."

"Old Man Ziegler swore on his deathbed that there was treasure."

I let out an exasperated sigh. If something valuable was buried beneath the winery, I'd bet dimes to dollars Ziegler's daughter had unearthed it before she skipped town. Unless, of course, she found a body buried there — another rumor — and that was why she'd really left.

"Let me show you what else I have planned." Meredith pulled a piece of purple haze paper with frayed edges from her tote and waved it.

The timer in the kitchen tweeted.

"Give me a sec." I hurried to the kitchen at the rear of the shop, pulled the quiches from the oven to cool, grabbed the quickie breakfast I'd intended to eat in the silence of my office, two floral napkins, a knife, and a bottle of Kindred Creek spring water, and led my friend through the stone arches into the wine annex that abutted the main store. I set the breakfast on one of the mosaic café tables, poured the water into two of our big-bowled wineglasses, and offered Meredith half a croissant swathed with soft Taleggio cheese and homemade raspberry jam. Melt-in-your-mouth goodness.

As I took my seat, Meredith handed me the list. In addition to the scavenger hunt, she'd written down sack races, tag football, and Frisbee contests. More than fifty people had been invited.

"Oh, I almost forgot the main reason I came to see you," Meredith said, her mouth half-full. A tiny moan of gourmet delight followed her words. "I want you to serve fondue at the party."

I gulped. She'd hired me at the onset to provide cheese platters and finger food for the event. Fondue was not your typical buffet item. It was lovely for an intimate group of six or eight, but fifty or more? On a day's notice? Oh, my.

"You can do it, right? Of course you can. You're so incredible. Nothing fazes you. I want lots of different kinds of fondues." Meredith ticked her fingers. "A cow's milk, a goat's milk, and a sheep's milk."

"Sheep's milk cheese doesn't melt well."

"Sure, you know best. Anyway, it'll fit into the party's theme. *Lost and Fondue.* Get it? We're *finding* a new college." She giggled, tickled with her cleverness. "And I want Matthew to add champagne to the wine tasting."

14

My cousin, a former sommelier, was my partner in The Cheese Shop and Meredith's flame.

"I know the additions are last-minute, but please say you can do it all. Please?"

How could I say no in the face of her excitement? I nodded.

Meredith leaped to her feet. "Yippee. Oooh, on the platters of cheese, you've simply got to include that Humboldt Fog and, hmmm, that rosemary-crusted sheep's cheese."

"Mitica Romao?"

"That's it. And that Red Hawk from the Cowgirl Creamery. I made an open-faced salmon melt, like you suggested. Major yum!"

Red Hawk cheese was one of my all-time favorites. It had a buttery flavor and the smoothness of a Camembert. The closer to room temperature it was served, the better. That was true for any cheese.

"Did I tell you that I've invited my niece and her art class from Ohio State University to commemorate the event?" Meredith said.

The last time I'd seen Quinn, I was her babysitter.

"I told you she's studying fine arts, didn't I? She's part of this tight-knit group that hopes to go on to the Sorbonne or the Pratt

Institute or the Art Center College of Design in Pasadena. They're coming to paint pictures of the winery before it becomes a college. Sort of like a Degas gathering. I've gotten them some press. Isn't that cool?" Meredith polished off her breakfast, swigged some water, then rose from her chair. "I can't wait to tell my older brother you said yes. You remember Freddy, don't you?"

I warmed all over, remembering my first kiss with Freddy onstage, behind the curtain, in the Providence Elementary auditorium. He was ten, I was seven. His lips had tasted like peanut butter.

"I always thought the two of you would have hooked up," Meredith said.

When Freddy was a senior in high school, he had asked a junior to the prom and not me, a lowly freshman. I'd cried for days.

"You and he would have been terrific together."

Except he married the junior the summer following graduation and had a child — Quinn — five months later. Freddy was charming but impulsive.

"You both have so much energy, and you're kindhearted, and —" Meredith's voice caught ever so slightly. "Did I tell you he adores the Food Network and classic

16

films and juicy mysteries, just like you?"

She had. Many times.

"But now you're with Jordan, and I'm so happy for you."

Over the past few months I'd been dating Jordan Pace, one of our local cheese makers, a man with the good looks of a movie star, the voice of a crooner, and the edginess of a gambler. Except in his case, he liked to keep his past — not his cards — close to his chest.

Meredith glanced at her watch. "Gotta go. Quiche?"

While I packaged a pie in a gold box and tied it with strands of raffia, she kept talking about Freddy and her niece and the other talented artists.

Seconds after she departed, Rebecca, my young assistant, trotted in dressed in a yellow raincoat and matching knee-high boots. She smacked the heels of her boots on the rug by the front door to rid them of water.

"Morning, boss." She whipped off her coat and hung it on a peg at the rear of the shop. Beneath, she wore a yellow crocheted sweater dress that fit her coltish frame perfectly and looked suspiciously new. I kept myself from commenting on her spending habits. She didn't need me to mother her. She set straight to work, unwrapping cheeses and laying them on the cutting board. "Beautiful day, isn't it?"

"Lovely," I lied. An inch of rain in less than twenty-four hours wasn't my idea of beautiful, just sloppy. A foot of fresh snow and a snowball fight with Matthew's twin girls — now, that would be fun. We hadn't had snowfall in weeks and probably wouldn't until next year.

As if reading my mind, Rebecca said, "How are the twins?"

"Super."

In the course of the past year, I had fallen head over heels for my young nieces — who weren't really my nieces, if the truth be told. Matthew was my cousin, which would make the girls my cousins once removed, or something convoluted like that. But Matthew was like a brother to me, so I'd settled on calling the twins my nieces the day they were born, and no one seemed unhappy with the arrangement. At the insistence of my grandparents, I had taken Matthew and the twins into my home when Matthew's wife abandoned him for a cushier life with Mumsie and dear old Dad back in their cottage in England. Cottage, ha! A twelve-acre estate complete with a bowling alley and a dressage ring. So far, having the four of us live under one roof was working out just fine. If only I could stop the twins from sliding down the white oak banister of my old Victorian home. Even beneath their frail weight, the banister creaked. I worried for their safety but pushed the angst aside. In many ways, children are like cheese. Wrap them too tightly with protective wrap and they'll suffocate.

I tied a brown apron over my chinos and gold-striped sweater and joined Rebecca at the cheese counter.

"Did I see Meredith leaving the shop?" she asked.

I brought her up to speed about Meredith's request to change the fund-raiser menu as well as her plan to add mariachis for entertainment.

"Do you know what I heard?" Rebecca began facing the surfaces of the cheeses with a fine-edged knife while I arranged the prepared cheeses in the display case. "I heard there's buried treasure at the winery."

"Rumors." I blew a loose strand of hair off my face.

"Have you ever been inside?"

"Not on your life." Back in high school a group of daring souls, led by Meredith's brother Freddy, stole in. I chickened out. I had no desire to skulk through cobwebbed rooms or socialize with the rodents that had to have taken over the place.

Rebecca said, "You know, on *CSI: New York,* there was this story about —"

The grape-leaf-shaped chimes over the front door jingled, and Grandmère chugged inside, wagging her finger. "Where is your grandfather?"

She strode to the back of the shop, the flaps of her raincoat furling open and revealing a bright pink sweater and patchwork skirt. I smiled. My grandmother might be in her seventies, but she still had the style of a hip gypsy and the energy of a locomotive going downhill with no brakes.

She peeked into the kitchen and into the walk-in refrigerator. "I need him at the theater."

"What's the play you're doing this spring, Mrs. Bessette?" Rebecca asked.

"A new playwright's work: *No Exit with Poe.*" My grandmother gave a dramatic flourish of her hand. "Edgar Allan Poe's poetry, as interpreted by the characters of Garcin, Estelle, and Inez."

"That makes no sense," I said.

"Why?" Rebecca asked. Before leaving her Amish community and moving to Providence, Rebecca had never been to the theater. Now she was an empty vessel eager to be filled with knowledge. In addition to being a TV mystery junkie, she read a play a week.

I said, "Because *No Exit* is an absurdist play about three people in hell who probe each other's painful memories. It has nothing to do with Poe."

Grandmère sidled up to me and tapped my nose with her fingertip. "That is where you're wrong, *chérie*. The playwright is focusing on Sartre's main theme, the suffering of being, as seen through the poetry of Poe. We'll get rave reviews, mark my words." She scuttled to the wine annex and looked inside. "Where is your grandfather?"

"Not here."

"He said he was going for a cup of coffee at the diner, but I know him. He can't resist coming to The Cheese Shop. Oh, Etienne!" she called in a singsong manner.

She was right. My grandfather loved spending time in the shop. He may have retired, but he needed to breathe the pungent air inside Fromagerie Bessette on a daily basis or he'd die.

"He's hiding, *non?*" Grandmère returned to my side and peered cynically into my eyes, like a snake charmer who was being conned by the snake.

"Oh, please," I sniffed. "You think I'm abetting him? Maybe he's taking a little stroll. You know how self-conscious he's become about the few pounds he's gained since his retirement." My grandfather loved to sneak slices of cheese from the tasting platters we set on the marble countertop. "Look, there he is." I pointed. Pépère was exiting the Country Kitchen across the street. "And you'll notice he's not headed this way."

Grandmère muttered something in French, chastising herself for not believing the love of her life, and I smiled. Theirs was the kind of relationship I craved, aged like a fine cheese.

"Charlotte," Rebecca said. "Did you tell your grandmother that Meredith wants local actors to be mariachis at the fundraiser?"

I cocked my head. Exactly when in the last few minutes did she think I'd had time to do that?

Color drained from my grandmother's face. "No, no, no!"

I flinched at the panic in her tone. "Why not?" I asked, unable to mask my concern.

She didn't answer.

A shiver coursed through me. When Meredith first suggested the idea of converting the college, my grandmother suffered the same reaction, but she'd never explained why. Not one to buy into rumors, I had let the matter drop. "Is it the music?"

"It matters not. It . . ." Her voice trailed off. She petted my cheek. "I must fly. *Au revoir.*"

As she scurried out, I turned the sign in the front window to Open. Customers bustled inside. Many sampled cheeses, while others came to hang out and chat. With the flurry of activity, the feeling of foreboding vanished. An hour later, I believed nothing in the world could go wrong.

Was I ever mistaken.

The door burst open, a gust of cool air invaded the shop, and in bounded Sylvie, Matthew's ex-wife.

With her you-owe-me attitude, enhanced lips, and augmented breasts, Sylvie, as Grandmère would say, was all huff and fluff. She adjusted a gargantuan leather tote over the shoulder of her faux ocelot coat — at least I hoped it was faux — flipped her acid-white hair off her shoulders, and in a shrill English accent that would make Anglophiles cringe, shouted, "Where are my babies?"

CHAPTER 2

Without a care, Sylvie swiped droplets of water off her coat onto The Cheese Shop floor and stomped toward me. "I want my girls now. You can't keep me away. You have no right. They're mine. Mine, I tell you. Give them to me. Do you hear me?"

Loud and clear. I bridled at her demanding tone. Not because her entrance had scared off half of my customers or because her ranting had frightened the rest of them so much that they'd retreated to the edges of the shop, but because her girls were no longer hers. She had abandoned them.

"Sylvie." I didn't attempt to hug her. "Why don't we go in the other room?" I did offer a hand to guide her. It was the diplomatic thing to do, and the wine annex was empty of patrons.

She wrinkled her refurbished ski-tipped nose as if she'd detected some horrid odor. "I want my babies, Charlotte. They aren't at your house. I thought they might be here because it's so early."

"They're at school." I kept my voice cool, although I felt anything but.

"They are not. It's Saturday."

"They've got pottery classes."

"Fine. I'll fetch them."

I gripped her elbow to stop her, pinching hard with my thumb. So much for diplomacy.

She wrenched free and, out of nowhere, burst into tears. Crocodile tears. She flung herself into my arms and cried like a baby. Reluctantly, I patted her back.

"I made a mistake. A huge mistake," she blubbered. Her tears soaked through my sweater. After a long moment, she pushed herself away and wiped streaks of mascara from beneath her eyes. "You believe me, don't you?"

I smoothed the hair cupping my neck. Did I? Did it matter?

"Let's talk about it," I said.

Giving Rebecca an over-the-shoulder *what can you do?* glance, I guided Sylvie through the brick arches leading to the wine annex and settled her at one of the tables nestled by the bay window. Rags, my adorable Ragdoll cat who'd dared to sneak from the office to see what I was up to, sprinted to the wine bar and crouched beneath one of the stools, ears perked.

Sylvie shrugged off her ocelot coat to reveal a silver lamé sweater so tight that it made her ample breasts look like pyramids. To complete the outlandish ensemble, she wore gold spandex pants tucked into matching gold ankle boots. I bit back a comment. Taste had never been one of Sylvie's strong suits.

"I was overwhelmed and so young when I had the girls," Sylvie said.

She'd had the twins at the age of thirty-four. Hardly young.

"Do they miss me?" Sylvie twirled her hand in a circle. "Of course they do." She rifled through her tote bag, pulled out a wadded-up tissue, and blew her nose — a big honking sound.

I searched for the most tactful way to make her leave town. "Look, Sylvie, the girls are happy now. They've gotten over your abandoning them."

"Abandoning? Is that what you told them I did?"

"You didn't call. You didn't write."

"I was soul-searching. I've been seeing a therapist."

I raised an eyebrow. Just because Sylvie had met with a therapist didn't mean she'd reaped the benefits of therapy. "Amy and Clair wanted their mother, and you —"

"Oh, can it." Sylvie's tears dried up faster than rainfall in a desert. Her face turned hard. She grabbed her coat and bounded from the table. "I don't need your permission to see them."

I sprinted after her, ready to tie her up if need be. I kept heavy twine in the storage room, and I was a master at knots. I'd macraméd a fishnet to get my Girl Scout badge when other girls had only made plant hangers. I caught up with Sylvie by the archway and spun her around.

"Release me." She batted my arm. The crown of her diamond ring stung like a you-know-what. "I'd expected the teary act would work with someone like you."

"Someone like me?" I sputtered.

"Weak."

"What?" My voice spiked.

"You know what I mean."

Actually, I didn't. I was not weak. I was considerate. There was a big difference.

"I'm going to see them, Charlotte." She thrust a well-sharpened fingernail at me. "Whether you and Matthew like it or not."

"What won't I like?" Matthew shuffled into the annex carrying a box of wine and came to a halt. He gaped at his ex.

"Hello, love." Sylvie sashayed up to him and traced her finger along his strong jaw, then dragged her finger down his neck and arm. "So lovely to see you. You've been working out."

I gulped. She was good. Matthew looked transfixed. Like a siren, Sylvie was pulling him in with her honey-toned voice.

"I've missed you so much." Sylvie pried the box of wine from his grasp and set it on the wine counter. "Come sit, and let's catch up."

As she waltzed him toward the mosaic tables, Matthew pulled free. "Stop it, Sylvie!" He backed up two feet and glowered at her. Gone was his boyish demeanor. No longer was he a puppy with a gangly lope.

I breathed easier. A year ago, when Matthew was vulnerable, he might have caved to her wiles. But not now. Not when he had Meredith for support. Not when the girls had turned an emotional corner.

"But lover —"

"Stop it, I said!" Matthew's words came out firm, commanding. "Why are you here?"

"Don't get cheeky with me, Matthew." Sylvie cocked a hip and streaked her tongue across her lips, making yet another attempt to lure him into her web. Matthew remained tense. "I'm here because I'm taking my girlie-girls ice skating at the Harvest Moon Ranch."

Not many people booked weddings at the Harvest Moon during the winter and early spring, so the owners had turned their old red barn into a skating arena, fitted with an artificial ice surface.

"You're doing no such thing," Matthew snapped.

"The girls love skating."

"And you hate it. Your parents put you up to this, didn't they?"

"Tosh!" Sylvie thrust her chin upward. "I don't have to explain myself to you. In fact, I don't have to explain myself to anybody." She strutted around him, marched through the main shop, and out the front door.

Matthew charged after her. "Now, you listen to me, Sylvie —"

The chimes over the front door jingled, and then the door slammed.

Seconds later, a shriek sliced the air. Female. From the street.

A current of fear shimmied down my back. I tore to the sidewalk and stood beneath the awning, protected from the rain. A blast of cool air hit my face. While peering for signs of Matthew and Sylvie, I spotted two young men in swimsuits and a bikini-clad young woman bounding down the street. All wore flip-flops. All were armed with water balloons. The young woman, whom I recognized as Meredith's niece Quinn, screamed — the sound matching the shriek that I believed had come from Sylvie. I breathed a sigh of relief that Matthew and Sylvie weren't exchanging blows, though I shivered at the sight of the students. What were they thinking, being out in the cold in such skimpy outfits?

Rain-wet red hair clung to Quinn's pretty face as she dashed toward the tallest of the young men. "I'm going to kill you, Harker," she yelled, raising her second balloon.

With his rippling muscles and surfer-dude blond hair, Harker looked like he should have been named Adonis. According to Meredith, Harker had more talent in his pinky than the rest of the artists put together. His fellow balloon thrower was Harker's polar opposite, dark-haired and lean. A third young man, zipper-thin with hunched shoulders and baggy trunks hanging low on his hips, towed a Radio Flyer wagon filled with latex ammunition and a pile of something covered with a tarp. Give the guy a hump and he'd look as miserable as Quasimodo.

"Goose, goose, duck!" Quinn hurled the

balloon.

"Missed, babe!" Harker laughed.

"Missed me, too," said the dark-haired young man.

Harker bolted to the wagon, snatched more balloons, and flung one of his missiles at Quinn. It splat near her feet. She squealed with delight.

"Okay, gang, that's enough." Freddy Vance, Meredith's brother, flew out of the Country Kitchen across the street. "Did you hear me?" He hustled between parked cars and clapped his hands. From a distance, he appeared the same as he had in high school, compact and energized. A star gymnast. "Enough, I said." He waved his arms overhead. His orange slicker, which was just this side of Day-Glo, made him look like a crossing guard on fire. "Let's not scare off the nice folk of Providence. Show some respect. Quinn, where are your clothes? Do not tell me you left them at the bed-and-breakfast."

"They're in the wagon," Quinn said.

"Put them on," Freddy ordered. "All of you."

"Yeah, yeah." Harker waved him off.

Freddy charged Harker and nabbed him by the shoulder. He must have pinched hard, because Harker instantly acquiesced. He jogged to the Radio Flyer wagon, reached beneath the tarp, and pulled out dry clothes. After donning them over his wet swimsuit, the other students did the same.

Rebecca exited The Cheese Shop and joined me under the awning. Plumes of her warm breath fogged up the cold air. "Are they the artists?"

I nodded.

"Hey, Charlotte!" Freddy strolled toward me wearing that familiar wry grin. "I leave the kids alone for one minute, and see what they do? Mind if we warm up inside your shop and grab a bite to eat? I heard it's *the place* to hang out."

Rebecca elbowed me. I got her drift. We didn't actually serve meals, and I didn't want to compete with the Country Kitchen on a regular basis, but who was I to say no to a little extra business during a slow season?

"Be our guests."

Freddy gave me a quick squeeze and a rain-soaked kiss. "Gang, inside." He pushed open the front door and allowed his flock to pass beneath his arm. Quinn, who had covered her teensy bikini with a long-sleeved T-shirt, jeans, and hiking boots, pulled up the rear. Before entering, she gave me a fierce hug. I could feel the dampness from her wet swimsuit seeping through the cotton.

Freddy lingered by the open door. "So you own The Cheese Shop. Wow! I always knew you had a bright future. And you're a knockout. Meredith said you were, but who could believe Sis? Say cheese!" He scooted inside.

Shaking off the chill that was cutting into my bones, I followed him and moved behind the counter. "What'll it be, everyone?"

Rags weaved figure eights around my ankles. I nudged him with my toe, and he got the message. Everything was fine. He could retreat to the office and nap.

Before one of the students called out an order, the front door opened yet again, and a statuesque woman in her late twenties flounced in. "Freddddddddy?" She reminded me of a luscious Italian diva, with lungs that could blast out a pitch-perfect aria. "It's as cold as a polar bear's nose out there." She approached the cheese counter, nestled beside Freddy, and assessed me with open amusement.

I considered checking a mirror to make sure I didn't have something caught in my teeth but fought the urge.

"How do you do?" she said. "I'm Winona Westerton."

"Winona's a potential donor for the college," Freddy said.

"More than potential, darlin'. I've already given a hundred" — she paused for effect — "thousand."

Exactly what did she do that she could afford to give so much money to a boutique college?

Winona gave me a sly, bordering on disdainful look. If she wasn't careful, she and Prudence Hart, Providence's new self-appointed society goddess, would have to duel it out for Witch of the Midwest.

Freddy said, "Everyone, let's order breakfast before we paint."

"We're going to paint in this weather?" Quinn said.

"Of course we are," Harker chimed in. "It's ideal impressionist lighting outside."

Through the eyes of an artist, I mused. To most, the rain would seem grim.

"I think it's more like Dalí meets Van Gogh." Winona winked at Harker. "Jewels melting on sidewalks."

He didn't seem to appreciate the comparison.

"That's what's great about art," Freddy replied. "To each his own."

As the students eyed the cheese selections, Quinn skirted around the counter. She drummed my forearm with her fingertips, and whispered, "Sorry you had to see us, you know, goofing around. We aren't smashed or anything."

"Not to worry," I whispered. "I've had my share of romps." In college, a group of us had decided hitchhiking to the big football game was a safe venture. Along the way, everyone backed out except for me, who stupidly showed her mettle by getting into a car with four men. Luckily, they were all businessmen with young daughters, each of whom lectured me about the dangers of the road. Throwing water balloons on a chilly spring morning was a minor infraction compared to that. "Now, what can I get you?"

"How about that big pear-shaped cheese?" Quinn said.

"San Simon, a cow's milk from Spain. Nice choice. It's from the Galician region and tastes creamy and smoky."

"Oh, rats. I can't have that. I'm allergic. I can only eat goat's cheese."

"We have lots of goat cheese selections," Rebecca said. "Goat Camembert and goat Brie." She leaned forward as if imparting a dire secret. "My personal favorite is Cypress Grove Purple Haze. Here, taste this." She cut Quinn a slice from an opened round of cheese and handed it to her. "It's got hints of lavender and fennel, and it's fabulous melted on a grilled portobello mushroom."

Quinn slipped the morsel into her mouth. "Oh, that's delish."

"Winona, what'll you have?" Freddy said.

"How about that sourdough roll?" She wiggled a fire-engine-red fingernail at the shelf filled with baskets of fresh-baked breads that we ordered from Providence Patisserie. "It looks crusty."

"Soft as cotton on the inside," I said. "Which cheese?"

"No cheese. It'll make me fat."

"A piece of cheese won't make you fat," I said, eager to dispel the rumor. "Though eating too much of anything will."

"I'll take that roll, too," the zipper-thin young man with the hunched shoulders said. "And some of that white cheese."

"The Collier's Welsh Cheddar." I pulled out a wedge. "Good choice. Nutty with a hint of crystallization."

"Nutty," Harker said. "That's perfect for you, Edsel. Don't forget to say please and thank you, man."

Harker poked Quinn. She snickered. Edsel shot Harker a stern look. Freddy shot Quinn one.

"Hey, Harker, you gotta see this room."

The dark-haired young man stood in the archway of the annex. On the back of his T-shirt the word DANE was painted in huge letters. Was it a statement of origin, or a tribute to a dark and brooding Hamlet? He had the look — the somber eyes, the familiar chip on his shoulder. "It's so retro," he went on.

Retro? I didn't think the way we had decorated was retro at all. The annex was chic yet rustic. We'd lined the walls with mahogany, laid the floor with travertine tiles, brought in an antique wood bar and stools from an old Irish pub, and created cubby holes for each wine bottle.

"Wait until we get into the winery, Dane," Harker said.

Aha. Dane was the young man's name.

"I hear it's *major* retro," Harker added.

"Don't make fun." Quinn nudged Harker with her hip.

If my romance radar was working properly, I'd say they had a little thing going, and moody Dane wasn't too pleased with that scenario. Neither, it appeared, was Edsel.

"Don't mind them, Charlotte. I like what you've done to the place," Freddy said. "Don't you, Winona?"

"How am I supposed to know, silly man?"

She flicked her fingernail on his sleeve. "I've never been here before."

Freddy snapped his fingers. "Right."

"What cheese do you want to order, Dane?" Quinn asked.

"Morbier," Dane said, with the proper French pronunciation — a kid after my grandfather's heart. Pépère loved the flavorful cheese with the layer of vegetable ash in the middle.

"And what about you, oh glorious treasure hunter?" Quinn asked. "What are you going to get?" She bumped Harker again.

He grunted. "I'm not a treasure hunter."

"Are, too," Edsel jibed. "You're the one who talked us into this little trek."

"Did not, dufus."

"Did so, bro. You've got cash on the brain. Ca-ching, ca-ching."

"Blame Quinn," Harker said.

"No way," Quinn countered. "Dane showed me the story on the 'Net."

"Only after your aunt said she was turning the winery into a college," Dane said.

Freddy clapped his hands. "Okay, guys, that's enough."

Dane's cheeks turned ruddy and his cocoa-colored eyes smoldered with hostility. What was his problem? Was he wary, like me, about the winery and its iffy history?

Or was he just plain angry at Harker for getting the girl? Quinn was gorgeous.

"What does it matter who told who what?" Edsel said, an edge to his voice. "We're here to paint. Remember, painting is our vocation. We're all going to be famous."

"Oh, man." Harker faked a sob. "I'm getting all choked up just thinking about how successful we're going to be. Not!" He honked out a laugh. "Edsel, wise up! Our vocation? We'll all starve."

"You'll only starve if you keep losing poker hands to Dane," Edsel said.

"I don't lose. You're the one who's a loser." Harker's gaze turned icy. "A little pirate's booty could help take the sting out of poverty for both of us, don't you think?"

"I heard the treasure is jewels," Winona cut in. Though older than the group of students, she looked eager to become part of the teasing. "Rubies and emeralds and diamonds."

"It's not jewels," Harker said, a bite to his tone.

"Nah, it's gold doubloons," Edsel quipped.

"Stowed by pirates in a skull-and-crossbones box," Freddy said as he painted the air with his fingertips.

"Pirates?" Winona sounded wonder-struck. "Are you serious?"

Freddy nodded.

"Pirates," Dane said. "Yeah, that's ripe. Yo ho ho."

When he smiled, I revised my estimation of him. He didn't remind me so much of Hamlet as he did a clean-shaven Johnny Depp. Outline his eyes, add a scruffy beard, and give him some dreadlocks, and he'd look just like Captain Jack Sparrow.

Rebecca drew close and said, "Were there really pirates in Providence?" The quaver in her voice made me turn. Her lower lip trembled.

"No," I said, though the chatter was unnerving me, too. As a girl, I'd heard the rumors. They had rattled me in the same way then, even though I knew they couldn't be true. Kindred Creek wasn't big enough for a houseboat, let alone a pirate ship.

"All this talk is giving me a bad case of the creeps," Rebecca whispered.

I forced myself to be the model of calm and patted her arm. "Don't worry. It's only a rumor."

"But rumors are based on fact."

CHAPTER 3

The next day, by the time we arrived at Ziegler Winery for Meredith's celebration, the rain had ended and dusk draped the earth with a soft purple light. The entrance to the mock castle on the hill looked exactly as Meredith had promised. Handmade Chinese lanterns on poles lined the driveway. Multicolored crepe paper encircled the Corinthian columns flanking the porch. A half-moon of hand-stitched flags representing the counties of Ohio stood sentry by the stairs to the portico. The counties didn't actually have flags, but Meredith believed imagination was the spice of life.

Meredith met me as I pulled up the driveway. I rolled down the driver's side window.

"I'm so glad you're here," she yelled over the music.

Local actors, dressed like mariachis, strummed guitars by the front door. As

41

planned, their music was being piped through rocklike speakers that had been hidden in the garden behind tulips and jonquils. I wondered if my grandmother had shared what worried her with Meredith but didn't want to ask and spoil Meredith's buoyant mood.

"Isn't it fun having a party on a Sunday evening?" Meredith said.

She directed us to park at the far side of the broad gravel driveway. We had arrived as a caravan — I in my white Escort, Pépère and Grandmère in their Audi, and Rebecca and Bozz, my teenage Internet guru, in Rebecca's MINI Cooper. She'd recently bought it and wanted to drive it everywhere. Matthew was supposed to trail the pack. Where was he?

Meredith eyed the colorful pots in the back of my Escort. "Oooh, what kind of fondues did you make?"

"As requested, one's a Humboldt Fog goat cheese fondue made with whipping cream, pepper, and chives. The other's a champagne fondue, with nutmeg and white pepper to give it a zing. I used a Black Label Gruyère de Comté."

"Yum!" Meredith adjusted her ruby red shawl over the thin straps of her matching red dress and hoisted a box of utensils from my trunk. She trotted across the driveway and up a set of stairs. How she could walk in her spiky high heels was beyond me, but she looked fabulous. Cold, but fabulous.

I fetched a second box of utensils and followed. When I reached the porch, I turned and understood why Zachariah Ziegler had settled here and why Meredith wanted to turn the place into a college. The 360-degree view was incredible. Gently rolling hills, freshly green and hinting at the promise of a lusty spring, could be seen for miles. The lights of Providence twinkled below.

A door squeaked open and I heard, "Wow!"

Bozz popped from the MINI Cooper and halted in his tracks. He wasn't taking in the same view I was. Quinn and the other art students had just arrived in an Explorer. Quinn, the first to climb out of the SUV, looked radiant in a pair of jeans, sky blue sweater, and multicolored knitted scarf. Bozz watched her, his mouth gaping open. I grinned. Who could blame the kid? Girls were on his radar. And he should be on theirs. He was growing handsomer by the month. High school wrestling had been good for him.

Harker bolted from the car, slung his arm around Quinn, and sneered at Bozz. "What are you staring at, dufus? She's mine."

Edsel clambered out and slung his thumbs through the loops of his jeans. "Bro, I'm not really up on today's possessive lingo, but claiming a girl is *yours* before you've put a diamond ring on her finger is a little premature."

Harker cut him a nasty look.

Dane slapped Harker on the back. "Hey, man, want to take a tour of the place? I hear the inside is pretty cool."

"Who did you hear that from?"

"My folks. They're Ohio history and architecture buffs."

"I thought you were from New York," Quinn said.

"I am, but my folks came from Ohio. Anyway, see, they knew I was coming to paint this place, and . . ."

As the group continued its conversation and headed for the front steps, Matthew tore into the driveway. He screeched to a halt and scrambled out of his Jeep.

"Bozz, give me some help. Now!" Matthew stomped to the rear of the Jeep and whipped open the hatchback door with such force I feared he'd tear it off.

"What's with Matthew?" Meredith whispered to me.

I didn't have a clue, but I intended to find

out. Lugging the box of utensils, I hurried down the stairs and cornered him by the Jeep. "Are you okay? The shipment of pinots from Washington State arrived, and you got the Bozzutos' wines, right?"

He gave a curt nod.

"They said they were supplying gewürztraminer and sauvignon blanc," I went on. Ohio vintners do best with grapes that require a cool climate. "The Bozzutos are here." All the local vintners were invited to the event. "Do you need to speak with them?"

Matthew shook his head.

"Then what's with the attitude?"

"Sylvie showed up at the shop right after you left and begged to take the twins for a night on the town. They already went horseback riding." He ran a hand along his neck. "What was I supposed to say with the girls within earshot? 'No, you can't go'? They'd have blamed me for ruining their plans. Or their lives." He muttered, "Can't win for trying." He blew a thatch of hair off his forehead, then handed a case of wine to Bozz, grabbed one for himself, slammed the hatchback shut, and strode toward the front porch.

"What's Sylvie's game plan?" I adjusted the box in my arms and kept pace. "How long is she here for?"

"Got me."

I adored my cousin. He truly loved his children. Seeing him this distraught tugged at my heartstrings. In the past few months, his relationship with Meredith had done him a world of good. The glow had returned to his cheeks, the humor to his life. He'd even put a little meat on his lanky bones. What would happen if Sylvie decided to move back to Providence? I wished I knew what her agenda was. Money, perhaps. Maybe Mumsie and Dad had cut her off.

"Hey, babe." Matthew met Meredith on the porch and, like a seasoned actor, forced a smile. He bussed her on the cheek. "You look great. So does the winery."

"Isn't it fabulous?" Grinning from ear to ear, Meredith glided into the foyer and twirled on the parquet floor. "Did I tell you there are winepresses and vats downstairs in the cellar?"

"You went down?" I said.

"No, no, not I. I'm not that brave. The folks from *Vintage Today* told me. They've set candles in the old sconces. *Très mystérieux.*" She poked a finger upward. "Oooh, and there's a ballroom that takes up the entire floor! I decided not to have any races and such, but won't a scavenger hunt

46

be fun?"

Her enthusiasm was infectious. The creepy feeling I'd had yesterday dissipated. As I took in my surroundings, I realized that the *Vintage Today* crew had surprisingly gotten this makeover right. Oversized oil paintings as well as portraits hung on the refurbished oak paneling in the hallways. A gorgeous spray of irises sat on an antique side table. A winding staircase with a thick balustrade led from the first floor to the second. The domed ceiling sparkled like it was encrusted with gems.

"Give me a quick verbal tour," I said to Meredith. "Where's the dining room?"

"End of the hall."

"And the tasting rooms?"

"Beyond the dining room. Untouched. The wood paneling was still in fabulous shape."

Matthew said, "Bozz and Rebecca, follow me."

"*Bon soir,* Meredith." Pépère scuttled into the mansion, his sparse white hair flying out like wings, his cheeks ruddy with excitement. "Where do you want this, Charlotte?" In his arms he carried a box of breads and dipping sauces.

Arms full, I gestured with my chin. Pépère took off. Grandmère bustled after him,

47

raincoat cinched tightly. The lower half of her burgundy corduroy skirt swirled around her calves and dark brown boots. She paused by the staircase and peered at one of the portraits. Though she stood in profile, I could see her nose wrinkle with distaste. She caught my gaze and started again for the dining room.

I dashed to her. "What's wrong?"

She shook her head.

"Grandmère, talk to me."

"It matters not, *chérie.* It is an old woman's superstition. That is all."

She disappeared around the corner and the feeling of foreboding that had walloped me yesterday returned. I headed back to Meredith but stopped to glance at the portrait that had spooked my grandmother. A gold placard beneath it read: *Zachariah Ziegler.* The old man reminded me of Ebenezer Scrooge with his gaunt cheeks, deepset dark eyes, and miserly mouth. A family portrait hung beside his. In it, the son's face was as stoic as his father's, his eyes as deepset and solemn. Thinking about his tragic death made me shudder, and I wondered again if the place should be razed and the land preserved. What kind of money would it take to erect a brand-new building without the tragic history attached to it? Could I talk Meredith and her fellow college committee members into the idea?

"In addition to the dining room and living room" — Meredith moved to my side — "on the main level, we have an observatory, a study, and a music room. What do you think?"

I giggled. For a second, I felt like I'd been plunked into the middle of a game of *Clue*. I said, "In the library with the candlestick, Ms. Scarlet."

"Stop. You're awful." Meredith swatted my arm. "Oh, speaking of the library, I've displayed the artists' works there. Make sure you see what Quinn created. Her style is reminiscent of Matisse. And Harker . . ." She swirled her hand in the air. "Jackson Pollock meets Picasso with a bit of Shakespeare thrown in."

"He's not only an artist, he's a playwright?" I grinned at her.

She tweaked me again. "You know what I mean — wild, unpredictable, yet whimsical. Brilliant."

High praise for a student around the age of twenty, I mused.

"Let me show you the dining room," she continued. "It's incredible!"

In keeping with the turn-of-the-century theme, *Vintage Today* had decorated the dining room with gold-filigree lighting fixtures and red and gold-flocked drapes. The dining table was massive, at least twenty feet long and ten feet wide, and draped with ecru linens. In the center of the table stood a spray of white iris, which was gracefully inserted into a burgundy crystal vase. French doors leading to the terraces that faced the vineyard's slopes stood open. A cool breeze swept inside.

For the next ten minutes my crew and I shuttled food into the grandiose room. Once our vehicles were emptied, I advised Rebecca and Bozz to set up the warming trays, the lazy Susans, the fondues, and the accompaniments toward the end of the table closest to the kitchen. Matthew chose the opposite end for his wine tasting. We left ample space for all the other potluck items to come.

As if on cue, a group of townsfolk entered the dining room. Each carried a covered dish.

Meredith joined me, brimming with good vibes. "Gretel brought her favorite chili," she said. The Congregational Church pastor's wife made chili that was triple-alarm good. "And Lois brought her yummy scones." The owner of Lavender and Lace, a bed-and-breakfast inn located next to my

Victorian home, was an incredible baker. Good scones, she said, were essential at high tea. Meredith leaned in. "And Tim supplied trays of his famous bacon-filled potato skins." Timothy O'Shea, owner of our local pub, was a fine chef. He created appetizers that made me want to give up eating dinner altogether. For his potato skins — at my suggestion — he used old-fashioned Fior di Latte Mozzarella, a creamy, meltable cow's milk cheese with a salty finish.

Meredith continued. "And Delilah brought —"

"Let me guess. Grilled cheese."

Meredith tapped her nose. Delilah, our friend and owner of the Country Kitchen, had been testing grilled cheese combinations for weeks. Holmes County was vying to host a statewide competition. Delilah had invented a number of new recipes, including a potato-bacon grilled cheese, lobster grilled cheese, and a portobello vegetarian grilled cheese. She'd even used one of my cheesecake recipes to make a grilled cheese for dessert.

"Uh-oh, what's she doing here?" Meredith's mouth twisted into a knot.

"Who?"

"Cruella de Vil."

Gripping the twins firmly by the hands,

Sylvie strode into the dining room, her ocelot coat flogging her calves.

Matthew charged around me to block her entry.

"Why, Matthew, you look almost apoplectic." Sylvie offered a sly grin. "What's the problem, love?"

Matthew muttered something unintelligible.

Sylvie released Amy and Clair and posed, head cocked, hand on hip, trying to look nonchalant, but she didn't. Her acid-white hair hung in straggly pieces around her face. Today's horseback outing with the girls must have taken a nip out of her. *C'est bon,* I thought with wicked delight. On the other hand, the twins looked energized. Dark-haired little Amy glowed with vivacity, and Clair, a head taller than her sister and typically pale, had rosy cheeks.

I crossed to the girls and whispered, "Did you have a good time?"

Clair nodded, but she didn't look me in the eye. Was she embarrassed that she had enjoyed being with her mother?

"Matthew, don't make such a big deal of everything." Sylvie pressed her palm to Matthew's chest, right over his heart. He reeled as if he'd been scorched. To cover, Sylvie nodded greetings to the assembling crowd. A spat never failed to attract lookie-loos.

My grandmother and grandfather pushed to the front of the throng. Grandmère seemed to be holding her breath.

"This is an adult party, Sylvie," Matthew hissed.

"Tosh!"

"It's not a place for children. Amy, Clair, I'm sorry. Charlotte, would you —"

"Laissez-moi, chérie." Grandmère warned me to stand pat. "I'll take the girls. After we eat, we're going straightaway to the theater." She crouched and opened her arms. Looking sheepish, the twins scooted to her. She ushered them out of the room, and Pépère trundled after them.

An instant later, Matthew grabbed Sylvie by the arm and swept her toward the exit.

If looks could kill, Sylvie wasn't long for this world.

I scurried after them, eager to watch Matthew put her in her place. However, before I had even reached the foyer, I heard the slam of a car door and the screech of tires in the driveway.

Matthew returned inside, his eyes smoldering, his mouth tight. He slipped an arm around me, whispered, "Fiasco avoided," and guided me back to the dining room.

The banquet table looked resplendent, like something out of a medieval painting. In addition to cut vegetables, Rebecca had suggested serving sliced apples and cooked and cooled fingerling potatoes with the fondue. She'd piled them high onto huge platters. Providence Patisserie had supplied hand-woven Amish baskets filled with crusty bread cubes.

Matthew squeezed my arm and left me to tend to the guests who were hankering for wine.

"Oooh, look who just popped in." Rebecca danced to my side and nudged me with her bony hip.

My heart caught in my chest. Imaginary butterflies took flight in my stomach. Jordan Pace stood in the doorway. Golden light from the chandeliers highlighted his striking cheekbones. Could any man look better in a white shirt, jeans, and boots than he did? Call me crazy, but I swear I heard a jangle of spurs and horses neighing in the distance.

I twisted away and plucked at my hair. "How do I look?"

"Sporty," Rebecca said.

Rats. I'd been going for Woman of Mystery. Or at least semi-sexy. I'd worn black jeans tucked into black boots, an emerald green turtleneck sweater, and for the first time in days, I'd applied eye shadow and blush. I'd even painted my fingernails and spritzed myself with Shalimar perfume. It didn't matter how long I'd been dating Jordan, I still felt as if every meeting was our first. I wanted to make a good impression.

"Wave," Rebecca said. "He's staring."

I spun around. Jordan gave me a two-fingered salute. We strolled along the edge of the dining table until we met halfway.

"Hello, gorgeous." He pecked my cheek and laced his fingers around mine. The instant our flesh touched, something inside me went hippety-hop, right down to my toes. That was followed by a rush of desire, the kind that begged for a pot of cocoa for two.

Alone.

In front of a roaring fire.

"Got a second before the gala begins?" Jordan escorted me toward one of the open windows by a terrace. "I thought we might plan that romantic getaway we've been talking about."

"Where are we going? Cleveland? Columbus?" Both cities were short driving distances from Holmes County.

"I was thinking someplace like Gruyères."

I gasped. "Switzerland?" The quaint village of Gruyères, known for its cheese, had topped my travel list for years. "A weekend isn't long enough."

"Then a week. Better yet." He winked. "We'll go snowshoeing at night. Or we could take the funicular to Plan-Francey. I was thinking we'd aim for next week."

"But it's the beginning of our tourist season."

"Uh-uh. That's not until May. C'mon, be spontaneous. Say yes." He ran a finger along my arm. I shivered with desire. "You form the word like this." Teasingly he mouthed the word: *Yes.* "Remember what we've been talking about. Spontaneity is the spice of life."

I wish I were impulsive. Really. Sometimes I was, like when Rebecca prodded me to snoop, but otherwise, I preferred a schedule. No surprises. Looking back over my life, I was pretty sure that my hitchhiking adventure had put me off being unstructured.

Jordan chuckled. "C'mon, you can do it. Repeat after me: Yes." He kissed me behind the ear, the exact spot that made my knees weak.

Before I could answer, Winona Westerton, clad in a tight gold dress, snaked her way into our twosome. I was struck by the contrast between us — she with dark hair that swooped along her face like a 1940s vamp, and I with my short feathery blonde cut. She clung to a wisp of a man with translucent skin and hair the color of butter.

"Hello, Charlotte," Winona said. "Remember me?"

As if I could forget. She looked like Venus de Milo with arms.

"May I introduce you to Wolford Langdon, a patron of the arts and a donor, like me," Winona added.

"Possible donor." The frail man offered a stiff nod as he nudged his thick-rimmed glasses back into place.

"Lovely evening, isn't it?" Winona fondled her dangly earrings and gazed appreciatively at Jordan. "What's your name, cowboy?"

"Jordan Pace." He didn't look moved by her charms, which endeared him to me even more.

"Jordan's a farmer and cheese maker in Providence," I said.

"But you didn't grow up here, did you?" Winona assessed him with a shrewd eye. "We don't grow them this good in Ohio."

"California," Jordan said politely, not responding to her overt attempt to charm his socks off.

"I love California," Winona gushed.

Since we'd started dating, I'd learned

about Jordan's past in snippets. He knew how to ski, liked the color blue, and adored Southwestern cuisine. His favorite author was Lee Child, his favorite movie *The Godfather,* followed closely by *The Bourne Identity,* and his favorite musical artist was Dave Brubeck. I craved to know more.

Winona turned her attention to the room. "Oh, my, with digs like these, I might reenroll in college. How about you, Wolford?"

Her slight companion stifled a yawn, peeled Winona's fingers off his arm, and shuffled toward the buffet. Winona didn't flinch at his rebuff.

"Hello-o-o-o, everybody!" Harker stumbled into the room. "Hey, Cheese Shop Lady, has anybody found the treasure yet?" He made a beeline for me.

"There is no treasure," I said with a tinge of exasperation.

"Sure, there is."

He reeked of beer. Was he drunk already?

"Isn't that right, Dane?" Harker looked behind him. No Dane.

He hustled out of the room and returned with Quinn and Dane in tow. Quinn whispered something to Dane, then buffed him on the shoulder and laughed. Dane, dressed in black and looking even more like a brooding Hamlet than he had yesterday, scowled. Quinn tickled Dane's chin with the ends of her multicolored scarf but he still didn't smile. Out in the hallway I spotted their friend Edsel drawing in a sketchbook, his shoulders hunched, forehead pinched with concentration, oblivious to his friends' exit.

Freddy appeared behind Edsel and prodded him toward the dining room. "Put it away, son," he said in a commanding tone. "Let's be sociable."

Edsel slapped his notebook closed and stormed off.

Freddy gave him a concerned look, then spotted me and strolled over. "Hey, Charlotte, what a place."

"Is Edsel okay?" I asked.

"Just a dedicated artist. The kid never misses an opportunity." He gazed around the room. "My sis did good, didn't she?" He offered his hand to Jordan. "Freddy Vance, Meredith's brother." He hitched his chin at me. "Charlotte and I go way back."

"How way back?" Winona said, her eyelashes batting at supersonic speed. Was there a man with whom she wouldn't flirt?

Freddy grinned. "Way, way back. I was crushing on Charlotte when I was ten." He elbowed me. "Remember when we would lie beside Kindred Creek and tell each other our dreams?"

I did. It was long before he'd entered high school. Long before he'd crushed my childish heart.

"You still dream, don't you?" he said.

Of course I did. Of cheeses and recipes and orders to fill. And Jordan. Perhaps a week away with him would spur me to abandon the other more mundane ones. I mouthed the word *yes* at Jordan, but he wasn't looking my direction. He was assessing Freddy.

"Are you married, Freddy?" Jordan asked with an obvious edge to his voice that made me smile. He was a teensy bit jealous. Hooray for me.

"Used to be," Freddy answered.

"Used to —" I gaped at his empty ring finger. Meredith hadn't told me anything was wrong between Freddy and his wife.

"She left me for a nine-to-fiver with a big paycheck," Freddy said. "Artists barely make enough to eat, and art teachers don't make much more than that. I'm a Bohemian, short and simple. I'm dealing with it."

Freddy sounded chipper, but I wasn't so sure he was. A muscle was ticking in his cheek.

Winona slipped her hand around Freddy's elbow. "I, for one, like Bohemians."

Jordan cleared his throat. With his eyes, he encouraged me to leave the pack, but before we could break free, his sister Jacky burst into the room.

She looked like a sleek horse running from a fire, black mane cascading down her back, gaze frantic.

CHAPTER 4

Jordan raced across the dining room to his sister. She whispered in his ear. He gave a curt nod and guided her to the terrace overlooking the vineyards. I couldn't catch a word of their ensuing conversation, but something in their need for privacy and the worry in Jordan's eyes sent a frisson of fear through me.

Meredith moved to the center of the room, clapping her hands. "Hello, everyone. Welcome. Get a bite to eat. The scavenger hunt starts in ten minutes!"

"We'd better get a move on," Freddy said. He nudged Winona and me toward the buffet, where another twenty stood in line.

As we arrived, I heard Rebecca, Grandmère, Pépère, and the twins arguing the finer points of Grandmère's upcoming theater production. The twins called their great-grandparents Grandmère and Pépère, like Matthew and I did, for the same reason

I called them the twins — the ease of it. Amy was still trying to understand why Grandmère wanted actors from another play to read Poe's poems. Pépère didn't think "The Raven" was the right poem to open the show. Rebecca suggested "The Bells." Clair said she preferred "Lenore." I didn't question that she'd read the latter. Even at the young age of nine, she was a serious reader. Grandmère pooh-poohed them all. She said it was the playwright's prerogative.

And who exactly was the playwright? I wanted to know. Grandmère was certainly being coy about the identity.

She turned to me. "What do you think, Charlotte?"

I knew better than to get into a debate with my grandmother. She hadn't become the mayor of our fine city by being a lamb in an argument. I said, "I think you should sample more of my fine fondue."

Grandmère chortled and patted her tummy. "I've done plenty of that." She elbowed my grandfather. "Etienne, we must leave. Find Bozz. He's agreed to help finish building the sets. Amy, Clair. Wash your hands and meet me at the car." She shooed them away. When they were out of earshot, she said, "What is Sylvie doing back in

Providence?"

All I could do was shrug. I hated feeling helpless. Apparently, so did Matthew. He and Meredith were huddled in a corner. She was stroking the back of his head while he talked nonstop.

"I don't trust her," my grandmother said. "She's up to no good. Mark my words."

She started to walk away, but I grabbed her elbow. "Wait. Tell me why this winery makes you anxious."

"I told you. It is an old woman's superstition. Let it be. Oh, look, there's Chief Urso," she said, deftly changing the subject. "How nice to see him out in a social setting. He is quite handsome in his brown suit, don't you think? My, my, he does have eyes for you."

I glimpsed over my shoulder. Our chief of police, Umberto Urso — or U-ey as he'd been dubbed in high school — was looking my way. I waved. He gave a nod.

"Throw him a bone," Grandmère said.

Urso was a good man with a firm grip on how to keep the peace. Since the murder of a prominent citizen a few months ago, we hadn't had as much as a jaywalker. It didn't hurt that Urso was so big and tall that he looked like he could snap even the heartiest of men in two with his bare hands.

"I'm in a relationship," I reminded her.

"But of course. I am forgetful." My grandmother was never forgetful. At the sprightly age of seventy-three — she'd only admit to seventy — she could dance rings around everyone in the brains department. She said, "Is Jordan here?"

I glanced at the terrace. Jordan and Jacky had disappeared. "I think he left," I said, unable to hide my disappointment.

"Ah, *c'est la vie, chérie.*"

Her tone caught me off guard. Didn't she think Jordan and I were a good fit? She had never mentioned anything to the contrary before. I eyed her and waggled my finger. "Oh, no, you don't. You're just trying to get my mind off what's bothering you about this place. C'mon, spill."

Grandmère sighed. "When we moved to Providence, I met Ziegler's daughter. Something wasn't right about her. I worried that she might cause problems, but then she left town. The last I heard, she joined some hippie commune."

"Having music at the fund-raiser bothered you."

"No, *chérie,* you got the wrong idea. It is the winery. This place. I must let it go. There has been nothing amiss since, and with this event, Meredith has set my mind to rest."

She brushed off her shoulders to rid herself of bad vibrations — a trick that a gypsy had taught her — then pecked my cheek and waltzed off.

"Charlotte." Freddy tapped my shoulder. "Which fondue should I have? Champagne or Humboldt Fog?"

"Both. Taste test. That's always the most fun."

Freddy loaded a plate with pieces of bread and florets of broccoli, grabbed one of the bamboo skewers that we'd placed in crystal vases, and spooned some of each fondue onto his plate.

"I never eat fondue," Winona said.

Oh, please. I bit my tongue. Not the *cheese will make me fat* thing again.

"You're missing a treat," Freddy said. "Communal eating is sexy."

"Communal?"

"I give you a bite, you give me a bite." He winked. "I love a good bite."

She tittered.

Get a room, I thought, and then another notion whisked through my mind. Had Winona become a donor so she could put the moves on Freddy, or had Freddy wooed her into becoming a donor because of his sudden single status? Did it matter? She was here. He was loving the attention. And her friend Wolford, from what I could tell, had no apparent interest in her.

"How do I do it?" Winona eyed Freddy with damsel-in-distress meekness, which, for an Amazonian-sized woman, was hard to do.

Freddy speared a piece of bread with a skewer, rolled it in the champagne fondue cheese, and fed the bite to Winona. All of the cheese didn't make it into Winona's mouth. Freddy used a knuckle to clean her chin and licked the cheese off his finger. Winona moaned with delight.

I reached for a plate, but paused when I heard Quinn yell, "Stop it!"

Dane had trapped her by one of the windows. With one hand, he held fast to the ends of her multicolor scarf. Using his free hand, he tried to feed her fondue. "C'mon, it's Gruyère de Comté. You'll like it." Cheese dripped off the skewer and onto Quinn's scarf.

Quinn pressed her lips together. Tears pooled in her eyes. She flailed at Dane. A ring on her left hand snagged in the knitted loops of her scarf. But Dane didn't stop.

"Ah, young love," Winona cooed. "They're never happy."

"They're not in love," I said. "He's being a bully." I remembered Quinn saying she was allergic to any kind of cheese but goat's cheese. She was downright scared. Where was Quinn's knight in shining armor, Harker? "Freddy, if you're not going to help out, then I will."

Freddy gripped my arm and chuckled. "You can't help yourself, can you, Charlotte? Even in grade school, you were a mother hen. Don't worry about Quinn. She can handle —"

"I said stop it, Cegielski!" Quinn pushed Dane away.

As he stumbled back, melted cheese splattered on his sweater and the skewer of fondue fell from his hand to the floor.

Abandoning her scarf, Quinn darted through the French doors toward the rear of the estate. Dane huffed and tramped in the opposite direction toward the foyer.

The gong of a bell blasted the air.

"Hey, everybody!" Meredith waltzed into the room carrying a metal rod and a cowbell. She clanged the bell a second time. "Yoo-hoo, let's gather in the foyer."

Like a majorette, she paraded ahead. Guests set their dinner plates aside and fell in line behind her.

I stood frozen in place, torn about what to do: chase after Quinn or follow the hostess? I chose the latter because Freddy was right. The argument was over, and Quinn was a big girl. She could defend herself.

When the guests had convened in the foyer, the mariachi music faded out and Meredith stopped her clanging. First, she introduced herself, as well as a few townsfolk who were investing in the college and the donors from Cleveland. Next, she offered a few inspiring words about education. Then, she said, "Providence, let's show our guests how to have a good time! Everyone, grab a partner and take a scavenger hunt list. You've got forty-five minutes to find the items. There are thirty total, but there are thirty-six rooms, and some rooms might have more than one item."

The crowd cooed with appreciation.

"Some things are hiding in plain sight! The first duo back to the dining table with at least seven items wins a wine-and-cheese basket from Fromagerie Bessette."

Matthew and I had agreed that, in addition to providing a fabulous meal, a prize basket was a great way for The Cheese Shop to advertise. Meredith gestured to the basket, which she'd set on an entry table. A few of the guests oohed. Rebecca, our basket wizard, had created a beribboned showstopper, fitted with a bottle of sauvignon blanc, a bottle of malbec, and rounds of lavender chèvre from Two Plug Nickels Farm, as well as accoutrements like honey and jam.

"Ready, set, go!" Meredith held up a fistful of lists on green paper and a handful of matching green bags.

Freddy grabbed one of each and hurried off with Winona.

Dane broke from the crowd and approached Harker. "Hey, you got a partner, dork? Quinn ditched me."

Harker's eyes narrowed, probably wondering why Dane had the gall to think he could pair up with Quinn. But he let the dark moment pass and said, "You don't really expect me to go on this stupid thing, do you?"

Dane jammed his hands into his jeans pockets. "No, guess not."

"Say, did you see that fake art they hung in the halls?" Harker said. "Klee and Kandinsky have got to be turning over in their graves."

"Those Vegas entertainers?"

"Very funny. No, you goon. The Expressionists. Does color theory ring a bell?"

"Color theory? What's that?"

Harker whacked Dane on the shoulder, and the two headed down the hall.

At the same time, Rebecca trotted to my side. "Got a partner?"

Hoping for a miracle, I searched again for Jordan, but it appeared that he and Jacky had left the event altogether.

"C'mon." Rebecca handed me the list of items to find. "Do you think we'll stumble upon the treasure while we — ?"

"There is no treasure."

"Okay, okay. Let's start in the library."

Like other guests who'd entered the intimate mahogany-lined room, we stopped for a moment to admire the students' artwork. Quinn's piece — a façade of the winery on the knoll — was fun, flirty. Meredith had pegged it when she said Quinn had a style similar to Matisse. Pastel sheep pranced about the building. Clouds sparkled with glitter. Edsel's depiction of the winery, which he'd situated on a grim hill, the skies filled with rain-soaked clouds, was uninspired, but his *E. Nash* signature had dramatic flair. Dane's artwork, a black-and-white portrait of himself standing in the foyer of the house, looked immature but promising. Harker's artwork was the most unique yet, in its essence, forlorn. He had focused on the winery cellar, most likely because he expected to find the rumored treasure there, but the cellar looked like a hollowed-out cave, lined with gray stone and floating in black nothingness.

Freddy and Winona stood closest to the piece, and I overheard Winona say, "It's a little disturbing, don't you think?" She didn't wait for an answer, opting to continue hunting instead. Freddy followed.

Soon after, Winona shouted, "Found one!" She stood across the room brandishing a painter's palette.

Rebecca peeked behind one of the canvases and discovered a paintbrush. "Me, too! Item number six on the list." She waved it and dumped it into our bag as she bolted from the room. "C'mon, Charlotte. Ticktock."

We scoured the old kitchen, which was empty of other guests. *Vintage Today* had refurbished the kitchen with spanking-new appliances. All for show, I was pretty sure. I doubted the television program's budget would cover an update to the ancient wiring and plumbing.

A few minutes into our search, we discovered a crocheted pot holder hiding in a storage closet beside the dumbwaiter.

Rebecca said, "Two down, five to go. How about we — ?"

"Quinn, wait," a young man yelled.

Quinn charged into the kitchen, scavenger bag swinging on her arm, and skidded to a stop. She looked left and right, like she needed a place to hide. I jerked my thumb at the dumbwaiter. She tried to yank open the handle, but it stuck. I pointed to the kitchen table tucked into a nook. She dashed toward it. Too late.

Harker ran in and grabbed her by the wrist. He paid no attention to me or Rebecca. We could have been flies on the wall. When had he abandoned Dane and partnered up with Quinn?

"Let me go!" Quinn twisted to free herself.

"Listen to me," he ordered.

"Young man, let her go," I said, channeling Meredith and her most authoritative teacher tone.

Harker did, but he jabbed Quinn with his index finger. "Apologize."

"I didn't do anything wrong. Cegielski came on to me. So did Nash."

Dane and Edsel knew Quinn and Harker were an item. Why were they hitting on Quinn and pushing Harker's buttons?

"You're breaking my heart," Harker said. He looked like he really meant it.

Quinn sniffed. "Oh, please. You're the one who goes around breaking hearts."

Harker jolted as if she'd slapped him.

Taking advantage of his momentary paralysis, Quinn darted out of the kitchen with a quick glance back at me. Was there terror in her eyes?

Harker sprinted after her. "Quinnie, wait, I'm sorry."

The fact that he was the one doing the apologizing made me breathe easier. Young love was like cheese; it needed time to mature in delicate, controlled conditions.

"We need to find an eight-inch matchstick." Rebecca pulled out a drawer to search.

"Let's try the study. I noticed a fireplace in there."

Vintage Today had staged the study to look like something out of Providence's Historical Museum, with a commanding oak desk, comfy chairs, and Tiffany lamps. As Rebecca searched behind drapes and under stacks of books, I was drawn to the lectern standing in the middle of the room. On it lay a document that my grandmother would salivate over, if it was real and not some *Vintage Today* fake. It was a map of Providence in the eighteen hundreds, with lines delineating the various homesteads. According to the map, Ziegler's Winery went for miles. The Bozzuto, Urso, and Hart properties abutted the Ziegler estate. And the town of Providence consisted of a few cross streets and the Village Green. In the 1950s, Grandmère and Pépère fled France and moved to Providence. She gave up a dream of being a prima ballerina for a chance at a peaceful life. She found that life in Providence, and she would love to own an historic document that would celebrate the town that had embraced her.

"Is a map on our list?" I asked.

"Nope. But I found the matchstick," Rebecca said. "Now we need a candle. C'mon, let's go. I want to win."

I grinned. "I can make you a cheese-and-wine basket, you know."

"Nah, this is all about winning. We need a candle. How about the ballroom on the third floor?" she said. "Maybe there's a candelabra up there with real candles." She raced into the hall and jogged up the refurbished staircase.

As we neared the second floor, we heard a man yell, "Ow!"

I gripped Rebecca's elbow. "Hold on a sec."

"Stop!" the man yelled.

Laughter. Male and female.

"Don't be such a goon," Quinn said. I only recognized her voice. I couldn't see her. I stole to the top stair and peeked around the corner.

Where was Harker? I didn't really care. Quinn was rid of him. Good.

Hunched over and carrying a silver-scrolled candelabra fitted with three flaming candles, Edsel slogged down the hall, dragging one foot behind him. He swung his arm like that ogre in Mel Brooks's *Young Frankenstein* movie, and said, "This way, mistress. We're going to the conservatory."

He lisped his *S*s, which made Quinn laugh harder. She whacked Edsel playfully on the arm. He recoiled. "Ow. Mistress, why do you punish me so?" They disappeared into one of the bedrooms as other party guests exited.

Happy that Quinn was enjoying herself again, I tiptoed back to Rebecca, who was standing at the landing halfway down the stairs, gazing through a lead-crossed window.

I peered over her shoulder.

"Aren't the grounds pretty?" she said. "The grandeur."

Moonlight shimmered through the clouds and highlighted the aged grapevines that spilled down the hill in all directions. Taking in the view, I wondered if Meredith and her donors intended to revitalize the vineyard. Maybe a division of the school should be devoted to viticulture. That notion vanished when my attention was drawn to something out of place.

To the left. In the driveway.

Not Winona, who was out for a smoke, fingers absentmindedly stroking her throat. But Sylvie's Lexus. It was parked beside Matthew's Jeep.

Rebecca followed my gaze. "Hey, isn't that Sylvie's rental car. What's she doing back?"

"No idea." But I did my best not to worry. Matthew had proven he could hold his own against her. And I'd seen the girls leave with my grandparents. Sylvie wouldn't be able to snatch them for another impromptu outing without a fight from my grandmother.

I prodded Rebecca upward. "Back to the game."

As we bypassed the second floor, where most of the other guests seemed intent on scouring the bedrooms, Rebecca said, "Why did Matthew marry Sylvie?"

"It was love at first sight. He was the sommelier at a high-end restaurant. She was a waitress."

"Was she always so horrible?"

"She was colorful and unpredictable." Those were the terms Matthew had used when he'd introduced us. "A month later, they were married."

"Were they . . . ? You know."

"No, not pregnant. Just impetuous."

"But he's not at all like that."

"Not anymore." Matthew had learned a costly lesson.

As we reached the third floor, a man said, "That's far enough!"

Though he wasn't talking to us, my heart leapt to full throttle. I peeked around the corner and spotted Freddy and Harker, who stood in the middle of the marble-floored ballroom, highlighted by slivers of moonlight that pierced the windows.

Freddy's gaze was dark, threatening. He stabbed Harker's chest with his index finger. "Stop jerking my daughter around."

"She asked for it. She's the one gallivanting —"

"Enough!" Freddy cuffed Harker on the shoulder. "This is not part of our agreement."

"Are you reneging?"

"I never renege. But do not think I won't make you disappear. Got me?" Freddy stabbed the kid one more time in the chest to make his point, then stormed in our direction. Without making eye contact, he hurtled past us and down the stairs. A cartoonist would have drawn hash marks and exclamation points in the bubble over his head.

"Whew," Rebecca said when Freddy was

out of sight. "I thought my father was tough."

Pépère had delivered a similar showdown to Creep Chef. I'd always wondered whether something he'd said had driven Chip to abandon me for Paris. My life was happier without him, and I had to face it: Charlotte and Chip just didn't sound good together. Neither did Charlotte and Chippendale, which was his given name. And whenever I added his last name — Cooper — I giggled. We had way too many *C*s in our combined names. But still, I wondered.

Startled that tears had found their way to the rims of my eyes, I said, "Let's press on."

We entered the ballroom, and I could almost imagine the grand balls that had been held there. I envisioned a string quartet playing at the far end. The French doors would have hung open to let in the cool air. Chatter would have revolved around the new harvest and the delicious wine, and gossip would have abounded about Ziegler's crazy wife. The latter realization doused my musings with icy water.

Eager to move on, I said, "There's a candle."

A slender white taper was pressed into a silver candlestick that stood on a lion's-footed buffet. We snagged it, stowed it in our bag, and hurried out of the room.

Back downstairs, we entered the living room and located a sheet of poetry by Longfellow tucked beneath the old oak desk.

After that, we ventured into a tiny room accessed beneath the staircase — for storage, I imagined. *Vintage Today* had done nothing to the room. There wasn't a stick of furniture in it. The panels on the walls were painted completely white.

"Bust," Rebecca said. She turned to leave, but I grasped her elbow.

"Wait. Remember how Meredith said something could be hiding in plain sight? What if there are hidden doors and compartments? You know, like that dumbwaiter in the kitchen, but painted white to fool us." Feeling like Nancy Drew, I circled the room, pressing every panel. Nothing opened. I was about ready to give up when right behind the entrance door, I found a pencil. A white pencil. "Aha!"

Rebecca edged around to see what I'd found.

"In plain sight," I said. "Now, let's head for the cellar. We only need one more —"

"Can we quit?" Rebecca said, her voice small and tentative. "I mean, we don't have to win, do we?"

I glanced at her. She'd gone pale. Her

forehead was beaded with perspiration. "Are you okay?"

"This place is giving me the heebie-jeebies. All the fighting. First Quinn and Harker, then Quinn's father."

Because of her plucky attitude, I tended to forget how innocent my assistant was. Raised Amish, Rebecca had rarely seen anyone argue.

"On *Ghost Whisperer,*" Rebecca went on, "a whole town of ghosts lived in the basement of a building. They sent out bad vibes. What if there's an evil spirit living here, you know, a pirate ghost making all these people argumentative?"

I shuddered. I wasn't a TV nut like she was, but I had watched tons of films. I'd seen something like what she described in *Ghostbusters.* The *slime* made them do it. Yet I didn't believe in hoodoo voodoo, and I certainly didn't believe pirates had buried treasure at the Ziegler Winery. The only way to prove my point was to keep going.

"Buck up," I said. "One more item. We're bound to find a wine box in the cellar. Item twenty-nine. C'mon, we're a team."

"Couldn't we scour the tasting rooms?" Rebecca chewed on her lip then, digging deep for an iota of bravery, shrugged her acquiescence. "Okay. Cellar first."

We blazed through the halls, passing other guests, looking for the door leading to the cellar. As we rounded a corner, a gust of cold air hit us. The lights went out.

Partygoers gasped.

"Ghosts!" Rebecca clutched my arm with a death grip.

"There're no ghosts, you ninny. Don't panic. I'll fix it." I rummaged through the scavenger hunt bag and withdrew the wooden match and the candle. I scraped the match on the stone floor. It ignited. I lit the candlewick. The flame danced in front of Rebecca's face. She breathed easier.

As other guests followed my lead and lit their candles, the door leading to the cellar swung open.

Dane bolted through the door, his face as white as parchment paper. "Have you seen Quinn?"

I said, "She's with Edsel."

"No, she ditched him. She was with me then charged off. She got spooked."

Why did I suspect he'd scared her? On purpose. After the scarf incident, what was I supposed to believe?

Bad Charlotte. Suspecting the worst of people.

"I've got to find her." Dane raced toward the observatory. "She hates the dark."

At the same time, somebody screamed from someplace below us. Female. A blood-curdling scream.

Dane skidded to a stop and spun around. "Quinn!"

Rebecca moaned with fear.

I said, "Stay here."

She clutched a handful of my sweater. "Don't leave me."

With Rebecca clinging to me, we hurried down the creaky stairs. *Vintage Today* hadn't done a stitch of refurbishing in the cellar. There were only the candles Meredith had mentioned, stuck into rusted iron sconces. Cobwebs hung from the stone ceilings. The smell of wet mildew filled my nostrils — not the yummy, earthy kind of smell I associated with cheese caves, but rather dank decay.

When we reached the bottom, shouts swelled to our right. I held the candle out. Its flame cast a soft arc of light across the flagstone floor. With Rebecca still gripping my sweater, I followed the sound, passing huge oak vats and deteriorating winepresses, until I reached a knot of people hovering in the far corner. They circled a stone wine cellar that was guarded by metal bars.

I ordered Rebecca to stay put, then pushed through the crowd. When I caught a glimpse of what they were staring at, my stomach knotted up.

A partial brick wall stood in the middle of the wine cellar. The tail of a multicolored knit scarf poked out from behind the wall.

Quinn's scarf.

CHAPTER 5

"Quinn!" I yelled. My voice echoed off the cellar walls. So did the gasps of the crowd. "Quinn!" I repeated.

Maybe she'd fainted.

I skirted the brick wall and stopped in my tracks. Quinn wasn't lying on the flagstone floor; Harker was, with Quinn's scarf pulled tightly around his neck. I darted to his side. In the dim light, his face looked the color of an overripe blue cheese. I loosened the scarf and pressed my fingertips to his neck. No pulse.

In the past few years, I'd started to worry about my grandparents' health. Though they were spry and sassy, I had taken some CPR classes in order to be prepared for an emergency. I straddled Harker, placed palm over palm on his sternum, and thrust hard in an effort to force breath back into him. Ten thrusts. He didn't budge. I pinched his nose and blew into his mouth. Three quick bursts. I sat back and listened for breathing. Nothing.

I repeated the process but, no matter how I tried, I couldn't revive him.

Coated with perspiration and riddled with sadness, I stumbled to my feet and fell backward. Rebecca braced me.

"Is Mr. Harker dead?"

"His name's Harker Fontanne." I recalled seeing his last name in his signature on the painting in the library. "And, yes, he's dead."

"What're those rocks on the ground?" she asked.

In my haste, I hadn't noticed them, but they looked like jewels. Emeralds, rubies, and sapphires. Six to ten of them. They lay near Harker's hands. Had Harker discovered the rumored treasure, or had he interrupted someone else's search? I scanned the crowd that swarmed the area to get a view beyond the brick wall. Was the murderer among them? Winona and Wolford hovered at the forefront, each holding a candle. The flames danced and flickered in front of their faces. Winona's mouth was working, but I couldn't catch what she was saying. Dane had slipped in on the other side of her. His eyes fluttered, like he wanted to shut them to block out the sight. Other guests stood near them, mouths hanging open, all of them reminding me of the sufferers in Rodin's astounding sculpture *The Gates of Hell.*

Edsel pushed past the front row of people and swallowed back a groan. "Oh, man, no!"

I broke free from Rebecca and said, "Somebody find Chief Urso."

"Don't bother, I'm here," Urso said. "Back up, people, to the edges of the room." His footsteps resonated as he crossed the flagstone. He marched around the brick wall to the body, crouched down, and checked for a pulse. He eyed me with concern, stood up, and grazed the sleeve of my sweater with his fingertips. "You okay?"

My mouth and chin started to quiver. No, I wasn't okay. I was horrified.

Urso gave a little nod. He understood my silence. "What happened? Take it slow. Who is this?"

"Harker Fontanne." It hit me that the artwork upstairs would be Harker's last piece, and a wave of sorrow rolled through me. I took a deep breath and worked my tongue around the inside of my mouth. When I calmed, I told Urso about the lights going out, Dane running past looking for Quinn, the scream, finding Harker. Once I started, the words wouldn't stop.

"There's a breeze coming from that stone wall, Chief," Rebecca cut in.

"What's your point, Miss Zook?" Urso preferred using surnames when conducting an investigation. He felt it helped him maintain objectivity.

Rebecca toyed with her ponytail. She wanted to be bold around Urso, but she told me in private that his mere size cowed her. "I'm just saying it might be worth checking out. See, I saw this TV show, *Bones,* and there were hidden compartments behind some walls —"

Urso held up a hand to stop her. Treading lightly, he moved beyond Harker and peered at the wall. I gazed back at the iron bars that protected the space. Why were they there? Maybe stealing wine had been a problem back in the late eighteen hundreds or during Prohibition. The thought gave me a jolt.

Urso fingered the wall. He tried to wiggle a stone free. None of them budged. He found a chunk of loose mortar on the floor and used it to draw an outline around the crime scene, then radioed his deputy.

Rebecca scooted beside me. "Poor Meredith," she murmured.

My heart ached for my friend. Meredith's hopes for making the winery into a new college would be dashed when news of the murder got out. Donors would withdraw funding. No one would want to send a kid to school here. Our current self-appointed society goddess, Prudence Hart, who wanted to micromanage every facet of the locals' lives, would relish the failure. If she didn't come up with the idea, it wasn't an idea worthy of Providence.

Urso returned to my side.

"What about the jewels?" I asked. "Do you think they're part of the treasure?"

Urso knew about the rumored treasure. He'd been one of the kids in high school who'd dared me to steal inside the winery. He peered down at me. He couldn't help himself; he was a whole head taller. He said, "Do you think Mr. Fontanne found it?"

"And someone murdered him to get it."

"But left some?" Urso shook his head. "That's a little sloppy."

"There were lots of people moving about on the scavenger hunt. Maybe he or she was in a hurry."

"If the killer was a she, she would have had to be pretty darned strong. Mr. Fontanne looks buff." Urso bent to retrieve one of the jewels and pinched it between two fingers. "Hmm. Paste."

He would know if the jewels were real or crafted. In high school during the summer, he'd helped out at the Silver Trader, an eclectic jewelry store in Providence.

"Why would the killer strew cut glass around Harker's head?" I asked.

"I'm not sure." Urso rose to his full height and faced the crowd. "Anybody see anything?"

"I was on the scavenger hunt," Winona blurted. She fanned her list and jiggled her hunt bag as if to corroborate her story.

"Who are you?"

"Winona Westerton," she said with perfect operatic pitch. She explained she was a potential donor, as was her companion, Wolford. She had come to the cellar to look for a scavenger hunt item — an empty wine box. "Harker was so . . . so . . . I can't believe something like this happened."

"Where's Freddy?" I didn't see him among the crowd. "You and he were partners on the hunt."

"We got separated when I went outside for a smoke," Winona said.

I remembered seeing her through the lead-crossed window on the landing. What she didn't seem to realize was that her story left Freddy in the lurch. Where was he? I'd seen him argue with Harker. Had he killed him? No, I couldn't believe it. Not Freddy.

"A guest must have seen Harker come downstairs with somebody, U-ey," I said.

"Shouldn't you question everyone?"

Urso said, "Don't worry. I'll handle —"

"What's going on?" Meredith burst through a cluster of people and charged Urso. "What happened? Oh, my!" She shoved a knuckle into her mouth. "Where's Quinn?"

In my haste to help Harker, I'd forgotten about Quinn being frightened in the dark. Where was she? "Quinn!" I yelled.

"Who's Quinn?" Urso asked.

"My niece, Quinn Vance," Meredith said. "My brother Freddy's daughter. Quinn!"

"Nineteen years old. Redheaded," I said. "Quinn!" Where was Freddy? Maybe he had found Quinn and was consoling her.

"Quinn!" Meredith echoed, her voice shrill with panic. "Quinn! Sweetheart!"

"Over here," a tiny voice said.

Like a school of fish, the crowd parted. Urso and I wound through them to the far end of the cellar. We found Quinn hovering in a recess that was filthy with soot. Her arms were wrapped around herself so tightly that I worried she'd squeeze the air from her lungs. Candlelight flickered on her tear-stained face.

Meredith crouched beside Quinn and enveloped her in her arms.

"Is it true?" Quinn asked, her voice barely

a whisper. "Is Harker . . . ?" She hiccupped.

Meredith nodded. Quinn burst into tears.

"Shhhhh." Meredith patted her niece's back.

When Quinn came up for air, she pushed Meredith away and said, "Who would want to hurt him?"

Urso knelt beside them, a knee on the ground, his forearms crisscrossed over his bent leg. "Did you?"

"Me? No!" Quinn rolled her lower lip under her teeth.

Meredith whirled on Urso. "How dare you accuse her!"

"She's obviously scared, Meredith." Urso's voice was calm, reassuring. "She saw something. What did you see, Miss Vance?"

"I didn't see anything," Quinn cried. "I was hiding."

"From Mr. Fontanne?" Urso pressed.

"No! I was hiding from . . . from everybody."

She looked to me for support. Why, I wasn't sure. Maybe because I'd seen her argue with Harker. With my gaze, I urged her to continue.

"I found a door upstairs, and I crawled inside. Before I knew it, I was falling." She gestured to another recess. "I landed there."

I squatted and inspected the area. "It

looks like an old coal chute."

"I scrambled out and hid in this nook," Quinn said.

I couldn't tell whether Urso believed her or not. His face was as stoic as Mount Rushmore.

"Are you hurt?" Urso asked.

Quinn's cheeks were scraped, her skin flushed. "I don't think so."

"Let's get you to your feet." Urso helped her rise then addressed the crowd. "All right, everyone, I'd like you to convene upstairs. I'll question you there. Try not to touch anything as you head up. Charlotte, please go with them. See to it that nobody leaves the premises until I've talked to them."

I felt honored that he would entrust me with the duty. During last year's fiasco, he'd made it more than clear that I was intruding on his investigation.

People herded toward the stairs. I led the way up while thanking them for their patience and understanding. Some were crying. Others whispered their shock. As we reached the foyer and the folks moved as groups into the various adjoining rooms, I realized there would be no way for me to corral them all. Would the murderer hightail it? Had he or she already split? And where in the heck was Freddy? Dread seared the edges of my mind as I again recalled the argument he'd had with Harker.

Rebecca rushed to my side. "Tell me every little detail you recall."

Glad that her heebie-jeebies had vanished but not thrilled with how much she loved being an amateur gumshoe, I said, "Later."

"At least admit that the story about buried treasure was true."

"We don't know that for certain."

"But the jewels —"

"— are fake." I wondered again why the killer would leave fake jewels around Harker. I hadn't seen jewels on the scavenger hunt list.

Rebecca drummed her fingers at the hollow of her neck. "You know, finding Harker tucked behind that wall reminded me of that short story by Edgar Allan Poe, 'The Cask of Amontillado.' "

I knew the story. In it, the narrator took revenge on a friend who had insulted him. He baited the friend, led him to the catacombs, and buried him alive. I said, "But Harker wasn't entombed."

"Your grandmother would say placing him behind that brick wall was allegorical."

"No, my grandmother would say you're reaching. You've got Poe on the brain because Grandmère's putting on her quirky show."

Rebecca mulled that over. "Do you think one of the guests lured Harker to the cellar?"

I glanced at the people who lingered in the hallway. One cluster was making a wager about how long they'd have to wait. I flashed on the conversation yesterday in The Cheese Shop when Edsel had revealed that Harker was a gambler. Did he have debts he couldn't repay? He owed Dane Cegielski. Did he owe others? Had someone followed him from Cleveland to recoup the money? Had that person lured him into the wine cellar?

From my vantage point in the hall, I could see into a number of rooms. Just inside the living room Winona whispered to Freddy. Although I was glad to see him, he looked wild-eyed. His gaze ping-ponged from Winona and back to the hallway door. Was he worried about his daughter or his alibi? Edsel paced the living room carpet, hands jammed into his pockets. He stopped, kicked an end table with his toe, then started up again, back and forth, as if working out a problem. Where was he at the time of the murder? Harker had verbally abused him at The Cheese Shop. Had Edsel taken all the abuse he could suffer? Had he snapped?

Guests spilled into the hallway from the dining room, some carrying plates of food. Though my appetite was all but squelched, I worried that there wouldn't be enough fondue to feed the crowd. However, I was not the hostess, and making everyone comfortable was not my problem.

Poor Meredith. She hugged Matthew near the front door, her face awash with tears. Matthew stroked her cheek with the back of his knuckles. I heard Meredith say, "It's ruined," at least three times.

Beyond the opened door, a number of smokers had convened on the front porch, Dane among them. He leaned against a pillar in profile. Wisps of gray smoke spiraled around his head. Had he run past me on the stairs, not in search of Quinn, but because he was running from the crime scene? He cut a look in my direction, as if he knew that I was thinking about him. To my surprise, his somber eyes were pooled with tears.

I spun away, my pulse ticking double-time, and gazed at the door to the cellar. What was taking Urso so long?

A minute later, he lumbered from the stairwell, his beefy hand gripping Quinn's slim arm. He guided her to a straight-back chair against the wall. She sat, shoulders hunched and trembling.

The trio from the living room hustled to the foyer. The throng from the front porch extinguished their cigarettes and reentered the building.

Dane sprinted to Quinn. Edsel, too. As they squatted beside her, I envisioned the scene in *Gone With the Wind* when Scarlet was besieged by men who wanted to take care of her. Freddy made a move toward Quinn, but Winona stopped him.

Urso clapped his hands. "May I have everyone's attention, please?"

I perked up my ears, hopeful that Urso would tell us he had found the killer and this horrible ordeal could end right now.

Someone shouted, "Was he really strangled?"

Wolford, who stood beneath the arch leading to the dining room, said, "Is the treasure real?"

Urso raised his hands. The crowd quieted. The hush was disconcerting.

"I'd like to talk to everyone individually," Urso said. "This could take time."

The guests groaned in unison.

"Folks, please be patient. I'm sorry for any inconvenience. Kid." Urso eyed his sole deputy, Rodham, who reminded me of the Road Runner, slim and leggy, with beaky lips and a tuft of funky hair. He had attended the party with his fiancée, a prissy woman who looked less than happy to be detained. "Go downstairs and guard the crime scene." He turned to Meredith. "Could you round up some paper and pens for me?"

Looking relieved to have a mission, Meredith broke from Matthew and raced off in search of the requested items.

"The rest of you, let's gather in the dining hall and take a seat. It could be a long night."

While the crowd obeyed, Quinn broke from Edsel and Dane and dashed toward me. "Charlotte!" She skidded to a stop. "I know who killed Harker. Your assistant, Bozz."

CHAPTER 6

"Bozz?" I nearly shrieked. "No way."

Everyone heading for the dining room turned. I caught Prudence Hart leering at me with a tartness usually reserved for vinegar. She whispered to a needle-nosed friend to her right, then snickered. What was Prudence's problem? Did she blame me for being detained at the event? She certainly couldn't blame me for her choice of clothing, which was an obnoxious hot pink pantsuit that wouldn't even look good on a mannequin. Taking over Providence's only upscale women's boutique after the owner left town — on what she liked to call a sabbatical — hadn't improved Prudence's sense of style one iota. She reminded me of a worn pencil: skinny, hard, and chewed around the edges. I swear she cut her hair with garden shears.

I pushed the catty thoughts from my mind and gripped Quinn by the shoulders. "Bozz is not a killer."

Matthew, Meredith, and Rebecca hurried to our huddle.

Urso joined us. "What's this about Mr. Bozzuto?"

Quinn blanched. Her shoulders started to shake. If I didn't know Urso was a teddy bear to his core, I'd have quavered at his harsh tone, too.

"Bozz and Harker were fighting," Quinn said.

"Says who?" Urso folded his arms across his massive chest, jaw set, his eyes revealing nothing. If only I could be so implacable.

"Edsel." Quinn wriggled with discomfort. "He saw Harker push Bozz down the front steps."

"When?" I demanded. Certainly not when we'd arrived. They had exchanged words, but Bozz had backed off, and Matthew had instantly put him to work carrying crates of wine.

"About a half hour ago," Quinn said.

"Edsel who?" Urso said.

"Edsel Nash. The guy with the shaggy hair." Quinn wiggled her index finger.

"Mr. Nash, get over here, now!" Urso jerked a thumb.

Edsel obeyed. Dane, like a shadow, shuffled behind him.

Urso said, "Explain, Mr. Nash."

"Harker was, like" — Edsel cleared his throat — "spitting mad at that nerd, Bozz."

"Where?"

"On the front porch." Even standing at attention, Edsel looked sloppy. His shoulders slouched. His eyes grew hooded like a cobra's. He wiped raggedy strands of hair off his forehead. "He said —"

"Who said?" Urso cut in.

"That dork, Bozz," Dane blurted.

Urso wheeled on Dane. "You saw this, too?"

Dane screwed up his mouth. "Uh, no."

"Then let Mr. Nash tell the story." Urso turned his glare on Edsel. "Nash?"

Edsel licked his lips. "He — Bozz — said, 'What's your problem, man? Why are you following me?' and Harker said, 'I saw you looking at her.' And Bozz said, 'Was not.' And Harker said, 'Were, too. I told you to back off.' Then Harker landed him one right in the jaw."

Urso's face remained impassive. I would bet he had seen his share of fights — seen them, not engaged in them. He was an Eagle Scout through and through. But he had gone away to college and he'd joined a fraternity that favored football players and heavy drinking. An occasional brawl was

101

inevitable.

After a moment, Urso turned to me. "How does Mr. Bozzuto know Mr. Fontanne?"

"He doesn't," I said. At least I didn't think he did. Bozz wasn't working at The Cheese Shop yesterday when the students came in for breakfast.

"They met tonight," Rebecca said. "When we drove up. He said Quinn was cute, and —"

I gripped her wrist to hush her from telling more. "Look, U-ey." I paused. Swallowed hard. "I mean, Chief. Bozz is the sweetest kid on earth, you know that."

Freddy sidled up to Quinn and put a protective, fatherly arm around her shoulders. Winona moved to Quinn's other side, but her arms remained lank.

Prudence and her needle-nosed friend clustered behind Freddy, Winona, and Quinn. Each of the women carried a plate of bread chunks dipped into fondue. While popping bites into their mouths, they leaned forward, looking eager to hear the dirt. Inwardly, I groaned. I could just imagine the gossip that would fly around town tomorrow.

Freddy said, "Bozz might be a nice kid, but I saw the altercation, too."

I gaped at him, upset that I couldn't defend Bozz if two witnesses came forward.

"Tell the chief what you know, Freddy," Winona said.

Urso zeroed his gaze on Freddy. "Got something to say, Mr. Vance? Where were you at the time of the incident?"

"C'mon, U-ey, you can call me Freddy."

"I asked you a question, Mr. Vance."

Freddy stretched his neck. His jaw flicked with tension. "I was outside for a smoke."

If he'd gone outside for a smoke when Winona had, why hadn't they gone together? Winona said they had gotten separated. That must have been when Freddy had the fight I'd witnessed with Harker. I thought of the words they'd exchanged. What agreement had Freddy and Harker made? Why was Harker worried that Freddy would renege on it?

"Outside where, exactly?" Urso said.

"Over by the Dumpster." While Freddy plucked strands of hair off Quinn's shoulders with his right hand, his left hand fidgeted in his pocket, something he used to do back in grade school whenever he was lying. Was he fabricating an alibi for himself? Why would he and Edsel tell the same story about Bozz if it wasn't true?

"Did you see Mr. Bozzuto and Mr. Fontanne go down to the cellar together?" Urso asked.

"They couldn't have," I cut in. "Bozz left for the theater with my grandparents."

"Charlotte, hush," Urso said. "He's your employee."

"Does that mean I can't defend him?"

Urso glowered at me. "Did you see him leave the premises?"

"Well . . . no." My arms, down to my fingertips, prickled with anxiety. I shook my hands to clear the uncomfortable feeling, but it was to no avail. "Pépère was looking for him. He wouldn't have left without him. Bozz is innocent!" I clapped my hand over my mouth, surprised at my outburst; but my Internet guru was no more of a killer than Gandhi was. Bozz listened to inspirational music, he was an eco-nut, and he wrote poetry. Heck, he sneaked little treats to my cat and helped old ladies across the street.

Urso huffed. Exasperation turned into beads of perspiration. He rubbed the back of his neck. "Tell me again, Mr. Vance. When did this altercation take place?"

"A half hour ago."

Rebecca elbowed me and twitched her chin toward the staircase. I got the hint. I replayed the scenarios she and I had witnessed while on the hunt. Right at the start, Harker had chased Quinn into the kitchen. About five minutes later, we saw Edsel and Quinn upstairs. Two minutes after that, Harker and Freddy were heard arguing. Had a half hour passed since then?

I said, "Quinn, where did you go after you and Edsel played Quasimodo upstairs?"

"Quasi what?" she asked.

"The candle thing. He was making you laugh."

"Oh." Her breath caught in her chest.

Was she surprised someone had seen her? Maybe her dalliance with Edsel had made Harker so mad that he'd come after her a second time. Had he chased her to the cellar? Had she lashed out? No, I couldn't see Quinn having the strength to kill him. Not by strangulation. But it was her scarf that was the murder weapon, and she was the one we found hiding in the coal chute.

But then I recalled the earlier scuffle between Dane and her, when Dane had tried to force-feed her fondue. She'd abandoned the scarf. Anyone could have picked it up. Even Bozz.

My shoulders tensed.

"Don't worry, Quinnie," Meredith said. "Charlotte's not accusing you of being guilty."

"I'm just trying to establish everybody's whereabouts."

"That's what detectives do," Rebecca chimed in.

"She's not a —" Urso didn't finish the sentence. He pursed his lips with minor annoyance. "I'm going to solve this puzzle right away." With a crook of his thumb, he rounded up the Road Runner and instructed him to get statements from everyone, then summoned Mr. Nakamura, the owner of Nuts for Nails, to help the deputy. When that was handled, Urso cornered Meredith. "I'm going to the theater to chat with Mr. Bozzuto. You guard the crime scene. Your party, your responsibility. Go."

Meredith looked like the world had caved in on her shoulders, but she moved toward the cellar door.

As Urso marched toward the front door, I said, "I'm going with you."

"Moi, aussi!" Rebecca sounded distinctly youthful and unpolished. She was always trying out new French phrases.

"Me, too." Matthew hurried to join us.

"Fine, whatever." Urso fetched his car keys from his pocket.

"What about us?" Winona said.

Freddy grabbed her hand. "We're staying with Quinn."

"And you'll give statements to my deputy," Urso said, his tone clipped and authoritative. "I'm not through with anyone here yet." He eyed Quinn. "Including you, Ms. Vance."

Freddy slung his arm around his daughter again. She folded into him.

As we headed for our respective vehicles, Rebecca scooted to my side and petted my arm. "Don't worry. I'm sure Grandmère will confirm Bozz's alibi. You know how she is with her timetables. She'll know exactly when they left the party and when they arrived at the theater."

But what if Bozz hadn't left with my grandparents?

CHAPTER 7

Providence Playhouse boasted a state-of-the-art main stage theater as well as a black-box theater. The black box was compact and accommodated fifty patrons. Urso, Matthew, Rebecca, and I hustled inside and came to a dead stop in the center aisle, nearly crashing into one another. All the lights were out. Not a sound could be heard. The aroma of garlic and herbs suffused the cavelike space. Pépère must have provided the crew with spicy homemade pizza.

"Grandmère?" I called.

"*Oui, chérie.* Lights!" Grandmère clapped.

Like magic, the stage working lights snapped on.

No wonder I hadn't seen my grandmother. She stood center stage, dressed in a black T-shirt, black leggings, and black work gloves. She twirled in the middle of three striped sofas that formed a U. "Thank you for the silence, everyone. I found it!" she yelled, then explained, "We have been searching for a cricket in the sound system. One's hearing is so much better in the dark, *non?*"

Noise resumed backstage. Hammering, shouting. Lots of people, all out of sight.

"Come this way, *mes amis.*" Grandmère beckoned us toward the mini proscenium. "Welcome, welcome." We moved as a unit and lined up in front of the first row of seats. She eyed me and gestured to the stage. "So, what do you think?"

She wasn't kidding when she said she was going to combine *No Exit* with Poe's work. In addition to the three sofas, a statue of an oversized papièr-mâché raven occupied the middle of the stage. A silver pendulum made of tinfoil hung overhead, upstage left. Two stark black walls jutted into the limited space.

"The sofas represent the worlds of our lonely protagonists," Grandmère said. "You will note that there are no mirrors. The actors must see themselves reflected in the eyes of the other players. The jet-black drapes outlining the stage represent the emptiness beyond."

Through a break in the drapes, I caught a glimpse of a snack table backstage. On it, Pépère had laid out sodas, chips, and his yummy pizzas. A couple of crew people were grazing.

I said, "Grandmère, we're not here for a tour."

Her smile tightened. She pulled off her gloves.

"Madam Mayor, where is Bozz Bozzuto?" Urso removed his broad-brimmed hat and held it by his thigh.

Pépère shuffled from behind one of the drapes, a hammer in his hand, a toolkit strapped around his girth. The tail of his striped shirt had come free of his trousers. "What is the matter?"

"There's been a murder," I said. "One of the art students. Harker Fontanne."

Grandmère clamped a hand over her mouth.

"The talented one?" Pépère said. "*Mon dieu.* His painting at the winery was quite special, with his broad-stroked style and his play with light."

Grandmère glanced at him, willing him to be quiet. My grandfather could wax poetic about art. He fancied himself as a student of Renoir, though Grandmère would never let him paint studies of nudes the way Renoir did. Free spirit though she may be, she drew the line at that.

Urso cleared his throat. "Madam Mayor,

I'd like to speak to Mr. Bozzuto."

"You cannot think Bozz did this." Grand-mère admonished him with her index finger. *"Every man has his fault, and honesty is his,"* she said. "Shakespeare."

Urso looked unmoved by her literary defense. "I need to speak with Mr. Bozzuto now."

A long hiss escaped my grandmother's lips. "Such formality." She let her hand fall to her side. "He is in the back fetching a ladder."

Pépère said, "I will get him."

"Wait," Urso said. "A few questions first. Can you verify when Mr. Bozzuto arrived to help you?"

"At the same time we did." Grandmère stretched her spine to add height to her diminishing frame. "We drove him."

"And what time was that?"

"Nine forty-two. On the dot."

"Was that when you left the winery or when you arrived here?"

Grandmère rattled off a string of French words, which meant she didn't like Urso pressing her. He tilted his head, the epitome of patience. She said, "That is when we ar-rived."

Rebecca whispered, "I told you she'd know."

111

Urso thanked my grandmother and said, "Now, please fetch him."

Pépère started to leave, but Grandmère detained him with a steel grip. "I will get him." She scuttled across the stage and disappeared behind the drapes. Seconds later, she returned with Bozz in tow. Like Grandmère, he wore a black T-shirt that read "Crew" on the back.

He finger-combed his hair off his face. He liked to wear it almost shoulder-length. No amount of nudging from me would get him to cut it. However, he would comply and wear a hairnet if he helped out at the counter. "Hey, Chief Urso. What's up?"

"Where'd you get the fat lip?" Urso asked.

Bozz's lower lip was cracked. A thin line of dried blood clung to it. Instinctively he started for it with his forefinger but dropped his hand to his side.

"Edsel Nash and Freddy Vance said they saw you and Harker Fontanne fight," Urso continued.

Bozz's shoulders caved. "Yeah, we fought. He thought I was making eyes at Quinn. I said she was cute, but I already have a girlfriend."

"You do?" I blurted.

Bozz blushed. He mumbled something like "flibbertigibbet."

Rebecca translated in a whisper, "Philby Jebbs, super brainy. Strawberry blonde hair. She's come into the shop a few times. Likes blue cheese."

"Go on, Bozz," Urso said, his tone gentle, fatherly. I could tell he liked the kid. He'd stopped using Bozz's surname. "What happened next?"

"Harker was drunk. He took a swing at me. I stumbled down the stairs."

"Is your jaw sore?" Urso said.

"I've been hurt worse in wrestling." Bozz rubbed his chin. His knuckles didn't have any bruises on them, but Harker hadn't died in a fistfight. He'd been strangled. With all the weightlifting Bozz did for wrestling, he was strong enough to have killed Harker. "Look, what's this about?" Bozz asked. "Is he pressing charges, 'cause I didn't take a swing at him. I took the high road. Ms. B" — he eyed me — "she's always saying, *'To thine own self be true.'*"

I had dozens of books filled with inspirational quotes that Grandmère had given me over the years. She urged me to memorize one a week, saying that I'd never know when one might come in handy.

"I'm not a fighter," Bozz said. "I didn't —"

"Mr. Fontanne is dead." Urso paused. He

watched Bozz's eyes. "Strangled."

Bozz turned the color of Swiss cheese. "I didn't do it. No way." He spun in a circle then rounded on Urso. "You've got to believe me, Chief. I would never do something like that. Never!"

I believed him. Did Urso?

"Someone must have seen Harker after the fight," Grandmère said. "Have you asked, Chief? But of course you have. You always ask questions before you make accusations, don't you?" Her tone was a little snide. Last year, when she was accused of murder, Urso had sort of skipped a few steps in the investigation, which again made me wonder why she'd been pushing Urso on me back at the party. Was she less a fan of Jordan than she was of Urso?

A burst of laughter from backstage yanked me from my thoughts. The twins, Amy and Clair, scampered onto the stage looking like street urchins in *Oliver Twist.* In all the confusion, I'd forgotten they'd left the party with my grandparents. They needed to go home and get into bed, not play dress-up with all the extra costumes stored at the theater.

They stopped, center stage, and glanced to their right. Their faces twisted in panic.

A scraggly looking person dressed as the

114

pickpocket Fagin darted onto the stage and danced a jig around the twins. I was struck by how much he reminded me of a tourist who'd come into The Cheese Shop back in January, a guy who hadn't said a word; he'd simply hovered by the cheese counter to snag a free bite of ash-laced cheese.

Amy said to the Fagin character, "Mum, stop." She waved a finger, indicating us.

"Sylvie?" I said, stunned at the transformation.

Matthew stiffened. "Sylvie, what are you doing here?"

With confidence befitting Meryl Streep, Sylvie whipped off the floppy felt hat and phony beard and jutted a hip. "I heard on the radio about the murder. I came straightaway to divert my girlie girls."

"Radio?" Urso groaned and looked my way.

I shook my head. I hadn't heard a thing. On the ride over, I'd driven in silence. I couldn't imagine who would have called the media. Some yahoo wanting fifteen minutes of fame, no doubt.

"I had to protect my babies," Sylvie went on. "After all, they're living in a town where two murders have happened in less than two years." She wiggled her fingers and beckoned the twins to her. "Come to Mumsie, girls."

Neither Amy nor Clair budged.

"Come!" Sylvie stomped her foot, but the twins remained huddled together.

"Let them be," Grandmère said.

Sylvie eyed my grandmother with outright disdain. "Who do you think you are, Bernadette, ordering me about? And stop looking like you swallowed a lemon. We haven't touched the *No Exit with Poe* costumes."

Matthew stepped forward. "Girls, your mother and I need to talk. Please get out of those costumes, put them away properly, then come back to the auditorium."

Amy and Clair scooted off the stage.

"You bet we need to talk!" Sylvie sprinted toward Matthew, claws primed. "You're obviously poisoning them against me."

Urso, who looked red-hot mad because his investigation had gone haywire, stepped in front of her to block her. He gripped her by the wrists.

Rebecca did a little fist pump beside me and whispered, "All right, Chief."

I eyed Bozz, who looked relieved that the focus had been removed from him. Poor kid probably wanted to duck under his bedcovers and hide for a week. At least he had a firm alibi.

"I've got this, Chief," Matthew said. "Thanks."

Urso reluctantly released Sylvie. She snarled at him, but she didn't do anything more. Smart on her part.

Matthew sighed. "Sylvie, why do you insist on breaking the rules?"

She fluffed her hair. "Rules. Tosh! Rules stifle creativity. Our girls need to be creative, not locked up into little cells saying, 'Yes, sir' and 'no, sir.' Look at Clair. She's as pale as milk and can't seem to stop crying. And Amy, poor dear, has absolutely no sense of style."

"She does, too," Matthew said.

"Not worth a grain of salt. She's gotten into bad habits with her color choices. Do I have Charlotte to thank for that?"

I nearly choked. If Sylvie didn't watch out, I was going to haul off and punch her. Even Urso wouldn't be able to hold me back. Deciding to take a more subtle approach, I said, "What were you doing back at the winery?"

Sylvie faltered. She gave me a scathing look. "I left my purse."

"Oh, please. Your flashy tote's so big there's no way you would have left it behind."

Sylvie's hand flew to her chest. "You can't

possibly think that I had anything to do with this boy Harker's death, Charlotte. I've never met him before."

"You just called him by his first name," I said.

She threw her shoulders back. "I have ears. Tell me, what's my motive?"

I couldn't think of one, but give me long enough . . .

I didn't hate many people, but I truly loathed Sylvie.

"Matthew has more motive than I," she snapped.

Like a beleaguered umpire caught between two warring team managers, Urso shot a look at Matthew and back at Sylvie. "What does she mean?"

Matthew's neck and cheeks turned splotchy.

"Matthew?" I said.

Before he could respond, Sylvie said, "When I came back for my purse, I saw Matthew fighting with Harker." She smiled a sugary smile, the kind that probably worked magic on getting Mumsie and Dad to open their checkbooks. "Did you kill him, love?"

Matthew sputtered then held out his hands, palms up to Urso. "Harker was drunk."

Sylvie thrashed a sharp fingernail at the air. "Harker accused Matthew of having eyes for Quinn."

"He did no such thing, you lying —" Matthew's hands fisted into balls. He blew out a long stream of air to compose himself. "I was in the dining room. Harker stumbled in and knocked over a stack of wineglasses on the tasting table. I pulled him into a corner and politely told him to sober up or leave."

"You didn't sound all that polite to me," Sylvie said.

Urso ran his tongue along his upper teeth and finished with a click. I could almost hear the voice in his mind saying, *Patience, Umberto, patience.* After a long moment, he said, "When was this?"

"Sometime around nine fifteen." Matthew glanced at his watch as if to confirm it was still ticking. "I have a slew of witnesses. Locals you know and trust."

Sylvie sniffed, suggesting a slew of witnesses wouldn't be good enough for her if she were sitting on the jury. "If you don't believe me, Chief, never mind. Justice will prevail. In the meantime, I have something else that might interest everyone here." She retrieved her silver tote from a chair in the front row of the auditorium and pulled out an envelope. She slapped it against Matthew's chest.

He instinctively grabbed the envelope to stop her.

"Matthew, snookums, consider yourself served. I'm suing you for custody."

CHAPTER 8

Although I was still shell-shocked by the evening's events, I couldn't simply go home and go to bed. I needed to return to the winery to clean up. Matthew, who had been driven into an inconsolable funk by Sylvie's pronouncement, asked if Rebecca and I would bring the extra wine and wineglasses back to the shop. I agreed, and he took the twins home.

An hour later, after stowing utensils, fondue pots, and assorted accoutrements into the gigantic dishwasher in The Cheese Shop's kitchen, I was too wired to sleep. And too depressed. Granted, I didn't know Harker Fontanne well. But he was so young, so full of promise, and I couldn't erase his blue-tinged face from my mind. I asked Rebecca to join me at the Country Kitchen for a soda. The little night owl readily agreed.

The jangle of chimes shaped like Elvis

Presley holding a guitar didn't buoy my spirits as we entered the diner. Neither did the silence.

Rebecca said, "Our favorite table is free."

We weaved our way to a cheery red booth, each of the booths fitted with a jukebox. As I fished for a quarter in my purse, "Twelve O'Clock Rock" rang out through the speakers around the diner. Per usual when a popular rock song started to play, the waitstaff stopped what they were doing, bounded from the tables they were serving, and marched through the restaurant, singing loudly and proudly — though a little off-key. My friend Delilah, a trained singer, was not among them. She was still at the winery with the other guests being grilled by Urso.

Once seated, I spotted Jordan and Jacky sitting at a booth at the far end of the restaurant. Jacky's pretty face still looked tear-stained and stressed. Jordan's mouth was moving, one hand cupped around it to help project his voice over the singing. I was dying to know what they were discussing, but I stayed put. It was none of my business, and I didn't think mentioning the murder was in good taste.

Seconds after the singing stopped, Rebecca and I ordered sodas. As our waitress brought them, Delilah sashayed into the diner carrying a platter wrapped in tin foil. She made a beeline for our table, her dark curly hair sweeping shoulder to shoulder. A couple of men turned to watch her walk. She didn't pay them any attention.

She stopped beside our table and whistled softly. "What a night!"

I was surprised to see her so soon. "Urso let you go already?"

"He said a kook like me wasn't capable of violence." She set the platter on our table. "If only he knew. We creative types can be pretty hot-tempered." At one time, for a nanosecond right after Delilah had returned — defeated — from trying to star on Broadway, Urso and she had dated. I would imagine he knew firsthand how hot her temper could get. Nowadays she was interested in Bozz's uncle, a local four-star restaurateur. Delilah removed tinfoil from the platter to display leftover grilled cheese sandwiches, cut into triangles. "By the way, Urso's in a real twist."

"Why?" Rebecca said.

"Uh-uh. Before I dish the dirt, you've got to try the Wensleydale with cranberries and turkey." Delilah pointed to a sandwich. "A good friend who owns a cheese shop tells me Wensleydale has the texture of Caerphilly, the flavor of wild honey, and melts like a dream. Or try this." She offered a second choice made with Butterkäse and loaded with jelly, turkey, and ham. "Still crispy. Even lukewarm, it'll taste great," she promised.

I wasn't in the least bit hungry, but I could never resist Butterkäse, which was creamier and less tangy than Havarti. I plucked one of the crispy sandwiches from the platter and bit off the corner. Heaven.

"Rebecca, do you want one?" Delilah said.

"No, thanks." Unlike me, the skinny snook merely slurped her diet soda. She'd told me on the way over that angst made her appetite disappear. I wished.

"Sit," I said to Delilah. "Now, tell us why Urso's upset, other than the obvious — having to solve another murder."

Delilah glanced over her shoulder at her father, Pops, who was picking up orders at the pass-through counter. He reminded me of a windblown sailor, hair sticking out in all directions, skin weathered from too much sun, ruddily handsome.

"The waitstaff just sang," I said. "You're good for at least fifteen to twenty minutes."

Pops glanced our way, acknowledged Delilah, and indicated with a free elbow that she could give her pals a few minutes. He didn't own the place anymore — he'd passed it on to Delilah — but she still honored his wishes.

"Okay. Here's the dirt." Delilah nestled into the booth beside Rebecca and brushed her raven curls over her shoulder. "Urso's looking for a couple of suspects."

"Who?" I asked.

"He wouldn't say."

"They weren't at the winery?"

"I guess they split." She leaned forward and ticked off points on her fingertips, rapid-fire. "But here's what I picked up after you left: that Edsel Nash likes Quinn. Dane Cegielski joined the art trip late, just so he could be near Quinn. And Freddy didn't like Harker — or anybody for that matter — hitting on Quinn. Edsel and Quinn were jealous of Harker's talent. Dane . . . I guess he's sort of so-so about the whole art thing. And by the by, that gal Winona, what a piece of work she is. She wants to jump Freddy's bones." Delilah sat back, smugly satisfied with her sleuthing capabilities. "Oh, yeah, a Eugene O'Neill drama is brewing, if you ask me."

I cocked my head. "You've been writing plays again, haven't you?" About six months ago, no longer content to simply star in Grandmère's theater productions, Delilah had taken up writing. About a month ago, she told me she hoped Grandmère would stage one of her works. I glanced at my friend, and a notion struck me like a frying pan to the side of the head. "The Sartre/Poe idea is yours, isn't it? You're the playwright."

She grinned.

"Wow, am I slow," I added, feeling dumber than a lox for not figuring it out before. "Grandmère loves it."

Delilah blushed.

"Yoo-hoo." Rebecca rapped the table with her knuckles. "Back to the murder. Is Urso looking for Dane? I think Dane did it. Remember how Edsel said Harker owed Dane money because of poker? Maybe the stakes for Harker and Dane's games were jewels."

"Jewels?" Delilah raised an eyebrow. "Real jewels?"

"The murderer scattered fake jewels around Harker," I explained.

Delilah tapped the table with her fingernails. "Maybe there was a girl named Jewel."

I buffed her on the shoulder. "That's why you're a playwright. You're such a romantic."

"Maybe Harker refused to pay Dane," Rebecca continued. "Maybe he said, 'No way, Jose.' "

I stifled a grin. Rebecca often came up with cockamamie expressions that she gleaned from late-night TV.

"So Dane scattered the fake gems symbolically?" Delilah said. "I like the theory."

"Ahem." Rebecca pointed discreetly.

Jordan had left his table and was heading my way. My heart flew to my throat. I adored this man. I couldn't wait for our getaway and wanted to tell him so, but what exactly was proper decorum after a murder? How much time needed to pass before life went back to normal?

Jordan stopped beside our table, acknowledged the three of us, then placed his hand on the back of the booth. His fingertips grazed my shoulder. "Charlotte, I'm so sorry we were interrupted back at the winery, and —"

"Did you hear about the murder?" I blurted.

He hadn't. I filled him in. He muttered his sympathy, and then his face screwed up. He glanced at his sister, who was staring out the window.

"Is Jacky okay?" I asked.

"She's fine. Under the weather." His gaze faltered. He was holding something back, but I kept quiet. "If you're not busy tomorrow, I thought we might grab a cup of coffee."

"I'll be at the shop."

"Great."

The Elvis-shaped chimes rang out.

All heads turned as Urso lumbered into the restaurant looking like a defensive lineman too tired to take on the opposing quarterback. He bypassed tables of patrons, stopped beside ours, and removed his hat.

Jordan stepped back to give Urso a wide berth. "Sorry to hear the news."

Urso said, "You're not as sorry as Mr. Fontanne's parents."

"You notified them already?" I said, feeling slightly ashamed. I hadn't thought once about Harker's family. I'd bet they were heartbroken.

Urso nodded. "Seems they're world travelers. They're on a trip in the Australian Outback. It could be days before they get here."

"I'll leave you to your conversation." Jordan squeezed my shoulder affectionately, offered a hint of a smile to me, then sauntered back to his sister.

Urso removed his broad-brimmed hat and combed his fingers through his thick hair.

"Sit," Delilah said.

Urso slumped into the booth beside me.

"Got any DNA on the murderer yet?" Rebecca asked.

Urso gave her a slow, withering glare. "Not yet, Ms. Zook."

Providence was too small to have its own forensics team. We had only Urso and the Road Runner to process a crime. The last time a murder had occurred in Providence, the Holmes County staff had come to help with the evidence.

"So who do you think killed him?" Rebecca asked. Sometimes she astounded me. She had the bulldog tenacity of an investigative reporter and the subtlety of a hammer.

"Quinn Vance is my bet," Urso said.

"Shut the front door!" The quaint expression — one my mother had used, according to Grandmère — popped out of my mouth. I couldn't remember much about my mother except a warm lap and the way she'd twirl my hair around her finger. I pushed the bittersweet memory aside, twisted in the booth, and poked Urso in his chest. "Quinn is not guilty."

"She and her father are gone," he said.

"Gone, as in *gone?*" I swallowed hard.

"Told you somebody split," Delilah said.

I couldn't remember seeing Freddy or Quinn when I'd returned to the winery, but I hadn't been paying attention. Why would they run? I couldn't believe Quinn was guilty. Not Quinnie. We'd read books, blown bubbles, sung "Itsy Bitsy Spider." She was an innocent.

"They left while we were at the theater," Urso said. "Deputy Rodham tried to detain them, but Freddy Vance put up a fuss. According to ten party guests, Quinn Vance was the last person seen with Harker Fontanne."

"But she's so sweet," I said.

"Sweet people kill, Charlotte."

"Sure, except —" I snapped my mouth closed, worried that condemning words might slip out. I'd seen Quinn quarrel with Harker. Had she abandoned her frolic with Edsel, only to return to Harker and have it out with him? Had she lured him to the cellar? Earlier I'd determined that she wasn't strong enough to have strangled Harker, but now I recalled seeing her in that bikini. She had tight abs and muscular arms. Was she capable of taking down someone Harker's size?

"Except what?" Urso demanded.

"Aw, shoot." I couldn't keep a secret. I mean, I could, but I wouldn't when it came to tracking down a murderer and bringing him, or her, to justice. "Rebecca and I saw Harker and Quinn fighting."

"In the kitchen," Rebecca said.

"But she fought with Dane, too," I added. "That was when she abandoned her scarf." I explained about Dane taunting her with fondue. "Anyone could have picked up the scarf after that."

"Including Quinn," Urso said.

"I'd wager a bet on Winona Westerton being guilty," Delilah cut in.

Rebecca waved a hand. "I agree. She's got a secret."

"Seconds ago, you said it was Dane," Urso reminded her.

"I'm allowed to change my mind." She flipped her ponytail for effect.

Sometimes I believed my lively assistant had dreams of becoming a private detective. I didn't dare ask what her Amish family would say about that. She'd had little contact with them since she'd left the fold.

"Did you know Winona tracked down Freddy to make a donation?" Rebecca went on. "I heard she was itching to go on this trip."

"I'm sorry. I don't understand," Urso said. "Did she have to donate to be included?"

"If she made a donation, how could Freddy say no?" Rebecca replied.

Good point.

"Winona Westerton looks strong enough," I said, backing Rebecca's suspicions. "And I saw her flirting with Harker at The Cheese Shop. She winked at him."

Urso smirked. "A wink is flirting? Hmmm, better watch myself." He deliberately winked at me.

I looked away, hoping I was misinterpreting his intentions, which got me to thinking. Maybe I had misconstrued Winona's brief exchange with Harker in The Cheese Shop. Perhaps she was the kind of person who winked at everything. They'd been talking about the treasure, not s-e-x.

The door to the diner whisked open, the chimes jangled again, and Edsel Nash slogged in, chin slack, his dress shirt rumpled and hanging out of his jeans. Dane shuffled in behind him, looking equally messy, his gaze dark with unease.

Edsel weaved toward our table and glowered at Urso. "You let that Bozz nerd go, didn't you, Chief?" He pounded a fist into his palm. "Why?"

"Because I didn't feel he was guilty, son. He had a solid alibi." Urso sniffed hard. "Been drinking?"

Dane slung an arm over Edsel's shoulders. "Man, let's grab some chow and chill out." He guided Edsel to the counter and nudged him onto one of the red leather stools. I had to admire the way he defused his friends.

Edsel teetered. Dane righted him. Edsel looked at Dane with weary eyes. "Harker was my best friend. Best in the whole world."

He had to be kidding. I remembered the demeaning way Harker had treated Edsel at The Cheese Shop.

Urso rose from the booth and drew near to Edsel. He perched a foot on the chrome rung of Edsel's stool. Like a stalwart musketeer, Dane slipped behind Edsel. If he'd had a sword, I had no doubt he would have laid a tip in Urso's chest to keep him at bay. All for one and one for all.

Edsel shoved Dane away. "I'm cool, bro."

"Mr. Nash, tell me more about your relationship with Harker Fontanne," Urso said, his tone laced with honey. He was fishing.

"We were freshman roommates," Edsel replied.

I wanted to hear everything, so I slid out of the booth and carried the remains of the grilled cheese platter to the counter. "Hungry, fellas?"

Delilah hopped up and hurried behind the red laminate counter. As she rustled up two sodas, Rebecca joined the huddle.

Edsel snatched a grilled Butterkäse triangle, finished it in two bites, and licked his fingertips. "Harker and me took art classes together. Ski and me —"

"Who's Ski?" Urso asked.

Edsel jerked his thumb at Dane. "Cegielski. If you ask me, those Germans have too many letters in their names."

"Polish," Dane corrected.

"I thought your grandparents were German. Whatever." Edsel wasn't slurring. He couldn't have been too drunk. "Ski and me, we were first in the class. Then Harker came in. He was great, right off the bat. He couldn't make up his mind whether he wanted to paint with oils or acrylics or watercolors, but our teacher, Freddy, said to do anything he wanted. Harker was that good. He had the talent. The rest of us are hacks compared to him."

"*Were* hacks." Dane's face twisted with pain.

Edsel nodded. "Yeah. *Were.*"

"Quinn's talented." Dane took a sandwich and stared at the different angles of it as if studying a piece of sculpture. "But Harker had the chops."

Urso pulled a notepad from his hip pocket. "What was your relationship with Harker Fontanne . . ." He consulted the pad. ". . . Mr. Cegielski?"

"We were friends."

"And poker buddies," Edsel said. "Harker owed Dane a wad of cash."

Urso's gaze sharpened with interest. "How much?"

"Five hundred," Edsel said.

"Liar!" Dane abandoned his sandwich. "We never bet that —"

"Chief Urso!" Lois, the owner of Lavender and Lace, darted down the aisle between the booths and counter. The hem of her purple poncho fluted up like an umbrella to reveal the lavender sweater and purple calf-length skirt she wore beneath. "Chief Urso! There you are. And Mr. Cegielski and Mr. Nash. Oh, my! I heard the news. Oh, my."

Freddy, Winona, and the artists were staying at Lois's bed-and-breakfast.

"Oh, my, oh, my, oh, my." Lois placed a bony hand on her narrow chest.

Urso rushed to her and steadied her by the shoulders. "Breathe, Mrs. Smith. What's the problem?"

"It's lost. Mr. Fontanne's art." Lois's partially blind eye fluttered open-shut, open-shut. "It's gone!"

CHAPTER 9

Lois talked nonstop from the diner to Lavender and Lace, covering the same ground. The artwork was gone, stolen. She couldn't imagine how a thief had gotten into her place. Her husband, a man whom I'd dubbed the Cube because of his solid, square stature, was home night and day and always watchful, she told the group of us who had accompanied Urso.

After fetching a set of master keys from the kitchen, Lois bustled up the stairs. The purple rabbit's foot on the keychain bounced in rhythm. She entered Harker Fontanne's room ahead of us. Her Shih Tzu, Agatha, bolted out of nowhere, weaved around our legs, and scuttled to her mistress's side. Without a command from Lois, Agatha sat on her rump and panted, totally attentive to the serious nature of the business.

Urso paused in the doorway, making it

difficult for the rest of us to see past him. Rebecca and I stood on tiptoe for a peek. Dane and Edsel hung back. I could hear them fidgeting.

Lois stopped beside the four-poster bed and folded her hands beneath her poncho. "Here we are."

Harker's room, like every other room at the B&B, was decorated in shades of lavender: floral bedspread, lavender pillow shams, sprigs of silk lavender in lavender-glazed flower vases. Light from a streetlamp glinted through the sheer curtains that tiered behind the brocade lavender drapes and created a path on the carpet. In every guest's room, Lois had set up a showcase of her collectible teacups on a floating bookshelf. Other homey touches included the makings of a fire in the hearth, ready to go with a single match, and a hurricane candle on top of the antique bureau. Two scones sat on a lavender-rimmed china plate beside the candle.

A few things looked out of place in the tidy room: Harker's jeans, socks, and paint-splattered work shirt were strewn on the easy chair; his mess of toiletries was scattered on the counter by the antique sink; his clothing spilled out of a suitcase that was tucked into the corner of the room.

"Are all the students rooming alone?" Urso asked.

"Mr. Cegielski and Mr. Nash are together," Lois said. "The others chose singles, don't you know. Anyway, as I said, I cleaned this room yesterday and then again today, and, well, I'm a snoop. I admit it. Terrible habit. But I am." She crossed to the pillows on the bed and automatically fluffed them. Agatha jumped to her feet and followed, her ID tags jingling merrily. "Anyway, I was cleaning yesterday and I saw Mr. Fontanne's . . . Oh, what do you call it?" Lois snapped her fingers. After a brief moment, she tapped her head. "Aha! Portfolio. He has this portfolio." She pulled a black leather case, which was about three feet by two feet with a finger-grip handle, from beneath the bed.

A number of artists I'd known at OSU had carried similar art cases, large enough to hold works in progress.

"Yesterday, I peeked inside," Lois went on. "His work was beautiful. Portraits and landscapes. And now it's gone, don't you know."

Urso strolled into the room to inspect the portfolio, giving Rebecca and me a chance to slip in, too. Eager to see the evidence, I set my purse on the mahogany ladder chair to the left of the door and started toward the bed.

"Stay back, Charlotte," Urso said, deducing my intention. He unfolded the case on the bed and thumbed through the cellophane sleeves.

Lois said, "See? Empty. There were paintings and sketches in it." She shook her head, obviously distraught with the circumstances. Without another word, she shuffled away and fussed with the drapes.

As I watched her, a prickle of curiosity nipped me. Had someone climbed the trellis outside and crept in through the window? Would there be fingerprints on the sill? I heard Dane and Edsel whispering and looked over my shoulder. They sealed their lips, and like men on a chessboard, advanced one pace forward.

It didn't take long for me to learn what they were whispering about. Quinn. She was hurrying down the hallway. Relief swept over me. She was alive, and she hadn't run away. She wedged through the boys and slipped into the room, her face blotchy, her red hair knotted and tangled.

"What's going on?" she demanded.

I crossed to her and gripped her shoulders. "Are you okay? Where have you been?"

"I was . . ." She sucked in a breath. "I

was . . . walking." Tears pushed at the corners of her eyes. "Oh, Charlotte, I can't believe Harker's gone. Dead. I can't believe it. I . . ." She curled into my arms and rested her head on my shoulder. After a moment, she pulled away from me. "What's everyone doing here?"

"Harker's artwork is missing," I said.

"Can't be," Quinn said. "He carried his portfolio everywhere. It was never out of his sight. He didn't want anyone to see what he was working on."

Except he hadn't carried it everywhere, I mused. He hadn't taken it to the water-balloon fight or to The Cheese Shop or to the fund-raiser.

"Was anything else stored in here?" Urso cocked his head. "Anything at all?"

"You mean like drugs?" Edsel edged closer.

"Harker didn't do drugs," Quinn said, her voice rising in pitch. "He rarely drank."

Except he had earlier. Matthew had spoken to him about overindulging. Had Harker discovered that his artwork was missing? Was that why he'd been drinking?

"He was very territorial about his work," Edsel added.

To my mind, Harker had been quite territorial about all of his possessions, including Quinn.

"Where's your father?" I asked.

"I don't have a clue. Doesn't that Winona know?" Quinn said, evidently not pleased that Winona was pursuing Freddy. But then what nineteen-year-old was happy with change? Quinn probably adored her mother. Freddy dating anyone but her mother would be considered a betrayal.

Urso moved closer, his size making Quinn cower ever so slightly. "You and your father disappeared from the winery when I gave strict instructions for everyone to stick around."

"I told you, I went walking. Not a very good alibi, I guess." Tears streamed down her cheeks. Her shoulders shuddered in distress. "I just couldn't handle being around so many people . . . I needed time to think." She hiccupped. "I'm so sorry." She jammed her knuckles into her mouth. "Ohmigod, Harker's really dead. I loved him so much."

Urso didn't look moved in the least. Did he still suspect Quinn was the murderer? He turned back to Lois. "Can you tell us what some of the art looked like?"

The Shih Tzu yipped.

"Hush!" Lois scooped the pup off the floor and petted her head. "There was a painting of a sunset, and another of towering buildings, and another of birds flying. A few of them were portraits of a pretty girl's face. No full figures."

Quinn said, "Harker didn't do torsos well. He had trouble with hands. They always turned into claws." The memory brought a pained smile to her face. She whispered, "Did you see what he painted at the winery? Masterful."

Dane stifled a snicker. Edsel slugged him with an elbow. Were they callous or jealous?

I remembered thinking Harker's artwork of the cellar in a black sea seemed forlorn. Had he foreseen his own fate?

A door slammed at the front of the bed-and-breakfast. Footsteps grew louder as the guests climbed the stairs. A man spoke — something low, unintelligible.

Rebecca said, "Sounds like your father, Quinn." I swear she had elephant ears sometimes.

"Daddy!" Quinn raced toward the door. Dane and Edsel parted to let her pass.

Rebecca nudged me. We popped into the hallway for a peek. Freddy and Winona halted at the top of the stairs. Winona looked flushed, windblown. A raincoat hung over one arm. Her tight gold dress had inched up around her thighs. She tugged the seams to draw the clingy material down.

Quinn threw herself into her father's arms. "Daddy, it's gone. Harker's art is gone. Stolen."

When confronted by his tearful daughter, Freddy reminded me of a punk being brought up on charges — shoulders taut, eyes wary. He patted her back stiffly.

What was up with that? The girl was heartbroken. *Hug her, for heaven's sakes.*

They shared a muffled exchange, then Quinn broke free and glowered at Winona. "What's she doing here?"

"Quinn, don't be rude," Freddy said.

"I'll be what I want." She aimed a stern finger at her father and then at Winona. "You don't belong here."

"Actually, I do, dear." Winona plucked a key from her purse and wiggled it.

"You should be with the other donors at Violet's Victoriana Inn," Quinn said. More tears erupted from her eyes. She tore past Winona and Freddy, rushed into a room, and slammed the door.

Winona smirked.

Lois, who'd sneaked into the hallway with Agatha for an eyeful, clucked her tongue. "Sad to lose the love of your life so young," she said, a wistfulness in her voice that I didn't understand. Was it born from experience? I didn't know much about Lois. I didn't know how she'd lost the eye, didn't know why she loved lavender. I was her neighbor, and yet I knew nothing about her. A knot of guilt caught in my throat and made it hard for me to swallow, but I couldn't address that right now. I was too concerned with Freddy and Quinn's situation. Why had he been so cold toward her? Was his stiff-upper-lip act meant to impress Winona? And what was Winona doing at the B&B instead of staying with the other donors?

As if sensing my agitation, Winona raised her chin, defying me to question her relationship with Freddy. "So-o-o-o." The way she dragged out the word, I expected her to break into an aria. "What are you all doing here?"

Dane said, "We're staying here, or did you forget?"

Winona narrowed one eye to admonish him — or was she winking at him, too? "I wasn't addressing you. Them." She gazed at me with malice. Did she view me as competition? Did she think I was vying for Freddy's affections?

"We're helping out Chief Urso," Rebecca explained. "Finding out who filched the art might be a clue. Whoever took it might be the killer." She looked to me to confirm her theory.

The timing of the theft did seem suspicious.

Freddy glanced over his shoulder toward Quinn's room. Was he regretting his behavior toward his daughter? Did he have to ditch Winona before he could deal with Quinn? He caught me watching him, offered a miserable shrug, and put his hands into his pockets.

"How can you be so sure the artwork was stolen?" Winona resumed smoothing the wrinkles from her stretchy sheath. "Maybe Harker threw it away."

"It was too good to throw away," Lois said.

"And how exactly did you see it, Mrs. Smith?" Winona asked.

I didn't appreciate the frosty prosecutorial tone she was using to grill Lois. I said, "It was in his portfolio."

Winona raised an eyebrow. "What portfolio?"

"The one Harker kept under his bed," Rebecca said. "There was artwork in it. Now it's gone."

"What does it matter who took the art?" Winona asked. "The murder didn't occur here."

"Maybe whoever made off with the art

wanted the theft kept secret," Rebecca said. "What do you think about that theory, Chief?"

Urso loomed in the doorway. What had he been doing all this time in Harker's room? Hopefully a little sleuthing without Lois hanging around. He ignored Rebecca's question and eyed Freddy. "Where have you been, Mr. Vance?"

Freddy whipped his hands out of his pockets and snapped to attention, a reaction that looked like a holdover from his days as a gymnast. He'd never been in the army. "I was upset. I needed some air."

"Why didn't you return to the winery?" Urso asked.

"He told you," Winona cut in. "He needed air. I found him taking a walk and having a smoke. I told him that you wouldn't mind if he came back here, since he didn't kill Harker."

Urso looked annoyed by her presumption.

I would be, too. How could she act so smug? Maybe she'd made her wealth working as a mind reader, I thought with a tinge of snarkiness.

"As long as he didn't leave town, of course," Winona hurried to add.

Another malicious thought flitted through my mind, but I erased it. Just because Winona sounded hip to the methods of the police didn't mean she was a criminal. She could come by that information the same way Rebecca did — by watching television — but her snooty attitude did make me wonder.

"Was I wrong to do that?" Winona asked.

Wait for it. Wait for it. I didn't have to wait long. Winona batted her eyelashes.

Urso sighed. He wasn't a pushover for a pretty woman's ploys. "Look, we're all tired." He addressed Freddy. "First thing in the morning, you and I powwow, Mr. Vance. Good night." Urso marched past them and headed for the stairs.

Dane and Edsel pivoted and entered a room down the hall.

"Wait, Chief." Rebecca ran after Urso. "You can't leave. Isn't this a crime scene?"

Urso glanced over his shoulder. "Mrs. Smith, please shut Mr. Fontanne's door and lock it. I'll review the crime scene again in the morning."

Rebecca said, "But —"

"No, Ms. Zook. It's time to go home. Sleep could do us all a world of good." Urso tapped the brim of his hat as a farewell and proceeded downstairs.

Rebecca sputtered and posed, fists planted

on her hips. She looked about as mighty as a moth.

"C'mon, Super Girl," I said. "Let's go."

"I'm mad," she hissed.

"Got that."

"The least we should do is guard the room."

"Don't worry," Lois said. "I'll set up a cot outside, don't you know." She looked more eager than Rebecca to get to the bottom of this.

I groaned inwardly. Just what Urso needed, another budding detective in town.

"Good night, Charlotte." Freddy pressed Winona at the small of her back. She moved forward, unlocked her door, demurely kissed Freddy on the cheek, and slipped inside. The door shut with a click.

Freddy did a U-turn and headed back to the room next to his daughter's. With his hand on the doorknob, he glanced wistfully at Quinn's door, but he didn't break stride. He entered his room and closed the door quietly.

In the gloomy silence, fatigue crept into my bones. I thanked Lois for her help, accompanied Rebecca downstairs, and we went our separate ways. I had made it as far as the front stoop of my house next door when I realized I'd left my purse sitting on the ladder-back chair in Harker's room.

I hurried to Lavender and Lace, slipped through the front door, which Lois never locked, and paused. *She never locks the door.* Anyone could have come into the bed-and-breakfast, stolen into Harker's room, and taken his things. Anyone. I'd bet the Cube was not as attentive as Lois had made out. I made a mental note to tell Urso in the morning.

In the meantime, I dashed upstairs. Lois had yet to set up camp, and — surprise, surprise! — she hadn't followed Urso's orders and locked Harker's door yet. I retrieved my purse, and as I returned down the hall, I paused outside Freddy's door, wondering whether I should talk to him about Quinn. I raised my hand to knock but realized his door was slightly ajar.

I heard him muttering to himself. I couldn't make out the words, but he clearly wasn't happy.

Ever so silently, I toed the door open. Peeking in through the three-inch slit I'd created, I watched as Freddy placed a large manila envelope — large enough to hold Harker's artwork — into the opened suit-case that sat on the four-poster bed.

CHAPTER 10

Sleep did not come quickly, but dawn did. I roused the twins and prepared one of their favorite breakfasts — omelets with fresh herbs that I'd plucked from the windowsill garden. I added their preferred cheeses. For Amy, Maple Leaf's Smoked Gouda. For Clair, Two Plug Nickels' Lavender Goat Cheese. Unfortunately, my attempt to spoil them didn't lighten their grumpy moods. They were snapping at each other, accusing the other of hiding a shoe or a sock, as if poison had been injected into them. In a way, it had. Not through a glass of orange juice but by the presence of their mother. Sylvie was such a negative force. I had to do something to remove her from their lives, but what?

"Why are Daddy and Mum angry at each other?" Clair said as she clambered into her spot at the breakfast table.

Amy said, "Because they're meeting with

attorneys, that's why." She stood beside the table, toying with a Chinese finger puzzle that her mother had brought her. She had her index fingers stuck into two ends of the bamboo braid and was pulling, which made the braid tighten, trapping her fingers inside. "Shoot, shoot, shoot." She grumbled her frustration. "I hate this game. Hate it!"

"Don't pull," I said. "Twist. It's a game about not resisting."

She did as I suggested and tossed the braid aside. "Why aren't you answering us?"

"Don't snap at me," I said calmly, knowing they wanted little-girl answers for big-girl problems.

"I'm sorry." Amy tucked her lower lip under her teeth. A single tear trickled down her face. Clair handed her a napkin.

I said, "Your parents aren't happy with each other."

"Were they ever?" Clair asked.

I smiled. "Once upon a time." I didn't offer anything more.

With a heavy heart, I sent them off to school and took a moment for myself. I sat in a chair on the wraparound porch of my Victorian home. Rain was not in the forecast, but the temperature — a brisk thirty-six degrees — wasn't quite up to spring standards. Dressed in a down parka, sweatpants, and a snuggly pair of Ugg boots, I sipped a cup of mint tea and stared at the B&B next door.

Yet again, the news of a murder in our fair town was drawing a curious selection of tourists. A dozen or more newshounds hunkered in vans along the street. Tourists dressed in winter clothing roamed past the inn with to-go cups of coffee in their hands. Some snapped photographs. Others plucked purple tulips from the Lavender and Lace garden as mementoes. I imagined there were lookie-loos lurking about the Ziegler Winery, too. The notion made me recall a quote by Oscar Wilde: "The public have an insatiable curiosity to know everything, except what is worth knowing."

Around seven fifteen, Freddy trotted out of the B&B. He was wearing jogging clothes and a bright orange ski cap.

Reporters descended on him like locusts to honey.

"Was Mr. Fontanne a gambler?"

"Were the jewels real?"

"What's the deal with the brick wall?"

I wondered where they had come upon their information. Last night, Urso had cautioned everyone at the winery not to talk about the investigation, but gossip was like a wildfire — hard to control.

Freddy didn't open his mouth. Didn't wave. Didn't stop. He bounded along the sidewalk and passed in front of my house looking rested and buoyant. I itched to know what he was hiding in his larger-than-necessary suitcase, but I didn't have time to snoop. I had a business to run. I tried to convince myself he was hiding something as innocent as underwear, but in my heart of hearts, I knew better.

When I opened The Cheese Shop doors to customers, more curious reporters and tourists appeared. I didn't mind the extra business — many purchased cheeses and breads and cups of mulled cider that Rebecca had insisted we serve on cold days. But I did mind that many were looking for Bozz. It didn't matter that Rebecca and I professed his innocence or that Bozz wouldn't arrive until he was out of school for the day. The reporters were dogged. At one point the noise level rose so high that Rebecca clanged a metal spatula against a baking pan and ordered them to hush. Occasionally Rags peeked out from the office, as if on alert so he could give Bozz extra emotional support the instant he arrived. Whenever I shook my head indicating we'd had no sign of Bozz, Rags retreated to his favorite spot on the desk chair and nestled down to wait a little longer.

Around noon, Pépère waved to me from behind the cheese counter. "Charlotte, your opinion, please." He was helping out while Matthew met with Mr. Nakamura over at Nuts for Nails. I hoped Mr. Nakamura, who used to have a big law practice in Cleveland, could make Matthew's custody battle problem go away. Pépère held up a wedge of Appenzeller and a wedge of Vella Dry Monterey Jack. "Which cheese do you want me to set out on the tasting counter?"

"The Appenzeller," Rebecca said. She was busy behind the counter finishing off a cheese basket, which she had filled with three artisanal cheeses, a chalkboard serving tray, an olive-wood-handled cheese knife, and a few of my favorite recipes. It was the prize for our first Internet contest. Anyone who signed up for our monthly online newsletter was eligible to win.

"I agree, Pépère. Appenzeller." Most people aren't familiar with the cheese, but I adored it. Appenzeller is a semi-hard Alpine cow's milk that looks a little like Gruyère but has a more pungent, farmlike aroma. The Swiss keep the recipe a mystery, though it's no secret that the recipe requires the cheese maker to continually brush the cheese with a special mixture of herbs, wine, and salt.

As Pépère started to cut the cheese into cubes and set them on a decorative platter, the grape-leaf-shaped chimes over the front door jingled.

Jordan sauntered in, carrying a nine-pound wheel of Pace Hill's Double Cream Gouda wrapped in yellow wax. He smiled his devilishly charming smile, and my heart did a little hippety-hop. "Brought my wares, Cheese Lady. Where do you want me to put the wheel?"

I took the cheese from him and stored it in the walk-in refrigerator. He followed.

As I was closing the door, he snuggled close and whispered, "Can you spend a few minutes in the garden?"

Could I ever.

I said, "Pépère and Rebecca, I'm taking a lunch break."

Pépère gave my spirited assistant a knowing wink. She giggled.

Let 'em giggle. I had a very handsome suitor wanting my attention.

"Are you hungry?" I asked Jordan.

"You bet."

I put together a small plate of sliced cheeses, flavorful crackers, and gherkins. Then I whipped off my apron, hung it on one of the hooks near the rear entrance, and slung on my parka.

The town owned a co-op vegetable garden and hothouse in the alley that ran behind the southernmost shops on Hope Street. Fromagerie Bessette took full advantage of both. We planted herbs, tomatoes, and assorted vegetables. The outside garden wasn't in bloom yet. The ground was still soggy from rain. But in a month or so, the scent would be heavenly.

After we settled onto the meditation bench at the far end of the garden, I put the plate of appetizers on a wrought-iron table to the right of the bench and slipped my hand into Jordan's. The touch of his skin warmed me to my bones.

"You look beautiful." He released my hand, wove his fingers through my hair, and pulled my face close. He brushed my lips with his, and a hunger rose within me.

A minute later, I came up for air, but I didn't move away. "Oooh, boy." My voice sounded husky with lust. He grinned. I playfully whacked his chest. "What are you doing later? I could use more of this kissing."

"Staff business dinner."

Pace Hill Farm took on the aging process for some of the smaller farms' premium cheeses. A couple of times a year, Jordan wined and dined his employees to show his appreciation for their hard work.

"Rats," I said. "I was hoping I could fix you dinner at my house. Fettucini Alfredo with a pear and blue cheese salad."

"Soon." He cuffed my chin.

"Is Jacky going to be at your dinner?" I asked.

"It's Girls' Night Out, isn't it?"

I snapped my fingers. "I almost forgot." Once a week, my girlfriends and I went to Timothy O'Shea's Irish Pub for drinks and gossip. "Can you tell me what's going on with her? I mean, why was she crying last night? I know you said she was under the weather, but I get the feeling it's something to do with being estranged from her husband." Last year, Jacky fled from an abusive relationship. Thanks to Jordan, she had a new identity in Providence. I didn't have a clue what her real name was. Didn't know what the ex did or even if he was an ex. For all I knew, Jacky could still be legally married. "I realize I don't have the right to pry. I just worry, that's all."

Jordan smiled and tapped my nose with his fingertip. "You are one of the best worriers I know." He stacked a piece of cheese onto a cracker, ate it whole, and licked his lips. "Love this cheese. Sheep's milk?"

157

"Kindred Brebis." It was a yogurty cheese with lovely flavors of caramel and clover from one of our local farmers.

Silence fell between us. So much for prying, I thought, as frustration swelled inside me. I wanted . . . needed to know more about Jacky. About Jordan. Why was he so closed off to me? Why was he so protective of her? How could I get him to trust me and open up? I didn't bite. Heck, I didn't even nibble.

After what seemed like an eon, he said, "Let's plan our getaway."

I was so surprised by the switch in topics that I worried I might fall off the bench.

"I bought two round-trip tickets," he went on.

"You did?"

"You said yes."

"For what date?"

"I was thinking we'd leave a week from Monday."

"A week from Monday!"

"Is your passport in order?"

A spate of emotions rose within me. When we'd first started dating, we had agreed to take our relationship slowly. We'd gone on picnics and to the movies — all very demure. Jane Austen would have been proud. Our romantic getaway was going to take us to the next steamy step. I couldn't wait, and yet I was scared half to death. I hadn't been with anyone since Creep Chef. Not a soul.

"You look like I've suggested you eat spoiled cheese," Jordan teased.

I laughed but my laughter sounded brittle.

"Don't you want to go?"

I gripped his hands. "Yes, I want to go, and yes, my passport is in order."

He looked like I'd given him the best Christmas present a boy could ever have. "Then Gruyère it is! We'll eat fondue to our hearts' content." He hugged me and kissed me hard on the mouth. When I melted into him, I could feel the pounding of his heart against my chest and knew, at the core of my being, that this man was the right man for me.

So what was keeping me from leaping with joy? Grandmère's reservation? Did she know something about Jordan that I didn't?

I broke free and lasered Jordan with my gaze. "Listen up, mister. I've said yes, but do not presume for a second that you can take me on a romantic getaway without me getting to know you better. I want to know what you used to do, why you moved here, and, well, everything. Got me? Full disclosure."

"Ruffles."

"Who's Ruffles?"

Jordan laughed a wholehearted hoot that made me hunger for him even more. "He was my first pet. You'd want to know that, wouldn't you?"

He was right. I would.

"Ruffles was a Wirehaired Terrier mutt. I was four when I met him at the creek. He was covered with mud. Didn't have a collar. Attached himself to me like glue. He lived a hearty fourteen years."

Jordan's eyes moistened. Mine did, too. Who couldn't love a man who took in a stray dog? However, I couldn't very well Google the name Ruffles and come up with clues about Jordan's past, could I? I'd need more.

"Go on," I said.

Jordan raised an eyebrow. "If I tell you everything now, you might be disappointed and back out of our vacation."

"Why would I be disappointed?"

"Because my life is so mundane."

"I doubt that." Nothing about Jordan was mundane.

"You're shivering." He brushed my arms to warm them. "Let's get you inside before you freeze."

I gathered the cheese plate, and we walked back into The Cheese Shop, hand in hand.

After I shrugged out of my parka, he pecked me on the cheek and whispered, "I can't wait." When he left, I felt a void so deep that I realized I loved him hopelessly, answers or no answers.

Although I wanted to reside on cloud nine for hours, I had work to do. I returned to my spot behind the cheese counter and told Pépère to take a break. "Do a little blogging. Boost our Internet presence." My grandfather may have been retired, but he couldn't stay idle. A social being, Pépère loved to leave comments on cheese makers', chefs', and foodies' blogs. "And give Rags some love, too," I added.

A little while later, as the newshounds and tourist crowd thinned, Prudence Hart flounced into the shop with Tyanne Taylor. Prudence was dressed in a spring frock hemmed with strips of chiffon that dangled around her bony ankles. I secretly reveled in the fact that her shawl-covered arms were pimply with goose bumps and her fancy shoes were soaking wet. More in keeping with the weather, Tyanne wore snug-fitting yoga pants, a long-sleeved sweater, and colorful tennis shoes. She'd worked hard to lose weight over the past few months. I was surprised to see her. I thought she had ended her rocky friendship with Prudence.

Tyanne was bright and should have known better than to rekindle an association with someone as prickly as Prudence, but she was also easily swayed. Her encounter with Hurricane Katrina and ultimate retreat to Ohio had left her emotionally vulnerable.

I said, "Hello, Tyanne. Prudence."

Tyanne looked like she wanted to say something. Instead, she wiggled her fingers about waist-high, as if she didn't want Prudence to notice. Was it a signal of some kind? A hint to get her away from Prudence? I had the urge to pull her aside and encourage her to link up with some of the nicer people in town. Maybe talk her into participating in one of the cooking classes that I had planned for the fall. My pal Freckles, who owned the Sew Inspired Quilt Shoppe, had registered. I was pretty certain Prudence wouldn't deign to join. Or maybe Tyanne would be interested in attending a class at A Wheel Good Time, Jacky's pottery place.

"What's the specialty today?" Prudence asked. She didn't truly care for cheese. I'd bet she had ventured in to keep current with the gossip.

"Sweet Grass Green Hill. It's a goat cheese." Rebecca plucked a round of cheese from the display case and waved her hand over it like a model. "Notice the fluffy white rind. Want a taste?"

"Sugar, don't mind if I do," Tyanne said, her sweet Southern accent drawing out the vowels. She split from Prudence and took the sample Rebecca offered. "Hmmm, I don't detect a scent."

"That's because the cheese is thin, like Brie," Rebecca said. "The mold that covers the cheese breaks down the fat and protein more quickly. It can also mute the aroma."

Tyanne ate the slice of cheese in one bite and let out a satisfied purr.

"It's from Georgia," I added.

"They make cheese in Georgia?" Tyanne giggled. "Who knew?"

"Hmph." Prudence sauntered to the cheese counter, her polished fingertips touching boxes of crackers and jars of jam as she moved. She wasn't a tactile person. She just liked having ownership over everything. Begrudgingly, she accepted a sample of the cheese from Rebecca and nibbled. I couldn't tell whether she enjoyed it or not. "Have you been to Georgia, Charlotte?" Prudence leveled me with a *gotcha* glare. "Oh, silly me, of course not. You don't travel much, do you?"

"Actually, I do, and I have been to Georgia. Atlanta, to be specific. We've been focusing on American cheeses this past year," I said. Matthew, Pépère, and I had taken a tour of the farms in the Northeast, too. Urso's mother, who owned Two Plug Nickels Farm, had joined us. I had asked Jordan if he'd wanted to tag along, but he'd had other plans.

Prudence sniffed. "American cheeses are all mass-produced."

"Actually, there are some fabulous artisanal cheese makers in America. In Wisconsin, Vermont, Oregon, California. You name it. Did you know that the United States is ranked number one in world cheese production?"

"I thought France —"

"Number two, followed by Germany in third place."

Rebecca rapped a cheese knife on the counter. "Ohio is gaining notoriety in artisanal cheese making, too. Amish milk is the difference."

"Your cheeses here are very expensive." Prudence took a second slice of the free cheese and downed it. As she chewed, she said, "How dare you charge so much?"

Rebecca gasped. Her fingers balled into a fist.

I grabbed her wrist while holding my breath to compose myself. Prudence really knew how to push our buttons. The *B* word came to mind.

When I felt I could answer calmly, I said, "Prudence, artisanal cheeses take time. The cheese makers have to accommodate for the availability of milk and —"

"Argh!" Prudence clutched her throat. Without warning, her eyes went wide and her face turned a funky shade of purple. She clawed at her bodice then gagged. She crumpled to her knees on the hardwood floor. Her purse toppled to one side.

I darted around the end of the cheese counter and knelt beside her, and all the panic I'd felt as a little girl rushed back to me. My mother ripping me out of the car. Blood dripping down her forehead. Fire flaming behind her. The smell of gasoline. Her arms clutching me so hard that I couldn't breathe.

"Prudence!" I yelled. "Are you choking?"

"Pills," she rasped. "In my purse."

Energy crackled through me. "Tyanne, call Doc Holloway. Rebecca, towels!" I rummaged through Prudence's expensive leather tote and found a vial of pills: Lorazepam. I'd heard of the medicine. It was for anxiety, not for a heart attack. Why was she taking it? Granted, she'd been through a lot in the past year. Her best friend had left town, she'd purchased the friend's clothing boutique, and just recently the manager of the boutique — which Prudence had renamed Le Chic Boutique — had quit. The woman had stomached enough of Prudence's rude behavior. But was that why Prudence was on the medicine? She gagged again.

"Oh, my, my, my," Tyanne muttered as she stabbed at the numbers on her cell phone.

I scooped out a pill and tucked it under Prudence's tongue. From what I understood, the medicine wouldn't work like a miracle drug. It would take time to calm her.

"Breathe, Prudence. Long, slow breaths." I gazed at her ashen face and wondered if something more sinister was troubling her. Guilt, perhaps? She was at the winery the night Harker Fontanne was murdered. Had she had a hand in it? What would her motive have been?

"Breathe," I said.

"Can't."

"Yes, you can. Breathe." I stroked her upper arm. "Rebecca, bring me a paper bag, too." My niece Clair often got overwrought and needed to breathe with a paper bag pressed to her mouth to calm her.

"Breathe."

Prudence glowered at me. She tried to stand.

I said, "Stay kneeling on the floor. Just for a bit."

"Don't . . . want . . . to." Her words were choppy and tense but not slurred.

"Sugar, the doctor's not answering," Tyanne said, holding out the cell phone like she needed to prove it to me. "Oh, wait. He's on the line. Dr. Holloway?" She stepped away from us and whispered into the telephone.

Rebecca brought a paper bag and cool wet towels from the kitchen. I folded a towel over three times and held it to the nape of Prudence's neck.

Tyanne returned to our little huddle and flipped her cell phone closed. "Doc can't come. He's delivering a baby."

"Shoot." I inflated the paper bag, twisted its neck, and held the opening to Prudence's mouth.

Prudence shoved the bag away, then me. "Just as well," she muttered.

It was well known that Prudence didn't trust either of the two doctors in Providence. She went to Cleveland for all her checkups. I gazed at her again and wondered whether, on one of those trips, she had met some out-of-towner who'd wanted to foil the conversion of the winery into a college.

Prudence struggled to rise. "I'm fine. Let me up." God forbid she look fragile in front of me or anyone. She teetered as she stood but found her balance. With her chin thrust upward, she grabbed Tyanne's hand.

Tyanne peered at me. Her mouth opened but no words came out, and again, I got the distinct feeling she'd wanted to say something. She didn't have time. Prudence tugged her out of the shop.

Needing a break from all the drama, I retreated to the wine annex to unpack the extra boxes of wine that we'd received earlier. Matthew planned to have a wine-tasting event in two days. He was focusing on the pinot noir wines of Ohio and California.

As I was setting a bottle on one of the mosaic café tables near the display window, I paused. On the sidewalk near What's In Store, an *everything* shop with the most wonderful knickknacks and gift items, I spotted Winona talking heatedly to Dane. She thrust her index finger into his chest. He knocked it away then spun on a heel and stormed off. It didn't seem like dialogue between strangers. Had they known each other before coming on the trip? Had one discovered something about the other that could be pertinent to the murder? Seconds later, Freddy emerged from What's In Store carrying one of the store's cherry red bags. He asked Winona a question, and she twirled one hand in the air, as if to say, "Who knows?" then she leaned in for a kiss. It wasn't passionate; more of a peck. I wondered if Freddy had been as curious about Winona and Dane's exchange as I'd been.

As they wandered off together, my gaze was drawn to Sylvie, who was skulking down the sidewalk, furtively peering into each car as she passed.

I felt the urge to rush to the street and confront her about the scene she'd made at the theater, but I couldn't because Meredith was charging down the street, her face racked with pain, mascara tears streaking her cheeks. She veered into Fromagerie Bessette. I raced across the annex and met her in the archway between the shop and the annex, my heart doing a triple-time step inside my chest.

"He's got her," she rasped. "He's got Quinn."

"Somebody kidnapped her?"

"No." Meredith took her hand away. "Chief Urso." She sobbed, shoulders heaving. "He took her in for questioning."

"Calm down. Questioning is normal. He hasn't arrested her." My heart rate settled down to a moderate shuffle-hop-step. I gripped Meredith's shoulders. "It's going to be okay."

"It's not. Someone overheard Harker dumping Quinn at the party."

"*Dumping her,* as in they broke up? So what? Kids break up all the time."

"There's more. Urso found out that Quinn takes karate classes."

"You and I take self-defense classes. That doesn't make us murderers."

Meredith shook her head. "You don't understand. Quinn has won competitions. She's strong." She gulped in air. "Strong enough to have choked Harker."

CHAPTER 11

Meredith said, "Please, Charlotte, you've got to help me pry Quinn from Urso's evil clutches."

How could I refuse? I glanced at Pépère and Rebecca.

"Go," they said. They could handle the flow at the shop.

Minutes later, Meredith was prodding me up the slate path to the Providence Precinct, which was located in a quaint Victorian house at the north end of the Village Green.

"Urso always listens to you," she said as she opened the front door.

Not always, I thought, but it was worth a try.

We took our first step onto the hardwood floor of the precinct's foyer and stopped short. As usual, the scent of cinnamon and coffee hung in the air, and also as usual, a platter of iced cinnamon rolls from Providence Patisserie sat on a side table. But unlike every other day, the place was busy — busier than I'd ever seen — probably because the precinct had started sharing space with the Tourist Information Center.

At one end of the room, a pack of tourists huddled near an antique oak desk, all vying for the attention of Gretel, the pastor's wife. Gretel was the reason that Providence had a Tourist Information Center. How else, she'd argued, was our burgeoning tourist population going to know about the treasures in our sweet town? With infinite wisdom, the town council had carved a space for the TIC at the precinct and put Gretel in charge.

"Where's Kindred Creek?" said a man wearing a fishing hat studded with travel pins.

"What're the best hiking trails?" asked a woman holding a toddler.

"I'm looking for the history museum," said an elderly gentleman.

Gretel, a dollop of a woman with wholesome good looks and the patience of Job, smiled sweetly at each and gestured to a rack of numbers. "I'll be with you shortly."

Whenever I saw Gretel, I had fond memories of the librarian who had introduced me to the wonderful world of books. She had the gift of being able to single out one child among a squadron of eager children and making her feel special and *heard.*

"When I call your number, folks, I will be glad to answer your questions. Promise." Gretel wiggled her fingertips at the toddler, who cooed with glee. "Meanwhile, take a brochure and thumb through it. We have so many fun things to do in Providence."

The tourists grumbled something that sounded like "watermelon, watermelon," then quieted.

At the other end of the reception area, a dozen pet owners and their pets were not so silent. They seemed to be trying to out-shriek a group of complainants, headed up by crotchety Arlo MacMillan, who owned a chicken farm on the fringe of town. On more than one occasion, Grandmère had asked Arlo, who was pasty-skinned and had a nose like a vulture's beak, to play Scrooge in her annual winter production of *A Christmas Carol.* Needless to say, he hadn't taken kindly to any of her offers. Arlo made no bones about wanting pets banned from the Village Green. The pet owners, led by our local pet rescuer, wanted the same privileges allotted to all Providence citizens — freedom to roam the outdoors. Theirs was an ongoing battle. I sided with the pet owners. I didn't like anybody — especially Arlo —

limiting a four-legged creature's right to frolic. On a leash, of course. Even I got spooked by big dogs rushing up to me for what their owners called a friendly sniff.

The receptionist, who wore a headset — I would imagine to block out the meowing, yipping, and sniping — was perched on a swivel chair, her back to the horde. She typed nonstop on her ancient Selectric typewriter.

Meredith circumvented the group and said to the receptionist, "Where's Chief Urso?"

The receptionist spun in her chair, and my mouth fell open. It was Freckles, the owner of Sew Inspired Quilt Shoppe, who was usually as slim as a prepubescent gymnast, but not today. She was in her sixth month of pregnancy and glowing.

She removed her headset and beamed at us. "Hi, ladies."

"We need to see Chief Urso," Meredith said.

"What are you doing here, Freckles?" I asked. "Where's your daughter?"

Freckles and her husband homeschooled their twelve-year-old.

"She and her dad are watching the shop for the A.M. My pal — the clerk — got sick. I offered to step in. What was I thinking?

Look at this mob." She snorted. Freckles finished every thought with a laugh. Nobody seemed to enjoy life more than her.

"Urso," Meredith repeated. "Can we see him?"

The roar of the feuding crowd grew by a decibel.

Freckles patted her bulging stomach. "There, there, munchkin. The noisy people will go away soon." She glanced at the antique clock on the wall. "Though not soon enough, I'm afraid." She tittered again. "Oh, Charlotte, isn't it wonderful? We're going to have a college nearby."

Not if the crime put a damper on the college's financial prospects.

"Our daughter won't have to move away from home."

I'd never tell Freckles, but I'd bet her little darling, come college age, would ache for a chance to fly the coop. Most kids did. I had, and I had adored my grandparents.

"We've got to see Urso," Meredith said, visibly at her wits' end.

"Oh, sure. He's in the interrogation room."

"My niece —"

"I know, poor dear. Her father arrived a few minutes ago. He's in back. Why don't you join him?" Freckles pressed a button

175

under the antique desk and a buzzer sounded. "I'm sure Chief Urso won't mind."

I was pretty sure he would mind, but I wouldn't be the one to put on the brakes. Taking advantage of Freckles's beleaguered state, I opened the door leading to the hallway and nudged Meredith ahead of me.

In ten feet, the hall dead-ended and split in two directions. One hall led to the holding cells; the other went to Urso's office and the interrogation room.

As we drew nearer, I saw Winona Westerton sipping from a water fountain by the ladies' room.

"Sheesh," Meredith whispered. "She's like a shadow Freddy can't shake."

"What's your take on her?" I whispered back.

"I don't trust her. It's something about that swoop of her hair. So deliberate," Meredith said. "On the other hand, she can't be after him for his money. He doesn't have a dime to spare."

A shout from behind the interrogation door drew us back to our task.

"Read Quinn her rights again!" Freddy ordered, his voice unmistakable.

"Don't have to," Urso snapped.

Winona didn't even look up. She continued to sip water.

I put my hand on the doorknob and glanced at Meredith. "Remember, take it easy with U-ey. He doesn't like confrontation. You'll trap more bees with honey, Grandmère says."

Meredith adjusted the collar of her blouse, smoothed the front of her jacket, and licked her lips. When she nodded that she was ready, I opened the door and we entered.

Without missing a beat, Meredith charged Urso. "Release Quinn at once."

So much for trapping bees with honey, I thought. How I wished I could rein her in. Urso looked peeved.

"What the heck?" He glowered at me. "How'd you get — ?"

"It's not Freckles's fault, U-ey." Heat suffused my cheeks. I hated bucking rules and regulations. But I also hated injustice. And I couldn't, for the life of me, believe Quinn was guilty of murder, no matter how physically strong she was. "It's pretty busy out front."

"Out. Both of you, get out!"

Meredith stiffened. "We'll do nothing of the sort."

Quinn sat hunched in a straight-backed chair at the distressed oak table. She looked fragile. Her skin was as pale as her snow-white sweater, her hair uncombed and straggly. With concentrated ferocity, she worried her fingers in her lap.

Freddy stood behind her, his right hand gripping the upper rim of Quinn's chair so tightly that his knuckles appeared drained of blood.

Meredith scooted to Quinn, bussed her on the cheek, and smoothed her hair, then she slid an arm around her brother's shoulders. "Chief, you can't possibly think Quinn killed Harker Fontanne. Okay, she's earned a black belt. I'm trained in karate, too."

"Me, too," I chimed in. The more the merrier, right? I didn't have a black belt. I only knew how to take down an attacker with a knee to his groin or a heel to his instep — not that I'd ever had to. I'd been warned it wasn't as easy as it looked. I added, "You don't think either of us killed Harker, do you?"

"She's got motive." Urso's gaze was hard, as if his mind were made up.

"So he broke up with her. So what?" Meredith said. "Lots of guys break up with lots of girls."

I liked that she was using my reasoning.

"They have for centuries," Meredith went on. "It's a time-worn tradition. They don't end up killing each other."

Urso eyed Freddy. "Mr. Vance, just this morning —"

"It's Freddy, U-ey."

Urso pursed his lips. "You said, Mr. Vance, that your daughter and Mr. Fontanne were always . . ." He consulted his notepad. " 'At it.' They were at it 'like cats and dogs.' "

"That's not what I said," Freddy protested.

"Verbatim."

"No, I said they *liked* cats and dogs."

Urso frowned. "Do I look like a fool? I'm sorry if you don't like having your daughter hear your opinion, but there it is. Black and white." He flipped his notepad closed and sat in the chair opposite Quinn. "Seems like we have a crowd, Miss Vance, but we might as well go through this together. One question at a time. Are you ready to answer my questions?"

"Quinnie, you don't need to," Freddy said.

"It's okay, Daddy," Quinn said, her voice barely a whisper. "I'm innocent."

Why wasn't that enough for Urso? It was enough for me.

"You were seen fighting with Mr. Fontanne around . . ." Urso consulted his notes again. "Eight forty-five P.M."

She'd had a second fight? Oh, my. What had prompted the confrontation? If only

179

she'd stayed with Edsel.

Quinn mumbled something.

"Give me a yes or no, Miss Vance," Urso said, his voice firm and coaxing.

Quinn looked up at him through tear-soaked lashes. "Yes."

"What were you arguing about?"

"I want a lawyer," Freddy yelled.

"For yourself or your daughter?" Urso said.

"For Quinn."

"She's not under arrest." Urso eyed Quinn. "Do you want a lawyer? Do you want to go that route?"

Quinn sat as tall as she could. "I don't need one."

Urso looked triumphant. "Go on, then. The argument."

Quinn sighed. "He didn't like me flirting with other guys."

It sounded like a continuation of the same argument that Harker and she had when they had run into the kitchen at the mansion. Were they, as Freddy said, always "at it"? Why would Quinn choose someone who treated her badly? Why did so many women do that? Me, included — up until Creep Chef left. For a couple of months after he ditched me, I went to a therapist to figure out why I was attracted to jerks. It turned out that I didn't think I was worthy of better, something to do with being orphaned as a young girl. I'd vowed, then and there, to change my pattern.

"Were you flirting, Miss Vance?" Urso asked, drawing me back into the conversation at hand.

"Sort of. I mean, yes. Not to make him jealous, though. Just because . . . well, it's what I do. My father does the same thing. He's not interested in that Westerton lady. But he's flirting with her. Right, Daddy?" Quinn twisted in her chair and gazed at Freddy, begging him to agree with her. "I mean, you've only known her a few days. It's not like it's serious or anything, is it, Daddy?"

I wondered if Winona was outside listening at the door to get the scoop. Her ears had to be burning.

"Daddy, answer me."

Freddy released the chair.

"Oh, Daddy!" Quinn folded her arms on the table and collapsed on top of them in tears.

Urso huffed, probably wondering how he'd allowed his interrogation to turn into a soap opera.

I was wondering the same thing. But I was more curious why Freddy was keeping mute. What hold did Winona Westerton have over him?

Urso patted the table. "Folks, please, can we stay on topic?"

I turned to face him. "Do you have anything else except hearsay?"

"We have an eyewitness who saw Miss Vance and the deceased arguing about a half hour before time of death."

"Who saw them?"

"Tyanne Taylor."

Oh, my. Slightly damning. After last year's fiasco, Tyanne had sworn off lying for life. I'd gotten the impression that she'd wanted to say something to me at The Cheese Shop. I wish she had. I wouldn't have felt so blindsided now.

"What did Tyanne say they argued about?" I asked.

"She couldn't be specific."

Good. That would give a lawyer something to work with. Did Quinn require one? I tried to decipher what was going on in her mind. She was massaging her left wrist, looking like a trapped animal that desperately needed to escape.

Urso referred to his notes again. "Mrs. Taylor believes she heard Miss Vance say that she was going to kill Mr. Fontanne if he kept hounding her."

"That's not —" Quinn gulped.

Meredith and Freddy blanched.

"I didn't mean it like that. I —" Quinn folded her hands in front of her. "Hasn't anybody here ever said that?"

"I have," I said.

Urso gave me a baleful look. He knew I was fibbing. On our sole date back in high school, I'd told him a deep, dark secret. The day before my parents died in the car crash, my mother had taken my doll away from me. Even at the tender age of three, I'd learned enough from television to yell, "I'm going to kill you." How was I supposed to know that she'd simply taken Dollie to wash the jam off of her face? When my mother pushed me from the blazing car, she said, "Don't watch too much television. Promise." All these years, I couldn't help but feel her death was my fault. Why had the car skidded? Had I somehow altered the universe with my petty vow?

"That's not enough to go on, Chief Urso," I said. "What else do you have?"

"Plenty."

"Like what?" I could be tough when necessary. According to Grandmère, I had inherited the stubborn quality from my mother's Irish side.

"Hard physical evidence," Urso said,

equally obstinate.

"What kind of evidence?"

"A ring."

"Which ring?" I snapped. Twenty questions was not my favorite game.

"A silver ring with a sapphire in it," Urso answered. "Inside it reads: *Mine, all mine.* Mrs. Taylor saw Miss Vance throw it at Mr. Fontanne. I discovered it clenched in Mr. Fontanne's hand."

I flashed on the moment when Dane was teasing Quinn at the fund-raiser. Her ring had gotten caught in the knitted loops of her multicolored scarf. Was it the ring in question?

Quinn's face twisted with pain. She pinched her lips together, but she wasn't strong enough to keep from blurting, "It was my ring . . . His ring. The ring he gave me a month ago. We were making plans to get married."

"Married?" Freddy yelped.

"We were in love. But then he got all bent out of shape, and I got angry, and, well, he started yelling, and I threw the ring at him. He didn't catch it. He let it fall to the floor." Quinn swallowed hard. "It wasn't like it was special or anything. It was a hand-me-down." She slapped her hand over her mouth and sucked in a sob. "I'm in real trouble, aren't I?"

Urso nodded.

Meredith ran to me and clutched my hands. "Do something!"

Urso gave a curt shake of his head, warning me off. But I had to do something. Meredith was like family. That made Quinn family, too.

CHAPTER 12

When Urso took Quinn into custody, I provided Meredith and Freddy with the number for Mr. Lincoln, the lawyer who had helped with Grandmère's defense last year. Clueless as to what else I could do, I returned to the shop. I puttered through the regular closing chores — wrapping cheeses, wiping down the counters, packaging quiches and returning them to the large refrigerator in the kitchen at the rear of the store. And though I wasn't hungry, I nibbled on a slice of day-old quiche. I needed to keep my brain fueled.

Around six, Rebecca reminded me that it was Girls' Night Out. I was reluctant to go, but Matthew said he'd take full charge of the twins for dinner, and Rebecca wouldn't accept no for an answer. Bozz, who looked as pleased as punch because he had deftly handled the few stalwart newshounds who had lingered around until he'd arrived at three thirty, said he would close up shop.

We met Delilah outside Timothy O'Shea's Irish Pub at six thirty. Rebecca quickly filled her in on the day's strange turn of events. She added that Meredith wouldn't be joining us. Mr. Lincoln had granted Freddy and her a late-night appointment.

"I'll bet Urso isn't happy about you wanting to help Quinn," Delilah said as she pushed open the antique oak door that Tim had bought from some defunct Irish castle.

"That's an understatement."

I paused in the entry to let my eyes adjust to the green-gelled lighting. Every day was St. Patrick's Day to Tim. He was proud to tell you that his great-great-great-uncle participated in the first celebration of St. Patrick's Day in New York City, which was held in 1756 at the Crown and Thistle Tavern. Once a year, Tim decorated for the holiday. He draped crepe paper on the half dozen televisions hanging over the bar, set little green hats on every table, and dangled green and silver tinsel from the wood-beamed ceiling. The décor would stay up for two months, minimum, and acted like a lure for locals and tourists. Everyone enjoyed a party.

In the corner, soulful musicians — one on an electric violin, the other on an electric flute — played Irish rock music.

Off to our right, a group shouted, "Erin Go Bragh!" Another group beyond them sang out, "Ireland forever!" A chorus of "Danny Boy" ensued.

"Where are we going to sit?" Delilah asked. "Looks like the whole town is here."

"If all else fails, we can join Urso and his parents." Rebecca elbowed me and sniggered — the imp.

Urso sat at a small table with his mother and father, a devoted couple with a zest for life. They were on their dessert course.

From behind the bar, Tim gave a shout of welcome. His voice, like his body, was husky. "Jacky's over there, Charlotte." He flicked his thumb toward the back of the pub.

"Looks like she's holding a table for us," Delilah said.

Jacky Peterson sat at a semicircular booth at the far end of the room. She waved and smiled, but her smile didn't meet her eyes.

The moment we arrived at the booth, Jacky excused herself. "Back in a sec. Nature calls."

As we scooted into the cushy booth, Rebecca said, "Is she okay? She looks flushed."

"Maybe she can't take the loud music," Delilah said.

I shook my head. "Jordan said she's a little under the weather."

"I'm sorry to hear that." Delilah grabbed the stand-free appetizer menu. "You know, I saw somebody hanging outside her house the other day."

I shot her a quick look. "Hanging how?"

"In a car. A blue sedan. Driving slowly. Like he was checking her out on the sly."

"On the sly?" I said.

"Whoops." Delilah chuckled. "I must be picking up TV jargon from Rebecca." She scanned the menu front and back, though I knew she had it memorized like I did. The pub offered a wide selection of cocktails and international beers as well as some of the best comfort food appetizers I'd ever tasted — potato skins, macaroni and cheese, and stuffed mushrooms.

A waitress wearing a jaunty green hat offered a list of St. Patrick's Day specials including a corned beef and Kerrygold Irish Vintage Cheddar sandwich that sounded incredible. If only I hadn't snacked earlier.

After the waitress took our drink order and left, I said, "Go on, Delilah. The guy in the car outside Jacky's. Can you describe him?"

"He was sort of shady, know what I mean? But muscular. I got the feeling he wanted to stop and get out, but he couldn't bring himself to do it."

"Maybe he's a secret admirer," Rebecca said.

"Or one of the reporters who needs a homey piece about new businesses in a small town," I suggested.

Delilah shook her head. "If that was the case, he'd hang around the pottery store and not Jacky's house, don't you think?"

An uneasy feeling crept into my psyche. I hadn't told my friends about Jacky running away from her abusive husband. Was it possible the guy had found her?

"I'm sure it's nothing," I said. But I wasn't sure at all. I desperately wanted to call Jordan and alert him.

"Shhhh," Rebecca said. "Here she comes."

Jacky looked tired. Lines creased her pretty forehead. She sidestepped the waitress who had returned and was setting our drinks on the table.

"Things at the Wheel going well?" I said, hoping simple questions might open up a discussion.

"Party-hearty." Jacky pushed aside the glass of water the waitress had placed in front of her. "Listen, do you mind if I bail?"

Delilah and Rebecca exchanged a look.

Jacky rose from the table. "You won't boot

me out of the group for being a flake, will you?"

"Of course not," I said. "Freckles couldn't make it either. The baby's kicking up a storm."

"What's she going to do with a teen and an infant?" Rebecca said.

While they talked babies, nagging doubt wormed its way into my mind. I tried to assure myself that Jordan was on top of anything concerning his sister, yet I couldn't erase the panicked look on Jacky's face at the winery last night and the pained expression there now. I said, "Is there anything we can do?"

"I . . ." Jacky forced a tight smile. "I've just been overrun at the pottery shop with birthday parties and such. Thanks for understanding." She gave the table a quick rap of her knuckles and turned on her heel.

As she exited the pub and another chorus of "Danny Boy" started up, I glanced at Urso.

Rebecca followed my gaze and punched my arm. "The chief looks pretty smug, doesn't he? Probably thinks he's solved the crime now that he's got poor Quinn in custody." She took a sip of her Cosmo. "But what if he hasn't? What if the murderer planted Quinn's ring in Harker's hand?"

"It's just like Quinn's scarf," Delilah said.

I shook my head. "I'm not following you."

"The scarf dropped to the floor." Delilah wadded a cocktail napkin and hid it in her palm, then dropped the napkin into her lap and held up her hands like a successful magician. "Anybody could have picked it up. Same with the ring."

Rebecca nodded. "Quinn said she threw the ring."

"What if Harker didn't retrieve it?" Delilah said.

"Right!" Rebecca thumped the table with her palm.

"Except if I were Harker, I would have put the ring in my pocket," Delilah said.

"Okay." Rebecca nodded in agreement. "If that's what happened, then the killer took it out of Harker's pocket and planted it in Harker's hand."

"To implicate Quinn."

"Exactly!" Rebecca cried.

They reminded me of a team of rookie investigators excited about working their first crime scene. *Cagney and Lacey, The Younger Years.*

"Or . . ." Delilah held up a finger. "What if Harker fought his attacker? He wouldn't have been able to hold on to the ring."

Good point.

"If he fought, there would be traces of the murderer's skin stuck under his fingernails." Rebecca thumped the table with her fist. "That means there'd be DNA."

Adrenaline mixed with hope percolated through my system. I glanced at Urso chatting amiably with his folks. Did he have the right to a quiet dinner while Quinn was cooped up in jail?

I slid from the booth and hurried to him. "DNA," I blurted.

"Hello, Charlotte, good to see you, too," Urso said, the exasperation in his voice impossible to miss.

I turned to address his parents. "Sorry for the intrusion, sir . . . ma'am . . . but do you mind if I have a word with your son outside?"

"You can speak freely, right here." Urso folded his napkin and plunked it on the table in front of him.

"Umberto," his mother said. "Be nice. Charlotte means well."

"No, she doesn't, Mama. She's sticking her nose in where it doesn't belong. Again."

"C'mon, U-ey . . . Chief Urso," I said, giving him the respect he was due. "Two minutes."

Without rising, he pulled an empty chair away from the table and gestured for me to sit. His gaze seared me like a hot poker. "Ask away."

I perched on the front edge of the chair. "I know you said that the Holmes County staff can't get results fast, but did Harker struggle? Was there skin under his finger-nails?"

Urso nodded.

"It would have been hard to hold on to Quinn's ring and fight, don't you think?"

Urso tilted his head, as if he were truly interested.

"What if Harker tucked the ring into his pocket, and the murderer found it and put it in Harker's hand? What if the killer is try-ing to pin the murder on Quinn?"

"Who would do that?"

"I don't know." I couldn't imagine Quinn had enemies, except the one she was mak-ing in Winona because of her disapproval of Winona's relationship with Freddy.

A waitress dressed in the pub's uniform of jeans, work shirt, and a kerchief set a bill on the table.

"Don't go away." Urso reviewed the charges then handed the waitress a credit card.

As she sashayed off, I noted the color of her kerchief — green, in honor of St. Patrick

— and an idea surfaced. I said, "Quinn's scarf."

"What about it?" Urso snapped.

His mother cleared her throat. She patted his hand, like Grandmère would do to me.

Urso snatched his hand away and folded his arms across his massive chest. "Please continue, Charlotte."

"The ring is like Quinn's scarf." I explained Rebecca and Delilah's deduction.

"Not enough to go on."

"Freddy," I said.

"What about him?"

I bit my tongue. Could I accuse Freddy of something I couldn't confirm? That wasn't fair. But Urso was being so prickly and making me antsy to come up with something that would force him to release Quinn.

Even still, I chose the high road. "Freddy's so upset."

"Tell me something I don't know." Urso rose from the table and pulled back his mother's chair. "Let's go, Mama. Pop."

Desperate to do something, I said, "You said the jewels were paste."

"So?" He helped his mother into her coat.

"Why were they there? More specifically, why would Quinn put them there?"

He didn't answer.

"U-ey, why would she do that?"

Urso escorted his parents away. Over his shoulder, he said, "I don't know, but I'll find out."

By the time I returned to the booth, Rebecca and Delilah had nearly finished a plate of goat-cheese-smothered potato skins. As I took my seat, they peppered me with questions. I started to tell them about almost implicating Freddy, but stopped when I spotted Winona and Freddy walking in the front door of the pub. A rash of guilt spread up my chest at the sight of him. His gaze met mine, and as if he knew that I'd contemplated throwing him to the police in lieu of his daughter, he made a beeline for me. Winona followed.

"Charlotte, thank you. The lawyer was great," Freddy said. "He's going to get Quinn out on bail."

"He'll *try-y-y-y,*" Winona said, dragging out the word in that irritating way she had. She was a real Miss Know-It-All. I'd bet she was the girl in grade school who always stuck her hand up before anyone else. She glanced at her watch. I expected a testy tap of her foot any second. What did Freddy appreciate about her, other than her luscious Rubenesque body? Or was he simply courting her to dig up more money for Meredith's project? A project that soon could be defunct.

"Hey, Mr. Vance," someone called.

Edsel and Dane shambled toward the group.

"Sheesh, is everybody in town here to-night?" Rebecca whispered.

Delilah said, "I don't see Ipo Ho."

Rebecca blushed. She had a little crush on our Hawaiian-grown honeybee farmer. I think he reciprocated the feelings, though they hadn't had a date yet. At least, not to my knowledge.

"Maybe I should consider having a St. Patrick's Day tradition at the diner," Delilah added.

I couldn't take my eyes off Edsel. He looked taller, less sullen, as if he'd mystically cast off his Quasimodo demeanor. Had he learned the beauty of meditation? Or had he come to grips with Harker's death? In contrast, Dane looked miffed. He glanced at Winona, who didn't seem to want to make eye contact. I wondered again about their spat on the street. What was going on between them?

"How's Quinn holding up?" Edsel said, his words clipped, tense.

"Not well," Freddy said. "Meredith is taking Quinn some books to read."

"That reminds me." Edsel snapped his

fingers. "Something came to me around two A.M. There was this poem we read in English last semester. We were discussing imagery, and you know how Harker was hidden behind that brick wall? Well, in the poem, there was this brick wall built around the hero, and it stood for his emotional barriers. Think someone built it specifically for Harker?"

"The wall did look new," Rebecca said.

Edsel agreed. "You know, you're right."

I understood Rebecca knowing something like that; she'd toiled on an Amish farm her whole life. But how would Edsel know? "Was it there when you went to paint the winery?" I asked.

"Who knows?" Edsel said. "None of us went down there."

"But Harker's painting," I said. "The one hanging in the observatory at the winery. It's a floating replica of the cellar with the metal bars and the same stones."

Edsel shrugged. "Maybe he sneaked down or saw a photograph or something."

"There's no brick wall in his painting," I said.

"Maybe he exercised artistic license and left it out," Edsel offered.

"My parents never mentioned a brick wall in the cellar," Dane said.

Edsel quirked an eyebrow. "Why would they?"

"They're Ohio history and architecture buffs. They know everything about the building. I told you, you dolt."

"You never told me, bro."

"Yes, I did, you dork."

"I'm telling you, you didn't."

I recalled Dane mentioning that tidbit to the group at the fund-raiser, but now wasn't the time to correct Edsel.

"Fellas, that's enough." Freddy stretched his neck, as if uncomfortable with the size of his shirt collar.

"Maybe the wall is symbolic," Rebecca said. "The wall and the jewels."

"Don't be ridiculous, Miss Zook," Winona said in a tone louder than necessary, as if she were trying to project to the rear row of a theater.

"I'm not being ridiculous," Rebecca countered, sitting taller and throwing her shoulders back to stress the point. "Every murderer leaves lots of clues."

"Is that so?" Winona's tone dripped with sarcasm.

I blocked their exchange from my mind and pictured the crime scene. If the jewels were symbolic, it made sense that the wall was symbolic, as well. Could the mention of imagery hurt Quinn's case? A psychiatrist might suggest that she built the wall to make a statement about how shut down Harker was. But how could she have built it? She had arrived in town only two days ago.

"Say, did the police ever find Harker's artwork?" Dane asked.

"I think whoever took it killed him," Rebecca said.

Edsel sneered. "I'll bet Harker tossed it."

"Why would he do that?" Rebecca asked.

Edsel worked the toe of his shoe on the floor.

"Come on." Rebecca ordered. "Out with it."

I smiled. At times, she reminded me so much of my grandmother.

"He was going to stop painting," Edsel said.

"What?" Winona nearly shouted.

I stared at her. Why would she care what Harker did with his art?

"Yeah, he wanted to ditch it all and become a comic book artist." Edsel's nose narrowed, like the idea reeked.

"But he was so talented," Rebecca said.

Quinn called Harker masterful. Dane said he had *the chops.*

"For heaven's sakes," Freddy cut in. "He was not going to throw aside his career."

"Yes, he was." Edsel clicked his tongue against his teeth. "He was chucking it all. The training. Everything. He said his quest for perfection in art was destroying his soul. He could do comic book work in his sleep and live a real life."

Before anyone could question Edsel more, the front door of the pub whipped open.

"Charlotte!" my grandmother shouted. Waving her fingers over her head, she plowed through the layers of people. "*Dèpèche-toi!* Come quickly! It's Etienne . . . your grandfather. He's had an accident at the theater!"

CHAPTER 13

Grandmère, Rebecca, Delilah, and I rushed out of the pub and across the Village Green toward the theater. As we ran, Grandmère relayed what had happened — half in English, half in French. She'd seen a vision of a gel light falling from the black-box theater's ceiling onto one of the crew. To make sure all the gels were secure, she prepared to go to the theater, but Pépère said he'd handle it and went to the theater alone. When he didn't come home in a timely manner, Grandmère searched for him and found him lying on the stage at the foot of a ladder.

"Mon dieu!" Tears streamed down my grandmother's aged face. "He is unconscious, but he has a pulse."

"Did you call the doctor?" My heart jackhammered my rib cage, but I kept my voice calm.

"The telephone at the theater is out of order."

"Did you think to use your cellular phone?"

"I did not have it with me."

I shook my head. Neither Grandmère nor Pépère could get with the twenty-first century. Either they forgot how to use their cell phones or they left them in the chargers at home.

"I came to find you, instead. Oh-h-h-h." Grandmère shook her head. "I am horrible. I left him alone. I am a monster." Her sobs made me ache deep beneath my solar plexus.

"No, you're not," I assured her. My grandmother was usually the steady one in a frantic situation. When I was eight, she hadn't flinched when I'd hobbled into the house, my shin looking like bloody pulp after a fall on my bicycle. Faced with Pépère's mortality, she wasn't as tough as she made out. Neither was I. I didn't know what I would do without him. He was my rock, my anchor. If possible, I wanted him and my grandmother to live to the ripe old age of one hundred and twenty.

I was the first to reach Providence Playhouse. I whipped open the front door and darted to the right, down the carpeted hall that led to the black-box theater. Doorstops held the entry doors ajar. Dim working lights lit the space.

I charged inside. "Pépère!"

Grandmère yelled, "Etienne!"

He lay in a heap by a rickety old wooden ladder that stood in the center of the three sofas that were set up for *No Exit with Poe.*

"Pépère!" I hurried down the aisle, leaped onto the stage, and knelt beside him. Rebecca, Delilah, and Grandmère gathered around.

Pépère stirred, then moaned.

"Are you okay?" I said.

He offered a lopsided grin. "I'm an idiot."

"That's not what I asked. Are you okay? Is anything hurt?"

"Only my ego." He snickered. "You've been telling us for a year that we needed to get one of those aluminum ladders, but did I listen?" He glanced up. The second-to-the-top rung of the old ladder had split in half. "My foot fell right through."

Grandmère settled onto her knees and stroked Pépère's messy white hair. "You were unconscious. I thought —"

He petted her cheek. "Do not write me off so soon, *mon amie.* And I wasn't unconscious."

"Then why didn't you speak to me? Why were your eyes closed?"

"The wind was knocked out of me. Before

204

I knew it, you had run from the theater."
He chuckled again. "It'll take more than a
fall from a ladder to end my life. Now help
me up."

Everyone assisted. Grandmère and I each
took an arm. Delilah and Rebecca propped
him up from behind. His knees gave way
twice as we shuttled him to a seat in the
front row.

"What's going on?" Bozz entered the
black box through the same door we had.

"The ladder broke," Grandmère said.
"Would you clear it from the stage?"

"Sure thing." Bozz raced to the stage.

Two teens trailed him into the theater —
a gawky boy and a leggy girl with luxurious
strawberry blonde hair.

"Philby?" I asked Rebecca.

She nodded. "Isn't she a knockout?"

"Her mother's head of the PTA," Delilah
said, huddling closer.

"But she's not the one who got caught
pole dancing at the men's club," Rebecca
added.

"No, she's the one who started that book
club I've been trying to talk you both into,"
Delilah said. "You know Prudence Hart and
she are related somehow."

"That's right," I said, now recalling how
the whole family went together. Philby had

two younger sisters about Amy and Clair's age, and an older brother who was on some mission in Timbuktu. Literally, in Timbuktu. The mother and Prudence didn't even share a hello if they passed in the street. I assessed Philby from afar. Bozz would be a lunkhead not to like her.

Bozz and his gawky pal returned to the stage. "What next?"

Grandmère said, "We need to repair that tormentor curtain on the right. The clips are coming loose."

"Gotcha, Gen." He saluted and grinned.

She narrowed her eyes, but I saw the twinkle. *The little general,* the crew called her. Secretly, she loved the nickname.

As the teens disappeared in the backstage shadows, Pépère said, "The show must go on."

Grandmère hunkered into the seat beside him and muttered, "Old fool."

He clipped her chin with his knuckles. "Who are you calling an old fool?"

"You think you are indestructible."

"Don't you worry. These old bones are as strong as bricks."

"Oooh, speaking of bricks." Rebecca beckoned us to gather in a semicircle in front of Grandmère and Pépère. "When we were at the pub, we were talking about the

206

crime scene."

I grinned. Leave it to my sly assistant to turn a dire situation into a discussion about murder. I wondered which television show she'd mention this time.

"I was thinking about the play you're doing and that got me thinking about Poe," she continued. "You know how in Poe's 'The Cask of Amontillado,' this guy exacts revenge on a friend who insulted him, so he baits his friend into believing something valuable is in the catacombs. In this case, a bottle of rare wine."

"Sherry," Delilah said.

"Sherry, right." Rebecca eyed me for confirmation, seeing as we'd already discussed the allegorical angle of the story. "Anyway, he says he wants his friend's opinion, but his friend is drunk."

"Like Harker was," Delilah added.

"Yes," Rebecca said. "He lures him to the spot and chains him to the brick wall."

"Except Harker wasn't chained," I said.

Rebecca brandished a hand to quiet me. "What if the murderer built that wall to mirror the 'Cask' story? What if the murderer wanted revenge against a friend?"

"Are you suggesting that Dane or Edsel killed him?" I asked.

Pépère sniffed. "Those boys aren't killers."

I said, "Agatha Christie claimed, 'Every murderer is probably someone's old friend.'"

"She was wrong," Pépère said. "You all are." He tapped his temple. "I know these things."

I grinned. What would he divine next? The winner of the Triple Crown?

"I was considering Quinn," Rebecca said.

"She's not a murderer," I snapped, but who else was? Freddy, Winona? A prior acquaintance from Cleveland? I doubted any locals from Providence knew Harker Fontanne. Meredith would have a meltdown if the killer turned out to be her niece. She'd disintegrate if it was her brother, too.

Rebecca said, "Whoever did it was familiar with the Edgar Allan Poe story."

"We don't know that." I broke from the pack and paced in front of the stage, my hands open, palms up. "It's all supposition." I stopped myself, befogged by the words and gestures spilling out of me. Who did I think I was, Clarence Darrow reincarnated? I hadn't gone to law school. Unlike half of my graduating class, I'd never even contemplated becoming a lawyer.

Delilah jabbed her forefinger toward me.

"You're missing the point. The killer tossed around jewels and built the wall."

Back to the darned wall. If it had been recently built, as Rebecca surmised, then who among the suspects would have had the time to do so? And how had he or she moved the materials into the Ziegler mansion without being noticed?

"I'm telling you, the killer set the scene," Delilah said.

"Set the scene. *Oui, oui!*" Grandmère popped up from her seat and barged through Delilah and Rebecca to the stage.

We spun around to watch her.

"It is so important to set the scene." Grandmère pushed one of the scenery couches off its mark. "Don't you see? Move this an inch, and there is too much distance between the characters. Move it too close, and we lose the distance so necessary for the underlying meaning."

"Mrs. Bessette?" Bozz pulled the tormentor curtain — a flat curtain in front of the upstage grand drape — toward the middle. It jerked and stopped. "I think all we need is WD-40."

"I just bought a case. It is under the workbench." Grandmère returned her focus to us, her rapt audience. "Where was I? Oh, yes, setting the scene. It is key. If we remove the couches entirely from the stage, we would not be doing *No Exit.* Do you see?"

"Not every version of *No Exit* has couches on the set," I argued.

"*Our* version does," Grandmère said.

"Yes, that's my point." Rebecca clapped with excitement. "That's what the murderer did. He set the scene for *his* play."

"Or *she* set it," I said.

"Or she," Rebecca conceded. "The murderer — whether it's he or she is insignificant — lured Harker Fontanne —"

I held up a hand. "You don't know he was lured. He could have gone there by himself to hunt for treasure. The murderer could have followed Harker and surprised him."

Rebecca huffed. "Fine. Then the murderer chained him —"

"Harker wasn't chained to anything," I barked, feeling more contentious by the millisecond.

"It's metaphorical," Delilah said.

"Right." Rebecca bobbed her head. "The murderer metaphorically chained Harker by choking him with that scarf and leaving him behind the wall with the jewels."

"And why were there jewels? Anyone?" Delilah wiggled her fingers, compelling us to answer.

I felt like we were in the middle of a

master class on the hidden meanings of a play.

"Because" — Rebecca held up a victory finger — "the murderer set the scene."

"Okay, fine," I said. "If the scene was staged, what do the jewels mean? Were they strewn beside Harker as a reminder of his gambling problem? Did they symbolize his constant hunger to find treasure? Or did they mean something else entirely? And what did the wall mean? Was it symbolic of some kind of emotional barrier?"

Pépère cleared his throat and struggled to his feet. He folded his hands in front of his belly. "You know, *chèrie,* there was a story about the treasure on the Internet today."

"I read it," Rebecca said. "It was in the *New York Times.*"

"I'm sure there have been plenty of stories, in plenty of newspapers," I said. "The rumor has been around for years. Old Man Ziegler said on his deathbed —"

"Perhaps word of our little play inspired the crime," Grandmère cut in.

"How so?" I asked.

"There were write-ups in the *Cleveland Plain Dealer* and the *Columbus Dispatch.* We also had Internet coverage from the regional reviewer." Grandmère focused on Delilah. "By the way, *chèrie,* that reviewer saw a

211

rehearsal a few weeks ago and is very excited. She said the playwright has courage."

Delilah beamed.

"I mean, how would your play inspire the crime?" I wished I didn't sound so snarky and out of sorts. I needed a meal or at least a slice of Manchego on warm toast with a drizzle of honey.

Grandmère gave me an appeasing look. "Maybe someone who knew about the treasure and read our rave review thought" — she tapped her head — *"Aha! I have a brilliant idea. I know a way I can get revenge. I will set the scene to baffle the police."*

"Maybe more than one person had the idea," Delilah added.

I held out my hands in a gesture of defeat. "What you're saying is everybody from Alaska to Madagascar could have known about the darned treasure and come looking for it."

My family and friends reminded me of a collection of bobbleheaded dolls as they nodded in unison.

"Don't forget," Rebecca said. "That includes everyone in Providence, too."

Her words took me aback. What if Harker wasn't killed by a friend or an acquaintance from Cleveland? What if someone from

Providence wanted to keep our little town insular? A local would have had plenty of time to build the brick wall. Was the murderer ruthless enough to kill a total stranger simply to ruin Meredith's plan to convert the winery into a college?

CHAPTER 14

As I headed home, I couldn't help thinking about what my grandmother and friends had said back at the theater. Urso wouldn't relish hearing the theory about the murderer setting the scene, but I left him a message to call me, hoping that when I did reveal the theory, I would create enough doubt in his mind that he'd agree to free Quinn on bail. I also reflected on Harker's stolen artwork. I hated to admit it, but Freddy topped my list of suspects for the theft. He had clearly disliked Harker, and he had something hidden in his room at the bed-and-breakfast.

When I turned the corner toward my house, the urge to find out what was in Freddy's suitcase plagued me. I paused in front of Lavender and Lace and stared at the windows upstairs. Lights were on in the two rooms facing the street, one of which was Freddy's. The drapes were pulled back, but the sheer lavender curtains hung closed. I didn't detect any movement beyond the curtains, but that didn't mean Freddy wasn't there. He could be in the restroom or lying on the bed. Or he could be among the guests in the great room having late-night tea. A soft glow spilled from that region of the B&B. If Freddy was there, I could steal in, take a peek, and slip out.

A minute. I'd be inside only a minute.

I started for the front door and froze. Someone moved in Freddy's room upstairs. Freddy, I assumed. And then another shadow joined him — as tall as he was, with round curves. Winona? She pressed into him. Their heads drew close. Their mouths met.

Upset that I couldn't try my hand at sleuthing, I shambled home. I found Rags fast asleep in his wicker kitty bed in the kitchen. I poured fresh milk into his bowl. Then, discovering I was out of Manchego, I made a quick Camembert and fig jam panini for myself, grabbed a Pellegrino water, and tiptoed upstairs with my snack. Expecting the girls to be asleep, I was surprised to see light coming from their bedroom. I peeked in and spotted Matthew sitting on the antique rocking chair between the twin beds, reading a story from the girls' favorite

Crafty Sleuth series.

Snuggled beneath her purple quilt, Clair looked like she was closer to six years old than nine. An angelic smile graced her lips. Amy sat upright, and per usual, her hands patted the bed with a little rhythm. She loved to sing. *Look out,* American Idol, I mused. In seven years, if the popular show was still on TV, Amy would be one of the first in line to audition. She was a talented ham, just like Grandmère.

I left them to their tender moment and padded into my room.

The moment I closed the door, a mischievous urge swept through me. I set my meal on the nightstand, and without turning on the light, stole across the Persian rug to my window. Doing my best to be discreet, I pulled back the brocade drapes and peeked at Lavender and Lace. The lights had dimmed in Freddy's room, but I still made out two shadows. They moved about the room as if they were doing the tango. Was it some kind of celebratory dance? Had they killed Harker together?

"Stop it, Charlotte," I whispered. "They could be in love."

Yeah, and Limburger cheese smells good.

Abandoning my Peeping Tom routine, I switched on the light on the nightstand, perched on the edge of my bed, and in less than two minutes, wolfed down my food. After that, I did my ablutions, spending extra time flossing — my dental hygienist would be so proud. Next, I donned a Victoria's Secret nightgown that Rebecca had given me for Christmas and slipped into the oak T-back armchair at my desk. If I couldn't sleuth in person, the very least I could do was an Internet search. Not only did I want to read what Pépère and Rebecca had mentioned they had seen online, but I wanted to know more about Winona Westerton.

In the past year, thanks to Bozz's guidance, I'd become pretty adept at Google searches. I'd learned that there were dozens of Jordan Paces and hundreds of Jacky Petersons. When creating their new identities, Jordan had been careful to choose common names.

Not so for Winona Westerton. I woke up my sleepy computer, clicked on my Internet browser icon, and typed Winona's name into the Google search line. There was only one hit with her name. She didn't have a Web page. She didn't blog. And she hadn't joined any of the social networking sites. But her name appeared in a newspaper article listing the donors for a regional theater in Cleveland and again as an alumna attending a reunion for Northwestern's class of 2005. The article said that as a teen, Winona and her sister Julianne won ballroom dancing competitions. Winona also placed fifth in a high school art competition. And she was fairly adept at baking, having won a pie contest at the age of fourteen. Hyperlinks to the various competitions were included.

Although I was disappointed not to have found a flagrant article declaring Winona a murder suspect in another case, I was intrigued by her art competition win. Perhaps art was her link to Harker. Granted, she was older than Harker, but she and he might have had art in common. Perhaps that was her link to Dane, too.

With a flick of the mouse, I clicked on the hyperlink to the art competition. The signal indicating that the site was loading whirled. And whirled. Two minutes passed. Three. Four.

The door to my room squeaked open.

I whipped around, heart pounding.

Rags skittered to my side and zigzagged around my ankles, meowing like it was my fault that he had been asleep when I'd arrived home.

"Hello, you little scamp. I wasn't ignoring

you. I didn't want to ruin your beauty sleep." I patted my lap. He leapt onto it and draped himself across my thighs. I scratched between his ears, and he hummed like a motorboat. If only I could feel so relaxed.

The computer message continued to read *loading.*

When another five minutes passed with no connection — our fair town was notorious for cellular dead zones and slow Internet hookups — I gave up and crawled into bed. I said prayers for Jordan, Jacky, the twins, and Matthew, and closed with a prayer for Quinn and Meredith. I really didn't want Quinn to be guilty. I would do everything in my power to prove she was innocent.

At 6:43, I woke with a start. Someone was pounding on the front door. I slipped out of bed and peered through the break in the drapes.

Sylvie, dressed in a skintight, futuristic getup that she must have purchased at a costume store, glowered up at me and waved a fist.

I moaned. Just what I needed, a not-so-cheery hello first thing in the morning. I massaged my scalp with my fingertips to fire up my brain cells and glanced at the computer. It had timed out and shut itself off — not a good sign. I could only hope the new day would go better than my night.

Quickly I dressed in black trousers, a scarlet sweater, and loafers. I liked the way jewel tones brought out the color of my skin and made me feel bold. I needed something to face Sylvie with a little more verve than I felt.

I rapped on Matthew's door and hurried past. "Wake up, Cuz," I rasped over my shoulder. "Guess who's here!"

Rags trailed behind me as I dashed down the mahogany stairs and skidded to a stop in the foyer. A peek in the oval gold-leaf mirror that hung in the foyer assured me that I looked strong and defiant. Good.

I whipped open the front door. "It's not even seven," I said.

Sylvie jutted a hip. "I have an order to obey."

Multiple meanings of the phrase ticked through my mind, but Sylvie snipped off my musings by flaunting a folded piece of paper.

"What's that?" I said, knowing full well what it was.

"The order to obey."

"To obey what?"

"Me, of course. Whenever I want time

with the girls, you have to give them to me." She tapped her foot. "And I want them. Now. I'm treating them to a tour of Amish country."

"They can't miss school."

"Yes, they can. I have an order. By a judge." She flourished the paper a second time.

A bit of the devil rose up inside me. I snatched the paper from her hands and ripped it in half. "Gee, oops." I grinned. "I guess you'll have to get another." I started to close the door.

Sylvie slammed her shoulder against it to prevent me from closing it.

I let out an *oof*, thinking with her sense of style and brute strength, Sylvie should consider becoming a Roller Derby queen.

"Don't get cheeky with me, Charlotte!" she said.

"I'll show you cheeky, Sylvie! I —"

The patter of small feet stopped on the landing above the foyer. I twisted and saw the twins at the railing. Amy rubbed her sleepy eyes with her fists. Clair looked bright-eyed, like she'd been up for hours — probably reading. I could see her becoming a librarian or bookseller or even a book editor later on in life. She'd be one of those people who could read a book a day and she'd retain every word.

"Charlotte, let me in." Sylvie poked her head through the front door's opening.

I considered using the door like a guillotine but nixed it. I wouldn't look good in prison orange. It wasn't jewel-tonish enough.

"Hi, my babies," Sylvie yelled. "Mumsie wants to take you on another trip."

Matthew bolted from his room, a chocolate brown robe tied tautly around the waist, brown paisley pajama bottoms bunching on his bare feet. "Girls, get ready for school." He bounded down the stairs, two at a time, and charged toward the entryway. "I'll handle this, Charlotte." He peeled my hands off the door and swung it open.

Sylvie stumbled into the foyer but righted herself and huffed. "I have an order, Matthew."

"It's not valid if it's torn in two." I offered the pieces to Matthew and winked.

"It says you have to obey me," Sylvie said.

"She wants to take the girls on an Amish tour," I countered. "I told her she couldn't."

"I've already paid for it."

Did I detect a hint of whine in Sylvie's tone? Score one for me.

"We're supposed to have a meal at an Amish house," she went on.

"Not happening." Matthew stuffed the torn document into his pocket.

Sylvie sputtered. Any second now, I expected her to stomp her foot and throw a hissy fit, but no words came out. What could she do? We were two against her one. After a long moment, she shook her fist and shouted, "I'm coming back with a policeman."

"Go for it," Matthew replied. "Chief Urso has so much time on his hands. Not!"

"You'll be hearing from me."

"I'm sure we will."

"And that Meredith —"

"You leave Meredith out of this!" Matthew said.

Sylvie started to leave and turned back. An evil grin spread across her face. "In the meantime, I'll use your credit card for a little shopping — an expense I'm sure you can ill afford." She spun on her silver stiletto heel and strutted out the door and down the path toward her rented Lexus.

I gaped at Matthew. "She's still able to use your credit cards?"

"No, I took her off all of them."

"She must have memorized the number and the security code. You'd better freeze your accounts."

Before pulling from the curb, Sylvie

whipped open the passenger window and yelled, "I hear Le Chic Boutique near The Cheese Shop is pricey. Watch me make Prudence Hart my best friend."

Just you wait, I mused with wicked glee, wishing I could be a fly on the wall as she went head-to-head with Prudence. Our local diva would suggest what looked right on Sylvie, and Sylvie, unable to restrain herself, would give Prudence a piece of her feeble mind. Oh, yeah, sparks would fly. Enough to start a forest fire. Maybe, if we were lucky, they'd both combust.

Matthew closed the door, his face pinched with concern. Sensing the tension, Rags brushed up against Matthew's bare ankles. Matthew bent over and kneaded Rags's neck as he glanced up at the landing. The twins hadn't minded him. They were crouched and huddled together, peering between the railings. Their sweet eyes glistened with tears. My heart ached for them, but even I, a fixer by nature, couldn't protect them from the cruel events that continued to alter their lives.

"Girls," Matthew said, his voice vibrating with pent-up emotion. "Get going. Now. Breakfast in ten."

"Gluten-free mascarpone pancakes," I added as an incentive.

As a unit, they scooted into the bathroom at the end of the hall.

When the door clicked shut, Matthew ran his hands through his mussed hair. "I've got to start early today. I'm making the rounds at the local wineries. Anything you need?"

I breathed shallowly in my chest, thankful that he was acting as if life was returning to normal, even if it wasn't. "I think a meritage would go nicely with that Irish blue cheese we got in."

"Consider it done."

"In our newsletter, I wrote seven o'clock for the wine tasting tomorrow. That's right, isn't it?"

"Yep." Matthew started up the staircase. On the second step, he paused. "Charlotte, I'm a good dad, right?"

A torrent of sadness clogged my throat. "You're the best, and the girls know it."

"Do they?"

"Of course they do." When Sylvie abandoned them, Matthew had turned a bad situation into a good one. He came home to a small town and a family that adored him. He became attentive to his girls' needs. At all times, he encouraged them to be their best. "They adore you, Matthew. More than you'll ever know."

■ ■ ■ ■

At The Cheese Shop, I put Sylvie and her threats aside, and went about my routine, making quiches and facing cheeses with a sharp-edged knife. Next, I set out the specialty dish — a new daily tradition that was fast becoming popular with the customers. The specialty of the day was a Brie fondue. I filled a white porcelain serving dish with the lusciously gooey mixture, placed it into a wire holder over a lit can of Sterno, and laid long wooden skewers on the plate below. Beside it, I set a basket filled with chunks of country bread. Within an hour, the customers had devoured the tasty treat, and I had to make another batch.

Rebecca slipped into the kitchen and leaned a hip against the counter. "Finally, we've got a lull."

"We deserve one." I fetched a wheel of Brie from the walk-in refrigerator and set it on the marble slab. As I removed the wrapping, I said, "What's on your mind?"

"I was thinking . . ." Whenever she used that tone, she was considering something nefarious. "We should go to the Ziegler Winery and check out that brick wall."

"We're doing nothing of the sort." I pulled

a sharp Wüsthof knife from the knife drawer.

"If it was recently built —"

"No."

"Maybe we could prove —"

"No."

"But the murderer —"

I gave her a warning look.

"C'mon, Charlotte. Didn't you hear the gossip? The town council is talking about not letting Meredith build the college."

I gaped. Was my theory correct? Had a local killed Harker Fontanne to put a damper on the new college plans? "Grandmère hasn't mentioned a thing to me."

"She might not know yet."

As mayor, she should.

"I only know because I overheard that old windbag Arlo MacMillan telling that local vintner about it." Rebecca frowned. "Why are they friends? Arlo's so —" She swatted the air. No one liked pasty-faced Arlo. "Anyway, if the college plan fails, the Harts have offered to buy the winery from the city."

I gaped. "Prudence?"

"Her brothers."

Prudence's brothers — she had two or three, I couldn't remember — were vintners and lived somewhere in Oregon. Why would they need another winery? Then I recalled the old map that I'd seen during the scavenger hunt at the Ziegler Winery. Back in the eighteen hundreds, the Bozzuto, Urso, and Hart families had bordered the Ziegler estate. Had the Harts lost their property along the way because of Ziegler? What if the Hart brothers wanted revenge? What if, to cast a pall over the transformation of the winery into a college, they indiscriminately killed Harker? Did Prudence know? Was she in on the plot?

"Here's what I think," Rebecca went on. "We've got to go inside the winery before the sale takes place. It's public property, isn't it?"

"No way. We're not going." I wadded the wrapping for the Brie into a ball and tossed it into a nearby garbage can.

"Don't you remember how your grandmother said it's important to set the scene? What if the murderer did that?"

Or murderers, I thought.

"What if doing that made him careless? What if he left even more clues than a brick wall at the scene? Shouldn't we know what story he — ?"

"Or she or they," I corrected, still stuck on thoughts of Prudence and her brothers.

"He . . . She . . . They . . . Whatever. Shouldn't we know what story the murderer was trying to tell? Jewels and bricks. There's something there. Time is of the essence."

The chimes jingled in the shop.

Rebecca looked in that direction and back at me. "Think about it, okay?" She scuttled out of the kitchen.

As I started to cut the Brie in half, I had to admit that my little assistant-slash-sleuth was on to something. Could I learn more about who killed Harker if I went back to the scene of the crime? Could I find something to prove Quinn's innocence?

CHAPTER 15

For the better part of the afternoon, I didn't think again of raiding the winery. But then Rebecca went missing.

"Rebecca?" I peeked out the rear door of The Cheese Shop and scanned the co-op garden in the alley. Other than tulips swaying in the breeze and a few daring birds searching for worms in the moist ground, there was no movement. Where had Rebecca gone? Usually she took a half hour break, not an hour and a half. I hadn't noticed her absence until now because we'd had a flurry of activity that had kept me hopping. The pastor had come in to order twenty cheese trays for a church function, and we'd had at least two dozen requests for the Brie fondue recipe.

I returned to the cheese counter and said to Pépère, "Do you know where Rebecca went?"

He shook his head, but I caught him eyeing me surreptitiously as he sliced a long tube of chili turkey pepperoni into wafer-thin slices.

"You do know, don't you?" I said.

"I have no idea."

"C'mon, tell me. Where is she?"

My grandfather did what I called his cute-little-boy pout, the one he used whenever he was trying to hide something. "Why do you not believe me?"

"Because it's not like her to be gone so long."

"Charlotte, she is a grown woman. Do not worry so."

"But she should have called."

"Perhaps she went exploring and lost track of time. She loves the outdoors."

"It's too windy."

"She likes a crisp breeze." He moved something from one hand to the other and chuckled.

But I didn't laugh, because an inkling of Rebecca's whereabouts came to me and sent a tremor of apprehension through me. I grabbed Pépère by the shoulders. "Are you speaking in code?"

"Code?"

"Did the little imp go to the Ziegler Winery?"

"Whatever for?"

"To explore!"

"*Chérie*, she wouldn't do that, would she?" Pépère laid his knife on the counter, wiped his hands on his apron, and strolled toward the refrigerator. As he moved, I noticed him stuffing a piece of Roaring Forties blue cheese into his mouth. He hadn't been trying to cover for Rebecca. He'd been sneaking a slice of cheese from the cheese-tasting platter.

"Pépère, I'm worried."

He swallowed and said, "Call her."

I did. She didn't answer her cell phone. Reception during a strong wind was spotty at best. Dread flooded my thoughts. What if Rebecca had sneaked into the winery and somehow locked herself in the cellar? Or fallen down stairs and couldn't get up? *Time is of the essence,* she'd said.

Kicking myself for not sensing what she was up to, I whipped off my apron, slung it on a hook, and grabbed my car keys. "Pépère, hold down the shop. I'll be back."

"*Chérie*, call Chief Urso."

And have him chastise Rebecca for breaking and entering? Uh-uh. I couldn't do that to her, and I wouldn't do that to myself. Urso would razz me or, at the very least, hold me responsible.

Because I wasn't keen on going to the

winery by myself, as I hurried to my car, I called Meredith and begged her to join me.

"Can't," she said. She was caught up in parent/teacher conferences. She tried to talk me out of going, but I wouldn't be swayed. Before hanging up, I asked the question that was pressing on my mind. "Meredith, do you remember seeing the brick wall in the Ziegler cellar when you started renovations with *Vintage Today*?"

"Remember? I told you. I didn't go down there."

"Could you call the *VT* crew and ask?"

"Why does it matter?"

I explained the theory.

She was silent for a long time. "I'll check and get back to you."

Banks of clouds blocked the late-afternoon sun as I drove toward the winery. Halfway there, the wind picked up in intensity. My insides felt just as rootless. As I swerved to avoid tumbleweeds frolicking across the pavement, I decided the best thing to calm my nerves would be to review what I knew about the case.

Because I refused to believe Quinn capable of murder, I put her relationship with Harker aside for the moment and focused solely on Harker. He was an artist. A good one. And yet, according to Edsel Nash, he was ready to abandon his fine art to become a comic book artist. Edsel said it was because Harker felt his quest for perfection in art was destroying his soul. Was that the truth or did Edsel have a reason to lie? If someone — Edsel — did steal Harker's art, had he killed him to keep the theft a secret? That seemed like an overreaction.

Harker was also a gambler. He had an outstanding debt with Dane Cegielski. Had Dane killed Harker because Harker refused to pay his paltry debt? At first impression, he'd reminded me of a brooding Hamlet in love with the beautiful Quinn. Had he gone crazy with jealousy because Harker got the girl? If Dane liked Quinn, why would he have set her up by planting Quinn's ring on Harker? No, I couldn't wrap my mind around that.

I reflected on how miffed Edsel had seemed when he told us that Harker was tossing aside his career, as if Harker were betraying other artists. Had he killed Harker out of spite? He was the one who had brought up the significance of the brick wall. Had he wanted us to focus on the wall? Was it a killer's ploy to show how clever he was?

Winona Westerton left me in a quandary, too. Rebecca said Winona had signed on as a donor the moment the trip to Providence came to fruition. Why had she been so eager to become a donor for a school that meant nothing to her? She seemed to have an intimate acquaintance with Dane. Had she become a donor to be near him? I had to find out more about their history.

And what about Prudence and her brothers? Had the Harts killed Harker to thwart the plan for a college? Were they in the process of trying to buy back the winery and its land from the city?

An S-turn caught me by surprise. Struggling to hold the road, I veered right then left. While I navigated the sinuous turns, a curious notion occurred to me. A complete stranger — a thief after the rumored treasure — could have killed Harker.

What if the thief had returned to search for treasure while Rebecca was exploring?

I stepped on the gas and sped ahead. By the time I reached the Ziegler Winery, tension whizzed through my bloodstream. I looked for Rebecca's red MINI Cooper but didn't see it. However, given her penchant for mystery, she might have thought it was clever to park the car out of sight, maybe even on the neighboring property. I decided to stash my car out of sight, as well, because I didn't want anyone — namely, Urso —

knowing I was there. I wouldn't put it past him to figure out what I was up to. Either he had a sixth sense about things like that, or he kept tabs on me by tailing me. For all I knew, he'd fitted my Escort with a tracking device.

Before slipping from the car, I fetched a flashlight from my glove compartment. Although I didn't need the light to make a tour of the exterior of the mansion, I would need it if I ventured inside. If . . .

Gravel crunched beneath my feet as I sprinted across the driveway and up the stairs to the front porch. After Urso was so cavalier about leaving Lois to guard Harker Fontanne's room at the B&B, I expected to find the entry door of the mansion unlocked, but I was sorely disappointed. It was sealed tight.

Either Rebecca hadn't entered the easy way, or she had, and she'd locked it after her. Drat! I'd have to break in.

I shivered as an unbidden memory flitted through my mind in full living color. A band of high school kids, led by Freddy, had decided to raid the winery. *Don't worry about the mice or skeletons,* Freddy had said. He and his partners in crime, which included Meredith, Mr. Boy Scout Urso, and a couple of others, had prodded me up the slope of dead vines, daring me to be the first to steal into the old estate. I promised I wouldn't chicken out, but in the end, I had. Freddy called me a scaredy-cat. Urso chortled deep as he slithered through the previously broken kitchen window. He never would have gone in if he'd had to break it himself — a major offense. When the group returned fifteen minutes later, they said I hadn't missed a thing. They hadn't found anything cool inside. No dead bodies. No buried treasure. But for weeks they had snickered at my spinelessness. The month before Creep Chef ditched me, I told him about the botched breaking-and-entering incident. I often wondered if my cowardice wasn't one more thing that had driven him away. While sitting at my kitchen table, he'd gawked at me with that sexy, toothy smile of his, his head tilted and his hair a mess of tangles. "My, my, Charlotte. I thought you were gamer than that."

Forget him, Charlotte. Hunky or not, you are well rid of him.

I yanked my thoughts back to the moment at hand. My young assistant was missing.

"Rebecca?" I whispered a few times as I traipsed around the perimeter of the mansion and attempted to open each door and window within reach. Nothing budged. I peered through the kitchen window. No sign of her. No drawers left open. No lights on anywhere.

Worried that I was right and she'd slipped and struck her head on something, I picked up my pace. Halfway around the mansion, I noticed movement overhead. A lacy curtain behind a closed window was dancing to and fro. The house didn't have air-conditioning. Air had to be getting into the building some other way. I heard a *clackety-clack* and moved away from the building. The doors on the second floor balcony were batting against each other, as if the latch had come loose in the wind, but I knew better. That had to be the way Rebecca had sneaked inside.

The Corinthian marble columns holding up the balcony were embellished not only with stylized acanthus leaves but with swirling grape vines that had been nicked by time. In high school, I wasn't very good in gymnastics class. I couldn't do flips or back-bends, and balancing on a four-inch balance beam was not my idea of a good time, but I could shinny up a rope like a monkey. I shrugged out of my rain slicker, then I kicked off my loafers, tucked the flashlight beneath the waist of my trousers at the small of my back, and gripped the marble vines with my hands.

Inhaling a long breath of courage, I wedged a toe onto a nick in one of the clumps of faux grapes and started my ascent. Good thing I'd worn trousers to work.

Minutes later, I scrambled onto the balcony, belly first. I rose to my feet, brushed paint flakes off my scarlet sweater, and took one long look at the valley below. The view was truly magnificent, but I couldn't stand there and think about how the view might inspire even the most moderately engaged college student to new heights of learning. I had to find my wily assistant.

I pulled open the doors, slipped inside, and closed the latch. As I faced the marble-floored ballroom, a notion hit me that anybody in town could have broken in like I just had — I was no Pink Panther — which only broadened the suspect list of who could have built the brick wall.

"Rebecca?" I hightailed it to the hallway and down the stairs, passing the gallery of photographs of the Ziegler family and wondering, ever so briefly, about the family's chilling history — the insane mother, the nutty daughter, the rumors of treasure. Had their insanity been inspired by the house? And now, decades later, had some evil spirit wormed its way into the psyche of a murderer?

Stop it, Charlotte. Find Rebecca.

It took me a few minutes to scan the bedrooms on the second floor. No Rebecca. I searched the observatory and library on the first floor. Still no Rebecca. I peered into the kitchen, thinking perhaps I'd catch sight of her from a different angle, but she was nowhere to be found.

She had come to the mansion to check out the brick wall, which meant she had to have gone to the cellar.

I hurried across the foyer, grasped the handle of the door leading to the cellar, and yanked it open. The candles that had burned brightly in their rusted iron sconces on the night of Meredith's event were now doused. The scent of must and dank decay swam out. I backed up a few paces, flattened myself against a wall, and clutched the flashlight to my chest. In my line of business, I'd visited a lot of cellars and been intoxicated by the aroma of ripening cheese, but this scent was dirty and tomblike. How had I erased the memory of the scent from my mind?

Battling nausea, I fumbled for the light switch. A single, outdated light flicked on, but its glow was dim.

"Rebecca?" I listened but didn't hear a sound. "Are you down there? Are you hurt?" I switched on my flashlight for extra illumination and coaxed myself down the steps. Cool air chilled me, and I regretted leaving my rain slicker outside. I crept forward, careful not to slip on the mossy stone floor, the beam of my flashlight scoping out what lay ahead.

"Rebecca?" I eyed the fireplace where we'd found Quinn hiding on the night of the murder. It was empty. I raced ahead to the wine cellar that was guarded by metal bars and peered inside. "Rebec— ?"

My cell phone jangled in my pocket. I whipped it out and felt a wave of relief sweep through me. A photograph of Rebecca's face stared back at me. I answered and said, "Where are you?"

"Where are *you?*" she asked.

"I thought you'd slipped off to check out the brick wall in the winery."

"Me? Break the law? *Au contraire.*" Her voice crackled with static. "Hello, Charlotte? Can you hear me? Are you still there?"

"Yes."

"Oh, good. I thought I'd lost our connection." She giggled. "Would I do something you specifically told me not to? Okay, maybe I would, but this time I listened. You aren't

241

— ?" She gasped. "You are. You're in the winery. Are you in the cellar? Is the brick wall new? Can you tell? Is there crime scene tape? If not, you can investigate. Remember, Grandmère said setting the scene —"

The reception ended.

"— is key," I whispered, finishing her thought for her.

Knowing she was safe, I followed her suggestion — I was at the winery, after all — turned my attention back to the cellar, and replayed the evening in my head. I imagined the path Rebecca and I had trod that night. I heard the shrieks of the crowd. Pictured my first sighting of the brick wall. I'd believed Quinn lay behind it because I'd spotted the tails of her multicolored scarf on the flagstone floor.

Re-creating my movements, I tiptoed to the far side of the brick wall. A sour taste flooded my mouth as I remembered Harker's blue-tinged face. At the same time, a flurry of questions zipped through my mind. Why were you here, Harker? Who put that ring in your hand? Who had time to build the wall? And how had that person gotten down here without being seen?

The wall was around six feet long by four feet high — long enough to hide the body of a man, yet short enough to see over. It was nothing like Poe had described in his short story. It was definitely not a crypt. Was the act of murder a simple case of vengeance? Edsel was obviously jealous of Harker's talent. Dane didn't appreciate that Harker had won the girl. Was Winona hurt that Harker, a younger man, had cast her aside? Had Freddy hated Harker dating Quinn so much that he had plotted to end Harker's life on this particular trip? He'd visited Meredith at the holidays. I hadn't seen him, but he had been here. Freddy could have slipped inside and built the wall then. Whatever he had hidden in his suitcase might reveal his dastardly plan, but how many breaking-and-entering expeditions could I carry out in one day?

I ran my palm along the brick wall. The mortar felt smooth, not craggy with age. For all I knew, it could have been built in the last week or the last few months, but I was pretty certain it wasn't as old as the house.

During the scavenger hunt, Rebecca had speculated that a place like the Ziegler mansion might have hidden staircases. I panned the cellar's gray stone walls with the flashlight's beam. The walls looked intact, but on the flagstone floor by the far wall there were gravelly particles. Had Harker made the mess? Had he discovered a trove hidden behind the wall? If so, he must have clawed at it with his fingers. I hadn't seen a tool beside him when I'd found him. I didn't see one now.

As I rushed to the stone wall and groped for a chink in the mortar, my pulse kicked into overdrive. Advising myself to be meticulous, I limited myself to small three-foot sections at a time. The first was intact. The second area proved no more fruitful than the first. Neither did the third. How I wished I had the wherewithal to just get the heck out and leave well enough alone. But I didn't.

Cursing my zeal for truth, I moved to a fourth area. Then a fifth.

On the eighth section, which was an area near the floor, a gray stone came loose. Then another. I examined the stones closely with the flashlight. They seemed to be façade stones, sawn in half to be applied to a flat surface. I squatted down, peered into the hole I'd created, and saw vertical wooden slats. Did they form a door? Was the elusive pirate treasure hidden behind the door?

Elation bubbled up inside me. I almost let loose with a scream of joy, but I bit back the sound when I heard something slam overhead. Had someone else arrived? The murderer, perhaps, returning to retrieve the treasure.

Heart pounding, I leapt to my feet and raced up the cellar stairs. No way was I getting caught in a dank cellar fitted with metal bars. I peeked out the door leading to the foyer but didn't see a soul. I scooted to the front door and peered through one of the etched windows that flanked it. No car stood in the driveway. Had I really heard a sound or had guilt from trespassing made me imagine it? How cliché, if that were true.

But then I caught a glimpse of movement to the right. Was it an intruder? Flattening myself against the door, I drew in deep breaths and begged myself to keep calm. Any normal person would have parked in the driveway.

If I darted now, I could hightail it to the main road before the intruder realized I was inside. I calculated time and distance to where I'd stashed my car and sighed. If only I had Harry Potter's cloak of invisibility!

Go, go, go!

Crouching low — like that would help me be somewhat invisible — I slipped open the front door and scurried out. Halfway down the front steps, I paused. Something overhead made a smacking sound.

I looked up. The sound I'd heard in the cellar was nothing more than a loose shutter banging against the house in the wind. The shadow I'd seen must have been the shutter's reflection.

Flush with embarrassment, I was ready to end my investigation, but I'd never live it down if Rebecca found out that I'd given up because a noisy shutter had scared me off. I willed myself to breathe normally and dashed back to the cellar.

With my flashlight trained on the wall, I peeled away four more façade stones and got a view of the entire wooden door behind them. In one of the slats, there was a finger hole. I slipped my finger through it and tugged. The door opened with a creak and a *whoosh.* Dust poofed out. So did cool air. The door opened to a shaft of some kind. I aimed my flashlight beam at the floor of the shaft.

It was empty. No treasure. No jewels.

Two cords hung down the back of the shaft and were attached to a pulley. Leading with my flashlight, I hunkered low and wriggled my head into the shaft for a peek. Before I could get a good glimpse, I heard another sound.

Footsteps. Stealthy footsteps. In the room directly overhead. I wasn't conjuring up the sound this time. It was real. Floorboards squeaked.

My insides — already ragged with stress — tightened. I slithered out of the hole and leaped to my feet. I was not a seasoned detective, but I wasn't a victim, either. I recalled Pépère's repeated warnings before I went on dates during high school: A good offense is the best defense.

My flashlight was too slender to use as a blunt instrument, and the façade stones were too thin to be of any use, but a full brick might work.

I bashed my flashlight against the brick wall. A corner loosened, which further convinced me that the wall had been recently built — with faulty mortar. I wiggled the bricks back and forth. Two came loose. One would do the trick.

Clutching a brick in my hand, I tore up the stairs.

As I pressed the cellar door open a crack and raised the brick to strike, a hand gripped my wrist.

CHAPTER 16

As the interloper yanked me from the cellar, panic burst up my throat and gushed out in a scream. My captor clapped a hand over my mouth, then spun me to face him and I melted. It was Jordan. Without removing his hand, he flicked his gaze to the right — a silent order for me to listen.

I heard the *click-click* of footsteps. Someone in heels was fleeing toward the back of the house.

A grunt. A rattle of a door. A curse by a female.

Glass shattered. The door the woman had selected must have been locked with a deadbolt key.

In seconds, I heard the roar of a car engine and the sound of tires peeling off. The woman was getting away.

Before I could ask the identity of the woman, Jordan cupped my head in his hands and kissed me hard. It was the most riveting kiss I'd ever experienced. I pressed into him and kissed back with equal intensity until the immediacy of the situation hit me full force.

I came up for air. "What just happened?"

"Besides us connecting on a deep spiritual level?" he teased.

"Be serious. Who was here? Winona? Prudence?"

"Your cousin's ex-wife."

"Sylvie? Why?"

"I'm not sure. While I was standing in front of the hardware store, I overheard her telling Prudence that she was up for a little adventure, but she looked like she had mischief on her mind. So I followed her."

Mischief was just the right word for what I'd witnessed earlier, when Sylvie was peering into each of the cars along the street. What had she been looking for?

Jordan rubbed my shoulder with his palm. "When she got here, she veered away from the driveway and hid her Lexus behind a stand of bushes on the left. I spotted your car tucked behind the clump on the right."

And I believed I'd done such a keen job of hiding it. Silly me.

Jordan continued. "I assumed you were up to no good, but I wasn't sure about her."

"What scared her off?"

"She must have heard you dashing up the stairs and panicked." He tapped my nose with his knuckle. "What were you doing here, anyway?"

"Looking for Rebecca."

"In the cellar?"

"Long story. How did Sylvie sneak inside?"

"Through the front door."

I groaned. When I'd checked for intruders, I'd seen the spastic shutter, and believing I was safe, had simply closed the door without locking it. What kind of lawbreaker was I? Rebecca would give me a ton of grief if she found out I'd been so careless.

Jordan wrapped a protective arm around my shoulders and steered me toward the front door.

I broke free of his embrace. "What do you think she was after?"

"I assume the treasure."

"That doesn't make sense. Her parents are loaded."

"Treasure hunters aren't always people who need money."

He said that like a man who knew. At one time, had he been a treasure hunter? Had his sister's dilemma cut short his life of carefree living? In the long run, would he, like Creep Chef, be disappointed in me? I was a homebody. I liked my life. My town. My family. I wanted to travel, but I didn't have wanderlust.

He stopped beside the door, traced a finger down my arm, and let it come to rest at the back of my hand. "Got time for dinner? My place, just the two of us."

A quiver of desire swept through me. *Yes, yes, yes! Dinner and dessert and . . .*

Reality blasted me like a cold shower.

"Can't," I said. "Grandmère always throws a cast party a few days before opening night. It's tradition. Want to join us?"

"Dinner with a horde of colorful theater folks?" He grinned. "I'm in." As he opened the front door, he eyed the brick that I was holding. "Please tell me you didn't plan to use that as a weapon."

"It seemed a better bet than my flashlight." I brandished the slender torch.

"You've got hands. They can be lethal."

"You're right." But I wasn't sure I would ever be calm enough or powerful enough to take down someone who wanted to hurt me without using a weapon of some sort. Take Harker, for example. He hadn't been able to overcome his attacker, and he was taller and much stronger than I was.

"Why are your fingers rubbed raw?" Jordan asked.

"I almost forgot." I darted across the foyer, yelling over my shoulder. "I found a shaft in the cellar."

"What were you doing down there?" He followed me.

I switched on the flashlight, and as I bolted down the stairs, I explained the theory about the murderer setting the scene.

Jordan said, "You're telling me you think someone built the brick wall as a metaphorical statement?"

"Or as a diversion."

"For what?"

"To keep us guessing why it was built. I think the shaft leads to the dumbwaiter in the kitchen." I guided him to the area behind the metal bars and showed him the opening in the wall. "The murderer could have come down the shaft, killed Harker, and escaped back through the shaft unnoticed."

Jordan raised an eyebrow. "And sealed the shaft with those half-stones after he left?"

I winced, feeling pretty foolish with my assumption. "Okay, what if the killer used the shaft to bring the bricks down to the cellar?"

"Why not use the stairs?"

"Because access to the kitchen is less steep, and he wouldn't have had to carry the bricks too far. A couple of trips using the dumbwaiter would do the trick."

Jordan crouched down and inspected the hole I'd created. "Okay, you've sold me, but why seal it up?"

"So no one knew he — the murderer — had been there."

"Except he left a wall as a calling card."

I gaped at the brick wall and hated to admit that its presence left me stymied. Why had the killer gone to the trouble?

Jordan said, "Call Urso and let him figure out the rest of the puzzle."

"I can't let him know I was here." A rush of fresh warm guilt crept into my cheeks. "He'll be angry when he learns that I've trespassed."

"Man up." Jordan grinned and cuffed my shoulder. "The theory about the brick wall should interest him."

"I've left him a message. When he returns the call, I'll come clean. Until then, will you keep mum?"

Though he didn't look pleased with my decision, Jordan said he would give me twenty-four hours. After that, he'd feel compelled to do his civic duty.

Grandmère met us on her front porch and bussed Jordan on both cheeks. "We're so glad you came." The warmth in her tone made me wonder if the other day I had misinterpreted her concern about my dating him. She patted his back and gave him a nudge to enter.

Theater folks, as Jordan called them, filled the house. Grandmère was using sixteen crew people and four actors for this particular production, but others who had performed or helped backstage in previous shows were in attendance, as well. They poured out of the study and living room into the hallway. A pair of crew people, playing a game of rock, paper, scissors, sat on a step halfway up the curved staircase. A cute couple huddled near the bathroom door. He whispered in her ear, then sneaked a kiss. She pushed him away, but her eyes were smiling.

"You're here!" Amy zigzagged through the crowd and scampered toward us, her royal blue cape billowing behind her, a matching pirate's hat falling rakishly over one eye. "Clair, Clair! Aunt Charlotte's here with Mr. Pace!"

Clair, dressed in a less flamboyant pirate's costume, appeared in the doorway of the study. She held a book tucked under her arm, one of Grandmère's leather-bound treasures — a century-old version of *Alice in*

Wonderland. A tentative smile graced her pixie mouth, but her eyes were moist. Had she been crying again? My heart wrenched at the thought. If only I could swaddle her in a baby blanket and protect her from pain.

"Pépère fixed incredible food." Amy slipped her hand into Jordan's and drew him along the hall. "Dr Pepper stew and cheese biscuits that Clair can eat."

Clair's diet needed to be gluten-free, which meant no wheat products in her food. Luckily, most cheese was gluten-free. Amy, older by a minute, was always watching out for her *younger* sister.

"And crème brûlée with shaved chocolate on top," Amy added.

"Sounds delicious," Jordan said.

"Take your coats off. Stay awhile." Grandmère waved her hand. "There are drinks in the kitchen. My specialty, of course." She kissed the tips of her fingers to show her appreciation. Recently she'd switched from her favorite drink, a gin fizz, to a beverage created "south of the border." Her margaritas packed a punch — only one was allowed per person. "And Matthew has brought some delicious syrah wine. Enjoy! *À votre santé.*"

"*À votre santé,*" Amy echoed. "Follow me!" She released Jordan's hand and sprinted ahead of us.

Grandmère gripped my elbow. "Take a moment to cheer Meredith. She's very low."

And why wouldn't she be? Her niece was in jail.

"Any sign of Sylvie?" I asked, wondering if that was why Clair was teary-eyed.

Grandmère shook her head. *"Dieu merci, non."*

I wondered where Sylvie had gone to after her foray into the winery. Did she know I'd been there, too? Was that why she was keeping her distance from her *girlie-girls* tonight? I didn't dare tell Grandmère about my breaking-and-entering episode. She'd scold me, although truth be told, she'd probably have done the same thing.

"Movie! Two syllables," someone shouted from the living room.

As we walked by, I peeked in. New posters for *No Exit with Poe* had been hung beside the other posters that decorated the wall. Actors, playing charades, sat on the Queen Anne chairs or perched on the burgundy sofa, their gazes riveted on the clue-giver who was miming by the fireplace. The group had made themselves signs denoting the two teams' names — the Ravens and Lenore's Ladies. Men against women. The stage manager at the theater, a squat woman with burgundy hair and more earrings in her ears than I had in my jewelry box, motioned: *first word.*

"*An Affair to Remember!*" a member of the women's team yelled.

"That's not two syllables, you ditz," one of the guys taunted.

"Colorful group," Jordan said.

"Like Grandmère." I nudged him at the waist. "Keep going that way."

We entered the kitchen, which blazed with light. Delilah, Bozz, and the two leads from *No Exit with Poe* huddled near the pass-through counter. On the countertop, Pépère had laid out platters of a selection of cheeses, roasted vegetables, crackers, and pinwheel-shaped appetizers skewered with toothpicks.

Delilah waved a slice of Edam at her audience. "No, no, no. Poe's parents died when he was young."

"I heard he was adopted," Bozz said.

Jordan moseyed to the group. "Actually, the Allans never adopted him. They just took him in. He was born Edgar Poe."

"Did he really die at the age of forty?" the actor who served as the town's only plumber asked.

"Sure did," Bozz answered. "He was a depraved, drug-addled drunk."

"Not true," Jordan said while he sandwiched a piece of Brie between Pépère's zesty three-seed crackers. "That was a lie spread by Rufus Wilmot Griswold, an editor and critic who hated Poe."

"That's right," Delilah said, eyeing Jordan with respect. "The letters that Griswold presented as evidence were later proven forgeries."

Jordan added, "Did you also know that Poe read Shakespeare and Zola and wrote fluently in three languages?"

I tilted my head, surprised by his knowledge. Perhaps in his former life Jordan had been an English teacher. I was dying to know the truth but afraid to press.

"No matter what, his words are glorious." The second actor, a bucktoothed local farmer, struck a pose. " 'All we see or seem is but a dream within a dream,' " he intoned. "Magnificent, don't you think?"

I bit back a smile, not sure if he was asking about his performance or Poe's words.

Jordan gripped my elbow and whispered, "While they emote, let's take a little walk outside."

He pushed back the kitchen door and let me pass through first. My grandparents' yard was L-shaped, with a patio that abutted the driveway and a grassy area that ran perpendicular to the rear of the house. Soon dozens of vibrant pink azaleas would blossom. We strolled to the edge of the patio, and he slung an arm around my shoulders.

"Warm enough?" he asked.

"Barely." I was glad that I'd retrieved my rain slicker from the bushes outside the Ziegler mansion. A few weeks hence, Pépère would start his Sunday barbecue tradition. For now, it was too cold to do any grilling.

"What a night!" Jordan tilted his head backward.

I copied him. The sky looked like black velvet that had been studded with diamonds. A scent of smoke from a fireplace hung in the air. Before I knew it, he was kissing me. I didn't resist.

When we came up for air, he said, "Make a wish."

"I have dozens of times."

"Make another. Wishes are always worthwhile. Close your eyes." He swept his fingers over my eyelashes. The musky scent lingering on his hands was intoxicating. "See it," he said. "Picture it coming true."

I imagined our trip to Europe, the two of us sitting at a café table, Jordan telling me all his secrets. He balked at one. My eyes fluttered open.

"Why the pinched forehead?" he said.

"Were you married before?" Over the past few months, I'd asked him all sorts of questions, but not that. Never that. At one time, I'd worried that Jacky was his wife, until I'd found out that she was his sister.

His gaze flickered. "Almost."

"What happened?"

"Let's just say I didn't do my homework." His mouth twitched with humor. "I was twenty and reckless. I met her at a beach resort. We had a bit too much to drink. I thought I was in love."

"I'm picturing a scene from the movie *Ten*."

"You're not far off the mark. She turned out to be married, on holiday for a little fling before" — he laughed hard — "before she settled down to have kids."

I gaped. "Are you telling the truth?"

He crossed his heart and pulled me to him. "Always the truth with you."

Hushed whispers growing louder kept us from succumbing to another round of passionate kissing.

I pressed away from Jordan and spied Matthew and Meredith rounding the corner from the rear yard. In the moonlight, Matthew looked wan and shaky. Meredith appeared equally haggard, nearly impossible for a woman who was so pretty. She held

Matthew's hand between both of hers. I doubted either had the wherewithal to console the other.

Remembering Grandmère's appeal to cheer up my friend, I said, "Jordan, Matthew. Would you guys get us a couple of glasses of wine?"

They eyed each other and shrugged. Neither of them was stupid.

While they headed into the house together discussing the Cleveland Indians' potential this season, I guided Meredith to the swing on the porch. The striped canvas cushions felt cold beneath my trousers but not unbearable.

"What's bothering you?" I asked. It was an insipid question, given the circumstances. "Is it Quinn?"

"Yes . . . No. It's Clair."

"Clair?"

Meredith drew in a shallow breath. "She's so brittle. She's crying in the classroom."

The thought of my niece hurting gave my stomach a twist.

"And she yelled at somebody who was taunting her on the playground today. She never yells." Meredith's lower lip trembled. "They think they want to be with their mother, but after being with Sylvie for any length of time, they're tense and grumpy.

261

She's like an evil spirit or something. I wish I could drive her away, but I don't know how." Meredith let out a tiny sob. She laid a hand on her chest to calm herself. "Oh, Charlotte, what are we going to do?"

"I saw her this afternoon."

"Sylvie?"

"She was at the winery."

"Why was she there, for heaven's sake?"

"For the treasure, I think. Matthew must have told her about the folk legend. What if she doesn't want custody of the twins? What if she came to town to sneak into the winery but needed a cover?"

A burst of laughter came from the kitchen. I glanced through the window and saw Jordan and Matthew standing amidst the huddle of actors. Jordan buffed Matthew good-naturedly on the shoulder. The sight warmed me to my toes. Chip had never liked anyone in my family. Jordan enjoyed all of them, including Rags and the twins.

"Wait a second," Meredith said, drawing me back to our conversation. "Do you think Sylvie might have killed Harker Fontanne? She couldn't have. She left the winery that night, remember? She showed up with the girls, and Matthew shooed her away."

"But she returned, ostensibly to retrieve her purse," I said. "She could have slinked into the cellar, surprised Harker, killed him, and hurried to the theater to establish her alibi. At the theater, when I told Urso I'd seen Sylvie's car on the winery property, Sylvie looked like she wanted to strangle me."

A shiver snaked up my neck. Had Sylvie shown up at the winery earlier to do just that? Kill me?

"Speak of the devil!" Meredith leapt to her feet. "Isn't that her in the driveway?"

Sylvie scrambled out of her rented silver Lexus and slammed the door. At the same time, as if tuned in by genetic code, Amy and Clair burst from the kitchen. They flew toward their mother like little birds seeking shelter. Sylvie swooped through the white picket gate and gathered up her girls.

"My babies!" With her feral gaze and the flaps of her coat opened like wings, she reminded me of a sharp-shinned hawk. "We're going for ice cream." She steered a withering glance in my direction. "Try to stop me."

I wouldn't. Not this time. But I'd keep a steady eye on her. If she wasn't restrained on a tight leash, she might devour her young.

CHAPTER 17

The following afternoon, when I'd finished putting together the trays of cheeses that the pastor had ordered, I helped Matthew in the wine annex. His mood was as dark as the clouds gathering in the sky. Noisily he unpacked crates of wine while I wiped down the mosaic tables in preparation for the evening's wine tasting. We'd had a rave response to the invitation. More than thirty people would be attending. Five of those reservations had come in since lunchtime.

"Sylvie's got to be stopped," Matthew said as he set a variety of pinot noir wines on the counter. He wasn't trying to start a conversation. It was the third time he'd made the pronouncement since Sylvie's arrival at my grandparents' house last night.

After Sylvie whisked the girls away from the house for a spur-of-the-moment ice cream, I told Matthew about Sylvie's raid into the winery. As much as he didn't like her, he couldn't believe she was guilty of murder. He said she wasn't a physical type of person. In the past, I would've agreed. I'd always thought she'd acted coolly toward the twins. But since she'd arrived, Sylvie couldn't seem to stop hugging them and kissing them. Was it all an act?

"What do you think she's up to?" I asked.

"I don't know. She was always into get-rich-quick schemes. The first year we were married, she almost wiped us out by investing in a junk-hauling franchise."

"I remember."

Grandmère had been appalled. She'd ranted for days on end that her grandson, an honored sommelier, should not lower himself to the level of a garbage collector. Numerous times, I'd had to remind her that garbage collectors made good money, and junk haulers did even better.

"The next year was hedge funds," Matthew said. "The year after that, a miracle cream that would erase wrinkles."

That memory from four years ago made me wince. Sylvie had urged me, at the age of thirty, to buy a case of the cream, which, of course, made me peer into the mirror to see if wrinkles had invaded my face. They hadn't then, and still hadn't now.

"No matter how many times I told her to

stop investing in these schemes, Sylvie did what she liked," Matthew said. "She's impulsive and out of control, but I still can't believe she could strangle someone. Though she's threatened to choke me a time or two." He offered a wry smile. "She's never put a hand on me, not so much as a slap. And yet . . ."

"Yet what?"

"Nothing. It's just that I remembered seeing her talking to Harker on the day of the murder. They were standing on the sidewalk. The rain had let up. She had the twins with her, so I didn't think much of it. Harker was showing them his paint palette." He scuffed his chin with a knuckle. "Why had she singled him out? Quinn was around. Wouldn't the girls have enjoyed hearing about painting from another girl and not a boy?"

"Good point. Do you think Sylvie knew Harker?"

"I'm not sure."

"I'll see if I can find out," I said. "In the meantime, what did Mr. Nakamura say about your custody issue?" Matthew had called the lawyer-slash-hardware storeowner first thing that morning.

"He said I shouldn't wait until things get worse." Matthew handed me two bottles of pinot noir from the Santa Rita Hills area in California and two more from local wineries. Thanks to the movie *Sideways,* Santa Rita had become known for its pinot noirs. I toted the bottles to the café tables and returned. "He said she's being unreasonable and is not a good candidate to negotiate, so I should use the hammer approach."

"Hammer approach?"

"Countersue." He pounded a fist into his palm. "Except that means going to court to prove her unfit, and that might involve bringing the girls into court. I don't want to do that. I can't do that."

"You'd have plenty of ammunition if you did."

Matthew had kept files on all of Sylvie's financial mishaps as well as a diary chronicling the girls' feelings about their mother from the moment she walked out of their lives. He'd never considered that he might have to expose those feelings to the world. He'd done it as a form of therapy.

"We'd all be there for you, too," I added. Grandmère, Pépère, and I each had stories to tell about Sylvie. I offered a supportive smile. "When is the lecturer from Cincinnati due?"

"No later than six."

Matthew had arranged for a guest speaker

to lead the evening's wine tasting, a representative who distributed wine in the Midwest. During the cooler months, red wines were preferred. Come May, our white wine stock would shoot out of the shop. I had prepared platters, each with three cheeses: a nutty and firm sheep's milk cheese from our local Emerald Pastures; a rich Le Moulis cow's milk cheese from the Pyrenees; and a tangy goat's cheese called Bermuda Triangle.

Matthew handed me printed note cards.

I read the top one. " 'Sunny, bursting with cherries and cloves.' Hmmm. The Shelton Nelson pinot, right?" Shelton Nelson, who owned a winery located at the upper west portion of the county, imported a variety of grapes from California and blended them with homegrown pinot noir grapes.

"You're getting pretty good at this."

"I've got an excellent teacher." I folded the cards, set them in front of the wine bottles on the café tables, and added a stack of comment cards and sharpened pencils. As patrons entered and paid their nominal tasting fee, they would receive order sheets and complimentary wineglasses etched with *The Cheese Shop*. "Speaking of teachers, how is Meredith today?"

"She took a sick day from school. She's at

the jail, keeping Quinn company."

If Freddy was doing the same, now might be a good time to sneak into his room at the B&B. On the other hand, business had remained steady all day. I wasn't sure Rebecca could handle the overflow without Pépère and Bozz. Both were at the theater helping Grandmère with her production.

Chimes over The Cheese Shop's front door jingled.

"Back in a sec." I passed through the annex archway and peered out.

Ipo Ho, our local honeybee farmer, sauntered into the shop. As the door swung shut, he said, "Stay, Buttercup." A beauty of a Golden Retriever, tongue lolling to one side, set her rump on the sidewalk and faced the display window. She knew what was coming. Every now and then, Ipo treated her to a taste of low-fat cheese.

From behind the cheese counter, Rebecca offered Ipo a quick "Hello" and returned to curling the ribbon for one of her specialty cheese baskets. I knew she liked the former fire-baton twirler, so why was she brushing him off?

Ipo hung back. To the untrained eye, he appeared to be checking out the different jars of jam, but I could see him eyeing my assistant from under his thick, dark lashes.

After a moment, he wandered nearer the cheese counter, tapping his oversized thigh with his hand, looking like a shy boy whose mom had told him he had to ask a girl to the prom.

I cleared my throat and gestured that Rebecca was going to have to take the lead if she wanted the relationship to move ahead, but she waved me off with a pair of scissors.

So much for my attempt at playing Cupid.

Ipo cleared his throat and said, "Hello, Rebecca . . . I . . ." In one fell swoop, he dropped to his left knee and fetched a small box from the pocket of his overalls. He popped open the box to reveal a shiny ring made of woven strands of gold. "Rebecca Zook, will you marry me?"

My mouth dropped open.

So did Rebecca's. She quickly snapped it shut and said, "Get up, Ipo."

"You didn't answer my question," Ipo said.

"We haven't even dated."

"But I love you."

Rebecca turned three shades of pink — her least favorite color. "Ipo Ho, you galoot, get on your feet, now. You look desperate."

He struggled to a stand and waggled the box with the ring in it. "Well?"

"Well, what?"

"Will you marry me?"

"Oh, for heaven's sake. You can ask me on a date, and if we still like each other a year from now, we can talk about it."

"A year?"

"You're on the rebound."

"My wife and I divorced more than three years ago."

"I rest my case."

Ipo frowned and snapped the ring box shut. The poor guy and his beautiful dog had come to Providence from Hawaii because Ipo fell in love with an Ohioan who'd wanted to start up an organic honeybee farm. Little did Ipo realize that the woman was famous for falling in love with just about anybody in trousers. Luckily, when she left, she didn't abscond with Buttercup.

"Now, which cheese do you want?" Rebecca cocked her hip and twirled her ponytail around a finger. "Might I suggest the Cowgirl Creamery ST PAT. It's their spring cheese offering." She pulled a small, green-smudged round from the display case. "Aren't they pretty? They're made with organic Jersey cow's milk and wrapped with nettle leaves."

Ipo winced. "Nettle leaves? Don't those have stinging hairs?"

271

"Relax. The nettles are frozen to remove the sting before they're wrapped around the cheese." She twisted the cheese in her hand. "Don't you love the color?"

While Ipo made up his mind, the chimes rang again, and Urso lumbered in. As the front door swung shut, I saw Dane sidle up to Buttercup on the sidewalk. He crouched to pet her.

"Afternoon, Charlotte." Urso removed his hat and fingered the brim. "Got a second?" Using his chin, he gestured for me to come closer.

Anxiety prickled my skin. He hadn't returned my phone call from yesterday. Had he figured out that I'd trespassed in the Ziegler mansion and decided to give me what-for in person? He didn't exactly look angry. In fact, he looked like he had to say something that was going to be hard to utter. Hoping a peace offering might soften his reproach, I snagged a chunk of his favorite cheese — Taleggio — wedged it between a pair of flax crackers, and hurried to him.

As I extended the morsel, he dropped to one knee.

Uh-oh. I skidded to a stop. My stomach did a flip-flop. He wasn't going to propose, too, was he? I wasn't as plucky as Rebecca. I couldn't make light of a proposal. We'd have to talk. I'd have to tell Urso how serious I was about Jordan.

"Don't do it," I blurted.

"Don't do what?" He picked something sparkly off the floor and flipped it in his hand.

"What's that?" I asked.

"A brand-new penny." He stood up and showed me the Abraham Lincoln side.

I felt like a fool. How could I have assumed — ?

"You said, 'Don't do it.' Do you have dibs on every penny in the shop or is it mine?" he teased.

"Yours. Of course." I waved for him to keep it as my heart rate returned to semi-normal. "Listen, about my phone call," I started, ready to blab everything, guilt weighing on me like a seventy-five-pound wheel of Parmesan.

He pocketed the penny. "In a sec. Do you — ?"

"Charlotte!" Octavia Tibble, part-time Realtor and the savviest librarian in all of Ohio, raced into the shop waving sheets of paper.

Gretel, her apple cheeks flushed and rain coat billowing, followed at Octavia's heels. She brandished similar sheets of paper.

"Do you know what Prudence is doing?"

Octavia said. "She's putting up flyers boycotting the price of cheese at Fromagerie Bessette."

I gaped. "You're kidding!"

"I'm not." Octavia brushed her beaded black braids over her shoulders and gave a quick tug to the lapels of her lime green linen suit. "The nerve."

Prudence had threatened that she'd take action against the shop, but I didn't think she would stoop so low.

"We've been following her around and yanking them down," Gretel said. "Don't tell my husband. He wouldn't approve. You know how he preaches about the blessing of freedom of speech."

Urso snagged one of the flyers. After scanning it, he said, "I'll warn her off."

"Pépère says any publicity is good publicity," I quipped.

"Not always. Besides, I don't like Prudence Hart bullying anyone in my town." Urso eyed the Taleggio cheese and cracker tidbit that I was holding. "Is that for me?"

I handed him the treat.

"Back in a few minutes." He marched out of the shop, looking for all intents and purposes like a sheriff in an old-time Western. All he needed was a pair of guns and a posse.

As the chimes settled down, I decided now was as good a time as any to go fishing for information. Octavia was an ace researcher and Gretel was one of the best sources of gossip in Providence. "Speaking of Prudence, do you know her brothers?"

"Can't say as I do," Gretel said.

"You wouldn't," Octavia said. "They live in Oregon. Nice guys. Health nuts." She eyed me. "Why do you ask, Charlotte?"

"Have you seen them in town lately?"

"No, they're never coming back."

"Why not?"

"They hate their sister. They wouldn't live within five hundred miles of her." Octavia snorted. "Can't say as I blame them."

"I heard they were trying to buy the Ziegler estate from the city," I said.

"Not a chance."

Buttercup barked so loudly, we all turned. Edsel had appeared on the sidewalk. Using his fist, he pounded Dane on the back. Dane jerked to a stand, his own fists primed.

"What's with them?" Gretel asked.

"Got me," I said, flinching automatically as Dane took a swing.

Edsel sidestepped the punch and glowered at Dane. He beckoned him closer and pointed to his chin, as if daring Dane to knock him for a loop. Was Edsel drunk? He poked Dane in the chest with his index finger. Dane grabbed it and held fast. Edsel didn't wince. Instead, he offered a malicious grin, and with his other hand, twisted his fingers on his lips like he was locking them with silence. Did they have some kind of a pact? I pondered what Jordan had said in the cellar. The murderer wouldn't have been able to seal up the hole leading to the dumbwaiter shaft after himself, but a team of conspirators could have done it. Had Edsel and Dane conspired to murder? Had one of them come down the shaft, killed Harker, and retreated to the kitchen while the other patched the wall? No, that didn't make sense. Why leave the murder weapon and the jewels? I felt as if I was fabricating a scenario out of cobwebs, easily shred to pieces.

"Earth to Charlotte." Octavia tapped my shoulder.

"Sorry. I was just —"

Out on the sidewalk, Mr. Nakamura dodged Dane and Edsel and burst into the store. "Where's Matthew?" he said, out of breath and flushed, as if his tie were too tight. Why he wore a tie to run Nuts for Nails was beyond me, but he and his teensy wife were all about decorum.

Matthew appeared in the archway. He

wiped his hands on a caramel-colored towel. "What's up?"

"Matthew, I —" Mr. Nakamura looked from me to Matthew and back to me. "In a minute, Matthew." He pivoted. "Charlotte, I heard Delilah's theories about the brick wall."

"What brick wall?" Octavia said. "What theories?"

"The brick wall in the cellar at the winery," Mr. Nakamura went on. "They're saying that the wall was recently erected."

"Who's saying?" Gretel asked.

I explained the theory in less than ten seconds. "Why do you care, Mr. Nakamura?"

"I thought you should know that a few months ago, Freddy Vance bought a flat of bricks from me. He said he planned to fix his sister's well."

Adrenaline sped through my bloodstream like a bullet train. Meredith had gone silent when I'd pressed her about the brick wall. She must have known that her brother purchased the bricks. When Freddy visited her for the holidays, had he built a well or a wall?

CHAPTER 18

I stood in the center of The Cheese Shop gaping at Mr. Nakamura. Rebecca, Octavia, Gretel, and Matthew gawked at him, as well.

"That's news that's fit to print!" Gretel clapped her hands. "Charlotte, we should tell Chief Urso."

Octavia agreed.

I nodded. *We should,* but first I needed to take a peek in Meredith's backyard. If her well had been rebuilt, Freddy was off the hook. If the brick was missing, he wasn't, and Meredith deserved a heads-up.

"Why don't you two track down Urso," I said. "I've got so much work to do."

Chatting excitedly, Gretel and Octavia exited through the front door. Mr. Nakamura headed into the wine annex to consult with Matthew. When the shop quieted, I told Rebecca I had an errand to run and to tend the shop. She was savvy enough to know I was on a mission, and she didn't look pleased to be left behind.

Meredith lived a few blocks from Fromagerie Bessette. Recently she had given her baby blue Victorian a facelift. It was no *Vintage Today* makeover, but it was a start — fresh paint, refurbished shutters, and a new fence. The grass in the yard looked spotty, however, and the evergreen bushes were in need of trimming. Meredith couldn't be blamed. On a teacher's salary, she didn't have the funds to do everything at once. Last November, for a birthday present, I gave her a dozen bags of daffodil bulbs. The showy flowers now flanked the front path and danced in the afternoon breeze.

I pressed the doorbell and waited, although I didn't expect Meredith to be home. According to Matthew, Meredith was at the jail entertaining Quinn. When she didn't answer, I trotted around the porch that encircled the house.

The backyard was filled with whimsical items — painted gnomes, inspirational stepping-stones, a rock pond, a bird feeder, and an old brick well that had been built in the eighteen hundreds. Only half of the well stood intact. Broken bricks and chunks of old mortar lay in a heap beside it. Its oaken bucket hung from a frayed strand of rope.

Beside the mess stood an empty flat that should have held a stack of fresh bricks.

Hoping Meredith could explain, I called her cell phone. She answered on one ring. She told me that after spending the morning with Quinn, she'd decided to take a little "me" time. She was having tea at Lavender and Lace and begged me to join her.

On my way to the B&B, in an effort to do my civic duty as Jordan had suggested, I dialed Urso's number. The cellular reception cut out. I left what could only be described as a sputtered message. It was sufficient.

Ten minutes later, I found Meredith sitting in the great room — with Freddy. She hadn't told me he was with her. The sight of him made me twitchy, but I had to proceed. I needed to know the truth. I wanted to believe the missing batch of bricks was an innocent mistake. I really did.

They sat hunched forward in wingback chairs and looked like they were plotting how to break Quinn out of jail. A pot of tea and a pair of Royal Doulton teacups were nestled on a tray in front of them. A fire crackled in the hearth, its smoke imbuing the room with a heavenly hickory scent.

In the adjoining room, Lois kept busy with a feather duster. If asked, she would probably claim she was hunting cobwebs, but I'd bet she was trying to hear Freddy and Meredith's conversation. Her Shih Tzu Agatha darted around the room behind her, nipping at the dust as it fluttered down. Her husband, the Cube, who was clipping hollies outside, looked as eager as Lois to get the scoop. Head craned, he hovered beside the great room window, which was open wide enough to get an earful.

Freddy rose when I entered and kissed me on the cheek. His lips felt clammy against my unusually warm skin. Nervousness had made me heat up like a campfire. He waited to sit until I settled into a lavender wingback chair.

One look at my face, and Meredith sensed something was off. "What's wrong?"

Though I felt nervous to talk about the brick wall in front of Freddy, I didn't think that he would harm me. Not in front of his sister. Not in the light of day. Using guarded words, I explained the situation.

"You've got to be kidding," Freddy blurted. "The bricks are gone?" His face blew up like a puffer fish. "Oh, man, I know what you're thinking."

"No, she's not," Meredith said, but her gaze told me she did. And I was.

"Yes, I bought the bricks," Freddy said.

"At Christmastime."

That confirmed what Mr. Nakamura had said.

"But I never started the project. I've only visited my sister twice since then, and both times there was snow on the ground. Needless to say, I didn't check the well on this blasted trip."

I swallowed hard, not keen to ask the next question. "Did you know they were gone, Meredith?"

Reluctantly she nodded. "I figured some kid in the neighborhood filched them over a period of time." Her voice cracked. "I didn't mention it to Freddy because . . ." Her voice thinned to a whisper. "When you called . . ." I could tell she wasn't sure if her brother was a killer, and the idea mortified her.

Not picking up on her worry, Freddy said, "I tried my hand at architecture once. I was horrible at it. I mean really bad. I couldn't draw a straight line to save my life. Even a ruler and a Craftsman level didn't help." He snickered.

"Do you think this is funny, Freddy?" Meredith snapped.

He sank back in his chair and shoved a hand into his jeans pocket. "Of course not."

"Any idea who might have filched the bricks?" I asked.

"Got me." Freddy's eyes blinked, and then his left hand began to fidget inside his pocket. He'd acted just as cagey at the winery when Urso had questioned him about Bozz's argument with Harker. I'd thought he was lying then. Was he lying now? Did he know who had taken the bricks? Was he trying to protect Quinn? She could have known about his purchase.

"Please tell me you had nothing to do with building that wall." Meredith flung her arms out in a pleading gesture and nearly knocked her teacup off the table. At the last second, she rescued it. Tea splattered, but the cup was preserved.

From the adjoining room, Lois gasped. She prided herself on her teacup collection. The Old Country Roses pattern was her favorite. She bustled in, pulled a dust rag from a pocket of her apron, and mopped up the spill.

"Thank you, Lois," I said. "I'll get it." I took the rag from her. She backed out of the room, nodding in deference like a scullery maid caught listening at a keyhole.

The front door slammed. "Where is she?" I heard Urso say from the foyer. Seconds later, he stormed into the great room. "Well, well. Isn't this cozy?" He threw me a sour look. "Did you think you'd handle this on

283

your own?"

"I called and left a message."

"Didn't get it. But thanks to Gretel and Octavia, I knew you would track down Meredith." He addressed her and her brother. "I know about the bricks. I saw the brick pallet. Mind you, I didn't go inside the fence. I'd need a court order for that."

Freddy blanched.

Urso said, "I also know about your little foray into the Ziegler Winery to check on said brick wall, Charlotte."

"How would you — ?"

"I do go back to crime scenes myself, and I have a nose. You smell like Camay soap and vanilla."

He was good. Before leaving the house, I'd dabbed vanilla extract behind my ears. Grandmère taught me that little trick. Everyone liked the aroma of cookies.

To exonerate myself, I quickly relayed how Grandmère and the others believed that the murderer had set the scene. I shared the various theories about the jewels being symbolic, either relating to Harker's gambling problem or his hunger for treasure. I left the discovery of the dumbwaiter shaft hidden behind the façade bricks for last. When I finished, I felt remarkably light. Confession was, indeed, good for the soul.

"My money is still on Quinn Vance," Urso said.

"Not Freddy?" Meredith asked.

Urso raised an eyebrow. "Should it be?"

"No," Freddy pleaded, "but Quinn is innocent, too."

Urso shook his head. "I went to Cleveland. I asked questions."

"Questions?" I repeated.

He glowered at me. "Yes, I actually do my job."

"I didn't meant to suggest —" I swallowed hard. "Who'd you talk to?"

"Mine to know."

"Bullheaded," I muttered.

"Meddlesome," he countered. "If you must know, I spoke to her former roommate. Miss Vance was not happy with Harker Fontanne, and she was quite vocal about it. She thought he was cheating on her. He'd painted portraits of another woman. I assume they were the same portraits that were stolen from Mr. Fontanne's portfolio."

Meredith started to weep.

Urso cleared his throat. "Meredith, I'm sorry if I'm upsetting you, but we've got to talk about motive for a moment."

"Quinn is innocent!" she cried.

"Then let's take a hard look at your

brother." Urso zeroed in on Freddy. "Mr. Vance, you didn't want Mr. Fontanne to get involved with your daughter, did you?"

Freddy looked like he wanted to disappear into his chair. "Harker was a student. We'd made a pact. No students were to get involved with other students. Not on my watch. I could lose my job. We didn't have chaperones on this trip. I was the only one in charge. I set the rules."

"Then why are you involved with a donor?" I said.

"We're not involved."

"Winona Westerton was in your room two nights ago. You looked pretty darned close."

Freddy scowled. "Spying on me, Charlotte?"

I sat taller. "You didn't pull the brocade drapes. The sheer ones provide a gauzy view."

He huffed. His hand twisted inside his pocket. When he caught me noticing, he pulled his hand free. "If you must know, Winona is teaching me to dance."

"Oh, please," I said. He couldn't really expect me — us — to buy that. "None of us fell off a turnip truck."

"Winona said all single men should know how to dance." He leapt to his feet and struck a ballroom dancing pose, arms extended, chin lifted. "Forward with my left foot."

I had to admit that his posture was excellent. Occasionally I watched ballroom dancing shows on television. I was almost as expert at judging as the judges, but then who wasn't from her living room?

Freddy said, "U-ey . . . Chief, it's true. I didn't like Harker Fontanne. I didn't trust him with my daughter. But I didn't kill him."

Urso lasered him with his steely gaze. I could see the wheels ticking in his head. He couldn't prove Freddy was outright lying. He had nothing to go on except Freddy's bravado and a stack of missing bricks, which I would bet he couldn't prove were the same as the ones in the winery. Brick was brick, right?

"Okay, I'll take your word, for now," Urso said. "But think hard about those bricks you bought. If you come up with a theory about who took them, I want to hear it."

"Let my daughter go. You know she didn't do this."

"I'm sorry, Freddy, but I've got enough evidence to hold her," Urso said.

Both Meredith and I breathed easier. At least Urso had resorted to calling Freddy by his first name, not his last. That was a step in the right direction.

Meredith rose and gripped Freddy by the forearm. Her fingers dug into his jacket. "Let's go back to the precinct to visit Quinn. Our attorney's working on her bail. We'll take a deck of cards with us. You know how much she loves to play gin rummy."

"Freddy, hold on." I bounded from my chair. "One more question."

"Sure, why not?" He spread his arms wide. "I seem to have a bull's-eye painted on my chest. Fire away."

"What do you think happened to Harker's artwork?"

"Don't have a clue. Why anyone would take it is beyond me. He wasn't that good."

Meredith looked askance at her brother. Apparently she believed that Freddy and she had held the same opinion about Harker — that he was gifted.

"Did you take it?" I asked.

Freddy coughed out a laugh. "I don't know where you came up with that idea, Charlotte."

I did. He looked so darned guilty. He hadn't liked Harker. He would have done anything to keep Harker and Quinn apart. Ruining Harker's career or at least setting him back a notch would have given Freddy great pleasure.

"Lois put you up to this, didn't she?" Freddy said. "She probably told you she saw me coming out of Harker's room."

"Are you saying you were in his room?" I glanced around, looking for Lois. She and the Cube seemed to have lost interest or were hiding out of sight, maybe in the kitchen with a glass pressed to the wall. Urso's arrival must have spurred their retreat.

Freddy shifted feet. "I don't have to tell you anything."

"Actually, you do," Urso said.

Freddy chuckled, but he was definitely ruffled. His neck had flushed bright red. "Fine. Here's the truth. I shot photographs of the Ziegler Winery for our painting session. Harker borrowed them. He said he wanted to sketch them. He told me he was through with them, so I went into his room and took them back."

"You're lying," I said. "Lois saw paintings in Harker's portfolio, not photos."

"He had my photographs, too."

Urso shot me a hard look, obviously not appreciating my interrogation style. "Want to show me what you took, Freddy?"

"Yeah, sure." Freddy beckoned Urso to follow him. I started after them, but Urso flashed a palm to stop me.

Minutes later, when they returned downstairs, Urso seemed satisfied, but Freddy's left hand was back in his pocket worrying the lining. Had he shown Urso what I'd seen him stowing in the suitcase or something else just to get Urso off his back?

"May I walk you to town, Charlotte?" Urso said.

A tingle of apprehension rippled through me. I recalled the moment when he came into the shop earlier. He'd wanted to discuss something, but Gretel and Octavia had rushed into the shop and he'd hurried off to censure Prudence. Was he hoping to talk to me about *us?*

"I have to borrow a recipe from Lois," I said. "She has an incredible scone that she makes with mascarpone cheese and cranberries." Granted, avoidance behavior and I were becoming fast friends, but I also wanted to take another look in Freddy's room.

"Sure. Another time." Urso gave a tip of his hat and left the bed-and-breakfast.

Seconds later, Freddy and Meredith departed, as well.

To secure my alibi, I located Lois and asked her for that recipe. While she went in search of it — I'd seen her disorganized filing system; the task could take her up to an hour — I hustled to Freddy's room. At the landing, I checked to make sure the hallway was clear. It was. All the B&B guests seemed to be out enjoying the day before the rain started to fall.

I dashed to Freddy's room and tried to twist the doorknob, but it wouldn't budge. I moved to the next room, hoping there was a connecting door between the two. I'd seen one in Harker's room. To my surprise, the door handle turned. I opened the door, expecting to walk into Quinn's room, and realized I'd confused the location. I was entering Dane and Edsel's room. I didn't care. I needed to get to Freddy's any way I could.

The scent of lavender sachets flooded my senses. A cool breeze swept through the open window. Even on cool days, when guests were away, Lois liked to air out the rooms. Avoiding the clothing and shoes that had been tossed on the floor, I tiptoed across the carpet to the door joining the two rooms and flipped the bolt, but the door wouldn't budge. It was locked from the other side. I quickly retreated to the hall and tried the room on the opposite side of Freddy's. Quinn's room. Unfortunately the door was locked, but the spring bolt was ancient and there was only a minimal door-frame. Rebecca would tell me to break in. I didn't think I was strong enough to knock down the door with my shoulder or with a hefty kick, but I remembered seeing a detective on some TV show open a door with a credit card. I slipped a laminated grocery store discount card from my purse — why destroy a good credit card if this ploy didn't work? — and wedged the card into the crack between the door and the skinny frame. Bending the card slightly, I slid it downward. The ploy would only work if the slope of the latch faced me. While wiggling the card and twisting the doorknob, I glanced over my shoulder to make sure no one was approaching. The coast was clear. Even so, perspiration broke out above my upper lip. I licked it away. Wiggled the card some more. And then, like magic, I heard a click. The knob twisted. The door opened.

I zipped inside, pocketed the discount card, and shut the door.

Quinn's room was as neat as a pin and as cool as Dane and Edsel's. Again, there was a lock on the door joining her room with Freddy's, but this time when I turned the knob, the door opened. Apparently Freddy wasn't concerned about his daughter entering his room. Maybe he was telling the truth about Winona's and his platonic friendship.

On a luggage rack in the corner of the

room sat Freddy's suitcase. As I headed toward it, I caught sight of a handful of photographs scattered on the bed: of the winery's hillsides, the vines, the mansion. Were they what he'd shown Urso to persuade Urso of his innocence? I wasn't so easily convinced.

I proceeded to the suitcase and reached for the zipper, but it was sealed tightly with a combination padlock. I tried the typical sequential combinations like 1-2-3-4 and 2-3-4-5. No go. I tested single-digit combinations: 1-1-1-1, 2-2-2-2. I was up to 5-5-5-5 when I heard the sound of footsteps padding along the hallway. The footsteps stopped outside Freddy's door.

My pulse skyrocketed. Was it Urso, back for a second look, or Freddy, ready to silence me forever? Or Lois, realizing how I'd duped her? Did it matter? I didn't want to get caught.

The doorknob started to turn.

I eyed the door to Quinn's room, but the distance was too far. Freddy's bathroom was nearer and the door hung open, but the bathroom would be an obvious place to search for an intruder. I darted to the window. Batting drapes out of my way, I peeked at the grounds below. I didn't see any sign of the Cube nor the guests.

Swiftly I clambered outside. Of course, in my haste, I hadn't considered the consequences. I would have to descend using the crisscrossed trellis, which was flimsy at best and prickly with leafless vines.

With my heart pounding so hard I could hear it in my ears, I swung around, stomach to the window, grabbed hold of a crossbar on the trellis, and stretched out a foot to the right. I lodged a toe into a diamond pattern, grabbed hold of another crossbar, and trusted my entire weight to the trellis. Blissfully, the wood didn't crack. The Cube was steadfast about yearly maintenance.

Thirty seconds later, I leapt off the trellis to the grass, my hands punctured and bleeding, and sprinted home.

As I tore into my kitchen and slammed the door, Rags appeared. He mewed at me as if asking what was wrong.

I scooped him into my arms and nuzzled him with my chin. "Nothing," I whispered. "Nothing." But I was lying. I was not cut out for a life of crime.

CHAPTER 19

Frustrated with my inability to crack the padlock's code and disappointed because I still didn't know whether Freddy was lying or telling the truth, I needed a little emotional boost. While driving to Providence Elementary to pick up the twins, I called Matthew. He sounded prepared for and excited about the evening's wine-tasting event. Another half dozen people had called asking if they could attend. He added that Pépère, who wanted to take a breather from Grandmère and her tech week craziness, had shown up to help. Grandmère had asked that he return in an hour, but for now, he was merrily tidying the store.

"The next onslaught won't be until the tasting," Matthew said. "And, hurrah, no Sylvie sightings."

"Life is good."

We laughed, the sound unique to both of us in the last few days.

Before he hung up, he said, "Please take Amy and Clair for a treat, Charlotte. Talk to them. Make sure they're okay. I'd ask Meredith to spend a little time with them, but she's preoccupied."

To say the least. I didn't tell him about the missing bricks.

All I said was, "I'm on it."

Once the girls were tucked into their seat belts, I offered them a choice of activities — going for a cup of cocoa at the diner or spending an hour at Sew Inspired Quilt Shoppe. The rain hadn't started, but a downpour was supposed to hit any time now, so we needed to do something indoors. Both applauded the second option. About a month ago, I'd bought each of them child-friendly quilting packages that included pre-cut patches, buttons, and thread. They stowed them in a cubby at the shop.

Inside Sew Inspired Quilt Shoppe, Freckles had created an atmosphere of fun and color and whimsy. Beanbag chairs, which were cozy places to knit, cluttered the multicolored carpeted floor. Sewing stations were set in each of the four corners for lessons or personal projects. Beautiful handmade quilts adorned the walls, each with a story to tell about the Providence area. Three were standouts — the first about the path to Ohio's statehood featuring the bicentennial wagon train, the second honoring the Sternwheel Festival of riverboats along the Ohio River, and the third depicting Amish farmers plowing in the midst of a blizzard. Every time I gazed at the beautiful pieces of art, tears welled in my eyes. Ohio's history was so beautiful and very much a part of my soul.

"Hey, Charlotte." Freckles sat on a stool by the store register, her hands folded beneath her very pregnant belly. Behind her were countless rows of fabrics, buttons, and thread, as well as a chalkboard filled with the week's activities — sewing, quilting, and crocheting classes. Beginner, intermediate, and advanced. I had never made it past the beginner level for knitting. I could purl one, knit two, and that was about it. However, I could sew. I would never forget my first sewing project — a wraparound denim skirt. At the time, Freckles's mother, now resting peacefully in Kindred Cemetery, had been our Brownie troop leader. She patiently instructed each of us how to use a sewing machine. *Through the rabbit hutch, around the big oak tree, and up the rabbit hole,* she'd say as she advised us how to thread the needle.

Amy and Clair made a beeline for the

book rack. Freckles, a clever saleswoman, stocked the Crafty Sleuths book kits that the girls enjoyed.

"Amy! Clair!" Freckles's twelve-year-old sprite of a daughter, Frenchie, whose christened name was Marie Curie, bounded down a ladder with a bolt of fabric tucked beneath her arm. She jumped to the carpet with a thud. Her red pigtails bounced on her back. Gold filigree threads and what looked like fairy dust poofed up around the hem of her corduroy overalls. I winced as I realized how difficult it must be to keep a fabric shop dust-free. "Come in the back." Frenchie set down the fabric and waved a hand. "I want to show you my latest creation." Frenchie, like her namesake, had gravitated to scientific experimentation at an early age. To feed her daughter's insatiable curiosity, Freckles had set up a science lab in the rear of the store.

"Is it okay, Aunt Charlotte?" Clair asked.

"Have fun."

"No Bunsen burners," Freckles shouted. "Not without your dad or me in the room."

As the girls disappeared through the velvet drapes, the front door to the shop opened. Sylvie paused in the doorway. A gust of icy air preceded her into the place.

How appropriate. She sent chills down my

spine. So much for no sightings.

"Where are my babies?" Sylvie waggled her arm. The dozen or more silver bangles she wore clanked like cymbals. "I want them now."

I pressed my lips together to prevent croaks of disgust from flying out.

"You give them to me now," she demanded.

Sadly, my lip-pressing didn't work. "No way!" I said as I marched toward her. "I'll do no such thing, and you'll stop ordering Matthew and me around."

Intent on pushing her out of the shop, I thrust an arm at her. But she was equally determined to stay. She flailed. Hard. Her bangles struck my skin and stung like a rattler's tail, but I wouldn't be deterred. I gripped her wrist and twisted her arm behind her. She yelped in pain.

Let's hear it for the one self-defense move that I'd mastered.

"Sit," I said.

Flummoxed, she fell backward, landing in a beanbag chair by the front window. The beanbag groaned beneath her weight and looked ready to swallow her whole. Sylvie scrambled to get back on her feet, but I knelt down and pinned her.

"Why did you come to town, Sylvie? The truth."

"To see my girls. I missed them."

"The truth," I hissed, fed up with her lies.

"That is the —"

"Did you know Harker Fontanne?"

"What?" Her face went as ice-white as her hair. "Are you insinuating that I killed him?" she sputtered. "No, I most certainly did not know him."

Freckles, who had left the safety of her position behind the register, drew near. She stroked her belly, as if to soothe the baby, and glowered at Sylvie with smoldering intensity.

"Freckles, I'm so sorry," I said. "I'll take my inquiry outside."

"Not on your life. Conflict is good. It stimulates the adrenal glands. Babies like that."

"Really?" I'd always heard babies liked calm environments.

"It's a new theory," Freckles said.

One she'd probably made up on the spot.

"Go on," she said.

I refocused on Sylvie, who was wiping mascara from underneath her overly made-up eyes. "Why were you at the winery yesterday?"

"How do you know she was at the winery?" Freckles said.

"Because I was there, too."

Freckles gaped at me. "What were you doing there?"

I didn't answer. I kept my gaze on my ex-sister-in-law. "Sylvie, answer me."

"I don't know what you're talking about." Sylvie jutted her chin, but lying in the beanbag chair diminished the effect.

"Jordan followed you from town. He saw you go inside. You ran out when I was running up the cellar stairs."

"What were you doing in the cellar?" Freckles asked, breathless with curiosity.

I gave a shake of my head, a tacit *not now*. She waved for me to continue.

"Sylvie, you're not here because you want the girls back," I said.

"I do so."

"You don't. Admit it. You're a treasure hunter."

Sylvie sniffed and tried to sit up straighter, but the beanbag didn't provide the essential structure. She slumped and started to cry. Freckles scurried to the front counter, plucked a tissue from a box, and raced back to Sylvie with it. Sylvie blew her nose.

"Mum!" Clair burst through the velvet drapes. She threw herself into the beanbag and cuddled with her mother. "Amy, Mum's

301

here!" she cried.

Amy darted out. She skidded to a stop and stared at her mother like she wasn't sure what to do next. Usually impulsive, she held her ground until Sylvie beckoned her with a finger.

"Please, baby, give Mumsie a hug. I could really use one."

Amy hunkered into the beanbag with her mother and sister.

Clutching the twins like a fox ready to protect her young from any danger, Sylvie glanced at me through wet lashes. "It's a long story."

"I'm all ears."

"Mum and Dad lost everything in the market two years ago."

In which scheme did she entice them to invest? I wondered, wanting to pinch myself for such a nasty thought. She wasn't the only person in the world who had made bad investments of late, except she made them with such regularity.

"They joined a group of investors that made iffy loans," Sylvie continued. "People didn't keep current with their payments. We had no recourse, no insurance. We've been scraping by ever since."

"Your folks owned twelve acres of land," I blurted. "And a castle."

"They leveraged it."

"What's leveraged mean?" Clair asked.

Sylvie ignored her. "All of it's gone. Repossessed."

"Couldn't they have parceled it off before losing everything?" I said.

"They tried, but to no avail." Sylvie jammed the used tissue into a hole in her fist. "We're broke, and I'm, well, destitute."

Was that why she had been peeping into parked cars on Hope Street the other day? Had she been looking for an unlocked car with loose change? Oh, my.

"Needless to say, I like to have a little cash on hand at all times," she added.

The tune "Baa Baa, Black Sheep" flitted through my mind. Sylvie didn't like a little cash on hand; she liked *three bags full.*

"Back in December, I saw the notice on the Internet about the fund-raiser for turning the winery into a college," Sylvie went on. "Now and then, I like to check what's happening in Providence. Call me a glutton for punishment."

I could call her a whole lot of other things, but not that.

"The fund-raiser got me to thinking about the treasure that was hidden in the winery."

"Allegedly hidden," I corrected.

"Right-o. Anyway, I got to thinking; maybe

303

I should check it out for myself. I could see my babies, and if I could find the treasure, I'd be able to help out Mumsie and Dad."

Amy and Clair beamed.

"It was the perfect storm," Sylvie said, misusing the term.

I stifled a snort. *She* was the perfect storm.

"I used my last penny to get a flight to the States to see you two." She kissed the girls repeatedly.

I thought I'd heave. Her affections, so lacking in the past, were a little over-the-top. Was she playing me? Playing them? Would she have stayed away from the twins if Matthew had paid her heaps of cash? Oh, if only.

I said, "The night of the event, you left your purse at the winery on purpose. That gave you a reason to come back."

She blinked an admission. "After the murder, the mansion was locked up tight, but I was pretty sure no one had found the treasure, or the discovery would have been all over the news."

"Which was what prompted you to go back yesterday."

She nodded. "When I was shopping, I got to talking to Prudence Hart about the treasure. She encouraged me to go for it. She said I was smart enough to figure out where the treasure was."

Prudence was craftier than I gave her credit for.

"How much did you spend while she stroked your ego?" I asked.

"I didn't —" Sylvie sputtered. "Of course, Jordan saw me with packages, didn't he? All those boxes were empty."

"I don't believe you."

"It was all in fun. Prudence and I hit it off, you might say."

"You're kidding!" Freckles giggled, but snipped her laughter short, her face blushing with embarrassment. "What I meant was, nobody hits it off with Prudence Hart, except, well, you know, b—" She slapped her hand over her mouth.

Sylvie shrugged. "Don't worry, love. I've been called the B word before." She turned her gaze back on me. "I wanted to hurt Matthew. I was mad at him and the world, but in the end, I decided to simply play a prank. I asked Prudence to play along with me. She gave me empty boxes, and I strutted out, hoping Matthew would see me and . . ." She swallowed hard. Her eyes pooled with tears. Huge droplets. "I'm a terrible person."

"No, you're not," Clair and Amy chimed.

"Yes, I am, sweethearts, but I'm going to

change. I am."

Why didn't I believe her?

I caught sight of movement outside the store. Meredith was peering through the window. She looked from the girls to me, her gaze peppered with confusion. I waved her inside, but she shook her head — vehemently — and scurried away.

I tore after her.

CHAPTER 20

I pushed through the front door of the quilt shop and sprinted down the sidewalk yelling, "Meredith, stop!"

She turned left and fled into A Wheel Good Time.

I charged into the pottery shop after her and promptly came to a halt. A birthday party was under way. Girls around the age of seven were seated at the tables. Sparkly balloons strung on curled ribbons decorated the shop. Mothers and fathers stood beside a long party table, draped with a Disney Princess tablecloth. I saw Meredith weave toward the back and veer into the restroom, but I squelched the urge to sprint after her. I could wait her out. The bathroom window was teensy. She couldn't slip out that way.

From my spot near the door, I could hear the parents, Tyanne Taylor among them, chatting about school and homework and the upcoming spring break.

Jacky, who owned the shop, wandered between tables. Though she was cheerily dressed in a blue-striped shirt, jeans, and paint-splattered smock, she appeared pale — sallow actually — and she seemed jumpy. In a span of a few seconds, she glanced out the window, up at the hand-glazed clock hanging over the kiln, and over at the parents beside the party table. When her gaze met mine, she smiled, but her smile was hesitant and not full of her usual zest.

In a flash, I remembered the conversation with Delilah about Jacky's possible stalker. Was that why Jacky was edgy? Had she told Jordan?

"Okay, girls, it's cake time." Jacky clapped her hands and forced one of her light-up-the-room smiles. "Let's turn in your pots. Make sure your names or initials are on the bottom, and then bring them to the counter."

As the party guests assembled in a line with their handmade works of art, Tyanne made a beeline toward me. She had a kid-friendly Parmesan porcupine appetizer pinched between two fingers. I glanced at the restroom. The door was still closed.

"I'm through with Prudence Hart," Tyanne said, waving the meatball in my face. "Do you know what she did?"

I could only imagine, since Prudence was fast becoming the town's looniest character.

"She said my little Thomas was a screwup. In front of customers in her shop. How dare she! I'll show her how cows eat cabbage." She popped the porcupine appetizer into her mouth and chewed furiously.

I shook my head. What was Prudence thinking? Purchasing the women's clothing boutique had not been a good move on her part. It was as if the previous owner's nasty spirit had lingered in the building and was seeping into Prudence's bones.

"Who will she attack next? My little girl, Tisha? Look at her. Isn't she sweet? Tisha wouldn't hurt a fly." Tyanne gazed at her seven-year-old, a spitting image of Mommy in her pink yoga outfit, her bobbed blonde hair framing her face. She must have grown an inch since I'd last seen her. Tyanne shook her head. "No! I refuse to let Prudence Hart ruin this town. If I have to, I'm going to start a petition and put her out of business. Or start a rival boutique. That would do her in, don't you think?" She clutched my arm and giggled like old times.

Secretly, I reveled that she was my friend again, as junior high school as that sounded.

Meredith shambled out of the bathroom with a wad of tissues in her hand. She noticed me and slumped onto the chair beside the pottery wheel at the back of the store.

I said, "Tyanne, we'll talk later." I hurried through the throng to Meredith and perched on a nearby stool. "Are you okay?"

"I'm fine." She spun the pottery wheel. "I thought, after this party, I'd talk to Jacky about helping raise awareness for the college."

"Good try," I said, not buying her half-baked lie. "Your face is a blotchy mess, and your blouse is still smudged and wet where you tried to wash out mascara." I brushed her arm with my fingertips. "C'mon, why were you so upset outside Freckles's place?"

"You know."

"Actually I don't."

"When I saw them . . . the twins . . . cuddling their mother . . . I . . ." She licked her lips. "I feel so guilty, Charlotte, wanting them to love me more than they love her."

"That's only natural."

"But she's their mother." Meredith gave the wheel an extra-hard spin. It made a wonking off-balance sound.

"She's not a very good one," I said. I told her about Sylvie's admission.

Meredith shook her head. "Do you believe her?"

"About the money being gone? Yes. She looked pretty miserable. However, I'm not sure I believe that she can change. She might promise, but I'm afraid the twins will be sorely disappointed."

Meredith ran a finger back and forth across her lower lip, a habit that had started way back in second grade when something was troubling her.

"Talk to me," I said.

"Do you think he'll get back together with Sylvie, you know, out of guilt? Because she needs him, and Matthew likes to be needed."

I laughed out loud. "No, my dear friend, there is no way in hell he'll reunite with Sylvie. He would give her half his future earnings before he would consider that. You are safe. Beyond safe. You are golden."

A chorus of "Happy Birthday to You" resounded from the partygoers. One little girl sang louder than the rest, and I thought of Amy, usually full of gusto yet hesitant to embrace her mother. Had she picked up on something I hadn't? Was Sylvie full of beans?

When the singing ceased, I said, "Meredith, the twins will always love their mother. That's a given. It's DNA. Even if she abandons them again, they will love her. But they adore you and will want you in their lives because you are smart and fun-loving and tender. They know they can count on you. And most important, they will love you because Matthew loves you."

A single tear slipped down her cheek. She brushed it away with a knuckle.

I said, "Now, let's retrieve them from Sylvie's clutches and take them out for hot cocoa."

Halfway to the door, I spied a man leaning against a lamppost kitty-corner from the shop, one ankle crossed over the other and a fedora pulled down over one eye. He clutched a newspaper in his hands and chewed a toothpick between his teeth. Everything about him screamed B-movie detective, and a tremor of fear shimmied up my spine. Was this the shady guy Delilah had seen in the blue sedan watching Jacky with such rapt attention? A tired-looking royal blue Chevy Impala was parked less than fifteen feet from him. Was he a stalker, or worse, Jacky's abusive husband?

"See that man at the corner?" I whispered to Meredith, unable to mask the panic in my voice. She started to turn her head, and I hissed, "Don't look."

"Then how can I see him?"

"Okay, take a quick peek. The guy with the newspaper."

She zipped her gaze to him and back to me. "What about him?"

"Does he appear familiar?"

"No. What's got you spooked?"

It dawned on me that she hadn't been at Girls' Night Out at the pub when Delilah, Rebecca, and I had discussed the mysterious man following Jacky. For the first time, it also occurred to me that if he was new to town, he, too, could be a treasure hunter. But why was he spying on Jacky? Or was he?

"Stay here."

"What are you going to do?"

I didn't know, but I dashed toward the front of the shop. I hurtled out the door, my feet picking up speed, and sprinted across the street. A Toyota truck came out of nowhere. Okay, it had come from somewhere, but I hadn't been watching. The truck screeched to a halt. I threw my hands out, like they could stop two tons of metal from trampling me. People on the sidewalk gasped.

The man in the fedora looked up. He tossed his newspaper on the ground and hotfooted it north on Cherry Orchard Road, toward the Congregational Church. Not to the blue Impala.

Dead set on finding out who he was, I

zigzagged around the Toyota and bounded after him. My heart battered my rib cage. My breathing was short and choppy.

The man in the fedora veered into the driveway beside the church.

I urged my legs to run faster and they did the best they could, but when I arrived at the driveway, I saw no sign of him. Not even a billowing of dust. I raced to the parking lot behind the church. Empty.

Where had the guy gone? Over the fence at the rear of the parking lot, or up the side of the church like Spider-Man? Either way, I'd lost him. I bent over my thighs, my lungs burning with overexertion.

Soon after, the predicted rain began, which of course put a perfect cap on a lousy afternoon.

While I headed back to the pottery shop, darting from awning to awning so I wouldn't get drenched, I called Jordan. He didn't answer, so I left a message telling him to check in on his sister and said that I was worried for her safety. I described the guy and the Impala, and with a nervous laugh, added that I could be wrong about the stalker. For all I knew, I might have just chased a total stranger who fled from what he perceived to be a crazy woman.

By the time I reached A Wheel Good

Time, I had convinced myself that was indeed the case, and I made an executive decision not to tell Jacky about the incident. She was immersed in birthday party activities and seemed, for the moment, happy and unstressed. Why rock the proverbial boat?

Meredith caught me by the elbow and tugged me to the far side of the shop. "What was that about?"

"Come with me and the girls to the diner, and I'll fill you in."

Her face tightened with worry. "What if they don't want me to join you?"

"They do. Believe me." I prodded her toward the front door. "C'mon, move those legs of lead. I need to get the girls fed before the wine tasting tonight." Thanks to keen foresight, I'd hired Philby Jebbs to sit the girls. With Bozz splitting his time between the shop and the theater, Philby was available for the evening and more than delighted to get the job.

After another trek through the rain, we found the twins in the back of Sew Inspired Quilt Shoppe, doing an acid versus alkali experiment with Frenchie. Clair twirled a strand of her blonde hair and watched with amazement. Amy looked at me, her face grim.

"Where's your mother, girls?" I asked.

315

"She had to run," Amy said.

Run or flee? A sliver of suspicion wedged its way into my thoughts. Had Sylvie lied about her parents' financial woes? Had she made up the whole story to dupe me about why she had really gone to the winery? Perhaps she had a link to Harker Fontanne that had yet to be discovered. Or maybe she found motherhood too darned difficult, yet again.

"She had an errand to do," Clair added. "At the pharmacy."

Bad Charlotte. Jumping to conclusions. Or was I?

"When will she be coming back?" I asked.

"She said she'd meet us at The Cheese Shop." Amy worked her tongue inside her mouth. "If that's okay."

If Sylvie returned — *if* — I'd deal with her then.

CHAPTER 21

As I exited the Country Kitchen carrying a sack of sugar cookies and a four-cup tray of hot cocoa, I silently cursed having left the house without an umbrella. What had I been thinking? Meredith, equally lax, had left hers at school.

The twins, finding adults funny, giggled.

"Okay, let's run for it," I said.

Hunched over the goodies, I bolted across the street to Fromagerie Bessette. Meredith and the twins followed. When we arrived, Rebecca was tending to a customer.

"Nice hairdo." She smirked as she proceeded to sell a pound of Pace Hill Gouda to her customer.

I shaped wet tendrils around my face — it was the best I could do — and scanned the shop. I spied Matthew and Freddy in the annex. Freddy was helping Matthew unload boxes.

"Look at them, Charlotte." Meredith

sidled to my side. "Chatting like old friends." Her voice was tinged with pride mixed with melancholy.

Freddy spotted me but acted like he hadn't. No doubt he was mad at me for considering him a murder suspect, but how could I not? I still wanted to know what he'd hidden in his suitcase.

I offered the snacks to the twins. "Why don't you hang your wet coats on the hooks at the back and go into the annex to eat? Give Freddy my cocoa." A peace offering was always a smart idea.

As they hurried away, I gathered a selection of slate boards and white chalk and moved to the kitchen. I set the items on the granite-topped prep station and started writing the names of the cheeses I intended to serve at the tasting.

Meredith perched on a stool beside the station. "You still haven't told me who you were chasing."

I brought her up to date about the possible stalker.

"Are you sure he didn't flee because you frightened him?" she asked.

"Oooh, I'm so scary. All five-foot-three of me." I wiggled my fingers in her face. "Yes, I considered that."

"You did look pretty scary." She laughed.

It was perhaps the first time I'd seen her smile since the night of the murder. But her face quickly grew serious. "Who do you think it was?"

"Got me." That was as honest an answer as I could provide. If it was Jacky's husband or a colleague of the husband, Jordan would know what to do. I continued to get the feeling that, prior to moving to Providence, Jordan had been involved in law enforcement. I'd heard him say things like, "Stand down," and I'd seen a gun in his top desk drawer in the office at his farm. He also knew how to apply CPR, but so did I and lots of other people I knew. However, his knowledge of cheese making and his chopping skills at our cooking classes at Bella Ristorante had me baffled. If I didn't know better, I'd swear he was an Iron Chef.

Meredith picked up a piece of chalk and worried it between her fingers. "What are we going to do about Quinn? She's not guilty. She should be out on bail. Freddy isn't guilty either. You've got to believe me."

I breezed to the refrigerator and grabbed a bottle of water. I offered Meredith one but she declined. As I cracked open the top, I said, "Why don't you hang out with the twins? I've got to call Urso and clue him in about the stalker." I wouldn't reveal Jacky's new identity to him, even though he was our chief of police. Jordan would have my hide if I did. But I figured that, no matter who the shady character was, Urso should be on the case. "While I've got Urso on the line, I'll see what's up with Quinn and bail."

She gave me a hug of thanks and trotted off.

Parched, I took a swig of water, then returned the slate boards to the cheese counter and retreated to my office. I sat at the desk and dialed the telephone. Rags leaped into my lap and purred for attention. I obliged with a nuzzle to his ears. After two rings, Urso answered and I brought him up to date.

Urso chuckled. "C'mon, Charlotte. He looked like a B-movie detective? Really?"

My face flushed with embarrassment. "Don't make fun."

"You and Rebecca crack me up. Shamus One and Shamus Two."

"Just do your job."

"Will do. Will do." He sniggered again. "I'll drop by Jacky's store. Deal?"

"Be subtle."

"I'm always subtle. By the way, she was married before, wasn't she?"

"I'm not at liberty to say," I blurted then bit my lip. Stupid me. My quick response had confirmed his guess. How had he known? It dawned on me that when I'd first met Jacky she had been wearing a diamond ring. Urso must have seen it before she'd decided to remove it altogether.

After I signed off, I realized I'd forgotten to ask Urso about Quinn and her bail. I was about to call back, when Bozz entered with a paper plate filled with bread cubes and a dollop of fondue. Today's daily special selection was blue cheese and garlic. Not for everyone. Definitely on the strong side, but ever so tasty and delicious added to a green salad.

"Hi, Ms. B."

"Why aren't you at the theater?"

"I'm taking my dinner break."

Rags dove off my lap and hustled to Bozz.

"Benedict Arnold," I muttered.

Bozz lifted Rags and slung him around his neck, then scooped up some warm gooey cheese with a piece of bread and plopped the morsel into his mouth.

"Isn't Grandmère having a buffet for the crew at the theater?" I said.

He licked his fingers. "Yeah, sure, but I wanted fondue. Man, this stuff is addictive."

"How's tech week going?"

"Your grandmother is a little cuckoo." He sputtered. "No disrespect meant."

I smiled. "None taken. I assume she's marching around the stage pounding her stick."

"You got it." He chuckled then took another bite of fondue and hummed his appreciation. "Hey, you'll never guess what I found on the Internet." He used his pinky finger to indicate the monitor.

I'd given him the task of updating our website to reflect our special events. In addition, I wanted us to have links to the websites of American as well as international cheese makers, and I'd asked him to add links to some of our favorite blogs. It was a big undertaking, one that I expected would take him at least a month. Pépère, of course, would disapprove. He feared expanding the scope of our business would lessen our ability to tend to our local customers. I argued that all of our customers seemed quite content.

"It's about Dane Cegielski and Edsel Nash," Bozz said. "I wanted to see if they had criminal records."

Great. Just what I needed. Another amateur sleuth working at The Cheese Shop. Soon I'd have to hang out a detective agency shingle.

"And did they?"

"I couldn't find a thing. Guess I need a

license to dig deeper. But I did find out they volunteered for Habitat for Humanity." He smirked. "Who knew they had it in them, huh?"

He didn't like those two, but why should he? They had accused him of murdering their friend. On the other hand, I didn't want Bozz thinking the worst of everyone and becoming a cynic. He had such a low-key nature.

I said, "Which means they're just like you."

"Sort of."

"You donate your time to Reading is Fundamental."

"Yeah, but —" He scuffed the toe of his shoe into the floor.

"Lots of kids give back to society, Bozz, not only the kids at your school."

"Guess so. You're right. I shouldn't judge, it's just —" He plopped another bite of fondue into his mouth and mumbled, "You're right."

I rose and strolled into the washroom that abutted the office. After any interactions with Rags, I made it a point to clean up before returning to the counter. Bozz finished his snack, then peeled Rags off of his shoulders, followed my lead into the washroom, and headed back to the shop.

In the doorway, he paused. "Do you like Philby?"

"She seems nice."

"We're working on a history project together. Genealogy." He furrowed his forehead. "Gee, I hope we're not related."

I raised an eyebrow.

"It was a joke, Ms. B. Lighten up. Besides, we don't look a thing alike." He snorted.

"Very funny." I tilted my head. "Oh, I should tell you that I hired her."

Bozz grinned like there was no tomorrow. "To work here?"

"To sit the girls tonight."

He shrugged. Mr. Cool. "You know, she'd probably like a job at Fromagerie Bessette this summer, if you could swing it."

In your dreams, lover boy. If I hired Philby, I wouldn't get zilch out of Bozz, he'd be so starry-eyed.

"We'll see," I said.

When I rejoined Rebecca at the counter, Fromagerie Bessette was bustling with a group of tourists wearing matching tour shirts. The flock chattered about the great purchases they'd made that day throughout Providence — exquisite antiques, excellent wines, handmade pottery and quilts. I was thrilled that our little town was prospering.

I said, "Rebecca, are you okay on your

own at the counter? I'm going to load the slate boards with cheese selections."

She nodded.

Moments later, Pépère entered the shop. He stowed his umbrella in the brass stand by the door and strutted across the shop, looking like the cat that swallowed the canary. He rounded the cheese counter and gave a proud cluck of his tongue.

"What did you do?" I loved when my grandfather felt he'd pulled off something clever. "Did you sneak out the back of the theater without Grandmère seeing you?"

"Not only that. I picked up these along the way." He revealed a handful of Prudence Hart's horrible flyers.

"You sly dog." I kissed both cheeks. "Just for that, you get a slice of Edelweiss Emmental." I plucked a piece of the firm but pliable cheese from one of the slate boards I was preparing.

"I had helpers, too," Pépère said.

Gretel, Octavia, and Ipo marched in, all drenched from the rain. I giggled. Apparently I wasn't the only one who was silly enough to leave home without an umbrella.

"That Prudence Hart!" Octavia sputtered. She waved soggy flyers. "She continues to put these up, despite Chief Urso's warning."

"Pfft!" Rebecca set a wheel of UnieKaas five-year-aged Gouda on the counter. "People think Prudence is certifiable." She wielded a ten-inch carving knife and waggled it in the air. "I've heard folks talking all over town."

"Let's not fuel the fire." I caught Ipo staring at Rebecca and nudged her with my hip. "Did you set your first date with our hunky honeybee farmer?"

"I did. He's taking me to the pub, and if that works out, we're going horseback riding."

She couldn't hide her joy. The cotton candy flush that suffused her cheeks revealed all. A warm glow radiated through me at the realization that with the onset of spring came new love. I hoped my romantic getaway with Jordan would secure ours. If he still wanted to go. With Jacky in possible peril, I feared he would change his mind.

"Charlotte!" Lois bustled through the knot of tourists, her face nearly as purple as her raincoat. Had she run the whole way from Lavender and Lace? She shrugged the hood off her hair. Raindrops flew everywhere. "We need to talk."

I moved from behind the counter and drew her toward a barrel stacked with a tower of pesto jars. "What's up?"

"I saw you," she said in a hushed, accusatory tone. Her bad eye blinked rapidly.

My pulse kicked up a notch. Had she seen me spying on Freddy from my bedroom the other night? She couldn't be referring to my covert lattice-climbing adventure or she would have mentioned it earlier.

"Actually, I didn't see you. My husband did."

The Cube? Oh, lord. I didn't want to imagine why the Cube would be watching me in my bedroom late at night.

"Actually, he didn't really see you, either. Mr. Nash did."

"Edsel?"

She nodded. "He told my husband that you were snooping in Mr. Vance's room, don't you know."

Aha. Edsel must have been the one I'd heard tiptoeing outside the bedroom door. Unless he'd raced outside, he hadn't actually *seen* me. I could try to lie my way out of this, but Lois was waving a finger. She seemed to have something else to say.

"You believe Mr. Vance lied to Chief Urso," she continued sotto voce. "You went to find out if he had that stolen artwork in his suitcase, didn't you?"

I remained mum, silently pleading the fifth.

"You didn't crack the combination, am I right?" She offered a smug smile. "Well, I did, don't you know." She folded her arms proudly across her chest. "I found Harker Fontanne's artwork."

It took all my effort to keep my voice in check. "Are you sure it's his?"

"Sure as rain." She crossed her heart. With a flourish, she whipped out her cell phone and stabbed the cell phone's screen. "See?" A photo emerged. "Mr. Fontanne's signature is on every piece. But . . ." She held the pause for a full half minute. ". . . it's not the same artwork I saw in his portfolio. These are purely scenery paintings. No portraits."

CHAPTER 22

What had Freddy done with the rest of Harker's work? Had he destroyed the portraits? Why?

I steered Lois to the cheese counter. "Let me handle this with Chief Urso, okay, Lois?" I scooted around Rebecca, who stood at the register, completing a sale. "In the meantime, would you like a slice of Etorki cheese? You're going to love it." It was a cheese I regularly used on pizzas for the twins.

"But —"

"Take a look at this, Mrs. Smith," Rebecca said, offering a quick wave of her fingers to the departing customer and zeroing in on Lois. "It's just the kind of cheese you like; creamy but firm." She held up a large wedge of Etorki and brandished a knife. "It's sheep's milk from the Pyrenees with a burnt caramel flavor."

Lois licked her lips in anticipation. She

was a sucker for free cheese of any kind, having fallen in love with cheese when she discovered she could have a little taste and not lose her slender figure. Everything in moderation, I told customers who were worried about the calories in cheese. If one eats too much of anything — even broccoli — one can put on weight. Well, maybe not broccoli.

As Rebecca sliced the Etorki, she tilted her head and gave me a *what's going on* look. I mimed that I'd fill her in later. I hurried to the wine annex, which was packed with wine-tasting hopefuls. Matthew was wiping down the wine bar.

I said, "Are the twins with Philby?"

"Yep. Amy and Clair took to her like ducks to water."

"Good." When I'd hired Philby, I'd given her the sparest of details about Sylvie's habit of showing up unannounced. Philby suggested she take the twins to her house and cleared it with her folks. Her father was an ex-Marine. Nobody messed with him.

I scanned the crowd. "Where did Meredith and Freddy go?"

"They left to visit Quinn."

"Shoot!" I dashed to the sidewalk and caught sight of them passing The Spotted Giraffe, a children's boutique just beyond

What's In Store. Thankfully the rain had abated and was no more than a drizzle, though a second wave of the storm was imminent. I hustled toward them yelling, "Meredith!"

I wasn't sure she'd heard me, because the *clip-clop* of an Amish horse-drawn buggy, moving slowly along the side of the street, drowned out my voice.

"Meredith, hold up!"

She turned and looked pleased to see me. I couldn't say the same for Freddy.

When I reached them, near the south corner of the Congregational Church, Meredith said, "We're off to see Quinn. Want to join us?" She reached to me for moral support. I squeezed her hand then released it. "What's wrong?" she said, obviously sensing my concern.

"Freddy lied," I blurted. No preamble. No hedging. No soft-soap sell. So unlike me.

Meredith glanced at her brother. He turned three shades of gray.

"You deliberately misled Urso about Harker's art, Freddy," I said.

"What is she talking about?" Meredith pursed her lips. "Don't you have those photographs you mentioned?"

"He does," I said. "But he also has some

of Harker Fontanne's artwork locked in his suitcase." I told them about Lois's raid and the incriminating photographs on her cell phone.

"That's an illegal search!" Freddy sputtered. The color returned to his face, this time three shades of red.

"So you're not denying it."

Freddy slammed a fist into his palm. "I didn't steal anything. You have to believe me. What I have is not the stuff that was in Harker's portfolio. I don't know where that went. Edsel's probably right, Harker tossed it."

A group of teenagers singing in four-part harmony, choir robes slung over their arms, ambled around us and continued toward the church.

Over the crooning, I said, "Freddy, you dismissed Edsel when he said that. In fact, you were adamant that Harker wouldn't have abandoned his art."

"If it's not the missing artwork, what *do* you have?" Meredith's voice trembled with worry.

Freddy opened his mouth and shut it. After a long moment, he said, "Harker and I had an agreement. We made it about two months ago. He would let me use some of his art as samples to teach certain techniques."

"His samples," I said.

"That's right. In return, I wouldn't give him a rough time about dating Quinn."

"Other than school protocol, why would you give him a rough time?" I asked.

"He had a bad rep with girls. He loved 'em and left 'em. I didn't want that for Quinn. She throws herself into a relationship heart and soul, like" — his shoulders slumped forward — "like me. I was afraid he'd break her heart."

"But in the end, you agreed to let them date," I said, guiding him to the truth. "They became a couple. They fell in love."

"And look what happened." Freddy sucked back a sob.

"Quinn did not kill Harker," Meredith said, her voice sharp, tense. "I'm sure of it."

I eyed Freddy. "Did you kill him?"

"I wanted to."

Meredith thumped Freddy's arm with a fierceness I'd never seen from her. "Don't say such a thing!"

A stark silence fell between us. Freddy jammed his left hand into his pocket. Within seconds, his fingers started worrying the lining, just like before, and a jolt of suspicion shot through me. Whenever I fibbed, my mouth fell open a teensy bit and my eyes turned dull. *Bad habits are like chains that are too light to feel until they are too heavy to carry,* Warren Buffett claimed — a quote from one of the inspirational books my grandmother had given me, though why it was inspirational was beyond me.

I said, "Freddy, on the night of the murder, you lied at the winery when Urso questioned you."

"No, I didn't."

"When you lie, you do that thing with your hand. You're doing it now."

With a shrug of surrender, he wiggled his cell phone out of his jeans pocket and held it out to me. "I play with my phone. Sue me."

"C'mon, Freddy, be straight," Meredith said.

"I am being straight."

"You don't want me to call the boys," she threatened. The *boys* were her other brothers — both younger, both meatier than Freddy. Did she consider them enforcers? Could they bully Freddy into a confession?

"Did you lie at the winery?" I said. "Did you really see Harker fight with Bozz or were you someplace else?"

"You mean, was I lurking in the cellar?" Freddy asked through tight teeth. "Waiting for my chance to kill him? C'mon, Charlotte. You sound like a dime store novelist." He stretched his jaw. "No, I did not build the frigging wall. Yes, I saw Bozz and Harker fight. After my argument with Harker, I went out for a smoke. I called my wife — my ex. Check the times. I don't erase calls. We must have talked for forty-five minutes."

"That's not a good enough alibi," I said. "You could have dialed your wife, reached her answering machine, and left your telephone on."

"She has one of those machines that cuts off after thirty seconds of talking," he said. "She doesn't like someone who chatters."

"He's telling the truth about that," Meredith said. "The machine cut me off last week when I was leaving a message for her."

Freddy swiveled his head. "You still talk to her?"

"Sometimes."

His eyes grew moist. "Look, Charlotte, if you don't believe me or the telephone company, ask the pastor. He saw me walking the grounds with the cell phone plastered to my ear. He's right over there."

The group of teenagers that had passed us had joined up with a dozen others on the Congregational Church lawn. Pastor Hildegard was hustling toward them, waving his hands and pointing at the sky. The pastor

335

was one of the most honest men in the world. Would Freddy have singled him out if he didn't feel absolutely sure his story would hold up?

As if he knew we were talking about him, Pastor Hildegard stopped shepherding the chatty teens into the church and turned. He nodded his chin in greeting.

"Well?" Freddy said. "Are you going to grill him or believe me?"

I swiveled back to face Freddy, who was gnawing the corner of his mouth, and another wave of distrust coursed through me. I felt like I was peeling back the layers of a very rotten onion. "Why didn't you tell Urso all of this up front?"

"Did you know that U-ey used to tease me in high school?"

"We were all friends."

"No, he was your friend and I was your friend. We did things together, but we were never friends. I was a gymnast. He was on the football team. He teased me a lot."

"Did he bully you?"

Freddy shook his head. "But if he found out that I was begging my wife to take me back now, he would call me a wimp."

"No, he wouldn't." I couldn't imagine Urso making fun of anyone, but people were different in high school. "Just so you know, a few years back, Urso was in the same situation as you. He wanted to reunite with his wife for a long time. I would imagine some pleading was involved."

Freddy worked his tongue along the inside of his cheek.

Meredith glanced at her watch. "Visiting hours are almost up. Let's walk and talk at the same time."

We turned the corner and headed toward the precinct, keeping to the sidewalk. Steady traffic prevented us from crossing the street.

"What if I had told the truth?" Freddy said. "I wasn't Urso's prime suspect. Quinn was."

"Urso wasn't considering Quinn at the time," I said. "You and the others had put the blame on Bozz."

"She's right," Meredith said. "You should have mentioned the artwork samples to Urso."

"If I had, Urso would have stopped looking for the art portfolio."

"That's not true," I said. "One truth does not discount the other."

Freddy huffed. "Look, if Harker didn't toss all the artwork, then someone took it. Not Quinn. Not me. Maybe the real murderer. Maybe that's your motive."

Rebecca had suggested the same.

"I've really botched things, haven't I?" Freddy's face grew tight, as if he was straining to keep himself in check. "If only I'd been with Quinn after she split from Edsel at the fund-raiser. I'd be her alibi."

And she'd be yours, I thought, but his words gave me pause. Something he'd said at the winery that night gnawed at the edges of my mind.

I pulled in front of him on the sidewalk and held up my palm. "Hold it. You said your wife left you for a nine-to-fiver because she wanted someone with a steady paycheck. Truth or lie?"

"Truth."

"Then why call her? Why plead with her? You're not going to change."

"She hasn't remarried yet. I thought . . ." Freddy stretched his neck. "I wanted to hear her voice. I miss her so much."

Meredith exhaled. "Tell Charlotte what really happened."

Freddy looked blankly at her.

"It's going to come out," she said.

"What's going to come out?" I demanded, wishing I didn't sound like a browbeating prosecutor, but what could I do? I had a reluctant witness.

"I have anger management issues." Freddy's shoulders sagged.

I gasped. "You hit your wife?"

"No! I hit a wall. Repeatedly."

His brothers were brawlers, too.

"Why did you hit the wall?"

"Because I couldn't stand the art I was putting out, okay? Because I was frustrated. I think I should have more talent than I do, but I don't. I've resigned myself to it now, but then . . . then I let things bottle up inside me and . . ." He rubbed his jaw. "I broke bones in my right hand." He held it out. A thin scar ran down the back of it. His knuckles looked oversized as if the swelling hadn't gone down completely. "That's why I borrowed Harker's artwork. I couldn't paint for two months. I needed samples to teach certain styles." He heaved a sigh. "My wife left me because she couldn't handle not knowing when I might explode again. I called her to apologize. To tell her I've changed." Freddy rolled his shoulders back and clicked his neck right, then left. "I'm in therapy."

"Meredith, why did you keep quiet about Freddy's problem? Why —" I halted as the reason dawned on me. "You did it because you thought the truth about the anger issue wouldn't help Quinn's case."

Meredith slipped her hand through the crook of her brother's elbow. "Urso would reason that Quinn had the same impulses as Freddy and my brothers. Or he would accuse Freddy of losing his temper and killing Harker. I couldn't risk telling you."

My heart felt heavy for her, for Freddy, and for Quinn. But if Freddy didn't kill Harker, who did?

As we neared the precinct, Dane trotted down the front steps, bouncing a set of keys in his palm. Had he gone to see Quinn? He looked upbeat, as if she had embraced his visit. He shrugged on his leather jacket, crossed the street, and strolled into the Village Green using the north path.

Right after his departure, Winona exited the building with Wolford Langdon. I was surprised to see him still in town. Had Winona encouraged him to get better acquainted with Providence? With her? They scanned what looked like a city map obtained from the Tourist Information Center, and without glancing in our direction, proceeded south. As flirtatious as Winona was, I wondered again about her relationship with Harker. I recalled the know-it-all wink she'd thrown him that first day in The Cheese Shop. There had been an intimacy between them I didn't understand.

"Freddy, talk to me about Winona."

"She's big, brassy, and bossy."

"But you like her."

"Yeah, she's okay. Look, it's not what you think between us. My wife —" Freddy wedged his left hand into his pocket, glanced at me, and quickly pulled his hand back out, shaking his fingers as if trying to break himself of the habit. "My wife always wanted me to learn to dance. I wasn't willing. But I thought if I showed her some good faith, she might reconsider. Like I said, she hasn't married the guy yet." His face pinched with pain. "Winona won some dance competitions. She offered to help me."

"She has designs on you," Meredith said.

"Nah. She's a tease. She comes on to lots of men. Look." He pointed.

Even at a distance, I could see Winona had looped her hand around Wolford's elbow. She teasingly tapped the handle of her red umbrella on his arm and tilted her head toward his.

"What else do you know about her?" I said.

Freddy smoothed his hair, clearly uncomfortable. "At one time she was an actress, working in Chicago. I don't think she was very successful."

"How does she have enough money to be a donor?"

"When she turned twenty-five, she came into family money."

That tidbit caught me off guard. "Were there any, you know, odd circumstances regarding the inheritance?"

"What do you mean?"

"Like, did she inherit because somebody died suddenly?"

"Ah, c'mon, Charlotte," Freddy blurted. "You can't possibly think she's a murderer. No, she isn't. I can't believe it."

Deep down, yes, I could.

CHAPTER 23

I left Freddy and Meredith at the precinct
and returned to The Cheese Shop. My timing was fortuitous. Seconds after I entered,
the storm arrived. Luckily, weather wasn't
putting a damper on the evening's wine tasting. Customers crowded the shop. More
filled the wine annex.

Using a dry towel, I blotted moisture from
my hair and clothing. Then I strolled to the
archway leading to the annex and listened
as Matthew gave his opening spiel. I saw no
sign of Sylvie and began to wonder if she
had hightailed it out of town to avoid
further scrutiny. Like Matthew, I couldn't
picture her as a murderer, but Lizzie Borden
had fooled a lot of people.

"Ohio does not have the showiness of
Napa," Matthew said in response to a question from the crowd. "Or the panache of
Europe, but we are a blossoming wine
culture. Our vintners are bursting with a

passion to learn. You'll taste some mature pinot noirs from California tonight, as well as some youthful and unapologetic pinots from around here."

Among the crowd, I spotted Dane leaning against the wine bottle cubbies near the window. Was he over twenty-one? He had to be. Matthew wouldn't have let him enter without carding him. He was strict about liquor rules. I scanned the room for his buddy, Edsel, curious whether he'd tried to sneak in. By my estimation, he was definitely underage, but I also thought women who were forty looked thirty and girls who were twelve appeared twenty. At the age of thirty-four, I wasn't sure I looked much older than twenty-nine, but I was probably kidding myself.

Dane swiveled and peered out the window, fixated on something on the street. I gazed where he was staring. Outside the Country Kitchen, Winona stood with Wolford beneath Winona's bright red umbrella. She laughed at something Wolford said. Dane scowled. What was Winona's and his story? I didn't think they were lovers or even former lovers, but there was something between them.

"Charlotte, can you help?" Rebecca tapped my shoulder. "We're swamped."

I peered through the archway. A troop of customers stood in line by the cheese counter. For the past year, I hadn't wanted to resort to using a number system, but with the crowds The Cheese Shop was drawing lately, I needed to reconsider the idea.

"Sure," I said. "Matthew's on firm ground."

Before I'd had time to sling on my apron, I heard a woman shriek, "Charlotte Bessette!"

Prudence Hart jabbed an umbrella into the container by the door and marched toward me. The bouffant skirt of her throwback-to-the-fifties floral taffeta dress swished noisily. I shivered at the sight of her. Wasn't she cold? The rain had turned the temperature outside to a brisk forty-two. All in the name of fashion, I guessed.

Accompanying Prudence was a reed-thin woman I recognized as the head of the Providence Garden Society, voted in because, at one time, she had been a landscape designer in Dayton. A title didn't necessarily mean she had talent, a number of people in town had confided. Prudence's friend also wore a vintage dress, no doubt pressed upon her by Prudence — hers was green-striped and too low-cut for a woman with practically no breasts.

Prudence pushed through the knot of people standing in front of the counter and wagged a finger at me. "Charlotte, this riffraff, this college influence, has got to go."

"Got to go," her friend echoed.

"Now isn't a good time, Prudence," I said. With all my might, I mentally telegraphed her the idea to leave of her own accord, but she didn't pick up on the signal.

"Now is the only time. You must control Meredith and that committee of hers."

"I must do no such thing. Talk to the town council."

"But you have to." Prudence's voice soared an octave.

"You have to!" her friend repeated.

I advised Rebecca that I would return in a second and hustled from behind the counter. Gripping Prudence and her friend by the elbows, I shuttled them outside the shop.

"What do you think you're doing?" Prudence sputtered, obviously surprised by my strength and determination.

I steered them away from the front door but remained beneath the awning. Prudence and her friend huddled together to stay dry as rain continued to spill over the edges of the awning. The nip in the air cut through my button-down shirt, but I refused to show any sign of weakness.

Gritting my teeth together to keep them from chattering, I said, "I will not have you disrupt Matthew's event. He has worked so hard to develop a clientele." When Matthew gave up his career as a sommelier, he worried that moving to a small town like Providence would affect how people viewed him. Since his arrival, he had toiled endlessly to keep up his relationships with wineries worldwide as well as the local wineries. One bad night could thwart his progress. "Before you go, let me add that I want you to cease and desist with the *Boycott Fromagerie Bessette* posters."

"Whatever are you talking about?" Prudence sniffed.

Her friend copied the sniff.

"You've been posting them all over town," I said.

"I've done no such thing."

"Let's make a pact. I won't buy anything in your store, and you won't buy anything in mine. I won't boycott your store, and you —"

"My *boutique*," Prudence hissed.

A car veered to the curb, splashing up rainwater. Prudence scooted out of the way, accidentally pushing her friend from beneath the protection of the awning. Her friend shoved back. Like a slapstick duo in an old-time movie, they swatted each other until they realized I wasn't the only one observing them. A pair of patrons clucked their tongues as they entered the shop.

Taking the highest of the low roads, Prudence's friend smoothed her dress and said, "Prudence, dear, you're getting off track. The college people. The riffraff. The museum."

Prudence snapped her attention back to me. "That's right! Charlotte, these college folk have ruined the Providence Historical Museum. They're traipsing in snow."

"We don't have snow. You mean mud."

In addition to running Le Chic Boutique, Prudence had put herself in charge of our local museum. It was a privately owned museum with mementoes from our town's illustrious, albeit quaint history. The owner, Lois Smith's sister and one of Prudence's best friends, had taken an extended vacation. Lois had no desire to manage the museum. The B&B kept her busy twenty-four hours a day. Out of the goodness of her pretentious heart, Prudence had taken the helm and was running the museum with a steel grip.

Prudence waved an agitated hand. "They're so scruffy. The language they use.

And they finger everything."

"Everything," her friend echoed.

"It's not a hands-on museum," Prudence continued. "It's for viewing purposes only. Their behavior is disrespectful."

I sighed. "Prudence, there are hundreds of books and photograph albums in the museum. What do you expect visitors to do? Stare at the covers? They're curious."

"I want them to put on Latex gloves, of course. We provide them. They're right by the front door as you walk inside."

I laughed. I couldn't imagine college students donning gloves to tour a museum.

"Tell her about the hot dogs," Prudence's friend prompted.

"My lord. They were eating in the study, gobbling down food." Prudence's nose thinned, as if she'd taken a whiff of something rancid. "Hot dogs smothered with cheese and baked beans that they'd bought at the diner. Delilah knows better than to let them do that."

"I'm sure Delilah didn't know they were heading to the museum." I checked my watch, itching to get back inside. How much longer did I have to listen to this tripe? My arms were cold. Wisps of hair clung to my face. A drowned rat probably looked better. Hopefully Jordan wouldn't put in a surprise

349

appearance. "Look, Prudence, why don't you complain to my grandmother? She's the mayor." *And she would tell your sweet sorry —*

I snipped off the thought. At times, I wished I had my grandmother's courage and could say what I felt. She'd tell Prudence in no uncertain terms to back off, and she'd rest easy at night. According to my grandmother, I had ended up with my mother's "nice genes," the genes that made me want to fix people's lives without hurting their feelings. An impossible task, she advised me, one that would leave me with burning indigestion if I wasn't careful. At night, I practiced saying bad things that cycled through my head in front of my bathroom mirror. I found it quite therapeutic.

"Your grandmother? Bah!" Prudence snorted. "She's too busy with that . . . that production of hers. What a farce!"

"Actually, it's a satire about an absurd play," I corrected.

"Absurd is right. It's a joke. Why our taxpayer money goes to support such junk is beyond me." She clucked her tongue. "She has absolutely no taste."

"No taste," her friend concurred.

My hands balled into fists. Prudence and

her pal were going too far. Nobody questioned my grandmother's artistic vision. Luckily for Prudence, a knot of my friends were walking en masse toward us. If Tyanne, Freckles, and Octavia hadn't appeared, I might have punched Prudence in the nose and cheered my spontaneity.

"Hi-yo," Freckles yelled.

"Hey, Sugar," Tyanne said.

Octavia eyed my fisted hands. "Problem?"

I rolled my eyes in exasperation. "Prudence is worried that having a college nearby will destroy our fair town."

"I think it's fabulous to have so many young people in Providence," Octavia said.

"Me, too." Freckles giggled. "They're so energetic. So curious."

"Pfft," Prudence muttered.

"Why, if we have a college here," Octavia went on, "it will give this town an injection of intellectual zing. More books, more discussion."

"My Thomas and Tisha can stay close to home," Tyanne said.

"So can my Frenchie." Freckles grabbed Tyanne's hand and squeezed, mothers-in-arms.

Prudence said, "You're hopeless. All of you."

Her friend echoed her yet again, making

me wonder if she ever had any actual thoughts of her own.

"If I wanted to," Prudence went on, "I'd buy that Ziegler property and end this fiasco waiting to happen."

"I heard you were already trying to buy it," I said.

"You heard wrong."

"What about your brothers?" I said. Octavia tilted her head, as if telling me we'd already covered this territory, but I still had my suspicions about the Harts. There was no time like the present to snoop. "The Ziegler Winery used to abut your property, Prudence. Rumor is that the Zieglers pushed your family off the land. I'll bet your family was upset about that."

"That's a lie," Prudence said.

"Maybe your brothers want to get it back."

"Prudence's brothers wouldn't move back to Providence for all the rice in China," Prudence's friend blurted.

Prudence looked at the woman as though she'd been thoroughly betrayed. She licked her lips. After a long moment, she said, "We don't speak." Her face grew pale, almost porcelain, as if the reminder of the feud was sucking the life out of her.

The urge to reach out and comfort her welled up inside me.

"Charlotte!" Delilah rushed across the street, dragging Wolford Langdon by the wrist. Where had Winona gone to? "You won't believe this." Delilah prodded the man to speak. "Tell her, Wolford."

He drew his chin down and arms to his chest, like a wimpy fighter protecting his core.

"Go on, tell her." When he didn't, Delilah said, "I overheard him talking to these tourists. You know, the one with the scraggly red hair and the other one with the bottle-top glasses? They were in here the other day."

Their faces sprang to mind. I nodded.

"Anyway, they were talking, and you know how I have an ear for gossip."

"It's not gossip," Wolford said.

"Tell her the story." Delilah tugged on his sleeve then ogled me. "It's about Winona."

"Weren't you at the diner with Winona?" I asked him.

"She left right away," Delilah cut in. "She bought a to-go milkshake and dashed out, like she had an appointment. Go on, Wolford. Spill."

Wolford drew in a deep breath and exhaled slowly, the air escaping through the space in his upper teeth. Whatever he had to say was making him highly uncomfortable. "Winona Westerton's sister dated

353

Harker Fontanne."

"And . . ." Delilah twirled her hand, encouraging him to continue.

"And they broke up."

"And . . ."

"And her sister committed suicide."

The collective group gasped. Freddy's words came back to me in a rush. Harker *loved 'em and left 'em.* Why hadn't Winona told Urso? Because if he found out, he'd consider her suspect number one.

"Why did you keep this a secret until now, Wolford?" I asked.

He sniffed. "Because I hadn't put it together before."

"Winona and her sister had different last names," Delilah explained. "Ever since Wolford signed on as a potential donor, he has been racking his brain trying to figure out how he knew her. See, he knew about the suicide."

"It was in all the papers," he said.

"Harker Fontanne was cleared of all responsibility," Delilah said.

"I'd put the memory behind me." Wolford worried his hands together. "It was such a tragic death."

"But here's the kicker." Delilah nudged Wolford to continue. "C'mon, tell her the capper."

He shuffled his feet. "Winona's sister's name was Julianne."

Big deal. I knew that from the Internet search I'd done. She and her sister had won ballroom dancing competitions.

Delilah spread her palms. "Her nickname was Jules."

CHAPTER 24

Jules. *Jewels.* Winona had spread the jewels around Harker as a reminder of what he'd done to her sister. He broke her heart. She took her own life. And Winona, exacting vengeance of the worst kind, took his.

"I'll bet Winona suspected you were on to her," I said to Wolford. Delilah nodded her agreement. "She's probably at the bed-and-breakfast packing up."

I excused myself from the group that was huddled beneath the awning in front of The Cheese Shop, taking pains to ignore Prudence's prune-faced disapproval, and hurried inside. I retrieved my purse and cell phone and called Urso. The precinct clerk answered and said Chief Urso was indisposed. The rains were flooding his family's farm — rains tumbling down Ziegler Winery hillsides, to be exact. I asked for the deputy but was informed that his sister was at the hospital having her first baby. I begged the clerk to contact Urso and tell him to meet me at the B&B, then stabbed END on the cell phone.

Rebecca said, "What's got you so hot under the collar?"

I filled her in. "I've got to stop Winona from leaving town."

"I'm going with you." She started to untie her apron.

"Uh-uh," I said. "I need you to make sure tonight's tasting runs like clockwork."

"It's not safe for you to go alone."

"Don't worry. I'll" — I glanced outside — "I'll take Octavia with me." Delilah was on her way to rehearsal at the theater. Tyanne and Freckles needed to go home to their families.

Rebecca pouted.

I hugged her. "This is not a showdown with Winona, okay? I'm simply going to detain her until Urso arrives. You aren't missing a thing. Slap a smile on that pretty face and get to work."

"But —"

The chimes over the front door rang out.

Rebecca wiggled her fingers with glee. "Oh, look, there's your grandfather."

Brushing rain off his slicker, Pépère bustled into The Cheese Shop and made a beeline for us.

"Is everything okay?" My stomach did a dive. With all the tension in the air, I instantly imagined another accident at the theater. "Is Grandmère — ?"

"Your grandmother is cuckoo. Someone said 'Macbeth' at the theater."

"Oh, no!" Rebecca clapped a hand over her mouth, then removed it and whispered, "Is that bad?"

Pépère said, "It is a long story, but it has something to do with Shakespeare and making fun of witches when he wrote *Macbeth*. Supposedly saying the name Macbeth inside a theater brings bad luck, not just to the play but to anyone acting in it."

"The only exception is when the word is spoken as a line in the play," I added.

"In order to change the luck," Pépère continued, "the person who said the word has to exit the theater, spin around three times while swearing, and ask for permission to return. Of course, your grandmother is beside herself, and I am the first target. Mind if I watch the counter?"

"Perfect." Rebecca whipped off her apron and thrust it at him. "Charlotte and I have an errand to run. C'mon, Charlotte, let's grab Octavia and go."

"Why are you taking Octavia?" Pépère raised an eyebrow.

"Um, it's an errand for the library," Rebecca said.

I gawked, amazed at the little scamp's ability to lie.

On the way to Lavender and Lace, I called Lois to confirm that Winona was at the inn. She was. Lois and her Shih Tzu greeted Rebecca, Octavia, and me on the front porch as we were folding our umbrellas. The strains of Beethoven's *Eroica* symphony floated from the speakers in the great room. The spicy scent of lasagna permeated the air. Every night, Lois prepared a modest dinner for guests who didn't want to venture out for a meal.

Lois leaned in. "I used that Mozzarella Company cheese you recommended, don't you know."

The raw milk cheese from Texas had the proper chew and stretch, with papery thin layers and a mild dose of salty flavor.

"Smells good, doesn't it?" Lois asked.

Agatha barked her approval.

"By the by, Miss Westerton is still in her room."

Taking the lead, I traipsed into the bed-and-breakfast and up the stairs. The other two followed me, Octavia tapping on her iPhone with lightning speed.

As we reached the second floor, Octavia held up her iPhone for inspection. "FYI, Winona Westerton is worth more than a million dollars." Octavia was incredible with research, but then what librarian wasn't?

"Do you think she'll attack us?" Rebecca asked.

"Not a chance. There are three of us, and we're in a busy place," I said.

"Being in a busy place didn't help Harker," Rebecca said.

A lump the size of a chestnut lodged in my throat. She had a point. Winona had lured Harker to the cellar and strangled him when there were dozens of people milling about the winery.

Doing my best to look confident, I marched along the lavender runner. A couple of guests walked along the hall toward us. I nodded a greeting. One of the men returned a clipped hello. I paused in front of the door to Winona's room, hand raised to knock. Was I being bold when I should have been frightened to death? What if she had a weapon? Just because she'd used a scarf on Harker didn't mean she wasn't packing a gun in her purse. Would she shoot all three of us? I considered not knocking and simply standing guard outside her room, ready to delay her if she tried to make a run for it. But what if she chose to make an escape via the trellis as I had?

Someone cleared a throat. I spied Lois and her husband on the landing and felt it was safe to continue with my plan. Expert snoops that they were, they wouldn't leave the area until they knew what was going on. Five against one felt like good odds. Safety in numbers, as the saying went.

I rapped on the door.

"Who is it?" Winona said from inside the room.

"Charlotte Bessette."

"I'm a little busy."

"This will just take a second," I lied.

I heard the sound of a zipper and a thud and a jangle of something that sounded like wind chimes. Footsteps followed, and the door opened.

In a black wool dress, one hand wedged on her hip, Winona reminded me of a human Grecian urn. "What do you want?"

Not ready to alert her to our intent, I pushed past her into the room that looked like all the others in the inn — floral and cozy and furnished with beautiful antiques. I stopped in the center of the woven carpet, and in my friendliest tone, said, "May we come in?"

"You're in."

"So we are," Rebecca said as she and Octavia joined me.

I glanced at the sealed suitcase standing beside the bed — the zipper and thud I'd heard. As suspected, Winona was ready to run.

Winona pivoted and strolled to us, leaving the door ajar. "I said I'm busy. What's up?"

"Leaving town?" Rebecca asked.

"I have a couple of board meetings to attend. I asked Chief Urso if it was all right. He said he was ready to wrap up the case and didn't need me any longer. Not that I have to report to you, but you seem interested." Winona tilted her head back and peered down the length of her aquiline nose at Rebecca and Octavia, then turned her gaze on me. "So-o-o-o, Charlotte." She dragged out the words in her divalike way. "Are you here to wish me a good trip?"

"What boards do you sit on?" I glanced at the suitcase again, prepared to hunker down on it if that's what it would take to keep her there. "That regional theater in Cleveland, I presume."

She raised an eyebrow. "How do you know about that?"

"I like to keep abreast of all the people who come to town." Another lie. I was getting good. Any day now, Grandmère would ask me to star in one of her plays. Actors needed to be expert liars.

Winona strutted toward me, one hand still anchored at her hip. "What else do you know about me, Charlotte?"

"You went to Northwestern. You were an actress before you became an heiress, and you have a sister named Julianne."

That stopped her cold.

"You and she won ballroom dancing competitions," Rebecca chimed in.

"My, my. Did you get all that from your iPhone?"

Octavia dumped her cell phone into the side pocket of her purse.

Winona sneered. "You don't know my entire résumé. Did you also know that I was a journalist? I wrote articles for the *Cleveland Plain Dealer.* And I was a photographer. I had photos displayed in *National Geographic.*" She walked a circle around the three of us. "I like rare steak and dry red wine, and I hate anything vanilla."

She sniffed. I hadn't used any eau de vanilla this morning. Perhaps the scent had clung to my clothes from a previous spritz. "Did Harker Fontanne know you and Julianne were sisters?" I asked.

"He didn't have a clue. We have different last names. Different fathers. We were five years apart in age. What else do you want to know?"

"Julianne committed suicide."

"That appeared on page twelve of the *Plain Dealer*. It wasn't earth-shattering. It didn't make page one." Winona's voice held an undercurrent of loathing. "What else do you want to ask?"

Rebecca inched ahead of the group. "Did you kill Harker Fontanne?"

I gasped as Winona reared up like a snake, hand raised as if she was going to strike. I tugged Rebecca by the collar of her ruffled shirt and pulled her back a foot.

"You have gall," Winona hissed. "Coming in here, accusing me."

"You didn't answer the question," Octavia and Rebecca said in unison.

"Jewels were strewn around Harker's body," I said, in for a penny, in for a pound. If she lashed out, I'd duck. "Symbolic jewels. Your sister was involved with Harker. Her nickname was Jules."

Winona barked out a laugh. "Involved? Is that the word you used? *Involved?* They were engaged, my nosy friends. They were going to be married. They'd set a date." Winona sucked back a sob. "But then he met Quinn Vance." She dragged the word out. "He threw Julianne over for that little redheaded bimbette, did you know that? Threw her over! I like Freddy, but really, his daughter is such an airhead."

"No, she's not," Rebecca said.

I gripped her arm to silence her as I reflected on what Winona had revealed. Harker and Julianne were set to get married. Quinn said the ring Harker had given her was a hand-me-down. Did she know he'd given it to Julianne first? When she found out, did she kill Harker in a fit of jealousy? Did she stuff the ring into his hand?

No. I refused to believe Quinn was the murderer. Winona had framed her.

I said, "You tried to pin Harker's murder on Quinn Vance by planting that ring in his palm."

"What are you talking about?"

"The ring. The evidence," Rebecca said.

"Are you saying you found Jules's ring?" Winona asked, her face suddenly vulnerable. Tears formed in the corners of her eyes.

"Chief Urso found it," I said. "You planted it on Harker."

"I did no such thing. I didn't —" Winona flicked away the tears that had trickled down her face and took a menacing step toward us. "I want that ring."

It was Rebecca's turn to pull me out of

the line of fire.

"Oh, my!" Lois said from the doorway. She flung a hand over her mouth. Her partially blind eye blinked furiously.

"Everything okay in here?" the Cube said, hovering protectively beside her.

Winona lowered her arm and snarled. "Come on in, folks. Why not invite the whole town? I was just telling Ms. Nosey-Nose and her friends that I did not kill Harker Fontanne."

"Your sister committed suicide," I pressed. "You blamed him."

"Jules was emotionally fragile. She was an artist, did you know that?" Winona painted an imaginary canvas in front of her. "Acrylics. Wild, exotic acrylics. Georgia O'Keeffe good. She had a future, but she threw it all away for him. She wanted him to be the star."

"You blamed him," I said.

"Darned right, I did. He could have encouraged her to keep painting. He didn't have to break her spirit and her heart."

"And you killed him. You threw the jewels on the floor. You built that wall to show how emotionally blocked he was."

"Me, build a wall? You've got to be kidding." She flashed her perfectly manicured fingernails at me. "I don't even garden."

"You signed on to be a donor for the college right after the art gathering was announced."

"That's right," Rebecca said. She had been the one to share that tidbit with me. "You knew Harker would be here."

Winona raised her shoulders as she drew in a long breath. She let it out in a gust. "Want to know the truth?"

"You bet we do," Rebecca said.

"Fine. I signed on for this ridiculous trip so that I could punish him."

"Punish him?" I said.

"For being so cavalier."

I gaped at her. "You strangled him."

"Strangulation is an extreme act of punishment," Octavia said.

Lois and the Cube bobbed their heads. A panel of Winona's peers couldn't have been more judgmental.

"Oh, for Pete's sake, I did not strangle him." Winona sighed, as if the act of explaining to a room full of idiots was exhausting. "The best place to hit Harker was in the art. That's right, the *art*. He loved his art. He would do anything for his art. I stole it from his portfolio."

"You stole it?" Rebecca said.

"Before he was murdered." Winona hoisted her suitcase onto the bed and unzipped it. On top of her clothing lay a thick brown envelope, about twenty inches by thirty inches — the same size as the leather portfolio we'd seen in Harker's room. She ripped open the Velcro latch and pulled out the contents — unframed canvases of Harker's artwork. She placed them on the bedspread. There were eight of them. Each was breathtakingly poignant and signed by Harker Fontanne. Freddy and Rebecca had said that whoever took the artwork had the best motive to kill Harker. The posthumous artwork would sell big on the open market. Harker hadn't been famous, but with his talent and an aggressive representative, he might have become famous. But Winona, being an heiress, didn't need the money.

"You stole the art to hinder his career," I said. "Having to paint new paintings would be time-consuming."

"Oh, please. That would be so mundane. I stole these pieces so he could never touch them."

I assessed the artwork again. Quinn said Harker had carried the portfolio everywhere. Why? Four of the pieces were landscapes; the others were portraits of a woman. They weren't of Quinn.

I glanced at Winona, suddenly seeing the

truth. "Are those portraits of your sister?"

Winona smiled a canary-in-the-mouth grin.

"Why didn't you tell Chief Urso?"

"For the same reason that's ticking away in your mind." Winona wagged a finger. "Don't deny it. I can see your eyes flickering. A thief could make millions selling the art on the open market once Harker's genius is realized." She collected the art and slid them back into the envelope. "I'm not keeping them. I plan to give them to a museum."

Rebecca muttered, "I'll bet."

Octavia said, "Yeah, right."

I shut out the murmurs of my companions and focused on the other thing that was bothering me. "Why were you arguing with Dane the other day?"

Winona threw me a sour look. "The kid made a play for me. I told him in no uncertain terms that I didn't date anybody younger than me."

"How long have you known him?"

"I only met him on this trip." Winona's gaze darted down and to the right, and then back to me. A psychology course I took in college taught me about eye signals. She was covering up something.

"I don't believe you."

Winona pursed her lips, as if weighing her options. Finally she said, "Dane knew about Julianne and Harker. He said he pegged me for her sister because we looked so much alike." Winona shook her head. "It was a line of bull, of course. We looked nothing alike. I'm dark and big. She was fair and slight. We have the same swoop to our hair, the same nose — got both traits from our mom — but that's it."

"Harker must have figured out who you were and told Dane," I said.

"That's my guess."

"Did Dane accuse you of killing Harker?"

"I assured him that I didn't. I told him I was here to ruin Harker, to humiliate him. He said my secret was safe." She jutted her chin. "I think he was ingratiating himself to me so I'd cave in and grant him a date."

"Did you?"

"No!" Her diva voice soared to a crescendo. "And don't get me started about that little creep, Edsel Nash."

I recalled Dane arguing with Edsel outside The Cheese Shop and imagined what his teachers must have written repeatedly on his report cards: *Doesn't play well with peers.* Edsel probably received the same kind of commentary.

"What about him?" I said.

"Never mind." Winona folded her arms across her chest and tilted her head.

"Did you know Edsel and Dane had an argument?"

"It had nothing to do with me."

Which meant she knew about it.

She glanced at the clock again. "If you don't mind, I have a train to catch."

The sound of footsteps running along the hall made me turn. Lois and her husband scuttled sideways as Urso burst into the room, his slicker and hat dripping wet.

"What the heck is going on?" he barked.

I gave him a twenty-second account. When I finished, Winona proclaimed her innocence yet again.

I said, "Tell her you believe her, Chief, as long as she tells us everything about Edsel Nash."

Winona gave me the evil eye.

"You're the one who brought him up," I said.

Winona's fingers tapped a rhythm on her biceps. "Fine. The kid said he saw me take the portfolio. He was blackmailing me."

CHAPTER 25

Neither Dane nor Edsel was at the inn. Lois hadn't seen them for hours. Urso said he would find them.

Before leaving Winona's room, Urso cautioned Winona not to leave Providence. He threatened to arrest her if she did. On the B&B's front porch, he also gave a warning to Rebecca, Octavia, and me. "Keep away from the investigation."

"C'mon, U-ey," I said.

"Don't 'U-ey' me. You approached a murder suspect alone."

"I wasn't alone."

Rebecca and Octavia raised tentative hands to signal their existence.

Urso frowned. "Promise me."

Playing the properly chastised citizen, I said, "I promise that I will not do anything rash."

He grunted his disapproval.

"I called you, remember?" I said. "I didn't

want Winona to flee. I acted quickly and responsibly. I also had two friends with me, and I knew there were people at the inn. Didn't you see Lois and her husband? They clung to us like shadows."

Urso grabbed my elbow and drew me to the railing. The rain, once again no more than a drizzle, splattered my hair, but I didn't protest. Urso peered into my face, his gaze concerned, his forehead furrowed. I worried for a moment he might lean forward and kiss me. A flock of birds in the leafless vines twittered, as if sharing my concern.

Don't, don't, don't kiss me. A kiss would ruin our friendship. *Don't, please.* A swarm of panicky butterflies fluttered wildly in my stomach.

As if intuiting my prayerful advice, Urso stood taller and said, "Your family can't afford to lose you. Your future family as well as your present, got me?" He kept his gaze on me for a long moment, and then he traipsed down the inn's steps to his patrol car.

After I bid my friends good night, I retrieved my umbrella and trotted toward home, wondering about my future. Would it be with Jordan? Why hadn't he returned my call about Jacky? Was I making a big mistake banking my heart on him? Perhaps that was what Grandmère feared. Perhaps that was why she favored Urso. She felt he was a better long-range choice for me. But did I want stability or passion?

I whipped out my cell phone, prepared to call Jordan, and noticed a missed call on the readout — from him. I listened to the message.

Jordan said, "Thanks for the heads-up about my sis. I'll check it out. On another note, my bags are packed. Are yours?" He laughed, blew a kiss, and ended the call.

As I stowed my cell phone, I glanced at the sky and imagined the stars behind the clouds. On the biggest, I made the kind of wish heaven reserved for children: *Make this man say he loves me.*

When I picked up the twins from Philby's house, Amy insisted I bring home her unfinished pizza. The aroma of pepperoni wafted up the stairs and snaked its way into the bedroom. My stomach grumbled with desire.

"By the way, Clair, what did you eat?" I peered through the crack into the twins' bathroom. The two stood at the sink brushing their teeth.

"Pasta," she said, her mouth filled with

toothpaste suds.

Amy said, "Philby's mom has to eat wheat-free, too, so Philby made Clair some of her mom's pasta with melted cheese."

Let's hear it for Philby.

Amy emerged first. Clair followed, switching off the light in the bathroom.

"Philby's nice, Aunt Charlotte." Amy scampered into bed and pulled the covers up to her chin. "Sort of bookish, but nice."

"She's not bookish," Clair said, taking her time to fold back the covers and smooth them with the palm of her hand. "She's intelligent. There's a difference."

"Speaking of Mum," Amy said, changing the subject with ease. "Why didn't she show up at The Cheese Shop for the tasting?"

I swallowed hard. "Your mother is going through some difficult times."

"Because she wants to marry Daddy again, but she can't because of Meredith?" Amy said.

"That's not quite it."

"She's got money problems, right, Aunt Charlotte?" Clair said.

"Your mother is dealing with some grown-up issues." I perched on the edge of Clair's bed while Rags performed his evening routine of leaping from bed to bed to say good night to the twins. He'd learned quickly that Clair preferred nuzzles to her chest and not her face. When he finished, he returned and curled by my side, his purring rivaling the rumble of a NASCAR engine. While idly plucking cheese from his whiskers — the rascal must have snagged a bite of Amy's leftover pizza — I added, "Grown-up issues are for grown-ups to discuss, do you understand?"

I could see in their eyes that they didn't. They wanted the whole story.

Clair toyed with a thread poking from the edge of the sheet. "Do you think there's really a treasure at the winery, Aunt Charlotte?"

"No."

"Yes, there is," Amy said. "Pirates put it there."

"Where did you hear that?" I asked.

"A couple of people were talking at The Cheese Shop while Daddy was setting up for the wine tasting. They said that Meredith's college idea had brought treasure hunters to town."

I revisited the reasons for Harker's murder. Had he simply gotten in the way of a treasure hunter? Sylvie said the Internet story about Meredith's plan to convert the winery into a college was what had piqued her interest to return to Providence. What if she wasn't the only one? Rebecca said that Winona Westerton had tracked down Freddy to make a donation because she'd been itching to go on the trip. I believed her when she said she was on the trip to avenge her sister, but what if that was only a half-truth? Jordan said rich people were treasure hunters, too.

And what about Dane or Edsel, or that curious Wolford character? Was it the treasure that had driven them to come on the excursion? Dane wasn't much of an art student. At the event at the winery, Harker had teased Dane because he didn't know Kandinsky and Klee were artists. Had Dane finagled his way into the group to get access to the winery? His interest in Quinn seemed genuine, but Winona claimed he wasn't after Quinn; he was after her. Which version of the story was true?

And Edsel Nash had me confused. If Winona was to be believed, he was blackmailing her. What if he hadn't pre-planned that? What if he had come on the trip to find the treasure but saw an opportunity for blackmail when he caught Winona stealing the portfolio? Or — and this idea made my insides tense — had he pretended to be a good friend of Harker's when, in reality, he hated him so much that he came on the trip with the sole intention of killing him? He was interested in Quinn. Had he killed Harker to remove the competition? That first day in The Cheese Shop, he'd said Harker was the one who had talked them all into coming on the trip. Had Edsel made Harker think that? Was he that manipulative?

"Hey, look who's still up." Matthew poked his head into the room. His eyes twinkled with good energy.

The twins squealed. "Daddy!" Both thrust out their arms for a hug.

Matthew kissed Clair first, then Amy. He knelt between their beds, reached for their hands, and said, "Prayers."

With bowed heads, the twins peeking between partially opened eyes as they always did, the trio recited Matthew's quickie version of vespers. "Thank you God for my wonderful day. Thank you for all my blessings. I love you. Amen." Matthew kissed each girl a second time and said, "Lights out."

As he headed for the door, he gestured for me to follow him. I scooped up Rags and strolled from the room. In the hallway, Matthew's mood seemed even cheerier.

"You must have had a good night," I said. "Did you sell lots of wine?"

"After you disappeared, we had double the number of walk-ins, and we tripled our orders from last time."

"Great news."

"We nearly sold out of the cheeses in the display case. You'll have to fetch the reserves from Pace Hill Farm."

Our business had grown so much in the past few months that we'd started stocking larger quantities of cheeses in Jordan's caves. He and his staff rotated and washed the wheels regularly to make sure the butterfat and aging process was perfect. Jordan had suggested we build our own subterranean cave in the basement beneath the shop. He'd help design it. Matthew and I were considering it.

"And no Sylvie sightings," Matthew added. He gave me a thumbs-up.

"Life is good."

"Yeah."

Matthew leaned against the moss green wall and folded his arms. "Say, Meredith filled me in on Sylvie's confession. Wild, huh? Mumsie and Dad blew through their wad."

I still wasn't sure if Sylvie was telling the truth about that. Was she trying to earn my sympathy to divert my suspicions? If she'd run into Harker in the cellar while searching for the treasure, she could have killed him. Wouldn't that have required a struggle? Harker hadn't struggled. Someone strong had sneaked up on him and strangled him.

"Are you okay?" Matthew asked. "Where'd you run off to tonight?"

I told him about going to the bed-and-breakfast and learning about Harker's connection to Winona's sister.

"Urso's right, you know. You've got to let him do his job."

"But when I find out things, and he's not available, they need to be acted upon, don't they? We only have a small police force."

"Give the girl a Citizen's Academy badge," Matthew teased.

"No, really. What if Winona had been the killer? What if she had skipped town?"

"Urso would have tracked her down. C'mon, Cuz, you can't be expected to run a successful business and save the world, too." He yawned. "I'm beat. G'night. See you in the morning."

"Not so fast." I gripped his elbow.

"What?"

"You're not telling me something. You don't look tired in the least. In fact, you look like you're ready to float away on cloud nine."

He grinned. "You are such a detective."

I tilted my head. "Out with it."

"It's for me to know." He chuckled then squeezed my shoulder supportively and sauntered into his room. The door closed with a soft click.

After a half hour staring into the bathroom mirror, picking apart my looks as well as my curious nature, I crawled into bed. Rags jumped onto the cover and padded in a circle until he found just the right spot beside my hip and plopped down. As I settled into the pillows with a new mystery in my hands, I could feel his rumbling purr through the quilt.

Before I finished paragraph one of chapter one, I glanced at the telephone on the bedside table. Only twenty-four hours had elapsed since I'd seen Jordan, but it felt like days — no, weeks. I craved to hear his voice, drink in his scent. Once Matthew and Meredith got married — and they would get married someday — I could see myself marrying Jordan. He'd move into my Victorian, or I'd move to his farm. We'd spend lovely evenings by a fire with a glass of wine and a plate of cheese and fruit. We'd chat about our days, our businesses, and our dreams. And we'd talk about having children. I wanted two. Did he want two, as well?

Anxiety ticked my insides. I slapped the book closed and sat upright. Did he want any? Why didn't I know the answer to that? Was I falling in love too fast?

Stop it, Charlotte. You're scaring yourself into spinsterhood.

I reopened the book and read the first paragraph for a second time, but I couldn't get Jordan out of my mind. It was too late to call him without seeming brazen. I decided a cold shower of talking to Urso was in order. I dialed his number and said, "What did you find out?"

"Charlotte?" he mumbled.

"Did I wake you? I'm sorry. I was eager to hear what you gleaned from Dane and Edsel."

"This is not your business."

"I know it's not, but inquiring minds want to know." I held my breath. He could hang up on me or talk. I was hoping he'd talk.

Urso let out a long sigh. "Mr. Cegielski —"

"It's me, U-ey. First names, please."

"Dane admitted that he made a play for Winona."

"Did he own up to knowing Julianne?"

"He said he never met her. He only heard about her from Harker. He thought Harker was a jerk, but he didn't think he deserved to die. He said suicide was something weak people did, and Harker shouldn't be blamed for Winona's sister's weakness."

"What about Edsel?"

"I couldn't track him down."

"Anywhere?"

"That's what 'couldn't track him down' means, Charlotte."

"Sorry." I chewed my lower lip, hating myself whenever I stated the obvious. "So we don't know if he was blackmailing Winona. That could be a story she made up."

"Could be."

"Dane didn't know anything about it?"

"If he did, he kept mum. I've got Deputy Rodham staking out the B&B. When Edsel shows up, we'll get answers. In the meantime, I'm checking into the guy you saw hanging around Jacky Peterson. Seems other folks near her store have seen him, as well."

"I don't think he's a local."

"I'll catch him. Promise." He yawned. "Get some sleep."

I began chapter one for a third time but froze on the second paragraph when I heard a scratch-skitter sound. From overhead. Somewhere between the attic and my room. Near the bedroom window.

Rags perked his ears, scrambled to a low

crouch, and eyed the ceiling, waiting with impish patience to pounce on the unsuspecting living toy that might appear.

"Down, boy." I patted the quilt.

He didn't obey.

"It's probably a squirrel that's found its way into one of the vents and is building a spring nest."

The creature overhead stilled, but I couldn't, too hyped up after the conversation with Urso, too worried that a murderer was still roaming Providence — a murderer whom neither Urso nor I could identify.

"C'mon, Rags, lie down. The excitement's over."

Obviously he didn't believe me. He kept his gaze fixed on the ceiling. When and if a plaything appeared, he would be ready.

Seconds later the scratch-skitter started up again. Exasperation forced me out of bed. I had to discover the source or I'd never sleep.

To ward off the chill in the air, I put on a sweatshirt over my Victoria's Secret nightgown. I grabbed a hanger from the closet and padded to my desk. Dragging the T-back armchair from the desk to the spot that I'd pinpointed for the noise, I climbed up on the cushion and banged the ceiling with the hanger. "You there, stop it!"

The noise paused but quickly started up again. Louder than before. As if a whole family of squirrels had decided to hold a sock hop overhead.

"Great," I muttered. *Bang, bang, bang!* "Out. Get out! Leave!"

My temper tantrum didn't work. The creatures leaped about with merry abandon.

"That's it!" I clambered off the chair and stomped to the window. The rain had ceased for the night. Storm clouds had exited. A sliver of a moon — God's thumbnail, Grandmère called it — glimmered overhead. I threw the window open and craned my neck to look for the site where the interlopers had invaded my home and spied a tile missing above the dormer window. I would bet dimes to dollars that was the point of entry. Tomorrow I'd insert a smoke bomb to drive out the rodents. I didn't want to kill them; I just wanted them to think twice about holding a party in my house again.

Ducking back into the room, I nicked my head on the window frame. I swiveled to rub my forehead and grew as still as a dormouse because across the street, on the sidewalk opposite Lavender and Lace, stood a figure in a hooded raincoat. Was it Urso's deputy, the one he had posted outside the bed-and-breakfast to wait for Edsel's arrival? He didn't look nearly as tall or leggy as I remembered, and he didn't seem to be staring in the direction of the B&B. He looked like he was gazing at my window. A bolt of fear shot through me. Was it the same guy who was stalking Jacky? No, the stranger's body looked misshapen. Either he had his arms wrapped around himself to ward off the cold or he had a hump. Like Edsel. Did he mean to frighten me because I'd stuck my nose into his affairs one too many times? He claimed to have seen me going into Freddy's room. Did he know that I'd first sneaked into his and Dane's room? Was he figuring out a way into my house?

Fear swirled inside of me, gathering speed. I plastered my hand over my mouth to keep from screaming and peered harder. Something glinted near the stranger's mouth. Seconds later, the stranger threw the *something* to the ground. A cigarette butt maybe? I hadn't seen Edsel smoke, but Freddy was a smoker. I eyed the B&B. The light was on in Freddy's room. Someone his size was moving about behind the sheer curtain. Dancing the tango, solo? I took another peek at the stranger. He hadn't moved.

I scurried to my desk and pulled out the pair of binoculars that I used to bird-watch, but by the time I got the focus right for a view of the sidewalk, the stranger was gone.

Fear — stronger than before, if that were possible — pummeled my rib cage. Where had he disappeared to? Was he touring the property, hoping to break in?

I raced down the hall and rapped on Matthew's door. No answer. I rapped again. Louder.

He shuffled to the door and opened it a crack. His hair was tousled, eyes hangdog. I'd roused him from a deep sleep. "What's wrong?"

I explained, including the bit about seeing something glimmer by the stranger's face.

Like the hero I knew he was, Matthew's brain cleared quickly. He donned a robe and tennis shoes, fetched a flashlight from the drawer beside his bed, and hustled down the mahogany stairs in front of me. "Let's make sure the first-floor doors and windows are secure."

In less than two minutes, we toured the interior and made certain that the house was as tight as Tut's tomb. Next, we raced to the front door.

Matthew grabbed an umbrella from the brass stand and wielded it like a sword. "I'm going outside. Stay here."

"Not on your life. I'm coming with you."

Rags wailed from the landing.

"I'll return, fella," I promised. I hoped I wasn't lying.

Matthew switched on the flashlight, and together we checked out the exterior of the house. As far as we could tell, the stranger wasn't lurking in the bushes.

When we returned to the front stoop, Matthew said, "I think we're safe. The guy was probably just a passerby who'd stopped to light up."

"Wait. The cigarette butt —"

"— unless it was a doused match."

"Fine," I said, not meaning to sound exasperated. "If it was a cigarette butt, do you think we could determine the brand?"

Being a good sport, Matthew sped across the street. He stooped down and inspected something with his flashlight. He scooped it up and called out, "It's nothing. Just a Hershey's Kiss wrapper."

Hershey's Kisses were my favorite candy.

CHAPTER 26

The next morning, though the rain had fled, clouds filled the sky and a gray gloom hovered over Providence. Inside The Cheese Shop, however, spring had arrived. I had tweaked the display in the front window by circling a stack of golden wheels of cheese with spring-themed paper chicks and bunnies. The woman who managed Emerald Pastures had suggested I add a small aquarium filled with eggs, warmed by a heat lamp to lure new customers. Soon baby chicks would hatch. I didn't have to do a thing, she assured me. She would take care of the hatchlings, and at the appropriate time, move them to her farm.

I lined a white porcelain bowl with green raffia and handed it to Rebecca.

"My money's still on Winona," she said as she nested colored hard-boiled eggs and small wedges of plastic-wrapped cheese on top of the raffia. We'd been discussing yesterday's events for the last half hour.

"You think she was the stranger outside my house?"

"Freddy said Winona was an actress."

"She'd know how to dress up in costumes. Maybe Urso can prove it was her. Matthew took the candy wrapper to the precinct."

Rebecca snuffled. "It's got to be near impossible to get fingerprints off one of those little foil things, not to mention the fingerprint would have to be in the system. And remember what Urso said about getting DNA results? Weeks." She held up one of the bowls she had created and, with a sculptor's critical eye, tweaked the raffia. "Winona said Edsel asked for a couple thousand dollars. Why would he settle for such a paltry amount?"

"You're right," I said. "He must know she has more money."

"If I were blackmailing her, I would have asked for a hundred thousand. I think she's lying about being blackmailed."

Rebecca toured the shop and set the bowls we'd arranged among the jars of jams and boxes of crackers. I followed and placed a one-pound chocolate bunny beside each.

"I'll bet your grandmother would know if Winona was lying," Rebecca said. "She has that sixth sense. You should tell Urso to consult with her."

I chuckled. "Oh, yeah, that'd go over well." With exaggerated politeness, I said, " 'Urso, your instincts stink. My grandmother could do better.' Uh-uh, no way am I having that conversation."

I returned to the cheese counter and sliced open a wheel of Wisconsin Cheddar. As I drank in the scent of roasted nuts and hay, I remembered, as I often did, my first day behind the counter. It was a Friday. I was eleven, and Pépère handed me a knife. "Tend to the customer, *cherie*. Say '*Bon soir, what will it be?*' " We were playacting, of course. No customer stood before me. He coached me for hours. On Saturday, when he unleashed me on the real customers, our sales had risen dramatically. Pépère said it was because I had a passion for cheese.

"Charlotte." Rebecca took up her post beside me and nudged me with her hip. "Don't forget about the jewels. The killer placed jewels on the cellar floor as a sign that he knew about Julianne, which means if Winona isn't the killer, then it's Dane."

"Not so fast." I cut a wedge of the Cheddar. "Dane, or Harker himself, could have told Edsel or Freddy about the relationship with Julianne." I recalled Edsel taunting Dane outside the shop and twisting an imaginary key to his lips. Was blackmail the secret he'd ordered Dane to keep?

"You said you saw Freddy in his room dancing the tango at the time your stranger appeared last night."

"I saw someone milling around his room, but the angle was funky. For all I know it could have been Lois."

"Cleaning that late at night?"

"She is a neat-freak. Lois and her broom are mythic."

Rebecca nodded. "Quinn probably knew about Julianne. But I don't believe for a second she killed Harker. She's just too darned nice. Besides, he left Julianne for her."

"Hey, Miss B." Bozz poked his head in the front door.

"What're you doing here?" I said. "Don't you have school?"

"I forgot to print out my homework. It's on the computer in the office." He scuttled across the floor. "You mind?"

I smiled. "Give Rags a nuzzle."

"Will do." He disappeared, and not long after, I heard the printer whirring.

The grape-leaf-shaped chimes over the door jingled the entrance of our first customers of the day.

Pépère traipsed in after them carrying a

cup of coffee from the Country Kitchen. *"Votre grandmère est folle."* He twirled a finger beside his head signaling just how crazy she was. "Keep a wide berth. If it's all right, I'm going to the kitchen to do inventory."

I never said no to an offer like that. I hated doing inventory.

As he disappeared, Gretel Hildegard bustled into the store, her braids bouncing on her shoulders. "Hello, Charlotte. I know it's early, but I need a basket of good cheer for the church receptionist. She's taken ill."

"Not seriously, I hope."

"The flu. My dear husband is having a mini meltdown without her to do his bidding." She grinned. "Men. How about a selection of three cheeses? You'll deliver it, right?"

"Of course."

"How about that one with the ash?"

"Taleggio?"

"No, the other one."

"Morbier."

"That's it, and a half pound of the Guggisberg Baby Swiss for my hubby," Gretel added. "That's the cheese you told me about, right? The family that came to America from Switzerland."

"Good memory." Back in the 1960s, the

Guggisbergs settled in Charm, Ohio, because Amish farmers needed someone to preserve the milk from their cows, and the Guggisbergs wanted to create a Swiss cheese like the one they'd had in their homeland. It was called Baby Swiss because Mrs. Guggisberg said that, compared to regular Swiss cheeses, the wheels they'd created looked like babies. It was soft in texture with a buttery, yummy taste.

As I carved the Baby Swiss, the chimes jingled again and Meredith entered. With Quinn.

"Yahoo!" Rebecca clapped her hands. "She's free, Charlotte. Quinn's free."

Quinn looked like a frightened deer, ready to bolt if anyone in the shop, including me, approached her.

In contrast, Meredith looked elated, like she was dwelling on a cloud, and if she wasn't anchored, a stiff breeze might blow her to the neighboring county. I believed Quinn's release was the reason, until I saw something sparkling on the fourth finger of my friend's left hand. Despite all the upset with Sylvie this week, Matthew had asked Meredith to marry him. Hallelujah! Hope reigned supreme.

Meredith released Quinn and dashed to the counter. "We're engaged."

"I can see that." After an apology to Gretel and quick instructions to Rebecca to wrap up Gretel's order, I skirted around the counter to give my best friend a squeeze. "Congratulations."

"Matthew said that having Sylvie in town made him realize how much he loved me."

"Small favors." I grinned.

"And, to add to my joy" — Meredith returned to the front door, and folding an arm around her niece, ushered Quinn toward the rest of us — "our Quinnie has been released. Mr. Lincoln got her out on bail. After the to-do with Winona Westerton, I think Urso has his doubts. He didn't put up a fight."

"But he's reserving judgment," Quinn said, the pain in her voice palpable. Up close, she looked haggard, like she hadn't slept at all since her incarceration. "I didn't do it."

"We know you didn't, sweetheart." Meredith petted Quinn's arm. "I feel badly about being this happy, with everything that's going on, you know."

"Don't feel guilty," I said. "You deserve every ounce of happiness. Did you set a date?"

"Not yet. It's too soon for that. Is Matthew here?"

I shook my head.

"Oh, my. He's not facing off with Sylvie again, is he?"

"He's visiting clients."

"Thank heavens."

"Speaking of Sylvie, have you seen her?" I asked.

"Missing in action. I hope she's slithered under the log she crawled out from."

Gretel giggled. "Meredith," she said in a mock-reproachful tone.

Meredith laughed, too.

"So how did Matthew propose?" Rebecca asked.

While Meredith described how Matthew took her to the wishing well at the center of the Village Green and got down on one knee, a sense of foreboding niggled its way into my mind. Had something happened to Sylvie? She'd acted quite desperate yesterday. As impulsive as she was, had she gone back to the Ziegler Winery to search for the treasure and met with an accident? Should authorities be alerted? I was about ready to dial Urso when I spotted an acid-white-haired woman in an ocelot coat exiting the boutique across the street, her arms loaded with bags. Prudence followed her out, handed her a small one, and blew her an air kiss. What was up with that? The bags Jordan had seen Sylvie carrying might have been empty, but these definitely weren't. The drag on Sylvie's arms was unmistakable.

My mouth fell open. Matthew had canceled his credit cards. No way could Sylvie have used them. She'd flat-out lied. She wasn't broke. Not in the least.

"Got it!" Bozz trotted out of the office, sheets of paper in his hand. "See you later."

Spying Bozz at the same time as Sylvie gave me an idea. Naughty, impulsive, but necessary. I snagged him and steered him to the archway between the wine annex and the shop. "Bozz, before you go, do me a favor. Go back to the computer and check out Sylvie's parents on the Internet. Find out what their financial situation is, if you can. Ascertain whether she's lying about them going belly up. If she's lying about that, she could be lying about a host of other things." Like why she had been checking out the winery.

"Last name?" Bozz asked.

"Jamison. Jamison and Gemma Jamison."

He snorted. "Can't be too many of those."

"J.J. to his friends."

"I'm on it." Bozz jogged back to the office.

"Charlotte," Meredith said. "Matthew

wanted us to share the news with the twins today. How do you think they will react?"

I rejoined the group by the cheese counter. "I'm sure they'll be ecstatic." I would make doubly certain that they were.

"Ladies, I need to get back to the church." As Gretel spirited away with a gold bag swinging on her arm, Delilah pranced into the shop wearing a bunny costume and waving flyers over her head.

I flipped a hand over my mouth to keep from bursting out in laughter. "Oh, my gosh. Have you glanced in a mirror?" At best, Delilah looked like a forlorn clown bunny at a circus. The whiskers sticking out of her plastic pink nose were nearly poking out her eyeballs, and the floppy ears, well, flopped.

Delilah glowered at me.

"Why are you wearing that silly getup?" I asked.

"It's a marketing ploy." She thrust her chin in the air. "May I post these on your windows? Our ticket sales are down. Your window display is drawing interest."

Indeed, a crowd of children and parents had gathered to watch the eggs mature, even though all of them were crackless. Watching water boil would be more exciting, in my humble opinion, but I wouldn't turn away potential customers. If even ten percent came inside, the display had succeeded.

"If we post these on the front door, we'll get some action." Delilah thrust them into my hand. "Please? You'll be at opening night, right?"

"Wouldn't miss it." I set the posters by the cash register. I'd hang them later.

"I've got to run." Delilah glanced at Quinn, nodded a hello, and then pushed her whiskers away from her eyes and took a better look. "It's you. You're out!" She eyed me. "Ask her about the brick wall."

One thing I could say about my energy-charged friend was that she didn't have a subtle bone in her body. Perhaps that was why Delilah and Grandmère had hit it off. She hippety-hopped out of the shop, sticking a theater notice on the door before skipping east.

"What about the brick wall?" Quinn shifted feet.

"We think the brick wall that was in the winery cellar was new," I said, speaking softly, treading lightly. "We think the murderer built it."

"Why?"

"As a metaphor," Rebecca said.

Quinn's face turned stony — my kind of

lying face — probably thinking that if she held it steady, nobody would sense that she knew something. I stared at her, intent on making her uncomfortable. Finally, her shoulders gave way. "Chief Urso asked me if I built it," she said. "I told him I didn't. I'm as inept as my father. I glue my fingers together with a glue gun. I can paint. That's all I can do."

"Did you know your father had purchased bricks?" I said.

"We all knew. Dad came back from winter break and told us the whole sorry story. He starts so many projects that he doesn't finish." She sighed, and in that sigh, I sensed a daughter's lifelong embarrassment. "That was when we started planning the field trip here."

"What about the jewels?" I asked.

"What jewels?"

"There were jewels strewn around Harker's body."

"We think those were metaphorical, too," Rebecca chimed in.

"I didn't see any jewels," Quinn said, her voice thin with panic. "I didn't see anything. Why were there jewels? Did somebody find the treasure? Did Harker? Was that why he was killed?"

Meredith wrapped a protective arm

around her shivering niece and explained about Harker's former fiancée, Julianne. "Whoever killed him might have been pointing out Harker's mistreatment of Julianne."

Quinn glared at each of us, as if we were a panel of Salem elders and she was the innocent witch being burned at the stake. "I didn't do it!"

"We know you didn't," I said. Despite her anxiety, I needed to coax the full story from her. "But you knew about Julianne, didn't you?"

With a growl, Quinn shook off Meredith. "Harker said she was a nutcase."

"You never met her?" I asked.

"Never!"

"But you were angry about him giving you her ring," I said.

She glanced at her empty fourth finger. "She might have been crazy, but Harker was obsessed with her. He painted her. All the time. Even after she was dead. When I called him on it, he said it was his fault she was dead."

"That's why he wanted to break it off with you," Rebecca said.

Quinn nodded. "Harker said he was damaged and I deserved better. I told him I didn't, but he blew me off. I flirted with the other guys to make him jealous. He got mad, all right. He called me a . . ." She fluttered her hand in front of her face. "That's when I threw the ring at him." She sobbed into her palms. "Oh, no, no, no. He's dead because of me."

Meredith wrapped her in her arms. "Sweetheart, it's not your fault."

But it was someone's fault. Someone had killed Harker. Someone who knew about the bricks as well as about Julianne. Any of the students. Freddy. Winona.

Meredith gazed helplessly at me. I screwed up my mouth as an apology and suggested she take Quinn into the annex. As they trundled off, hunched together like a team in a wobbly three-legged race, the front door opened again.

"Charlotte," Jordan called.

I grinned, more than pleased to see my hunky boyfriend strut through the door. A sexy sheen of perspiration clung to his face and neck. As he drew near, I detected the scent of freshly mown hay.

"Tending to the cows?" I teased.

"Do I smell bad?"

"You smell incredibly good."

He kissed me on the cheek, and unbridled thoughts of the two of us tumbling around a hayloft swept through my mind.

"Um, Charlotte?" Rebecca toyed with her

ponytail. "Why don't I whip up a batch of champagne fondue to put out on the tasting counter, okay?" She didn't wait for my answer. She retreated to the kitchen.

Thankful for the privacy, I cozied up to Jordan. "Where've you been hiding?" The second the words fell out of my mouth, I wished I could scoop them back in. I didn't want him to think I was keeping tabs on him. But I missed seeing him and hearing his yummy voice in person.

"Tending to business. A couple farms to the north are thinking of selling."

"And you're going to expand?"

He quirked a smile.

I wondered how a man who was trying to stay incognito could do so if he became the wealthiest landowner in Holmes County, but I kept mute. It wasn't my business, right?

"Yipes!" Bozz yelled from the office. He tore out and cut around the cheese counter. "I just saw the time, Miss B. Sorry, but I've got to go. I left the search you requested open on the computer." He flew out of the shop.

"What search?" Jordan said.

"Into Sylvie's financial claims."

Jordan tapped my nose. "You are becoming an A-One snoop."

"I'll take that as a compliment."

"Bozz has certainly gotten more handsome in the last year," Jordan said. "He's going to break hearts one of these days."

"Or get his broken." I explained that he had a crush on brainiac Philby Jebbs. "You know her father, don't you?"

"In passing." Jordan ran a finger down my sleeve. "Now, let's talk about this man stalking Jacky."

"Outside." I threw on a sweater and led Jordan into the co-op garden behind the store. I paced in front of the bench at the far end of the garden. Jordan stood at one end, arms hanging at his sides.

"Describe the guy," he said.

I did. "When I left the pottery store to confront him, he ran."

"And you chased him?"

"I lost him at the church. He must have hopped the fence."

"What did you expect to do if you'd caught him? Were you prepared to take him down? Prepared to fight off his counterattack?" He stopped me from pacing and grabbed my shoulders, his gaze dark with concern. "What am I going to do with you?"

I had a list. A very steamy list.

He kissed me firmly and pulled me into a warm embrace. He stroked my hair and kissed my forehead. "Charlotte, Charlotte." He held me at arm's length. "You can't be so rash when it comes to your own safety."

"But I was worried that it might've been Jacky's husband."

"No way." He shook his head. "For one thing, her husband would never dress in a B-movie detective outfit. For another thing, his colleagues are typically larger than the man you described."

"Are they still husband and wife?"

"In former name only."

"What does her husband do?" I said. "You haven't told me."

"It's better if you don't know."

"Come on. I've kept Jacky's secret safe. I haven't told a soul."

His eyes narrowed. "If you must know, he's a very powerful lawyer."

With large colleagues. Did he represent a sumo wrestling gym? Fight obesity? Did he hire only associates who were larger than himself because he was as big as Jabba the Hut?

"And you? Who are you?" I asked, hoping I could catch him off guard.

"A man with no power."

"But you had power once upon a time."

"Never." He paused. A cloud of uncertainty suffused his face. As quickly as it appeared, it disappeared. "I never had power," he said, his voice controlled.

I snuggled up to him. "You've got to let me in. Tell me something more about you. Who are you? Why should I trust you? I think I'm falling in love with you, but there's a piece of me holding back because I'm afraid of you."

"You never have to be afraid of me." He ran his knuckles gently along my jaw.

I melted. "At least tell me how you learned about cheese."

"A Frenchman taught me."

I pulled away. "Very funny."

"That's the truth."

If it was the truth, had I ever met his teacher in my travels? Had Pépère? Jordan eyed me with an impish gleam. I knew him well enough to know that I would get no more. Not today. I would have to be satisfied with that teensy shred of a clue.

"Back to Jacky," Jordan said. "Don't worry about the guy in the fedora. I think I know who he is."

"Who? I've never seen him before."

"He's from two counties over. He just signed on at the Quail Ridge Honeybee Farm."

"Why did he run away from me?"

"He's sort of simple, you know? I don't

think he realizes that hanging around Jacky isn't cool. He's got a little crush on her." He laughed. "But who doesn't? Including Urso."

"Chief Urso? Umberto Urso? You're kidding. Really?"

There went my theory that Urso was interested in me. I wasn't upset, just curious.

"It's rather obvious," Jordan said.

Not to me. Not to my grandmother, who would be shocked that she had missed the clues.

"He's always making excuses to stroll by her shop and peek in the window," Jordan said.

And here I thought he was always dropping into Fromagerie Bessette to have a chat with me. Talk about being a little narcissistic. Sheesh!

Jordan scratched his chin. "Though I'm not sure he'll be as interested once he finds out Jacky's pregnant."

CHAPTER 27

"Pregnant?" I slumped onto the bench in the co-op garden and gazed at the birds searching for worms. Being pregnant would explain why Jacky had been crying at the diner and why she'd looked so tired at her pottery store. Except the timing was all off. I glanced at Jordan. "How can she be pregnant? It can't be her husband's. She's been here nine months, and she's certainly not showing." My mouth fell open as Jordan's last statement clanged in my head. "Is it Urso's?"

"No." Jordan sat beside me and took my hand in his. "The father isn't anyone you know."

"He doesn't live here in town?"

"He's not here at all."

"I don't understand."

"The father of the baby died."

I gasped.

Jordan perched beside me on the bench

408

and took my hand in his. He caressed it with his thumb. "I told you that Jacky's husband was abusive. Ultimately, she looked elsewhere for affection and fell in love with another man. She and her lover were going to run away together, but he died."

So much mystery and sadness surrounded Jacky. My next thought made my breath catch in my chest. "Did her husband . . . murder him?"

"No, he had a car accident."

"A real accident or staged?"

Jordan chuckled. "That Rebecca has really done a number on you. You see conspiracies in everything. He was hit by a drunk driver, who died, too."

"How horrible."

"I made plans to move them both here, but —"

"I still don't understand. He died before Jacky moved here? Then how could she be pregnant with his child?" Before he responded, the answer came to me. Jacky and her lover had planned for the future. "They banked his sperm in the event her husband did something dastardly to her lover, right?"

He nodded. "They didn't have a clue that fate would intervene. She's dealing with it. And though she's feeling a little sick to her stomach, she's excited about having a baby."

"Wait a minute. She's not fully divorced, is she? She must be terrified that her husband will find her and claim the child is his."

Jordan squeezed my hand. "We've taken pains to make sure the paternity is documented. Besides, her ex —"

"Her husband."

"He won't find her. Her past is over."

Tacit in his tone was the fact that his past was over, as well. Would I ever know who he was or who he had been? Was I ready to take a leap of faith and trust that he was a good guy and not a made man?

Listen to you, Charlotte. A made man? You've seen The Godfather *one too many times.*

Jordan traced my jawbone with his finger.

"What?" I said, my insides growing hot with longing.

"I adore you and your good heart."

He kissed me, full-throttle, and out of nowhere, I heard imaginary violins and pictured the two of us walking along a moonlit country lane.

When we took a breather, he said, "I hope that was okay."

"Better than okay."

And yet I felt so conflicted. I was happy for Jacky yet sorry for her at the same time.

I felt guilty that I had found love when she had lost it, but I was also exhilarated, because only a year ago, I'd believed my chances of falling in love with a fabulous, albeit mysterious, man were slim to nil.

Jordan pressed me to him, my hands to his chest, and kissed me again. Deeply. Passionately. His heart pounded beneath my palms.

When we broke apart this time, a smidgen of fear crept back into my psyche. I said, "Are you sure about the guy in the fedora?"

"Yes. Don't see evil in every nook and cranny. It doesn't suit you." He tapped my forehead with his finger. "Neither does that frown."

I didn't know I was frowning.

"I'll check on my sister. Happy?"

"Ecstatic."

"Good. Now go inside. It's cold out here." He pecked my cheek then rose from the bench.

As he strolled past the hothouse toward the street, I found myself humming a deliciously wicked tune.

I returned to the shop and was surprised to see my grandmother sitting at the cheese-tasting counter, a tiny pot of fondue in front of her, a basket of bread chunks nearby. She dipped a piece of bread into the pot and ate hungrily.

Rebecca jerked a thumb at the kitchen and held a finger to her mouth. Apparently Grandmère hadn't discovered that Pépère was doing inventory in the kitchen.

I suppressed a smile. Ah, the secrets we kept in the name of peace. "Where's Meredith?"

"She and Quinn went to find Freddy. You know, I couldn't help thinking again about that Winona Westerton. Stealing Harker Fontanne's portraits of her sister wouldn't be enough to satisfy her."

I chuckled. "You're a psychology expert now?"

"House would say —"

"House? As in Gregory House from the TV show? You're quoting a fictional character?"

She shot daggers at me. "House would say Winona had a deep-seated need for vengeance."

"But someone else might have an equally strong motive." If only I knew what it was.

"*Chérie,* hello!" Grandmère beckoned me with a piece of cheese-drenched bread between thumb and forefinger. Her gloomy face struck a chord. What was wrong?

I patted Rebecca's arm. "We'll continue our discussion later, okay? In the meantime, why don't you put together the gift basket for the church receptionist." I sauntered around the counter and kissed my grandmother on the cheek. The black peasant blouse she wore over her leggings sapped the color from her face.

"Give me some consolation," Grandmère said as she eyed the ladder-back chair beside her.

I perched on the chair. "Why do you need consoling?"

"After last night's tech rehearsal, our play received a bad review on the Internet."

"Grandmère, you know that you don't give a hoot about reviews. You never have."

"This time . . ." She shook a finger.

"You already had a good review. Why did you need another?"

"I am a fool. She said she liked avant-garde plays, but I think she was plotting against us. This review is harrowing." She pulled a piece of paper from her pocket and flapped it at me. "See what she says about our leading man."

I took it and read: *Barton Burrell, the star who is a farmer by day, has the emotional depth of one of his cows. Throw in an inappropriate amount of moaning and the performance was bucolic, at best.*

"So she didn't like an actor, big deal."

"*Non!* Read on . . . about the playwright." She stabbed the paper.

I dragged my gaze down the page and read: *The playwright believes she's hit upon a novel idea, but she mixes her metaphors like a hack. Poe does not belong in a Sartre play. Give up and get out of show business, lady.*

"Of all the gall!" I blurted.

Grandmère snatched back the review and stowed it in her crocheted satchel. "Delilah might never write again. She is devastated."

Delilah hadn't seemed at all worried when she'd come into the shop earlier in her bunny costume, but then she was an actress. A very good actress. "She'll come around," I said, hopeful that I was right. "And your regulars are open-minded, savvy theatergoers. They'll adore the play."

"I am not so sure." Grandmère grabbed both of my hands. "Please. I am having an impromptu rehearsal right now. Will you come? We need your objective opinion."

I felt honored that she would even consider asking me, but I couldn't. "We're a little short-handed this afternoon."

"No, you are not." Pépère popped from the kitchen. "I am here. I could not help overhearing your dilemma."

I squelched a smile. He'd probably been leaning against the kitchen wall, straining to hear every word.

"Go, Charlotte," he said. "Rebecca and I will see to the customers. Your grandmother needs you."

And you need a little time away from the craziness at the theater, I thought. I kissed his cheek.

Rebecca, who was busy preparing a lacy basket of cheeses, jams, and crackers, winked at me and gave me a signal that she had everything under control.

I glanced at the office, eager to learn what Bozz had dredged up on Sylvie's parents, but Grandmère tugged on my sleeve.

"Please, *mon amie,* it is life or death."

Okay, now she was being a little overdramatic, but who was I to argue?

When we arrived at the Providence Playhouse, the black-box theater was semi-dark. In the dim light, I made out crew people with paintbrushes and paint cans scurrying along the fringes of the stage, dabbing and fixing. The aroma of turpentine permeated the air.

Delilah, no longer in her bunny outfit, bristled with manic energy as she and the stout stage manager with the burgundy hair roamed the stage checking light cues.

"Cue seventy-seven," the stage manager

yelled. "Go."

A rose-colored light illuminated the statue of the raven.

"Excellent," Delilah said and headed upstage. "Moving on."

"Cue seventy-eight," the stage manager shouted as she wrote a note on a pad.

Grandmère said, "Sit with the others in the audience, *chérie.*"

Five people, whom I recognized as cast members' family, occupied the last row of the theater.

"We will start in minutes." Grandmère handed me a program then sashayed to the stage and clapped her hands. "Everyone, come together. Form a circle. *Tout de suite!* Delilah, set aside the lights for a moment. It is time for good vibes." As crew and cast gathered around her, Grandmère grabbed hands with the people on either side of her. Each, in turn, grasped a neighbor's hand until the circle of *good vibes* was complete. "Remember," Grandmère said. "Edgar Allan Poe said, 'Those who dream by day are cognizant of many things that escape those who dream only at night.' We are daydreamers. Never forget."

I nestled into one of the loge chairs in the front row and opened the glossy pages of the program. On the left-side page was an explanation of the settings: *Massachusetts and Maryland,* as well as an explanation of the play. *No Exit is about the inscrutable gaze of others and how constant attention restricts one's freedom. The characters will constantly look for mirrors in order to avoid the judgment of the other characters. Our one-act play will use this template to explore Edgar Allan Poe's life.*

The right-side page displayed the biographies and photographs of the actors, none of whom were professionals. The piano teacher and the hair stylist had appeared in more than twenty productions between them. Barton Burrell, the local farmer who was playing Poe and was panned by the reviewer for his bucolic performance, had appeared in dozens of plays. In his bio, he thanked his wife and sons for allowing him to pursue his passion at night.

Something about Barton's picture struck me as odd. I stared at it for a long moment. It wasn't the same old picture I'd seen in previous programs. In this one, he wore a baseball cap with his farm logo. I couldn't blame him for trying to get a little free advertising out of the production. The actors received only a nominal amount of money to perform. Gas money, Grandmère called it. That was typical around the United

States for any production that wasn't run by the Actors' Equity Association. But it wasn't Barton's cap that bothered me, and it wasn't his nose, which was big and prominent. I tilted my head and realized that his teeth were different. In real life, he had a cavernous gap between the top two teeth. In the photograph, they were smooth and perfect. If he'd added a beard, I wouldn't have recognized him at all. Vanity wins out, I thought and chuckled. I'd have to give him a little grief. Barton had never come across as narcissistic. Quite the opposite.

"We're starting." Grandmère clapped her hands. "Places."

Lights dimmed. Three actors convened on the stage, each taking a seat on a different striped sofa. The lights came up in a gray, tepid hue, and then switched to a bright, burning orange, which I assumed was symbolic for hell.

Barton, wearing a rumpled shirt, raggedy suit, and unpolished shoes — an outfit that, according to a footnote in the program, Poe had worn on the night of his death — sat hunched on a ruby red sofa. He rubbed his scruffy face and grunted as he rose to his feet. Somberly he approached the statue. "Once upon a midnight dreary, while I pondered, weak and weary," he began, quoting from Poe's "The Raven." "I took a look inside my soul and hated what I saw," he continued, diverging from the poem. It was the twist that my grandmother had promised. Delilah had used Sartre's theme without using his words directly.

Through the opening monologue, the female characters listened with rapt attention, but when Barton finished, they leapt upon him with ferocity. Verbally they tore him to pieces for making a mess of his life.

Barton — Poe — denied that he had and draped himself on the statue of the raven. "Open here I flung the shutter, when, with many a flirt and flutter, in there stepped a stately raven of the saintly days of yore."

The women peeled him away from the statue and assailed him with more invectives.

I glanced at my grandmother, who stood to the right of me, leaning against a wall, her hand cradling her throat. As each character spoke, she mouthed the words. She would know every one by heart.

As I continued to watch the performance, I pondered what the reviewer had written. Barton wasn't moaning. He wasn't even over-emoting. He was delivering an impassioned plea for help. Over the course of the one-act production, Delilah led the characters through conversations of suicide, betrayal, drug addiction, and lost love. No decisive commentary was made about Poe's death. Delilah had left his mysterious demise open to speculation. But in the end, I decided that Delilah's playwriting ability would stand the test of an audience.

Grandmère and Delilah rushed to question me. What did I think? Did I like it? How were the actors?

I said, "Stop worrying. The play, no matter what the reviewer says, is going to be a success. And you, Delilah, are a talent. The reviewer was mistaken."

Delilah blushed.

"You will write many more plays, my friend," I assured her.

"Who said I wouldn't?"

Grandmère clucked her tongue.

"You-u-u-u." Delilah shook a finger at my grandmother. "You thought I'd give up because of one review? How little you know me."

We all laughed.

"Got time for a soda?" Delilah pinched my elbow, a clue that she needed to talk. Privately.

"Sure."

I kissed my grandmother goodbye. Over

her shoulder, I saw Barton, cleaned up, his face scrubbed, his white shirt crisp beneath his overalls. He was talking to his wife, who had been in the audience. I considered razzing him about his photograph in the program but stopped short. Something still bothered me. Not about Barton. About Harker Fontanne's murder.

I couldn't pinpoint the connection.

CHAPTER 28

Cheery rock-and-roll music blurred the chatter of tourists and locals in the Country Kitchen. The gloomy skies of earlier had vanished, and the late afternoon sun's rays blazed through the windows. I sat in a red booth with Delilah, our purses on the banquette between us. She inserted another blue-cheese-smothered French fry into her mouth, having insisted on a snack to carry her through the grueling opening weekend of her play, and I did the same, though I tried to restrain myself. I really did.

"About the review," she said, as she licked her fingertips.

"Hold it," I said. "Are you really upset about it? Did you lie to me back at the theater?"

"I'm a little upset." She clicked her tongue. "Okay, I'm a lot upset."

"And I thought you wanted to talk about your love life or something. Shoot. I was ready for gossip." I mock-frowned then leaned forward. "Listen up, all kidding aside. You can't believe reviews. Good or bad. Remember that one Fromagerie Bessette received last year? You told me to discount it. It was only one person's opinion. Your reassuring words pulled me out of the doldrums."

Delilah believed Prudence Hart had paid the woman to write the ghastly review. Honestly, I couldn't ever remember the woman visiting The Cheese Shop, and I had a memory, not only for labels and cheeses, but for names and faces as well.

"I guess I have first-time-playwright jitters," Delilah said.

"Well, get over them!"

"Okay, okay!" She laughed.

I sipped my cream soda, relishing the thick foamy head and natural vanilla flavor. The Bozzuto Winery, in addition to wine, made natural sodas that tasted like dessert. The Country Kitchen had been the first place to offer them in Holmes County.

"On another note, what was up with Meredith yesterday?" Delilah asked. "Before rehearsal, I stopped in the diner and saw all of you getting your to-go dinners. Meredith's face was splotchy. She looked a wreck. Is Sylvie causing more chaos?"

Sylvie. A notion swirled around in my mind.

"I never considered her," I mumbled.

"Huh?"

"Could Sylvie have been the stranger on the sidewalk?"

"What stranger? What sidewalk? When?"

I glanced at my puzzled friend. "Outside my house." I remembered the Internet search that was waiting for me at The Cheese Shop. What if Sylvie had lied about her parents' financial woes? What if there was a link between Harker Fontanne and Sylvie? What if she thought I'd discovered what that link was? "I've got to go." I scrambled out of the booth.

"Wait!" Delilah caught up with me by the coat rack. "Is someone stalking you like he's stalking Jacky?"

"No one's stalking Jacky." As I shrugged into my tweed jacket, I gave Delilah a quick recap of Jordan's explanation for the guy in the fedora.

"Well, that makes me breathe a little easier," she said. "Now, what about this stranger outside your window? Why would you think it was Sylvie?"

I told her my iffy theory.

Delilah's head bobbed in rhythm to my words, as if I were making sense. "She knows you eat Hershey's Kisses. The killer likes leaving little symbolic clues. If Sylvie is the killer, she could have left that wrapper as a warning."

Chills cascaded down my back.

"Are you going to confront her?"

"Not without proof." I hugged Delilah goodbye and told her to break a leg.

As I darted from the diner, I heard her say, "Be careful."

When I entered The Cheese Shop, three customers waited in line at the counter. Rebecca was offering tastings of Pace Hill Farm's Double Cream Gouda. I skirted behind her and headed for the office but stopped when Pépère whistled from the kitchen doorway.

"*Chérie,* come here." His face was flushed with concern. "I'm afraid I have bad news. It's about Quinn."

My pulse was already doing a hop-skip-jump. I skidded to a stop. "Is she hurt?"

"She has been arrested again. Urso discovered a letter she wrote to Harker about Julianne. In it she wrote that she wished Harker would choke on his inflated ego."

Oh, my. How incriminating, seeing as Harker was strangled. And yet I still didn't believe Quinn was guilty. She couldn't be. But how could I convince Urso?

Pépère gestured toward the annex, where Matthew cradled a crying Meredith in his arms.

At the sight of them, my heart grew as tight as if it had been shrink-wrapped. I had to help Meredith. If I could prove that Sylvie was involved . . .

I kissed my grandfather and started again for the office. Before I'd gone three paces, the front door opened and Prudence Hart marched in.

"Charlotte, stop this instant!"

Why should I? I continued toward the office.

"Charlotte, please stop."

The *please* caught me off guard. I hesitated.

"I want a word with you." Raising her left arm overhead, Prudence strode through the shop and behind the counter as if she owned the place. She wore a green charmeuse cocktail dress — totally inappropriate for the temperature. In her hand she clutched something that resembled a torch. The Statue of Liberty couldn't have looked any more righteous.

On closer inspection, I could see Prudence's torch was a sheaf of rolled-up papers. Flyers. The ones she had been posting around town.

"Truce," she said.

My mouth opened. I snapped it shut. Didn't a truce require two sides being at war? I hadn't done a thing to counteract her initial assault other than offer not to shop in her store if she stayed out of mine.

"I do not need your friends saying bad things about me," she said. "Don't deny it. They're insinuating that I'm crazy."

"Who?" I sputtered.

"Tyanne, for one."

I bit the inside of my cheek to keep from laughing. Prudence shouldn't have lambasted Tyanne's little boy. When challenged, a mother bear always defended her cub. I said, "Anyone else?"

"That Sylvie Bessette, too."

Oooh, interesting. Sylvie had switched allegiances.

"I want a truce." Prudence thrust the flyers at me and offered a conciliatory, alligator-with-a-sour-stomach grin.

Something about her smile made me pause. I gaped at her teeth. They were so straight and smooth. I flashed on the picture of Barton Burrell in the theater program and realized what had bothered me about it. "Prudence, you were in here the other day."

"I'm allowed to roam our fair city," she hissed.

"Time out." I formed a T with my hands. "You mentioned how upset you were with the college people visiting the museum."

"Riffraff."

"You said they were scruffy. Did one have a beard?" I remembered thinking that I wouldn't have recognized Barton if he'd had a beard in his photograph. Not that I believed Barton was one of the riffraff. I was focused on Sylvie.

"If that's what you'd call it." Prudence instinctively stroked her chin. "It was so thin and sparse it looked fake."

"Could one of these so-called riffraff have been a woman?"

"I guess so."

I pictured Sylvie at the black-box theater, on the night of the murder, prancing about the stage dressed as Fagin.

"The other was shorter, sort of hunched," Prudence added.

"You said that they tracked in snow. We don't have snow right now."

"It was during the winter. January, I believe."

And Prudence was still upset about it? I let that slide.

"By the way," she went on. "Why were

they here in January?"

Why, exactly.

I recalled the tourist who had come into the shop in January — long hair, scruffy beard, wide nose. At the time, he'd struck me as a little odd, standing hunched over like he was tall and trying to be smaller. He'd snagged a slice of Morbier from the cheese-tasting counter, but he hadn't purchased anything. Was it one of the riffraff Prudence had seen? Was it the same person who had stood on the sidewalk outside my house? Was it really a man? He hadn't spoken. He'd loitered and left. Sylvie said that she'd read about Meredith's intent to convert the winery to a college way back in December. Had she come to town in January and disguised herself as a man to — as Rebecca would say — case the joint? On the night of the winery event, had Harker stumbled upon Sylvie while she was looking for treasure? To cover her tracks, had she strangled him? I still couldn't fathom a reason for her to build a brick wall, but I pushed that detail from my mind. For all I knew, the bricks could have been filched from Meredith's by a team of high school hellions and the wall built as a prank.

I said, "I've got work to do, Prudence. Nice talking to you."

"What about our truce?"

Impulsively I pecked her cheek. "Truce, yes, fine. We've got a truce."

She fanned herself with the flyers.

Once inside the office, I nudged Rags to the back of the desk chair. He waited until I was settled, then tiptoed around me, nestled into my lap, and yowled his *pet me, pet me now* sound. Like a well-trained human, I obeyed.

While stroking him, I hit the return button on the computer keyboard. The monitor came to life. At the top of a series of Internet searches was a *London Evening Standard* article Bozz had pulled up. Eager to see if Sylvie was in Providence in January, I read it word for word. As it turned out, not only had Sylvie not lied about her parents being broke, but during the entire month of January, she had been by their side in court. There were photographs of her and public statements outlining her deals with creditors. She wouldn't have had a spare moment to fly across the Atlantic to visit Providence. Despite my dislike of her, I was relieved to learn that the twins' mother was not a murderer.

Exhausted and ready to close up shop, knowing my time would be better spent comforting Meredith, I clicked on the X at the upper-right corner of the Internet page. Beneath it were layers of other Internet search pages. I groaned. What was I going to do with Bozz? I hoped I wouldn't stumble upon any teenage boy searches that might make me blush.

The first was Bozz's genealogy project that he was doing with Philby. So were the next two. The Jebbses had come from Derby, England, and the Bozzutos had come from Castelpagano in Italy. There was no possible connection between the two families. Lucky Bozz.

A few pages later, I came upon Bozz's discovery about Dane and Edsel's volunteer work with Habitat for Humanity. A photograph of the students involved in the project appeared in the center of the page. Dane and Edsel stood together, each carrying tools and layered with perspiration. I halted, my finger hovering over the X that would close the page as I remembered something Prudence had said. One of the scruffy riffraff who had come to town in January was hunched. Had Edsel Nash and Dane made a trek to Providence together? They were rooming together at Lavender and Lace. They did volunteer work as a team. Edsel said they had been the first two to enroll in the art class.

Or better yet, had Dane come to town with someone else and pretended to be Edsel? That would have been the sly thing to do. Although he was smooth-faced, I remembered thinking a few days ago that, with a little makeup, he might look like Johnny Depp in *Pirates of the Caribbean.* Scruffy. Had he plotted Harker's death back in January? Given his volunteer experience, he could have learned how to put together a brick wall.

I replayed a conversation between the students at the onset of the event at the winery. To defuse Harker's anger at Bozz, Dane had suggested they take a tour of the mansion. He told Harker that he'd heard the layout was cool. When Harker asked how he knew that, Dane replied that his parents were Ohio architecture buffs. What if he had lied about that to cover up the fact that he was personally intimate with the winery's structure? Except at the pub, when a group of us were discussing that the wall looked new, Dane hadn't played it down. He'd reiterated that his parents knew the ins and outs of the structure. Had he hoped his openness would deflect suspicion from him?

I flashed on something else. The stranger who had come into The Cheese Shop in

January had tasted the Morbier. The first day that Freddy and the students had visited Fromagerie Bessette, Dane had asked for Morbier. It was an unusual request.

As I moved my finger, ready to close the Internet page, I paused yet again, my gaze riveted by the picture of volunteers. I zeroed in on Dane. As I peered at his somber face, I stiffened. I'd seen eyes like his before. In a portrait. At the Ziegler Winery. Zachariah Ziegler's eyes and his son's eyes were like Dane's. Deep-set and dark.

Could it be? Was Dane a Ziegler?

I worked through the theory. He said he was from New York, but he also said his parents were originally from Ohio. In the 1950s, Ziegler's daughter Cecilia had moved to New York. Had she married someone named Cegielski? Dane would be about the right age to be her grandson.

A genealogy search like Bozz's was in order. I typed the name *Cecilia Ziegler* into a Google search line, added a plus sign, and typed *ancestry.* Up came Zachariah and his wife as Cecilia's parents. Cecilia married in the 1960s, but like many hippies, she kept the maiden name of Ziegler. She bore one child, whom she named Zeb. She died in the 1970s. There was no mention of anyone named Cegielski.

I typed *Dane Cegielski* into a search line. Over two hundred thousand Cegielski references emerged. The first specific one for Dane Cegielski was the same article that Bozz had found about volunteering for Habitat for Humanity. I was ready to dig deeper, when I noticed another article, about halfway down the first page of search items, that read: *Cegielski: surname.* The first line of the article: *Cegielski, in Polish, means tiler or bricklayer.*

The killer liked leaving clues. Had Dane built the wall to telegraph that he was the killer?

Fingertips tingling with excitement, I double-clicked the article and couldn't believe what I found. According to the website, during the Middle Ages, as people moved north, surnames adapted to the languages of the people. *Cegielski,* a Polish name, became *Ziegler* in Germany. Was Dane the grandson of Cecilia Ziegler? The son of Zeb? Had he changed his name to Cegielski to hide his identity? Had he come to the winery to claim the treasure that he believed was rightfully his?

I typed *Dane Ziegler* plus *ancestry* into a Google search. A host of articles appeared. One made my teeth tingle. Dane's mother had committed suicide. The journalist who wrote the article noted that Dane's great-grandmother had committed suicide after killing her son. The journalist added that, of course, a history of insanity could not be concluded because Dane's mother was not a Ziegler. But the coincidence was bizarre.

I sat back in the chair, my breathing shallow, certain that Dane killed Harker. But why? I couldn't chalk it up to mere family insanity. By my estimation, there was a tremendous amount of premeditation. One: Dane came to town in January. He stole the bricks in small increments — possible because snowfall had hidden the theft. Two: He built the wall. Three: On the night of the event, Dane toyed with Quinn. He tried to get her to taste the fondue. He must have known about her allergy. He purposely dripped cheese on the scarf, hoping she'd abandon it. All along, he planned to use her scarf in the murder. Four: He placed fake jewels around Harker. That was the capper. If they'd been real because he'd been searching for treasure, I could have seen Dane leaving them in haste. But the jewels were fake. That made them significant. I believe they represented Harker's ex-fiancée: Jules. Dane had known about her.

A tremor of anxiety shot through me as I realized Dane could have been the stranger who had stood outside my house. He might have thought that I had put two and two together. He would have been wrong, of course, unless he believed I'd seen something when I'd stolen through his room to get to Freddy's — something linking him to Harker's murder.

Rags yowled his *I'm starved* squall.

I scratched his ears and whispered, "Good idea. I'll take you home and feed you. Then I'm going next door to snoop, okay?"

To make my visit to the B&B look legitimate, I would take a basket of cheese for Lois.

CHAPTER 29

With Rags trailing me, I raced from the office and fetched a basket from the shelves behind the cheese counter.

"Whatcha doing?" Rebecca strode from the kitchen with a fresh white towel to clean the counters. Soft afternoon light bathed her in a radiant glow.

"I'm making a basket." My voice sounded a little too singsong. I cleared my throat.

"I can see that."

"Time to close up."

"I'm on it." She waggled the towel.

"Of course you are." I set the basket on the cutting board and swiped rounds of Camembert and Brie from the cheese display. Lois preferred soft cheeses.

The Cheese Shop was empty of customers. So was the annex. I spotted Meredith and Matthew sitting at a booth in the Country Kitchen across the street. Jordan and his sister sat in the booth next to them.

As if sensing me watching him, Jordan looked up and smiled in my direction. I remembered our last delicious kiss in the co-op garden, and my insides turned warm, like the center of a molten lava cake made doubly rich with a powdered sugar and crème fraîche center.

Soon, I reminded myself. We would leave for our getaway soon.

"Where's Pépère?" I asked.

"He went back to the theater," Rebecca said. "What's up? You're acting funny."

"Nothing's up."

"Liar."

How could she tell? I was the model of calm. Chin high, shoulders back. My hands weren't even trembling.

"You're doing that lip thing. And your eyes . . ." She twirled a finger. "They're all glazed over. You're keeping something from me."

I had to practice lying more. Maybe a few sessions in front of my mirror would help. "Don't you have a date with Ipo tonight? You're going to the pub."

"Oho! Trying to change the subject, are you?"

Indeed, I was.

"Have you tried the pub's Brie-stuffed mushrooms topped with herbed crumbs?" I hummed my appreciation. "To die for."

Rebecca clucked her tongue.

I ignored her curious gaze and stuffed the basket with gold raffia. Next, I inserted balls of crumpled paper. They would serve as props for the cheese. I rewrapped the Camembert and Brie, sealed them with our special gold labels, and positioned them against the crumpled paper just so. I added a box of whole-grain crackers, a jar of raspberry jam — Lois's husband, the Cube, would appreciate that — and a package of cute cocktail napkins. I tied a mixture of gold and burgundy raffia around the handle and said, *"Voilá."* The result was festive and fun.

"You forgot the gold cellophane."

"I'll skip it this time."

"Who's it for?"

"Lois."

"Aha!" Rebecca drummed her nails on the counter as punctuation. "I knew it."

"Knew what?"

"You're going back to Lavender and Lace."

"I'm paying a social visit to Lois." I pressed my lips together. Hard.

"Hogwash." Rebecca flicked my arm with her fingernail. "Why are you keeping me in the dark?"

I swooped up the basket and headed for the exit. Rags galloped to catch up with me. "Have a fun time on your date. I'll see you tomorrow."

"I'm going with you. Ipo will understand."

"No," I said firmly.

"You're investigating something." She darted around me, locked the door, and flipped the closed sign. Then she faced me, hands on her bony hips. My grandmother couldn't have struck a more demanding pose. "At least tell me what you're doing."

Fully aware that I wasn't getting out of the shop unless I did, I relayed what I'd learned on the Internet.

She agreed with my deduction. "The mother's suicide, the bricklayer clues. Oh, yeah. You've nailed it. Dane thinks you saw something in his room. Go, go." She unlocked the front door. "Make sure you look under the bed. And between the mattresses. And don't forget to check the bottoms of his shoes for trace evidence from the cellar. Urso didn't think to check our shoes that night."

"That's probably because so many of us had been in the cellar."

"Good point. Oh, don't forget to check the nooks and crannies."

"Good night, my little Sherlock." I

scooped up Rags and flew out the door.

As I trotted north toward home, I saw Dane, Edsel, Freddy, and Quinn entering Timothy O'Shea's Irish Pub, and I nearly cheered out loud. Their little gathering would keep them out of my hair while I snooped. Perfect.

After I fed Rags, I sped next door to Lavender and Lace. The dinner hour hadn't quite arrived. I heard the lovely strains of "Clair de Lune" playing on the stereo in the great room but saw no one occupying the couches or chairs. I searched for Lois in the kitchen to deliver my basket but didn't find her. The spicy aroma of cloves mixed with cinnamon drifted from a pot of stew on the stove. A low gas flame fluttered beneath it. Agatha, the Shih Tzu, raised a sleepy head from where she lay on her checkered pillow by the kitchen door. I crouched to scratch her ears, and she settled back down.

"Lois?" I called.

No answer.

As I turned to leave, I noticed a keychain with a purple rabbit's foot tucked onto a hook in the back of the telephone cubby. Lois's set of master keys. She'd had them when she'd let us into Harker Fontanne's room. It was my lucky day. I wouldn't have to employ the credit-card-entry trick again. I'd been worrying about that all the way over. Dane certainly wouldn't have left his room door unlocked a second time.

As I reached for the keychain, I heard giggling. My pulse kicked up a notch as I tiptoed to the hall to locate the sound. It was coming from Lois and the Cube's living quarters. They lived at the rear of the inn. The giggling, both male and female, came from behind a closed door. So did the sound of a shower. Oh, my.

My cheeks grew warm, but I wasn't one to waste an opportunity.

I snagged the keychain and dashed up the stairs to the second floor. Using the key marked with Dane's room number — Lois was such a trusting soul — I let myself inside and closed the door. A cool breeze wafted in through the opened window, but it did nothing to calm me. I set my purse, the cheese basket, and the keychain on the dresser, put a hand to my chest to still my beating heart — could it pound any louder? — and surveyed the room.

If I was right and Dane thought I'd seen something, what was it and where was it now?

Nothing on the surface of his bureau or bed or bathroom counter screamed out to me. As before, a stack of receipts was piled on the bureau. This time I fingered through them. None showed that he had visited Providence prior to this visit.

On the floor lay a pair of tennis shoes, moist from rain, but no moss on the soles. Pebbles and what looked like bits of mortar stuck in the grids. Would any of it match the material that I'd chipped out of the cellar wall by the dumbwaiter?

That's a reach, Charlotte. Move on.

I inspected Dane's black leather toiletries kit. It contained the usual things. Razor, comb, toothbrush. Nothing out of the ordinary.

I rifled through his suitcase, which was half full. Where were the rest of his clothes? Had I seen something among his laundry? In the top drawer of the dresser, I found a wad of dirty clothes, including the sweater that he'd worn the night of the winery event. There was cheese on the collar, but it was nothing that would incriminate him or get him to confess to murder. I peeked into the remaining drawers, but each was empty.

Working my way around the room, I grew increasingly tense. I felt like I was dallying. *Go, go, go. Time is of the essence.*

I clicked my neck to relieve the stress and made another visual tour. What had I missed? *Check the nooks and crannies,* Rebecca had said.

I peered behind the tissue box. Under the bureau. Inside the cabinet beneath the sink. Nothing.

My gaze landed on the mirror and zeroed in on Dane's toiletries kit from the backside. It had a zipper pocket that I'd missed. Energized with hope, I reached inside and felt the edges of a photograph. It was of Dane and a pretty girl in a blue sweater, mugging for the camera. The girl's hair swooped like Winona's. Like the girl in Harker's paintings. It was Julianne. I flipped the picture over and read in chicken-scratch writing: *Frailty, thy name is woman.*

A chill scudded through me. Not from the uptick in the breeze from the open window, but because I recognized the line from Shakespeare's *Hamlet.* At Grandmére's insistence, I had taken an intensive Shakespeare class in my sophomore year at college. Hamlet was fed up with his mother's infidelity. Was Dane comparing Julianne to his mother? Had his mother had an affair? Had her lover abandoned her? Was that why she had committed suicide?

I was ready to call Urso, but paused when I saw something knobby protruding at the bottom of the zippered pocket. I set the

444

photograph down on the bathroom counter and rummaged for the item. I found two things — a blue jewel, similar to the fake jewels that had been strewn around Harker Fontanne, and a teeny sapphire ring. Quinn's ring. He must have stolen the ring from the precinct. I had to call Urso.

But before I could spin around, a strong arm circled me. Yanked me backward. My attacker shoved a wad of something into my mouth — paper towels, if my palate was correct. He snared me with both arms, and squeezing like a boa, said "Gotcha."

I caught a glimpse of him in the mirror. Dane.

I grasped his biceps and pulled down as I'd been taught in self-defense class, but his hold wouldn't weaken. He was too powerful.

"Find what you were after?" he hissed.

I cursed inwardly. At the time I'd found the photograph, I'd felt the breeze kick up. Why hadn't I realized someone had entered the room? Why hadn't I heard Dane's footsteps?

"I hoped when you saw me standing outside your house, you'd be scared and back off," he said. "My mistake."

I moaned.

"Uh-uh. None of that. Hush!" He

strapped his forearm across my neck and jerked.

My breath caught. My knees gave way. A blackness enveloped me.

By the time I came to, he'd lashed my hands behind my back. It didn't feel like he'd used rope. The material was softer, a silk weave. Maybe a scarf.

"Let's go." He yanked me to my feet. The photograph, jewel, and ring had vanished. "Stand up."

I couldn't. My knees felt like jelly.

He braced my knees with his. "I'll sling you over my shoulder if I have to. Nobody's around."

I ordered my legs to grow strong. Without the use of my arms, I needed my legs.

"That's a girl," he whispered. "I saw you as we were strolling into the pub. You looked like you were up to something. You shouldn't have pried. You should've known better." He slung his arm around my shoulders like we were best friends. "C'mon, we're going to take a little trip."

On the way out the door, he hefted the cheese basket and my purse from the dresser. "We don't want to leave any evidence behind."

CHAPTER 30

Dane led me down the hallway toward the rear staircase. I wriggled in protest and tried to jam my heel into his instep, but he was quick and dodged the assault.

"Nice try," he said. "Downstairs." He lifted me around the waist. My feet dangled above the steps.

At the exit leading to the parking lot behind Lavender and Lace, he set me down and yanked on the door handle. The door squeaked with a vengeance as it opened, but no one came running to save me. Where was the ever-industrious Cube when I needed him? Playing footsie with Lois in the bedroom, I thought miserably.

Dane peeked outside then shoved me forward. Gravel crunched beneath my feet. A lone Toyota truck was parked in the lot — the same truck that had almost plowed me down in the street the other day. Too intent on catching the B-movie guy who I'd mistakenly thought was stalking Jacky, I hadn't registered that Dane was the driver of the truck. Had he wanted to kill me then? Did he have a last-minute change of heart? I wished he would this time, too.

"Get in." He swung open the passenger door and gave me a shove.

I clambered up — hard to do without the use of my hands — and pitched forward. My face smacked the seat. Dang, but it smarted. Blood trickled from my nose. Angry, I kicked backward, but Dane anticipated the attack. He ducked out of range then came at me with a firm hand and pressed me to the floor. "Stay out of sight like a good girl."

For the first time in my life, I was sorry I was a good girl. Why wasn't I tougher? Why wasn't I the female counterpart of James Bond? Oh, to be strong and —

Buck up, Charlotte. Now! Think!

If only I could get my hands free and pull the wad of paper towels from my mouth. I had lungs. I could scream. The fabric handcuffs around my wrists were soaked with perspiration. My first instinct was to stretch the bonds to slip free, but then I recalled Amy at the breakfast table, playing with the Chinese finger puzzle her mother had given her. The more she'd struggled,

448

the tighter the bamboo braid had become. I'd told her to relax and twist. Would that strategy loosen my fabric handcuffs?

Dane opened the driver's door, tossed my purse and the basket of cheese onto the seat, and slithered in. "Be glad I didn't dump you in the truck bed."

Yeah, like he'd do that. I wasn't stupid. He hadn't put me in the truck bed because he knew I might roll around and make a ton of noise.

Like a law-abiding citizen, Dane exited the parking lot slowly. He drove with the same caution. No way was he going to get pulled over for a traffic violation.

Inside the truck, light waned. The sun was setting. Dane began to hum a tune that sounded like a dirge. Visions of funerals — mine, in particular — played in my mind like a bad movie. Determined to change my fate, I twisted like a worm until my back faced away from Dane. Next, I squeezed my wrists together. The silky material slipped down an inch. Hallelujah!

Dane glanced at me and grinned. "Getting comfy?"

I grunted.

"Edsel wasn't as curious as you. He was willing to drink away his sorrow. He actually liked Harker, the dolt. More than liked, if you really want to know."

I didn't. I wanted to break free.

"He had the hots for him." Dane snorted. "Harker missed the signs."

I had, too. Was he sure?

"Harker was such a jerk. He only cared for himself."

I worked at my bonds. They felt looser but not lax enough. The wad of paper in my mouth was wetter, though. I tried to compress it and gagged.

"Julianne was my dream," Dane went on. "My everything. She loved the color blue. Did you know that? Of course you didn't. You didn't know her. Nobody did. She liked music by Usher. And dancing. Man, she loved to dance. And then *he* came along. Did I tell you Julianne was an artist?" He glanced at me and back at the road. "Me, I sucked at art."

On the night of the murder, Harker had teased Dane about not knowing the difference between famous artists and Las Vegas nightclub performers. Why couldn't I have figured out then that he was a phony?

"I only took up art because of her. But Harker had the chops. He swept her right off her feet. She cried when she dumped me, but she said he was so talented, so clever, so handsome. She couldn't help herself."

The way he was talking, I wondered if he'd murdered Julianne and made it look like suicide, but then he slammed the steering wheel with his hand. "She shouldn't have killed herself! She had me. She could have had me forever. But no. If she couldn't have him, she didn't want to live." He glowered at me. "Do you know how that feels?"

Creep Chef hadn't wanted me, and the rejection still stung, but I'd never contemplated suicide. Not once. Julianne was fragile, Winona had said. When Harker dumped her, she couldn't face life on her own.

"We're here." Dane pulled the truck to a stop and looped the basket of cheese over two fingers. "Want to have a picnic?" He climbed out of the truck and slammed the door. I heard his footsteps on gravel. Seconds later, he opened the passenger door and tugged me by the ankles. The floorboards ground into my right hip, scraped my cheek. I groaned from the pain.

When I was fully out of the truck, Dane yanked me to a stand and I saw where we were. At the Ziegler Winery.

"Apropos, don't you think?" he said.

"Back to the scene of the crime." He grabbed my elbow with a firm hand. "Move. We're going to the cellar. I don't think I'll kill you. I think I'll let you rot there. How do you like that idea?"

I didn't like it a whit.

"Until the rats are done with you, you can contemplate your stupid decision to stick your nose in where it didn't belong."

I'd been doing that for the past half hour.

He dangled the basket of cheese in front of my nose. "Maybe they'll go for the Camembert. What do you think?" He sniggered. "No one will find you. This place is a pariah now. Quinn's aunt will never get her college off the ground."

When I first met Dane, I'd figured him for a malcontent, but I had no idea he was as crazy as the rest of the Ziegler family.

He pulled a keychain from his pocket. One of Urso's identifying tags hung from the loop, and I moaned. He must have filched those at the same time he took the engagement ring. If windows weren't broken in the mansion, no one would guess I was trapped inside.

"Let's see, which one? Aha! Here it is." He slotted a key into the front door lock and twisted. "Success." He pushed open the door. "You know the way. Go." He propelled me forward with a jolt to the middle of my back.

I coughed hard.

"Oh yeah, you don't need that gag anymore. Nobody will hear you. Scream all you want." He plucked it out with two fingers and winked.

I didn't scream. He knew I wouldn't. What good would it do? I wanted to save my vocal cords in case I needed them when I was fleeing to the road. I felt the scarf handcuffs give a little bit more, but still not enough. Dang!

He opened the cellar door. "Down we go, lady first."

The dank odor hit me head-on. My throat swelled with fear. I didn't want to be buried alive. I tripped over the threshold.

"Uh-uh, no falling." He grabbed my forearms.

I prayed the dim light would keep him from noticing how loose my bonds were.

"Harker had it so easy," he said as he prodded me forward. "A classy family. Girls falling all over him. He didn't deserve it so good. He deserved to die."

"Nobody deserves to be murdered," I said.

"Sure they do. Bad guys do."

"Do you?"

"I'm not bad. I'm making a judgment call.

453

Trust me; the world will thank me for my noble act. Harker used women."

"So do you."

"Bull."

"You used Quinn."

"Did not."

"You used her scarf as a murder weapon and set her up to take the blame. That's not a noble thing to do."

"She was a minx. She toyed with me." Dane pushed me forward and forced me to sit on the flagstone floor next to the brick wall. He set the basket of cheese beside me.

"I know why you built the brick wall," I said.

"Do you really?" He chuckled. "Enlighten me."

"You built it to honor your surname. Cegielski means bricklayer." With my hands out of sight, I jammed my wrists together. The handcuffs slipped another half-inch. "You thought you were so clever."

"I was." He grinned. "I am. What about those jewels that were scattered around? They kept everyone guessing, didn't they? By the way, there is no treasure here. No jewels, no gold doubloons, no pirates. Believe me, I've searched."

"In January, when you staked out Providence and the winery, you went to the museum. Who were you with? I don't think it was Edsel or Winona. Another student?"

He kept mute and eyeballed a spot beyond me. "Let's see. Shall I tie you to the iron bars? No. I'll stuff you in the hole for the dumbwaiter and seal it up so nobody will ever find you. I still have a bag of mortar in the truck. On your feet."

"Why did your mother commit suicide?"

Dane stiffened then forced a smile. "You've been doing your homework."

"I left an Internet page open on the computer at The Cheese Shop. My staff will see it."

He sighed. "The Internet is way too helpful. I'll make sure it's erased."

"Chief Urso will get here soon. He put a tracer in my shoe," I lied.

Dane snorted. "Don't make me laugh. This isn't some stupid TV show."

His words made me think of Rebecca and a nervous titter burbled out of me.

"What's so funny?" he said.

If only I had one of those silly plastic bracelets with WWRD emblazoned on it. *What would Rebecca do?* She'd tell me to use my environment, as I'd been taught in self-defense class. Except there was no environment in this cellar. There were no lamps, no chairs. Not even a blasted shovel.

"On your feet." Dane whacked my upper arm.

I flinched.

"Don't make me hurt you."

He had to be kidding. My nose wasn't bleeding any longer, but every bone in my body ached. I tried to stretch my scarf handcuffs wider. This time, they came loose and fell softly to the floor.

"Get up," he ordered.

As he straddled me to hoist me by the armpits, my elbow nicked the cheese basket, and I nearly cheered. The cellar had *environment*, after all. I groped for the cheese basket handle, snagged it, and swung out. The rattan crackled as the basket made contact with Dane's ear. The jar of jam sailed into his jaw.

He wailed and released me. He stumbled backward.

I swung again, but he grabbed the basket out of my hands and hurled it away.

"Sorry, Charlotte. An empty basket doesn't have the same sting."

He dove at me.

I dodged him and sidled, like a crab, along the brick wall. I groped the top ledge to keep my balance and felt a brick give under my hand — one of the bricks I'd loosened when I'd broken into the winery in search of Rebecca. Wasn't it ironic that, for a guy with bricklayer as his surname, he wasn't very talented at the craft? He'd probably used too much water in the mix. I swung the brick with force. It made contact with the side of his head.

Dazed, he careened into the iron bars. He slumped to the ground.

Moving fast, I unknotted the scarf I'd shed, pulled Dane's hands through the iron bars, and fastened them with a set of knots that would have made my Girl Scout leader proud.

Let's hear it for macramé!

Footsteps resounded overhead. In the foyer.

I glanced at Dane. Did he have an accomplice? Had he been pulling my leg with all that talk about Edsel being his enemy?

The door to the cellar creaked open.

"Anybody here?" a woman called with operatic gusto.

Was it Winona? Was she Dane's partner in crime? Had she snowed me? Snowed all of us?

I charged forward, prepared to hurl the brick at her, but stopped when I made out Sylvie, not Winona, in the dim light.

"Charlotte, are you all right?" Sylvie scuttled down the stairs and squinted into the gloom. "I saw that ratty purse of yours in the truck outside, and I got worried that something had happened to you."

Ratty? I didn't think it was ratty. It was well loved.

"Oh, dear, you're hurt." Sylvie tapped under her nose, indicating the dried blood on my face.

"I'm okay."

She spotted Dane. "Who's that? Did he force you down here? Is he dead?"

"He's going to wake up with a very bad headache."

"I'm so glad you're okay." She threw her arms around me.

Within seconds, the two of us became quite uncomfortable. I couldn't remember the last time we'd hugged, if we ever had. We pushed apart.

I cleared my throat. "What are you doing here?" I didn't need to ask. She was dressed in camouflage, complete with boots, and she carried a tote, most likely filled with tools to search for treasure. "You truly believe the pirate rumor."

"I don't just believe it. I *know* it. I found the doubloons."

"You what?"

"I thought I'd take one more look since my last try was, well, cut short. See, I read

Zachariah Ziegler's diary at the museum. Lovely place, by the by. The museum docent let me read it because I was wearing gloves. Such a silly rule. Anyway, the old man gave clues as to the treasure's whereabouts."

"Clues? What kind of clues?"

Sylvie pulled a diary from her tote and waved it at me. "Shhhhh. I'm just borrowing it."

Yeah, that's what the Grinch said.

"He fancied himself a pirate." Sylvie flipped to a page and showed it to me. "He wrote where he'd stashed the treasure using paces. You know, forty this way, ten that. I figured his paces would have been much longer than mine, so I added a few here and there, and I found it buried outside the mansion. Just beyond that fireplace, in fact."

I glanced where she pointed, the nook where Quinn had hidden on the night of the murder.

"I think that used to be an entrance to the cellar," Sylvie said. "Ziegler sealed it up. Clever old chap, don't you think?"

Clever Sylvie, was what I was really thinking. I hadn't given her enough credit.

Sylvie chewed her lip. "I'm not going to keep the money. It belongs to the town."

"That's noble of you," I said, though I wondered what her game plan was. Did she think that her gracious act would win back Matthew's heart? Surely he was smarter than that.

She fluffed her hair. "Should we call Chief Urso?"

Oh, no, you don't. She would not use this little scheme to win over Urso. Not on my watch.

"I'll call him," I said. After making sure Dane was still out for the count, I bolted past Sylvie, up the stairs, and out of the mansion to the truck. I fished my cell phone from my purse and dialed. Urso answered. I'd never been so happy to hear his voice.

CHAPTER 31

The next night, a crowd huddled around the buffet table in the Providence Playhouse foyer. The table had been draped with a white linen tablecloth and decorated with multiple vases of daffodils. Colorful platters of appetizers held bite-sized pizzas, prosciutto-melon-Havarti kebabs, and macaroni-and-cheese tarts. I stood amid the throng, my ears peeled for disgruntlement regarding the play they were about to see, but everyone seemed primed to enjoy *No Exit with Poe.* Talk of the bad Internet review circulated, but most of the patrons dismissed it. Many of the guests said that Bernadette Bessette knew what she was doing, words that filled me with pride.

As I stood at a beverage table waiting to pick up a cup of juice, Freddy, Winona, Quinn, and Edsel strolled into the venue. Freddy gave a nod, and I smiled back. Winona whispered something to him and he laughed. I noticed Edsel had his arm around Quinn, and lo and behold, she didn't seem to mind. In fact, she seemed to be enjoying his attention. When Freddy and Winona split off toward the buffet, Edsel turned to Quinn and looked at her so lovingly that I was sure the gossip Dane had spewed about Edsel was faulty. I chalked it up to sour grapes. Dane was the kind of person who felt if he couldn't be happy, then nobody deserved to be.

I caught sight of Meredith and Matthew entering the theater. Both were smiling. Their gleeful moods worked like a magnet. I abandoned my quest for a beverage and made a beeline for them. We met in the center of the crowd.

"What's got you jazzed?" I said.

Matthew grinned so broadly that his pearly white teeth reflected the gleam of the chandelier. "Meredith gets to go ahead with the college plans."

"Isn't that great?" Meredith's smile grew megawatt bright.

"Congratulations." I high-fived her.

"The town council is behind it," Matthew continued. "And with the new influx of cash from the treasure that Sylvie found, money is not an object."

"Share your news, too." Meredith elbowed

Matthew.

"I won the custody suit. Mr. Nakamura was, in a word, brilliant."

"Brilliant," Meredith echoed.

"The girls will be staying with me. Sylvie can have visitation rights, approved by me." Matthew beamed with confidence.

"Wow! That's super." I squeezed my cousin's arm. "Have you told Amy and Clair?"

"Are they here?" Meredith slipped her hand into Matthew's. "I heard this production might be a little, you know, adult."

"Don't worry," I said. "Pépère is playing cards with them in the green room. The broadcast speakers have been turned off." I gazed at Matthew. "So how did Sylvie take the news?"

"Charlotte!" Rebecca glided to my side and hitched her chin. "You've got to see this."

I followed her gaze and spotted Jacky entering with U-ey. Dressed in a pinstriped suit and soft blue shirt, he looked like a hunk, and I felt a little tickle of something. Not jealousy. Delight, perhaps? I couldn't remember him ever looking so self-assured.

"Yoo-hoo, Rebecca," my grandmother said as she waltzed between the guests. As always on opening night, she glowed with energy. "Somebody's looking for you." She jerked a thumb then proceeded on.

Ipo Ho, his impressive chest pressing at the seams of his Hawaiian shirt and leather jacket, stood by the far wall. He held a single rose in his hand and seemed to be mumbling words, as if rehearsing a speech.

Rebecca said, "Not again."

"Not again, what?" I said.

"He's probably going to propose again. He's such an innocent." She glanced at him. "Isn't he cute?" She giggled and trotted toward him.

Left out in the couples department, I felt my heart grow heavy. Jordan and I hadn't made plans to meet at the theater, but I'd hoped he would appear. He knew I'd be there. Maybe he was having second thoughts about asking me to go on the trip to Gruyéres. After the run-in with Dane, my picture had made the front page. Maybe Jordan figured that being with me might blow his well-designed cover.

I turned back to Matthew and Meredith. "So, where were we? Oh, yes, how did Sylvie take the pronouncement? Not to tragedian proportions, I hope."

"In her inimitable Sylvie way," Matthew said. "With a tight smile and a flip of her ice-white hair." He mimicked the gesture.

"Thankfully, she's going back to England today."

"No, I'm not." Sylvie strutted to our group, her faux ocelot coat replaced with a chartreuse knee-length coat, her hair streaked green to match.

I bit back a laugh. Had she glanced in the mirror? Did she really think she looked fashionable? Maybe at the age of sixteen. In Soho.

"What do you mean, you're not going back to England?" Matthew gulped.

"My luck's changed while I've been here," Sylvie said. "So I've decided this is where I should settle."

"Settle?" Matthew's voice bordered on strident.

Sylvie grinned. "I negotiated a twenty percent finder's fee for the treasure I found."

Of course she did. She was no dummy. Her self-sacrificing speech to me was a sham.

"I've rented a little place near Charlotte."

"Near me?" I chirped.

"And I've put the down payment on a lovely shop on Cherry Orchard. Poor dear was going under." Sylvie leaned in. "Bad money management."

"Which store?" Matthew clenched Meredith's hand so tightly he was draining the color out of it.

"The candy shop. I'm turning it into a women's boutique. I'll call it Under Wraps, specializing in items that go under or over anything. I'll give that old nag Prudence Hart a run for her money."

My heart started going pitter-pat as I worried about the repercussions for Matthew, Meredith, and the twins. And yes, for me, too. Prudence would be less than pleased with this little turn of events and blame me.

Sylvie fluffed her hair and eyed me with disdain. "Guess what? I'll give you a make-over for free, Charlotte."

"I don't need —" I snapped my mouth shut. The gall. I would not rise to the bait.

Sylvie smirked. "Isn't it wonderful? I'll be here for my girlie girls. What that old court said doesn't really have to stand, you know."

"Uh, yes, it does," Matthew blurted. "They'll be living with me. Full time."

"Whatever. You'll let me see them as much as I want. You'll want them to know that I love them and cherish them. After all, I am their mother, and we all know, after this week's tragedy, how negligent parenting can influence children." Sylvie twirled a finger. "Oh, Charlotte, by the by, come take a look at the gift I gave the girls."

Matthew said, "Aren't the girls with

Pépère?"

"They were, but I can always find them." Sylvie sniffed. "It's a mother's instinct."

Matthew snorted. "Stink is right," he mumbled.

I heard the comment and giggled. So did Meredith. She thwacked his shoulder.

With a firm grip, Sylvie grasped my wrist, drew me outside, and gestured toward the side of the theater where there was a narrow strip of grass. On it stood a massive brown puppy with long hair. It was flanked by the twins, who were using wide-toothed combs to groom its hair.

"He's a Briard," Sylvie said. "And get this. He's named after Brie, the cheese."

"The city," I said.

She frittered a hand at me. "Who knew there was a cheese dog? It's a herding dog for cheese. Well, for sheep, actually. I got him from that breeder in town."

"You mean the animal rescuer," I corrected.

"Whatever. She said the Briard is a fierce defender of family and farm, and he's so fast, I've named him Rocket. Isn't he a cute little thing?"

Little? By the look of his paws, he would grow to more than one hundred pounds.

I shook my head. "Sylvie, you can't start a

new business *and* take care of a puppy, too."

"Oh, I don't intend to. I told the girls that Rocket would be staying with them and their father."

I.e., *me.*

"What?" The roots of my hair twitched with anxiety. Any second now, I'd explode.

"Say yes. You wouldn't want to break their sweet hearts, would you?" Sylvie offered a sly *gotcha* smile.

"You can't. *I* can't," I sputtered, doing my best to keep myself under control. "I can barely manage a career and the twins and Rags. And Clair's allergic."

"Tosh! Not to dogs. Besides, kids need pets. Oh, look at the time." She didn't even attempt to give a cursory glance at her watch. She was on the run, yet again. "Amy, Clair! Mumsie's got to be off. Work calls." She swept them up in hugs and kisses, and seconds later, flew away, leaving emotional destruction that wasn't visual to the naked eye in her wake.

As a team, the twins tugged on Rocket's bright red leash and drew him toward me.

"Isn't he beautiful, Aunt Charlotte?" Clair said.

"And friendly," Amy added. "Bend down. Let him sniff you."

I wriggled my skirt to mid-thigh and

crouched next to the dog.

On cue, Rocket licked my face and stole my heart.

"You're going to let us keep him, aren't you, Aunt Charlotte?" Amy said.

Rocket nuzzled up to me and laid his huge puppy paw across my thigh.

By the impish gleam in the twins' eyes, I could tell that they knew I would. And Clair, surprisingly, wasn't sneezing. Maybe she truly was allergic to her mother and nothing else, I thought with sinful glee.

"Clair." I handed her the leash. "Take Rocket to the rear of the theater. We'll deal with this matter after the show, okay?"

They scampered off with Rocket — a wobbly mass of adorable — trotting between them.

I spun around to return to the theater and spied Jordan traipsing up the stairs toward the entrance. The golden glow of floodlights hit the planes of his face and magnified the strong cheekbones and the energy in his gaze. Ripples of joy swept over me. He spotted me and paused, one hand in his trousers pocket. Could any man look more stunningly sexy?

But then his mouth twisted down in a frown and his gaze turned hard. He said, "I run a little late and you replace me?"

"Replace you?"

"I saw the kiss he gave you."

"Who gave me?"

"The dog."

Like an idiot, I cut a look over my shoulder at the retreating dog, and back at Jordan, whose mouth twitched as his eyes now sparkled with mischief.

He swept me into his arms and planted a killer of a kiss on my mouth. "Tell me I'm a better kisser."

"You're definitely better," I mumbled into his lips.

"Now tell me you're ready for our trip."

"Am I ever." Unwarranted, a list of chores flew through my head.

"Uh-uh." Jordan tapped my nose. "No list-making. When the show is over, you're racing home and putting a few things into a suitcase. We leave tomorrow morning."

"Tomorrow? But I have to iron, pack, and bake muffins and casseroles for the week I'd be gone just in case Matthew doesn't have enough energy to put a hamburger together for the twins."

"Uh-uh. You're off the hook. I've arranged for my sister to check in on Matthew," Jordan said.

"Jacky would do that for me?"

"She's in nesting mode." He hugged me again.

"What about airline tickets you purchased? You can't possibly switch them at such short notice."

Jordan twirled an imaginary mustache. "I have my ways."

"Charlotte!" Grandmère appeared outside the front of the theater. "Curtain!"

"Coming." I gazed at Jordan and realized I needed a promise from him. One simple promise. I walked my finger up his chest. "Remember, I said I'd only go on this vacation on one condition."

He tilted his head in that sensual way that sent delicious shivers to my toes. "What's the condition?"

"You tell me everything about you. What you did before you moved to Providence. What your real name is. The truth."

He paused, as if the request was too much, then held up his palm and said, "I swear to tell the truth, the whole truth, and nothing but the truth, so help me God."

A different kind of shiver shimmied through me. Why did I get the feeling that he'd said those words a lot of times? To a judge.

And why didn't I care?

RECIPES

PORCUPINES

1 lb. chopped turkey
1/2 cup rice
1/2 cup Parmesan cheese, shredded
1 tablespoon parsley
1 teaspoon salt
1 teaspoon pepper
1 egg

For Spicy Catsup

6 tablespoons catsup
1 tablespoon Worcestershire sauce
1 tablespoon horseradish sauce

For Porcupines

Preheat oven to 300 degrees.
   Mix everything together. Easy.
   Roll into balls the size of walnuts.
   Place the balls on a cookie sheet, slightly apart.
   Bake 30 minutes.

Turn the heat up to broil.

Broil for 5 minutes.

Remove the cookie sheet from the oven. Place baked porcupines on paper towels to drain.

Serve with spicy catsup.

For spicy catsup

Mix catsup, Worcestershire, and horseradish and serve. (Really easy.)

CHERRY SCONES
MAKES 6–8 SCONES

1/2 cup dried cherries

4 tablespoons butter, softened

2/3 cup milk

2 tablespoons orange juice

1/3 cup sugar

1 egg, beaten

2 1/4 cups flour

1 teaspoon baking powder

Powdered sugar

Whipped butter

Pre-soak dried cherries in 1/2 cup hot water for 10 minutes. Drain and discard the water.

Meanwhile, preheat oven to 375 degrees.

Mix butter, milk, juice, sugar, and egg. Add in flour and baking powder. Beat until all flour incorporated. Add in cherries. Mix well.

Drop large dollops onto a cookie sheet. Bake for 15–17 minutes until golden brown.

Dust with powdered sugar. Serve with whipped butter.

GOAT CHEESE FONDUE
(REGULAR OR GLUTEN-FREE)
SERVES 4

3/4 cup heavy cream
8 ounces goat cheese
1 tablespoon white pepper
1 tablespoon green onion (green tips only)
1 tablespoon white wine
2 teaspoons flour OR 2 teaspoons tapioca flour (for gluten-free)
1 baguette bread OR 20–30 gluten-free crackers
Broccoli florets, steamed
Carrots, sliced raw
Celery, sliced raw

Warm the heavy cream in a pot until hot but not burning. Use low heat, about 3–4 minutes. Add the goat cheese in chunks.

Stir with a whisk to prevent clotting. Add the pepper, green onion tips, wine, and flour OR tapioca flour. Stir approximately 5–7 minutes until the mixture is as smooth as it can be.

Prepare your plates with vegetables and bread cubes OR gluten-free crackers. Eat family-style.

Note: The thickness of the fondue might vary. If it's too thick, add a little cream. Too thin, add a little more cheese.

Second note: I like to snip the green tips of onions with scissors for even cuts.

Third note: To steam broccoli perfectly every time: Bring to boil 1 cup water in a 6 quart pot with 1/2 teaspoon salt. Cut up 1–2 heads of broccoli into bite-sized pieces. Add to boiling water. Cook 4 minutes. Pour off boiling water. Cover again. Let sit for 4 minutes. Remove lid and rinse broccoli in cold water to stop the cooking process.

BLUE CHEESE AND GARLIC FONDUE

2 cloves of garlic
1/2 cup half-and-half
2 ounces Point Reyes Blue Cheese (or your favorite blue cheese)
1 tablespoon tapioca flour

Cut garlic cloves in half. Rub garlic around

the inside of a fondue pot. Heat fondue pot to medium heat. Add the half-and-half. Add cheese and stir until it is all melted. Add tapioca flour and stir again so there are no lumps. This all takes about 5–7 minutes.

Serve warm in a small crockpot with cut vegetables like broccoli florets, celery sticks, carrot sticks, and asparagus. It may also be served with crackers and/or bread cubes.

Note: This tastes delicious as a warm dressing on a green salad.

VIDALIA ONION AND BACON QUICHE
SERVES 6

6 slices Applewood-smoked bacon, cooked crisp
1/4 cup sliced green onions
1/2 large Vidalia onion, sliced thinly
2 teaspoons olive oil
1 teaspoon white pepper
4 ounces shredded Swiss cheese (use more, if desired, to taste)
1 pie crust (home-baked or frozen)
1/4 cup cream
3/4 cup milk
4 eggs
1 teaspoon cinnamon
1/2 teaspoon salt
1/4 teaspoon ground pepper

Preheat oven to 375 degrees.

Bake or sauté bacon until crisp. Remove from heat and cool on a paper towel. Break pieces into thirds.

Slice the green onions and Vidalia onions.

Sauté the green onions and Vidalia onions in olive oil at medium heat until they turn limp and slightly brown/caramelized. Remove from heat and drain on a paper towel.

Sprinkle white pepper and 2 ounces of the shredded cheese in the unbaked pie crust.

Lay onions on top of the cheese. Lay bacon on top of the onions.

Mix milk and eggs and seasonings together.

Pour milk mixture into the pie crust.

Sprinkle with the remaining cheese.

Bake 35–40 minutes until the quiche is firm and lightly brown on top.

ABOUT THE AUTHOR

Avery Aames loves to cook and enjoys a good wine. She speaks a little French and has even played a French woman on stage. And she adores cheese. Visit her at www.averyaames.com.

We hope you have enjoyed this Large Print book. Other Thorndike, Wheeler, Kennebec, and Chivers Press Large Print books are available at your library or directly from the publishers.

For information about current and upcoming titles, please call or write, without obligation, to:

Publisher
Thorndike Press
10 Water St., Suite 310
Waterville, ME 04901
Tel. (800) 223-1244

or visit our Web site at:

http://gale.cengage.com/thorndike

OR

Chivers Large Print
published by AudioGO Ltd
St James House, The Square
Lower Bristol Road
Bath BA2 3SB
England
Tel. +44(0) 800 136919
email: info@audiogo.co.uk
www.audiogo.co.uk

All our Large Print titles are designed for easy reading, and all our books are made to last.